ACCLAIM FOR JEFF SMITH'S

BONE

Named an all-time top ten graphic novel by Time *magazine.*

"As sweeping as the 'Lord of the Rings' cycle, but much funnier." —*Andrew Arnold,* Time.com

★*"This is first-class kid lit: exciting, funny, scary, and resonant enough that it will stick with readers for a long time."* —Publishers Weekly, *starred review*

"One of the best kids' comics ever." —Vibe *magazine*

"BONE *is storytelling at its best, full of endearing, flawed characters whose adventures run the gamut from hilarious whimsy . . . to thrilling drama."*
—Entertainment Weekly

"[This] sprawling, mythic comic is spectacular."
—SPIN *magazine*

"Jeff Smith's cartoons are irresistible. Every gorgeous sweep of his brush speaks volumes."
—*Frank Miller, creator of* Sin City

"Jeff Smith can pace a joke better than almost anyone in comics."   —Neil Gaiman, author of **Coraline**

"I love BONE! BONE is great!"
—Matt Groening, creator of **The Simpsons**

"Every one of the zillion characters has a unique set of personality traits and flaws and dreams that are developed amid the pandemonium."
—Kyle Baker, **Plastic Man** cartoonist

"**BONE** moves from brash humor to gripping adventure in a single panel."   —ALA Booklist

"**BONE** is a comic-book sensation. . . . [It] is a classic of writer-artist craftsmanship not to be missed."
—Comics Buyer's Guide

OTHER **BONE** BOOKS

Out from Boneville

The Great Cow Race

Eyes of the Storm

The Dragonslayer

Rock Jaw: Master of the Eastern Border

Old Man's Cave

Ghost Circles

Treasure Hunters

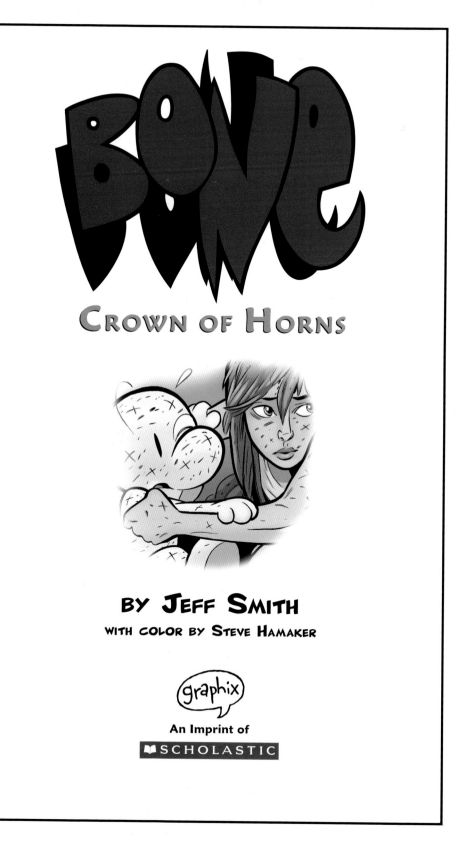

BONE

CROWN OF HORNS

BY JEFF SMITH

WITH COLOR BY STEVE HAMAKER

graphix

An Imprint of

SCHOLASTIC

This book is for Paul Pope and Terry Moore

Copyright © 2009 by Jeff Smith.

The chapters in this book were originally published in the comic book *BONE* and are copyright © 2003 and 2004 by Jeff Smith. *BONE*® is © 2009 by Jeff Smith.

Library of Congress Catalog Card Number 9568403.
ISBN 978-0-439-70631-5 (hardcover)
ISBN 978-0-439-70632-2 (paperback)

ACKNOWLEDGMENTS

Harvestar Family Crest designed by Charles Vess
Map of *The Valley* by Mark Crilley
Color by Steve Hamaker

20 19 18   18 19

First Scholastic edition, February 2009
Book design by David Saylor
Printed in Malaysia 108

CONTENTS

- CHAPTER ONE -

THE DUNGEON AND THE PARAPET - - - - - - - - 1

- CHAPTER TWO -

MIM - 53

- CHAPTER THREE -

GAPS - 58

- CHAPTER FOUR -

ESCAPE FROM THE CITY - - - - - - - - - - - - 85

- CHAPTER FIVE -

CHAMBER OF HORNS - - - - - - - - - - - - - - 117

- CHAPTER SIX -

HOMECOMING - - - - - - - - - - - - - - - - - - 169

- CHAPTER SEVEN -

SOLSTICE - 197

- CHAPTER EIGHT -

RIVER CROSSING - - - - - - - - - - - - - - - - 201

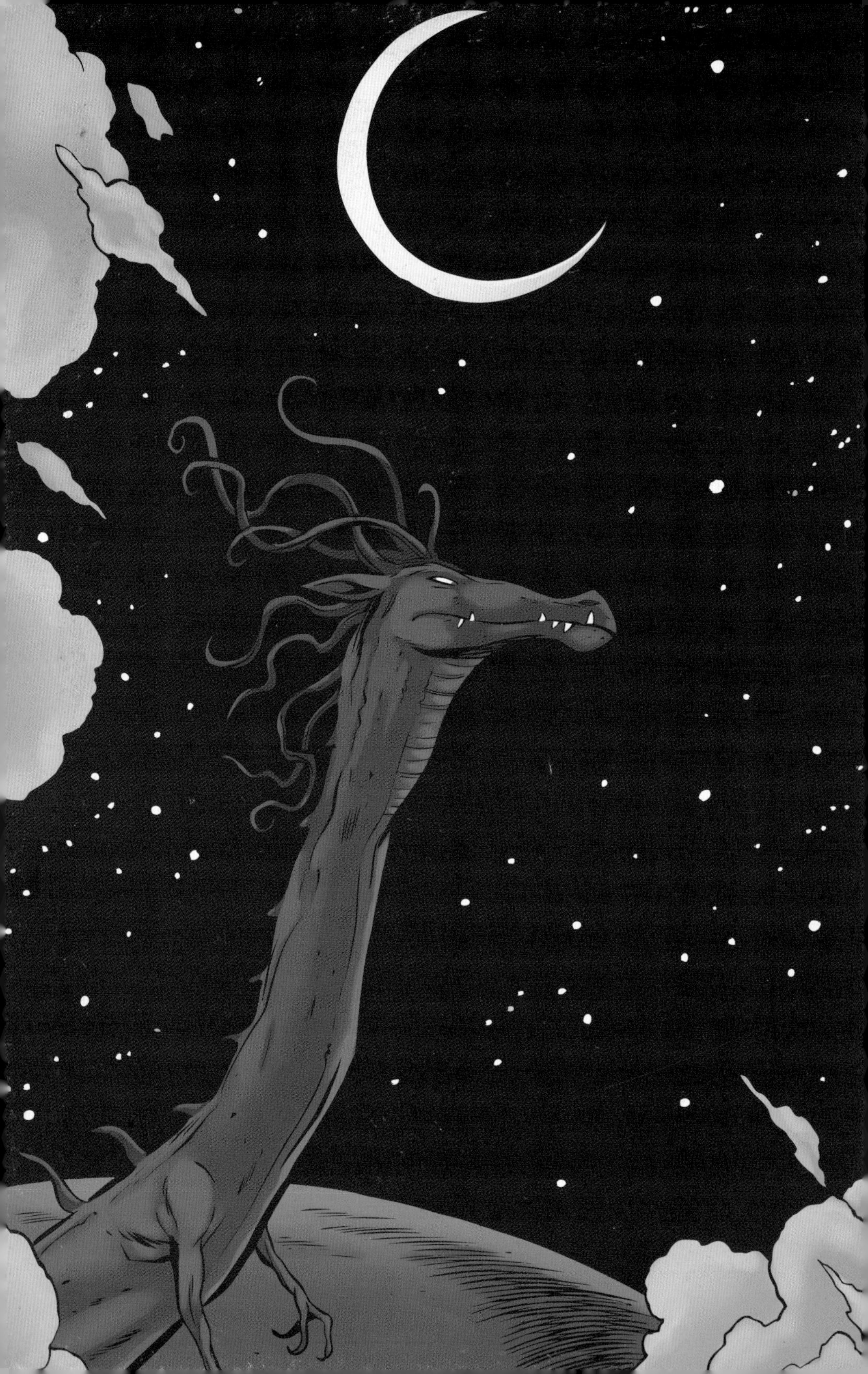

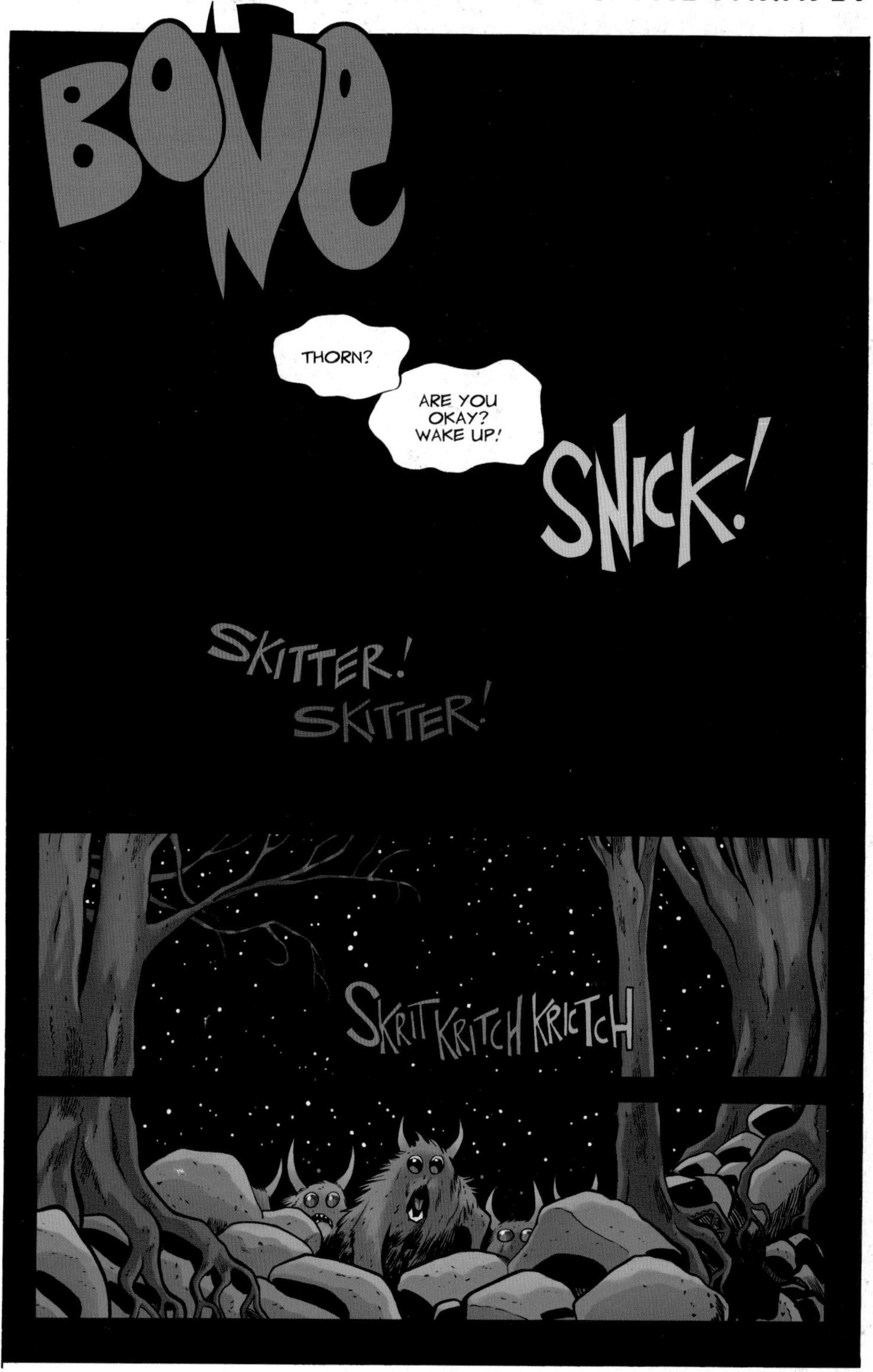
BONE
THORN?
ARE YOU OKAY? WAKE UP!
SNICK!
SKITTER! SKITTER!
SKRIT KRITCH KRICTCH

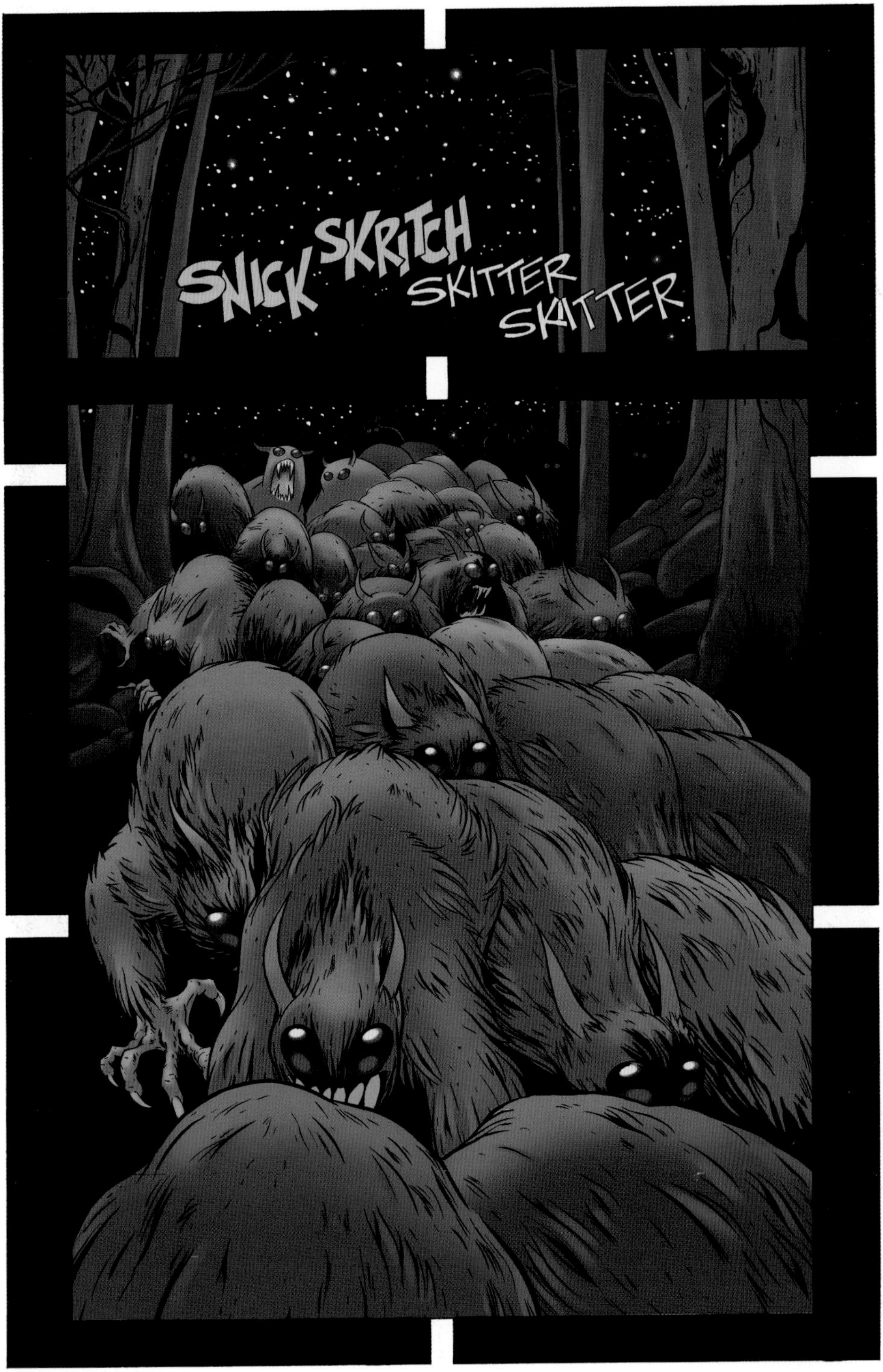
SNICK SKRITCH
SKITTER SKITTER

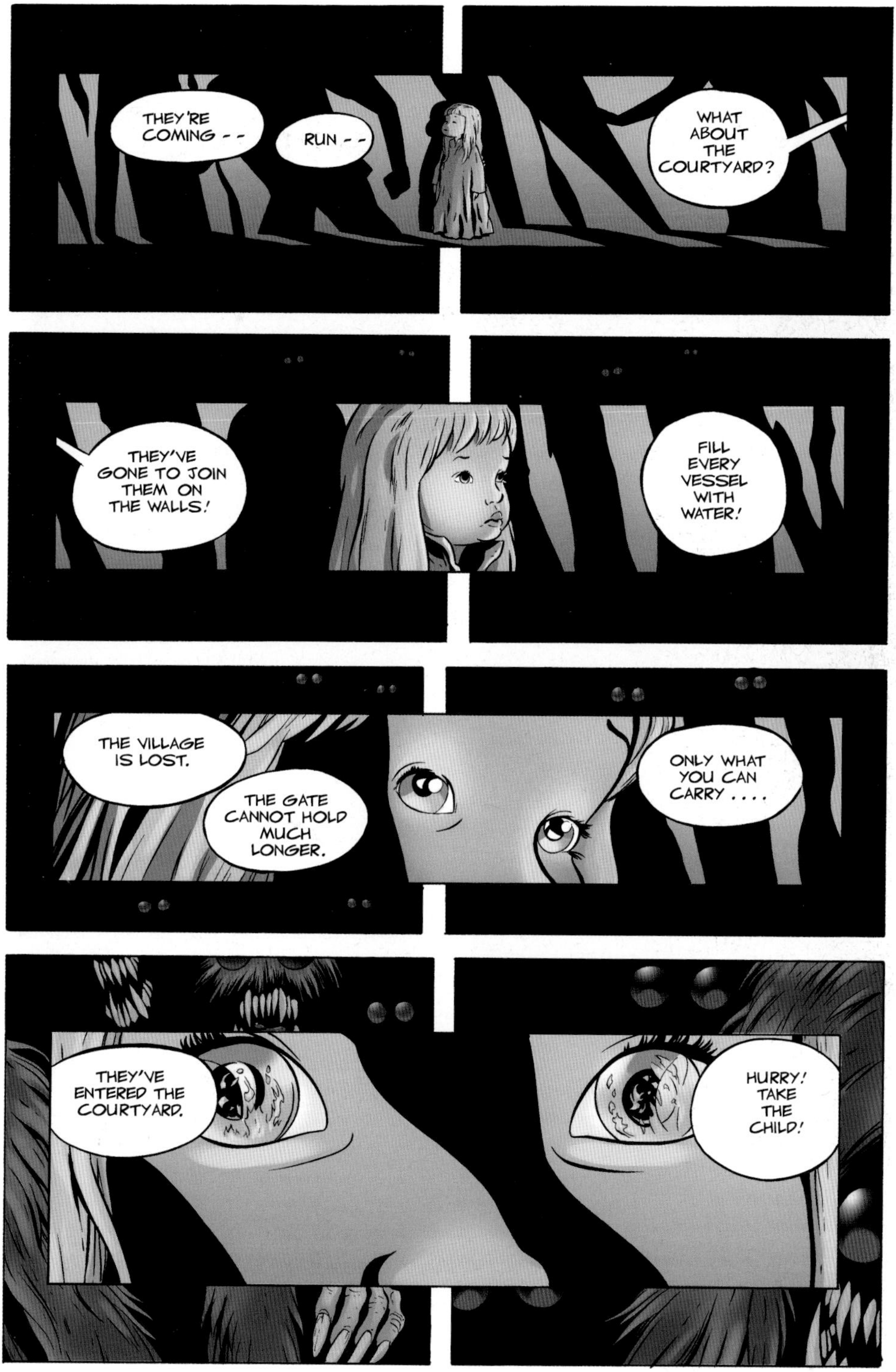
THEY'RE COMING - -
RUN - -
WHAT ABOUT THE COURTYARD?
THEY'VE GONE TO JOIN THEM ON THE WALLS!
FILL EVERY VESSEL WITH WATER!
THE VILLAGE IS LOST.
THE GATE CANNOT HOLD MUCH LONGER.
ONLY WHAT YOU CAN CARRY . . . .
THEY'VE ENTERED THE COURTYARD.
HURRY! TAKE THE CHILD!

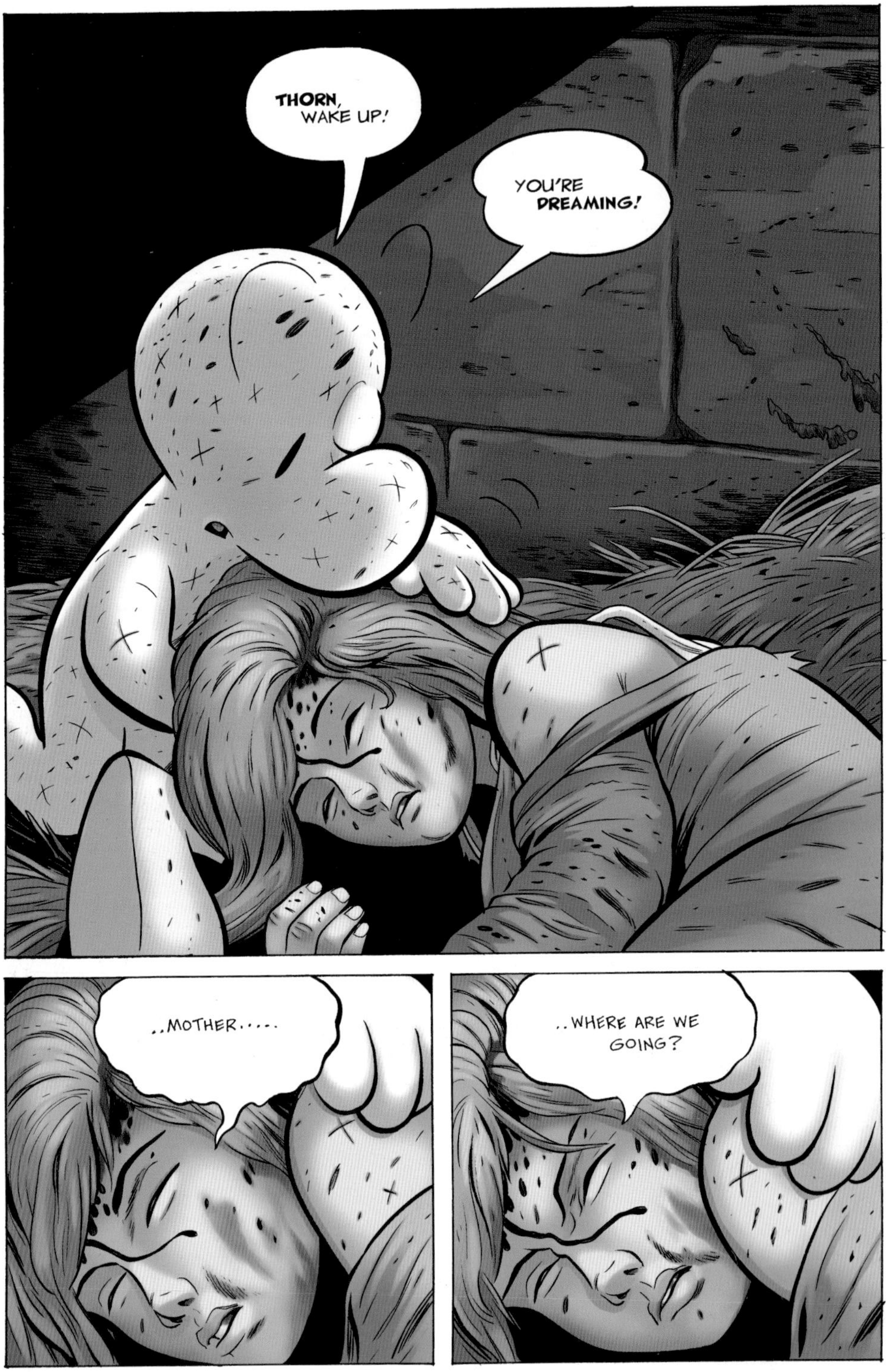
THORN, WAKE UP!
YOU'RE DREAMING!
..MOTHER.....
..WHERE ARE WE GOING?

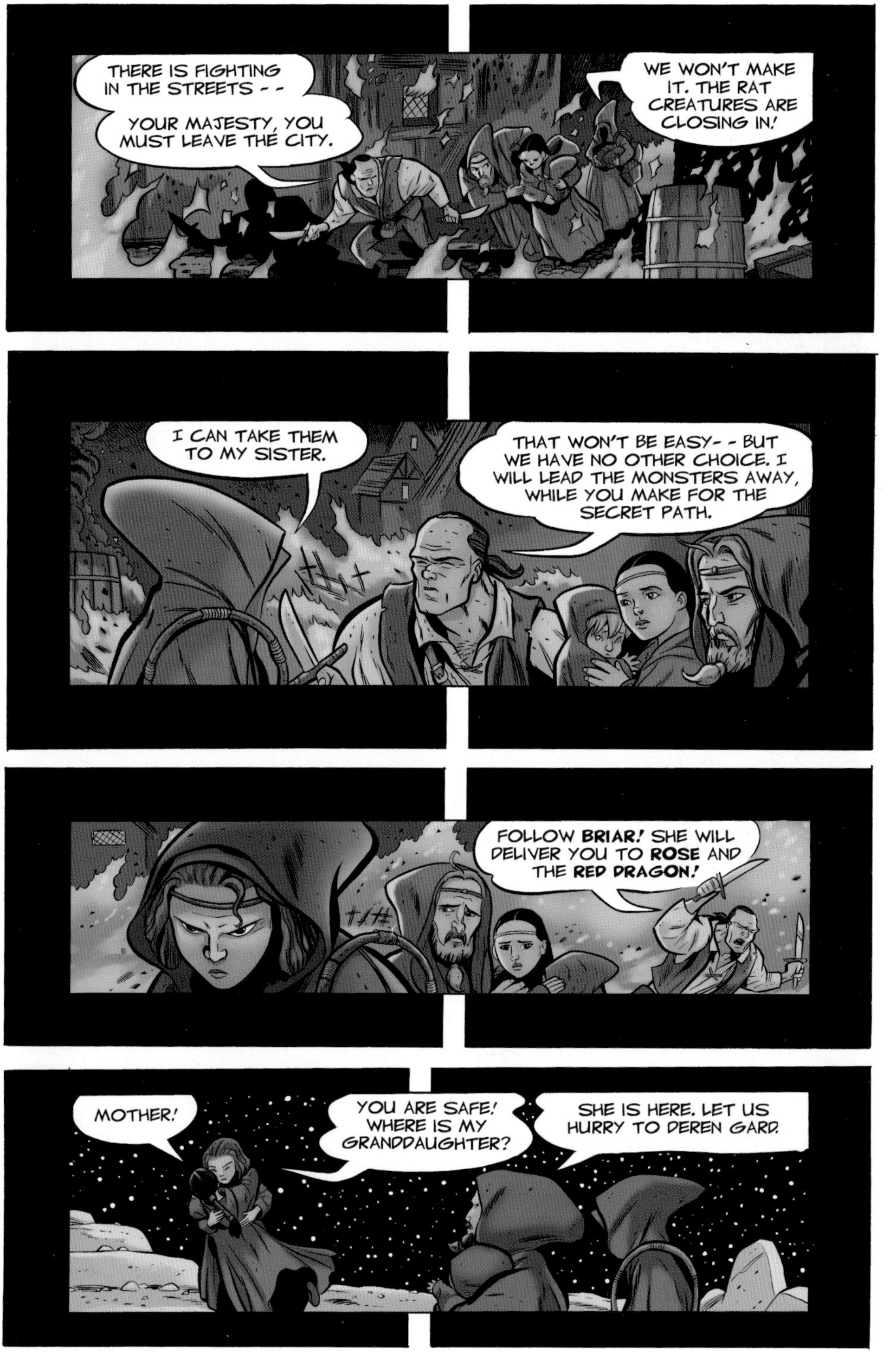
THERE IS FIGHTING IN THE STREETS - -
YOUR MAJESTY, YOU MUST LEAVE THE CITY.
WE WON'T MAKE IT. THE RAT CREATURES ARE CLOSING IN!
I CAN TAKE THEM TO MY SISTER.
THAT WON'T BE EASY- - BUT WE HAVE NO OTHER CHOICE. I WILL LEAD THE MONSTERS AWAY, WHILE YOU MAKE FOR THE SECRET PATH.
FOLLOW BRIAR! SHE WILL DELIVER YOU TO ROSE AND THE RED DRAGON!
MOTHER!
YOU ARE SAFE! WHERE IS MY GRANDDAUGHTER?
SHE IS HERE. LET US HURRY TO DEREN GARD.

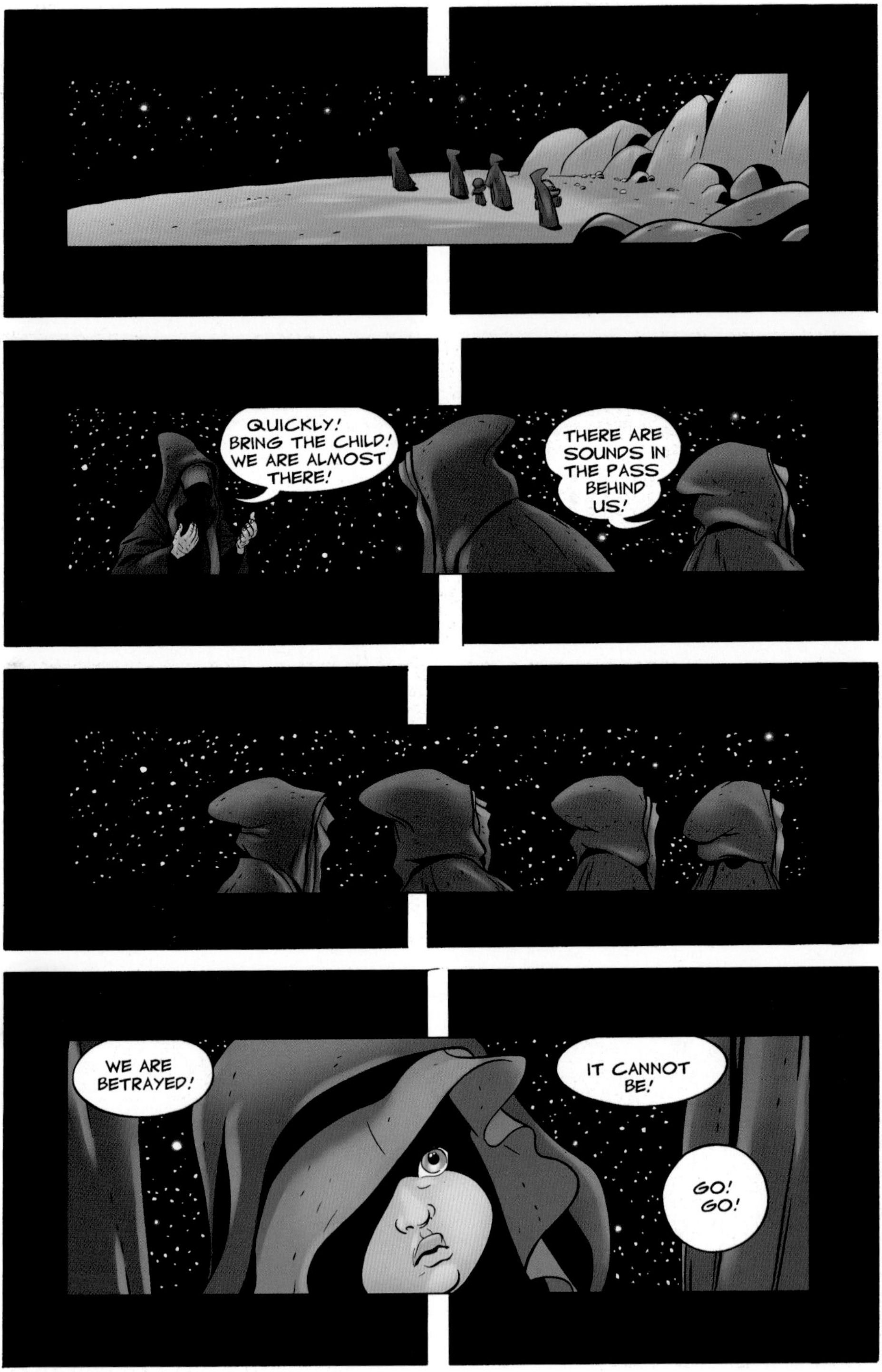
QUICKLY! BRING THE CHILD! WE ARE ALMOST THERE!
THERE ARE SOUNDS IN THE PASS BEHIND US!
WE ARE BETRAYED!
IT CANNOT BE!
GO! GO!

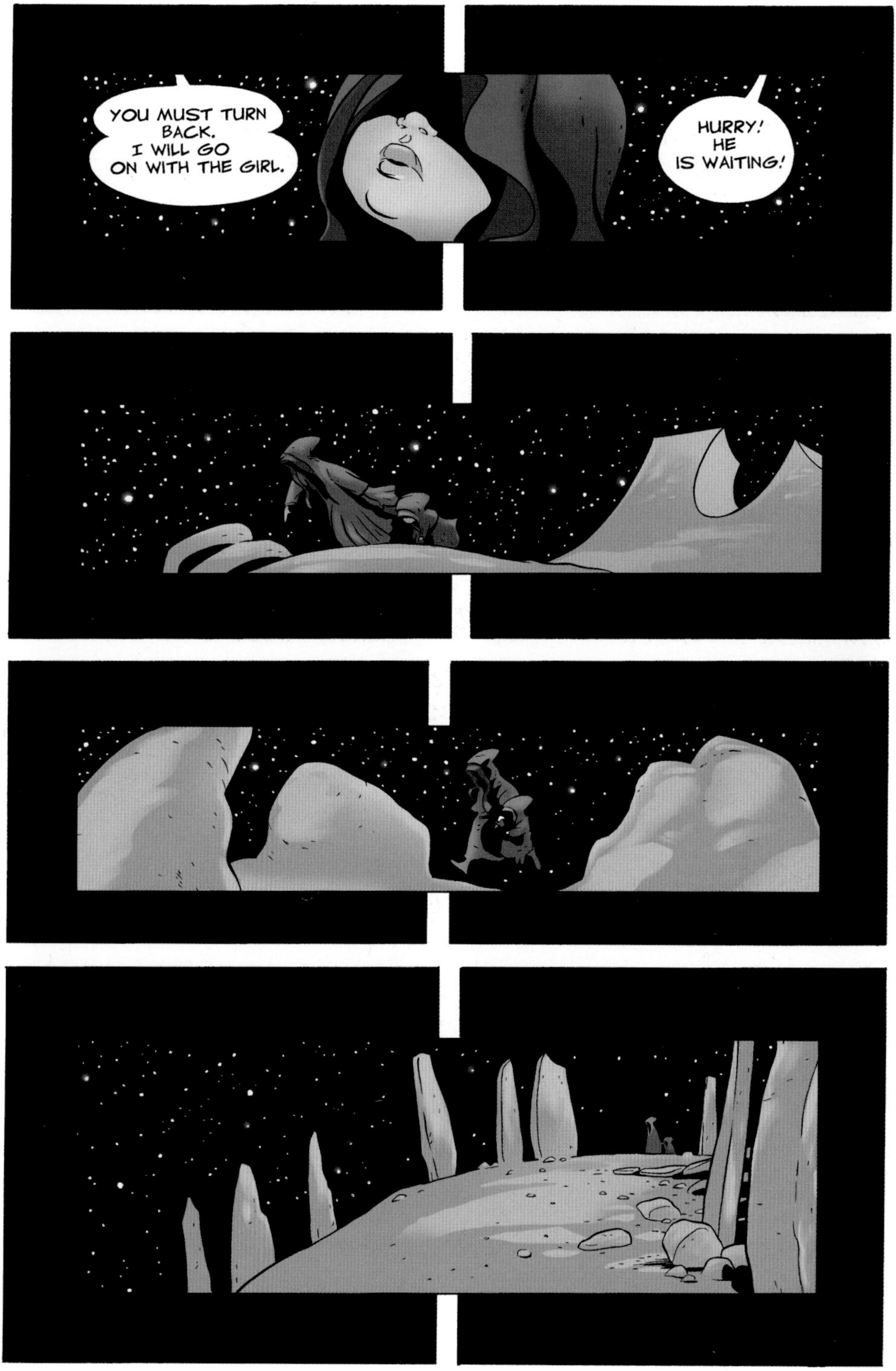
YOU MUST TURN BACK. I WILL GO ON WITH THE GIRL.
HURRY! HE IS WAITING!

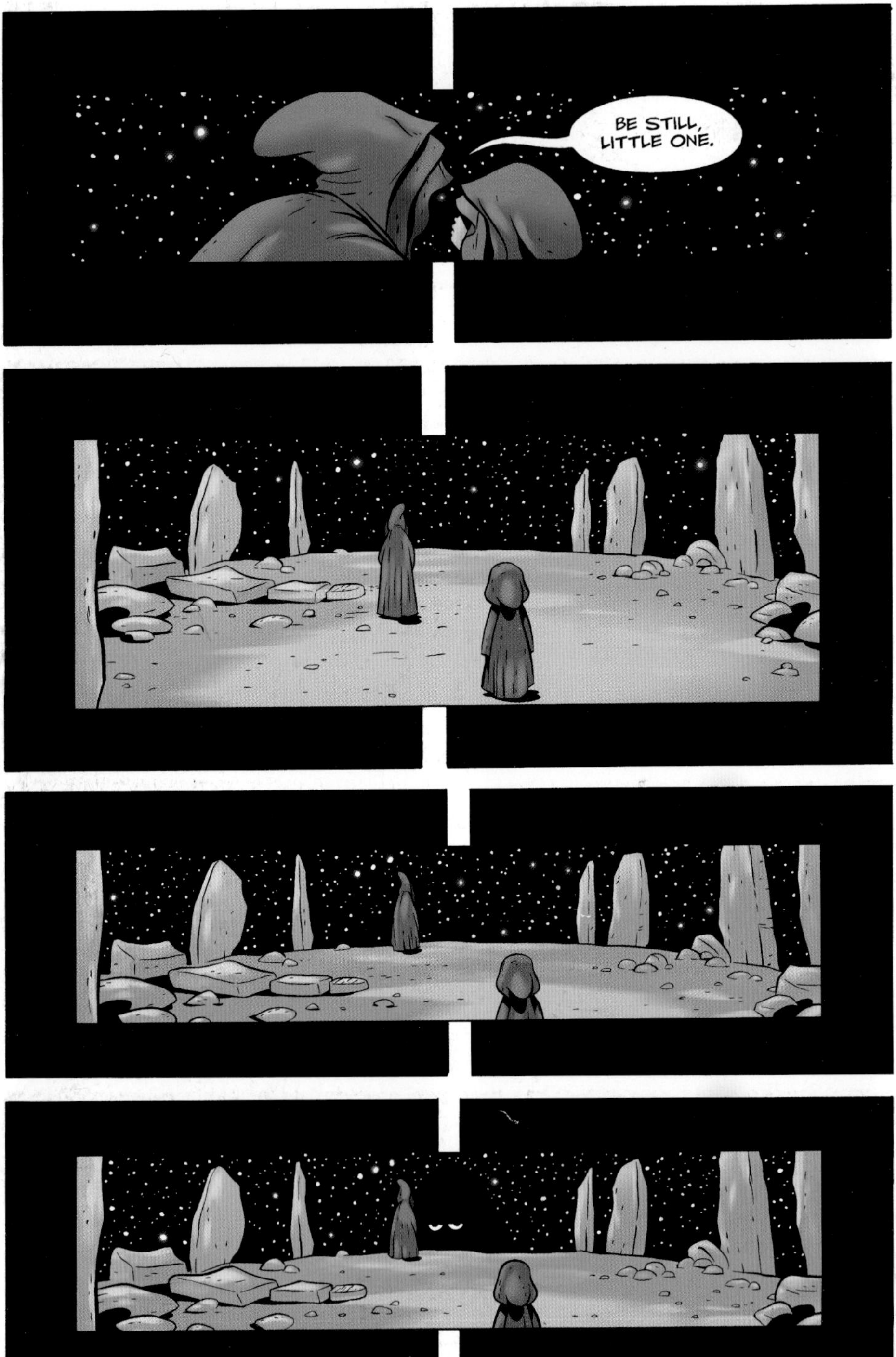
BE STILL,
LITTLE ONE.

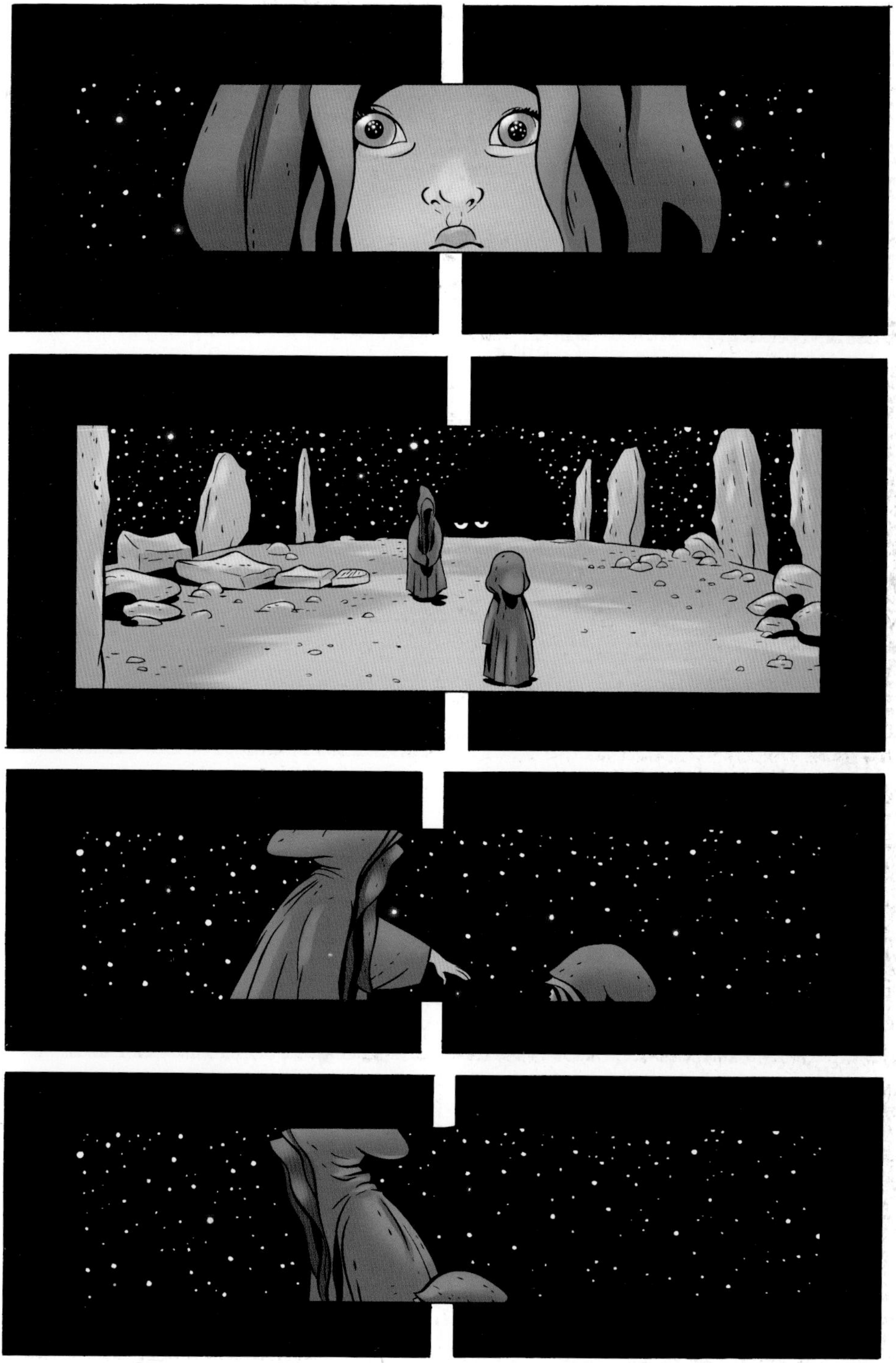

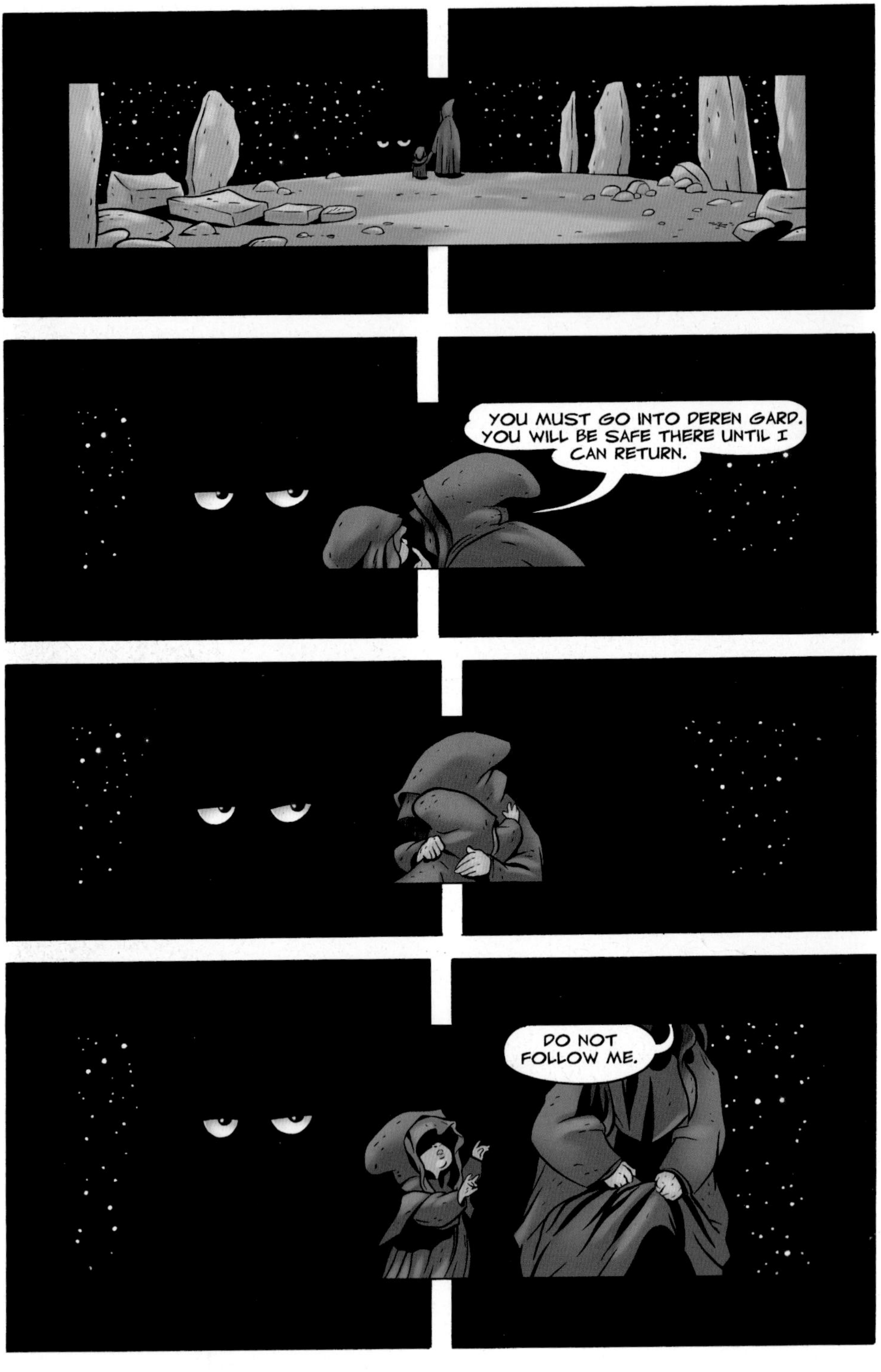
YOU MUST GO INTO DEREN GARD. YOU WILL BE SAFE THERE UNTIL I CAN RETURN.
DO NOT FOLLOW ME.

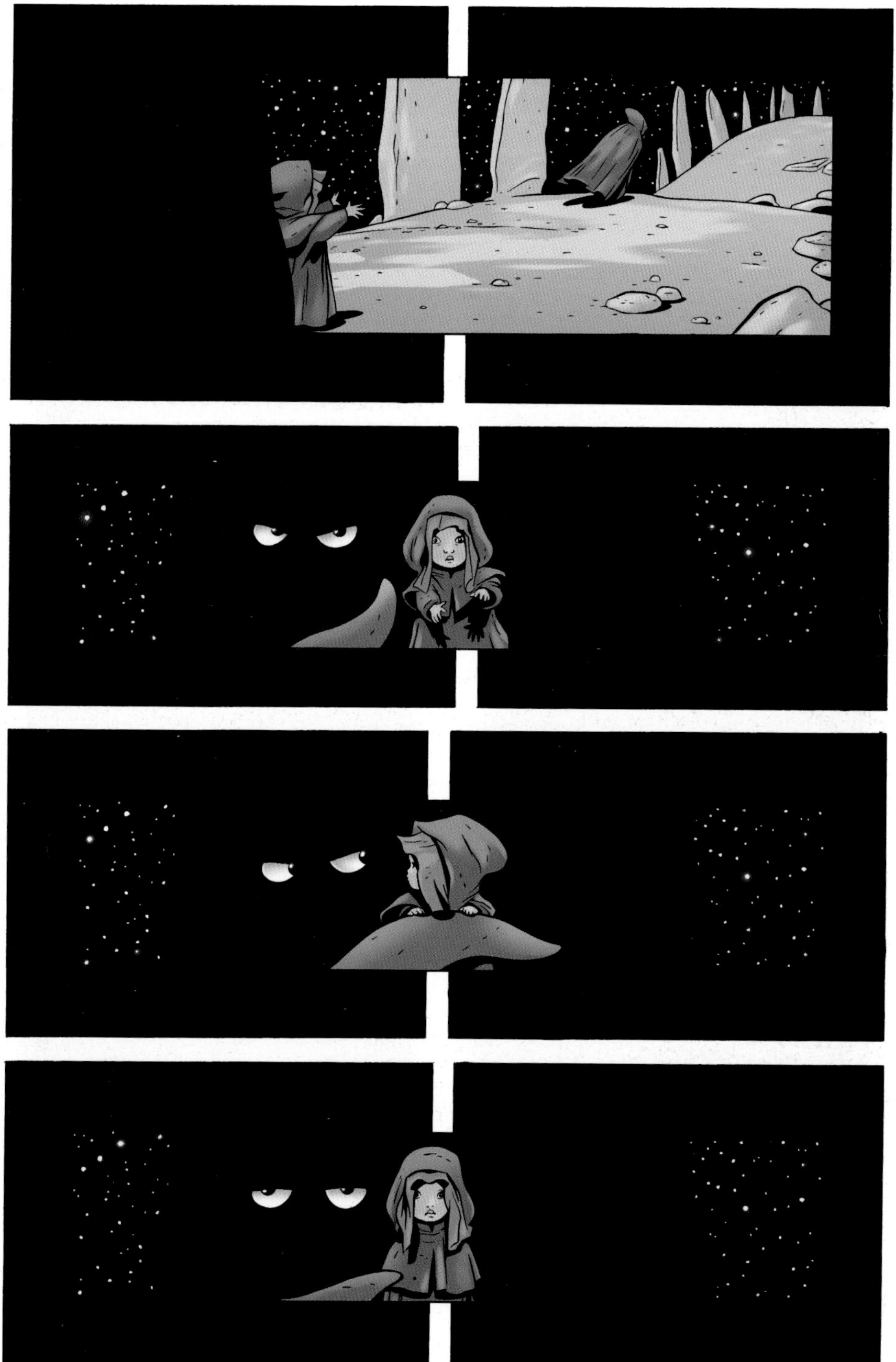

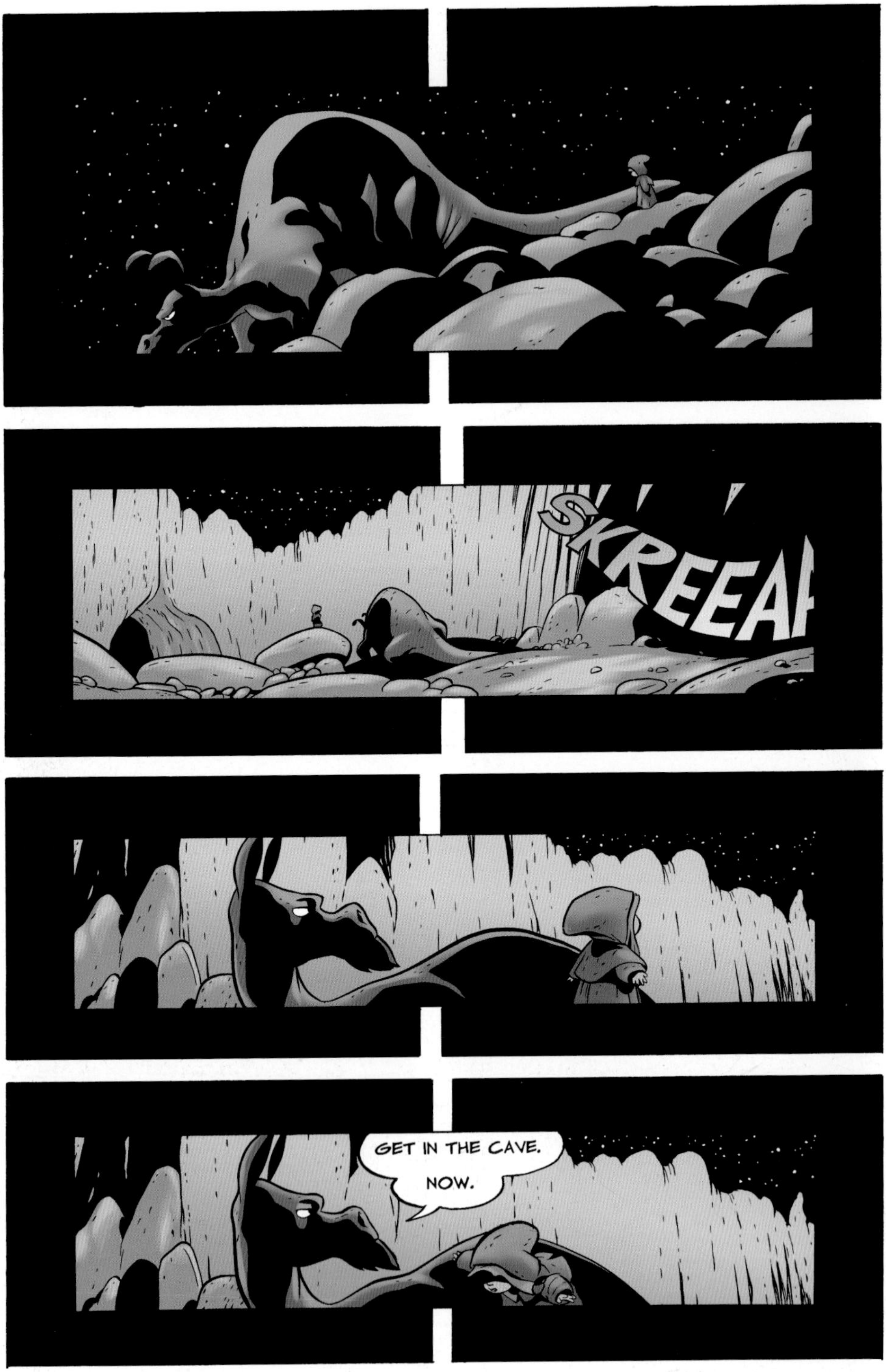
SKREEAH
GET IN THE CAVE.
NOW.

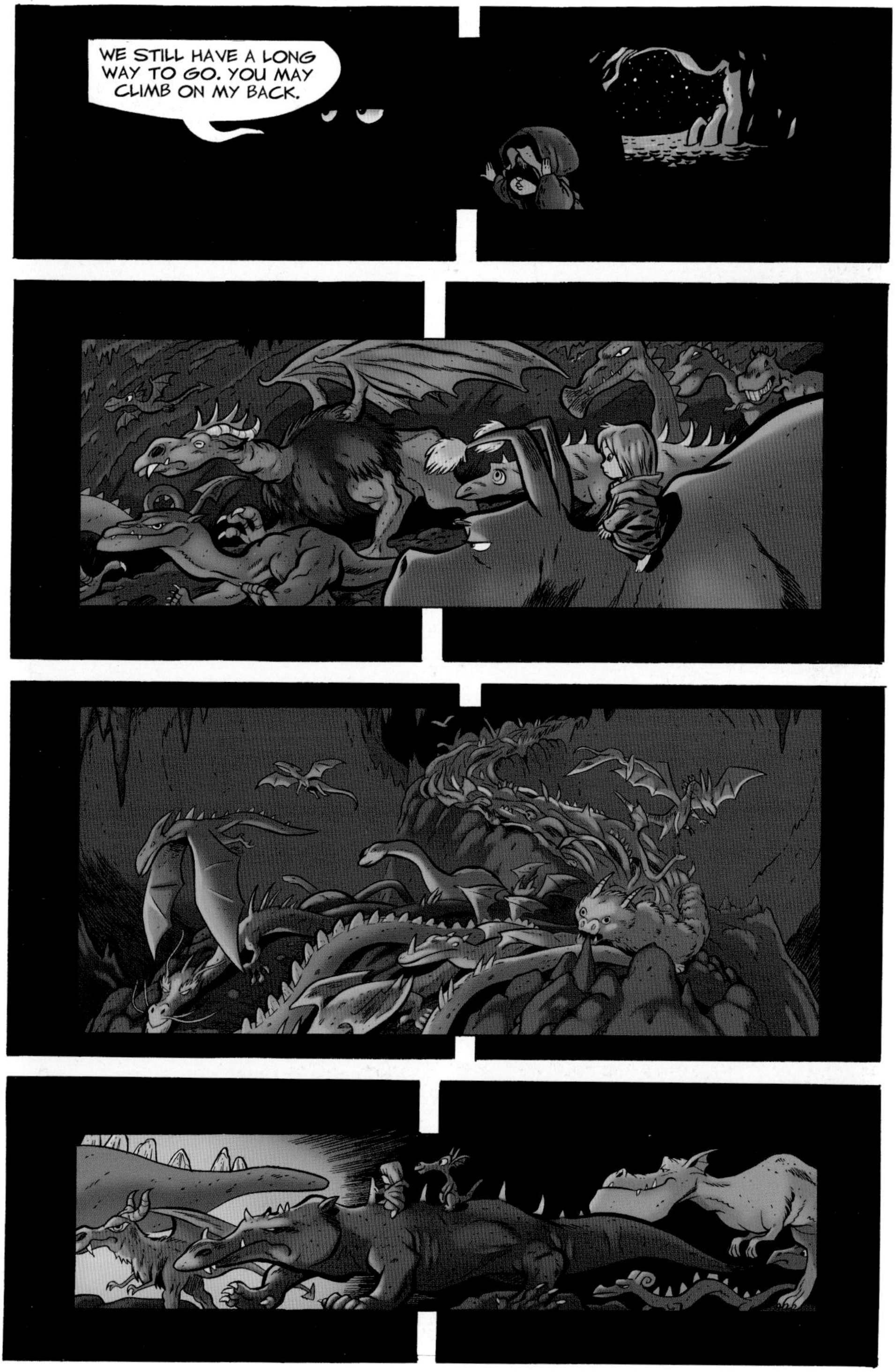
WE STILL HAVE A LONG WAY TO GO. YOU MAY CLIMB ON MY BACK.

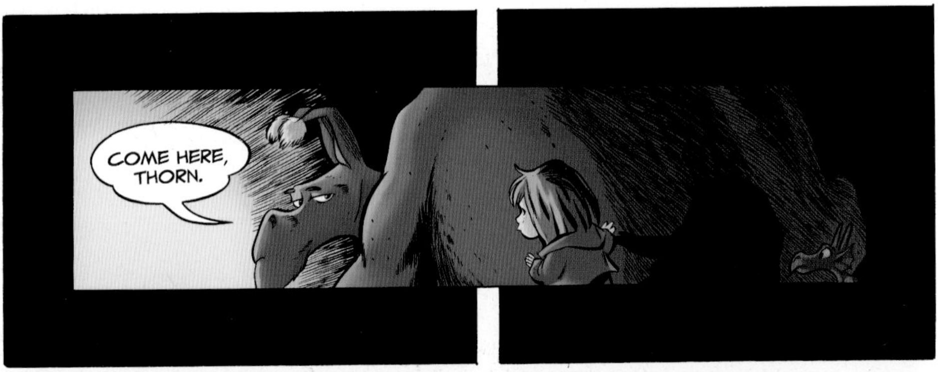
COME HERE, THORN.

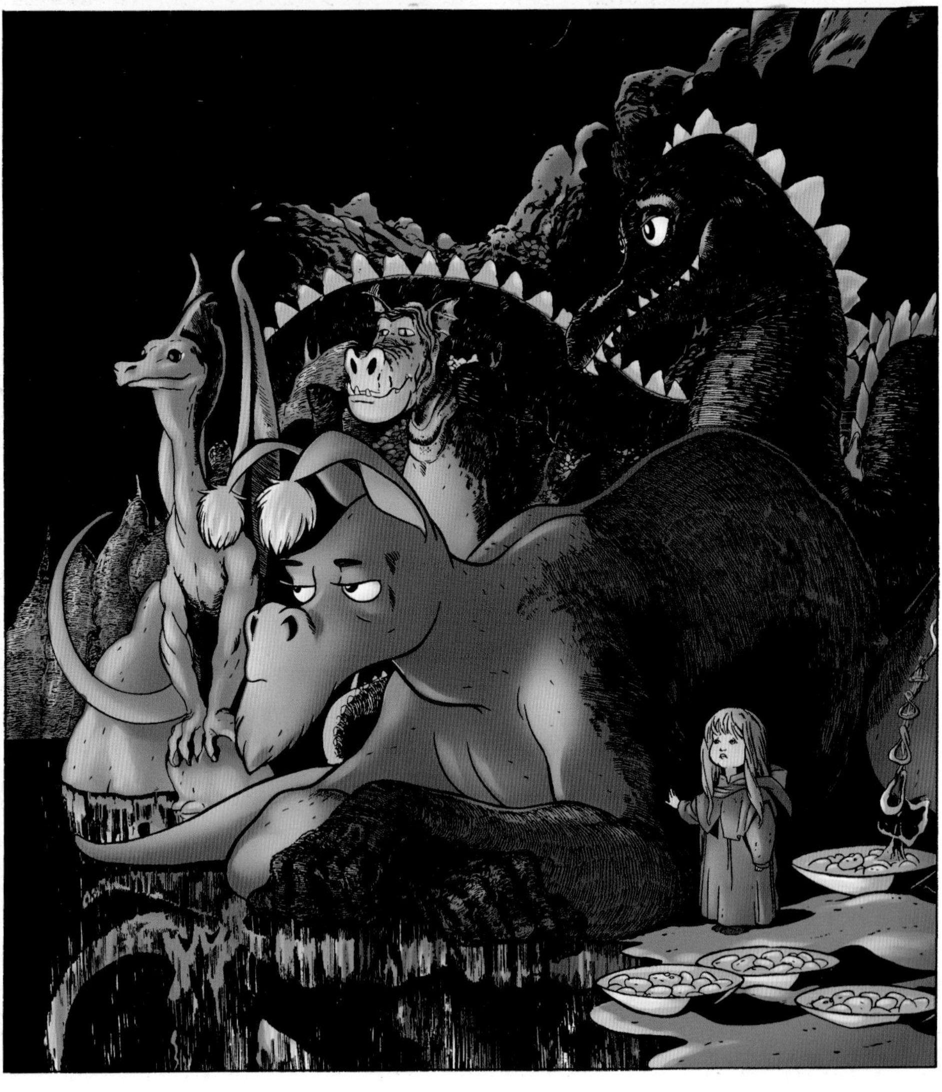

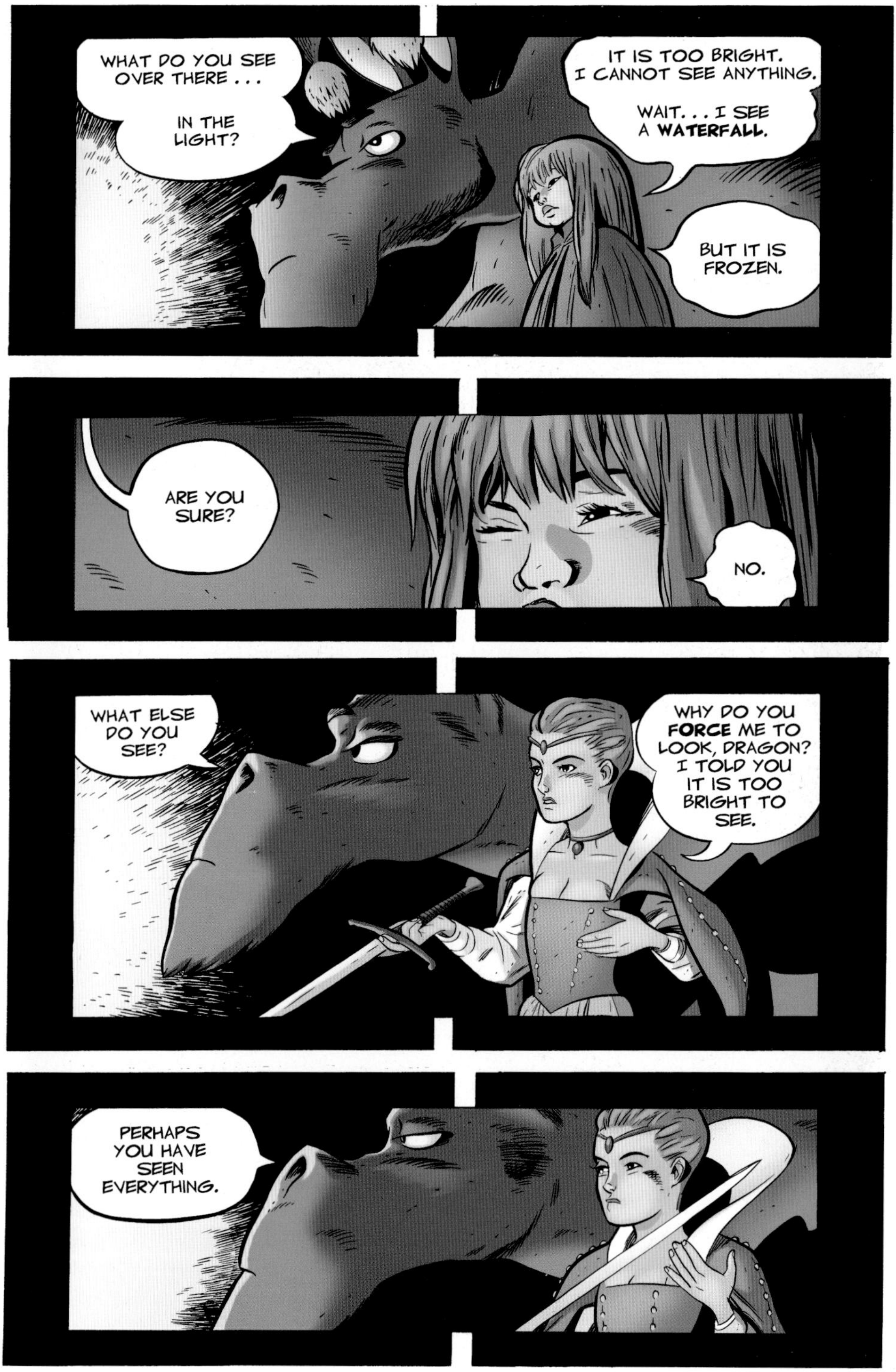
WHAT DO YOU SEE OVER THERE . . .
IN THE LIGHT?
IT IS TOO BRIGHT. I CANNOT SEE ANYTHING.
WAIT. . . I SEE A **WATERFALL.**
BUT IT IS FROZEN.
ARE YOU SURE?
NO.
WHAT ELSE DO YOU SEE?
WHY DO YOU **FORCE** ME TO LOOK, DRAGON? I TOLD YOU IT IS TOO BRIGHT TO SEE.
PERHAPS YOU HAVE SEEN EVERYTHING.

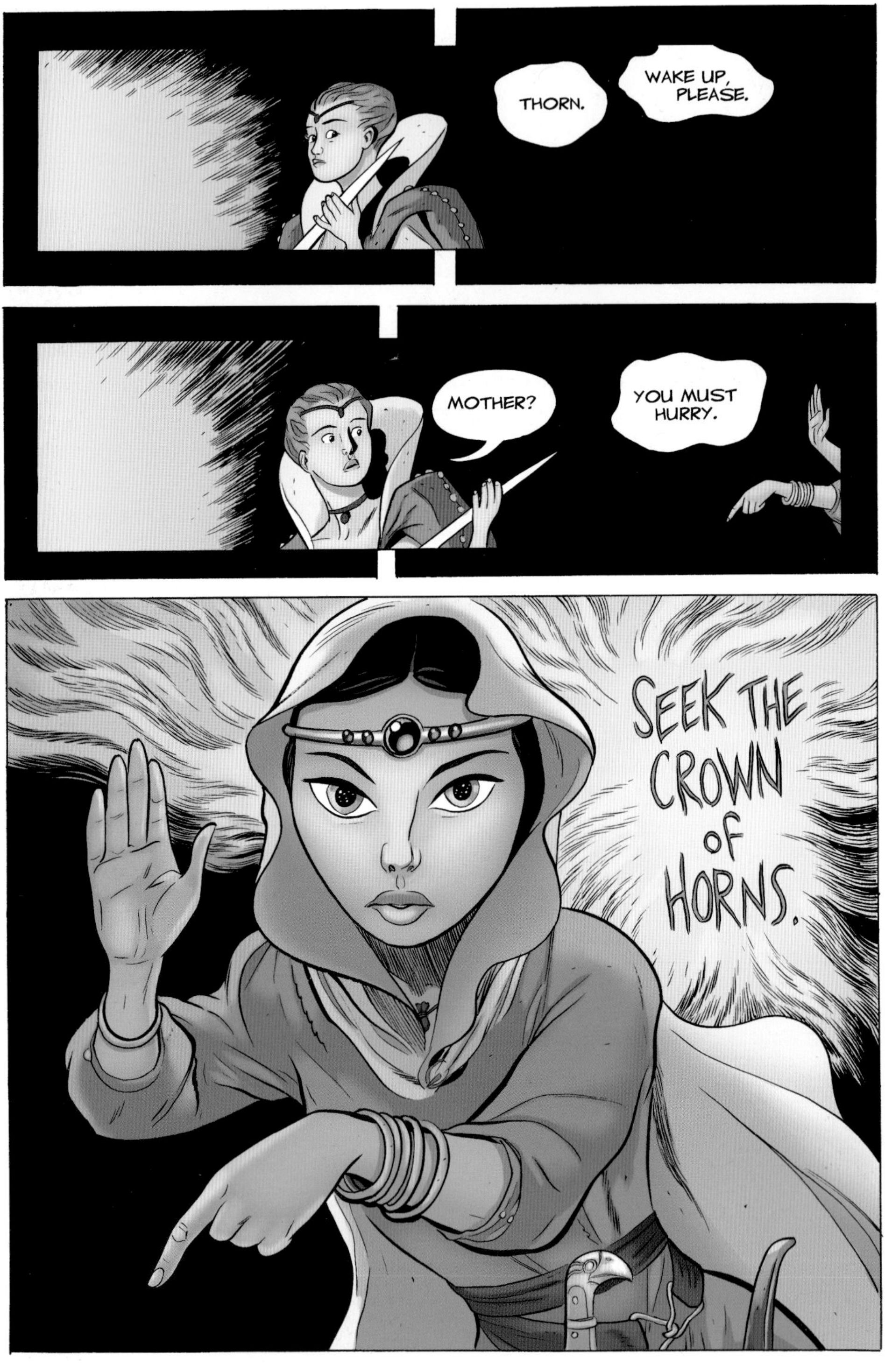
THORN.
WAKE UP, PLEASE.
MOTHER?
YOU MUST HURRY.
SEEK THE CROWN of HORNS.

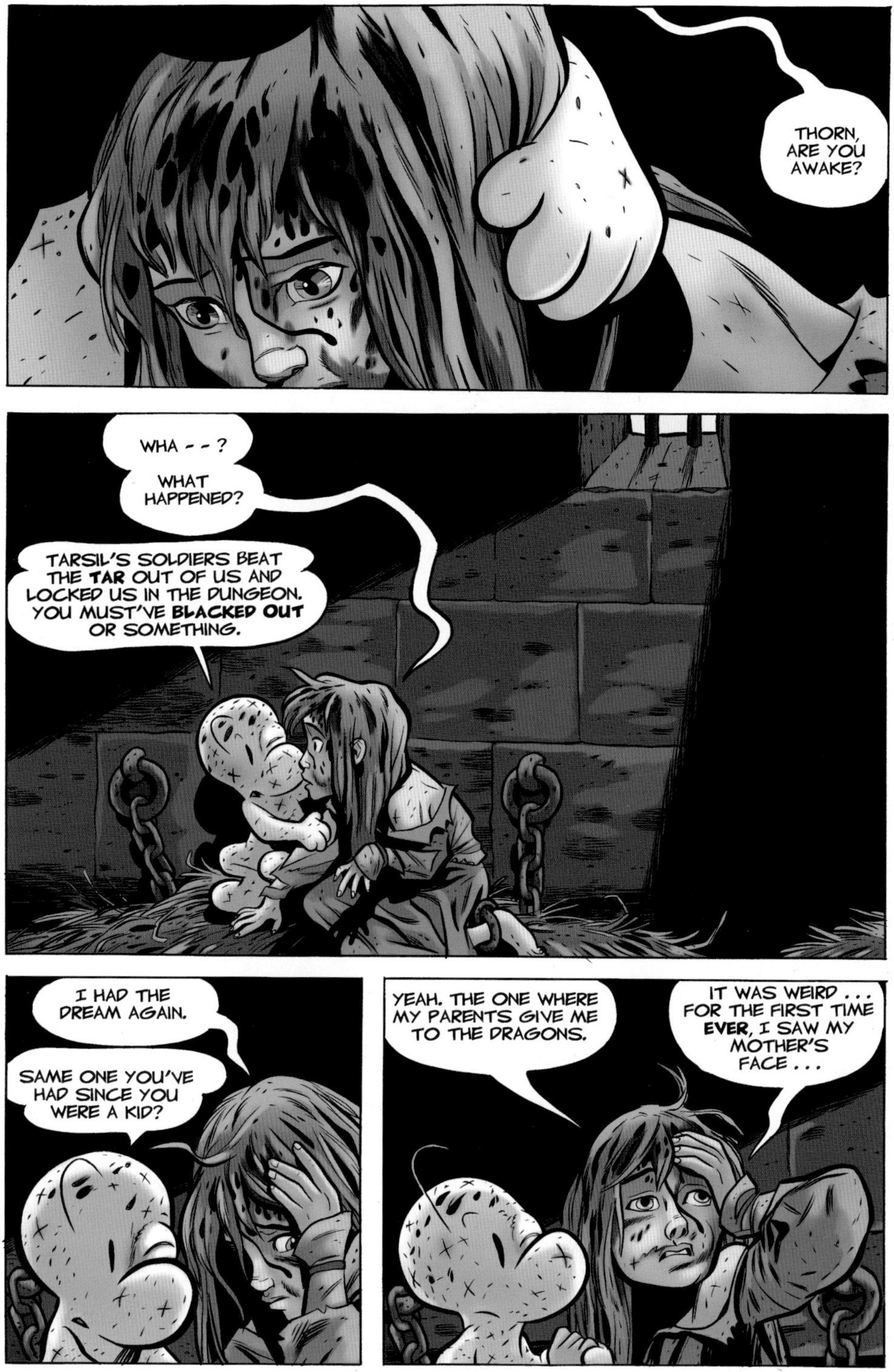
THORN, ARE YOU AWAKE?
WHA - - ?
WHAT HAPPENED?
TARSIL'S SOLDIERS BEAT THE TAR OUT OF US AND LOCKED US IN THE DUNGEON. YOU MUST'VE BLACKED OUT OR SOMETHING.
I HAD THE DREAM AGAIN.
SAME ONE YOU'VE HAD SINCE YOU WERE A KID?
YEAH. THE ONE WHERE MY PARENTS GIVE ME TO THE DRAGONS.
IT WAS WEIRD . . . FOR THE FIRST TIME EVER, I SAW MY MOTHER'S FACE . . .

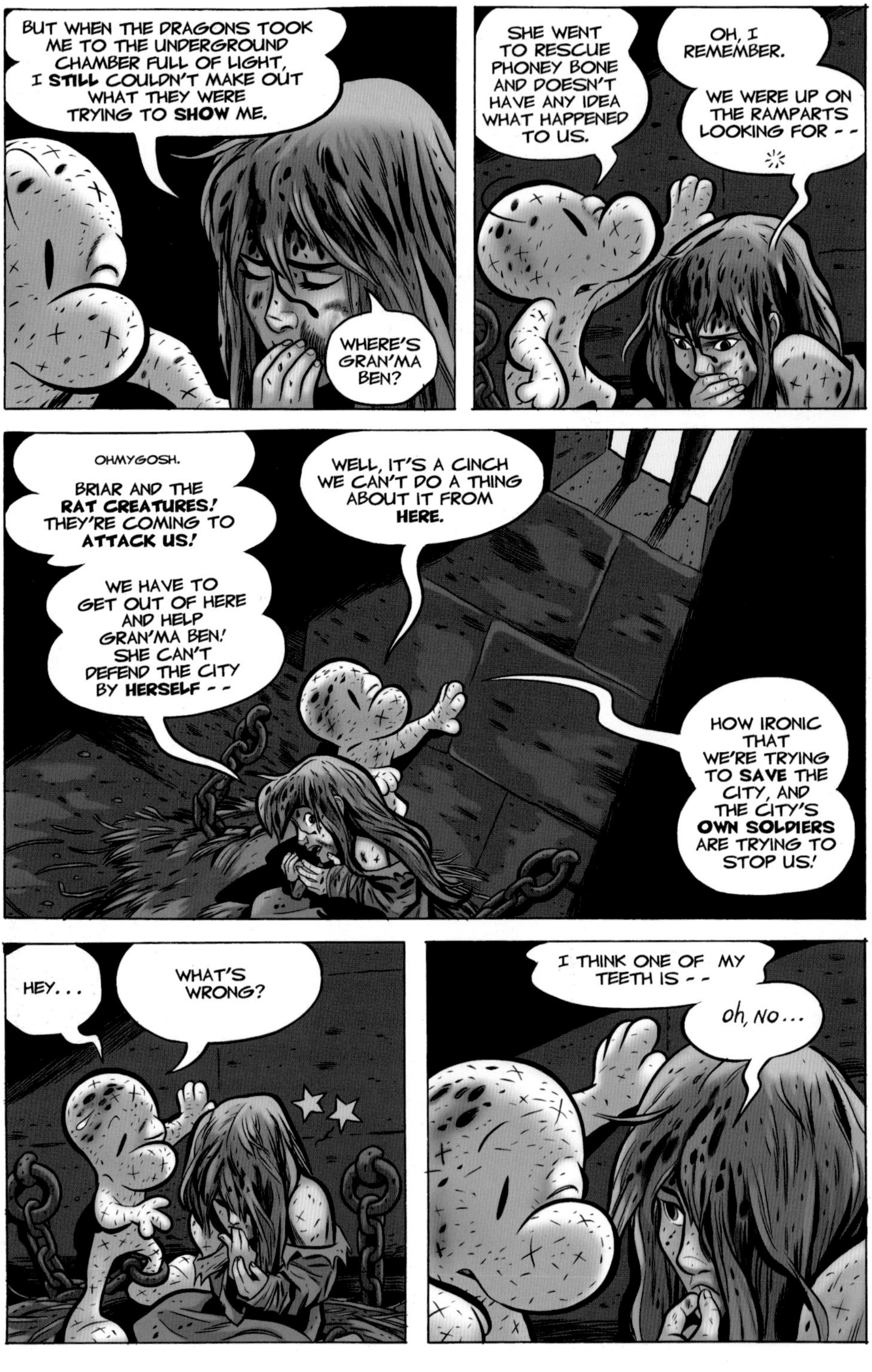
BUT WHEN THE DRAGONS TOOK ME TO THE UNDERGROUND CHAMBER FULL OF LIGHT, I STILL COULDN'T MAKE OUT WHAT THEY WERE TRYING TO SHOW ME.
WHERE'S GRAN'MA BEN?
SHE WENT TO RESCUE PHONEY BONE AND DOESN'T HAVE ANY IDEA WHAT HAPPENED TO US.
OH, I REMEMBER.
WE WERE UP ON THE RAMPARTS LOOKING FOR - -
OHMYGOSH.
BRIAR AND THE RAT CREATURES! THEY'RE COMING TO ATTACK US!
WE HAVE TO GET OUT OF HERE AND HELP GRAN'MA BEN! SHE CAN'T DEFEND THE CITY BY HERSELF - -
WELL, IT'S A CINCH WE CAN'T DO A THING ABOUT IT FROM HERE.
HOW IRONIC THAT WE'RE TRYING TO SAVE THE CITY, AND THE CITY'S OWN SOLDIERS ARE TRYING TO STOP US!
HEY...
WHAT'S WRONG?
I THINK ONE OF MY TEETH IS - -
oh, no...

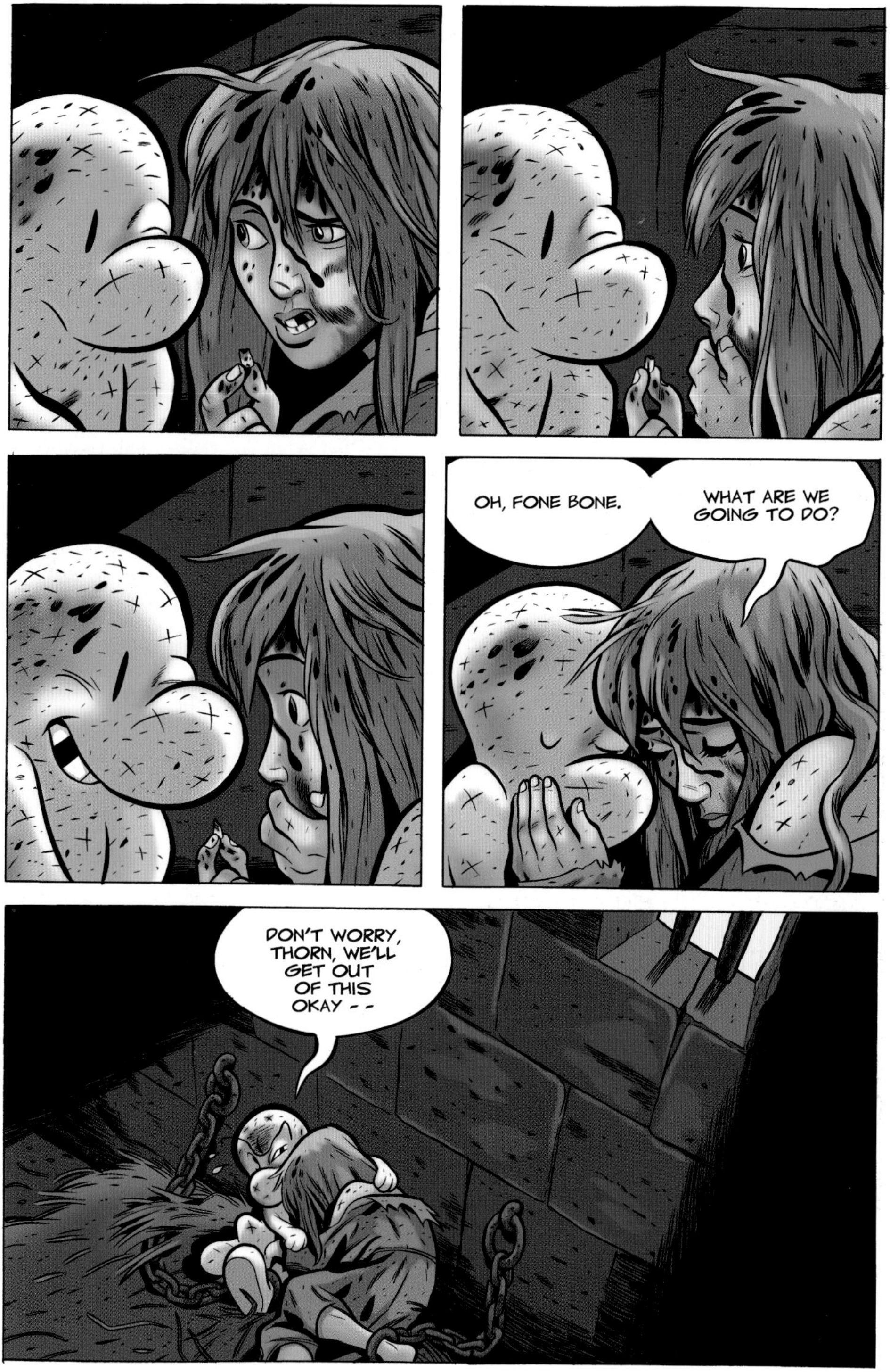
OH, FONE BONE.
WHAT ARE WE GOING TO DO?
DON'T WORRY, THORN, WE'LL GET OUT OF THIS OKAY --

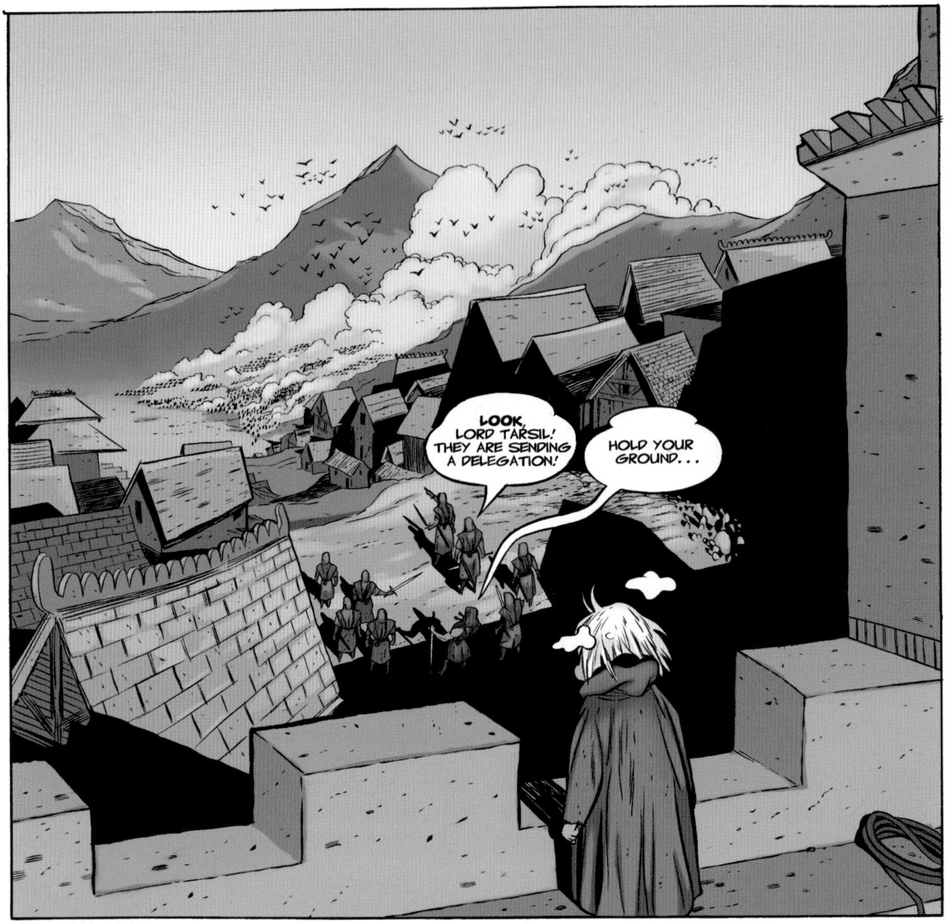
LOOK, LORD TARSIL! THEY ARE SENDING A DELEGATION!
HOLD YOUR GROUND...

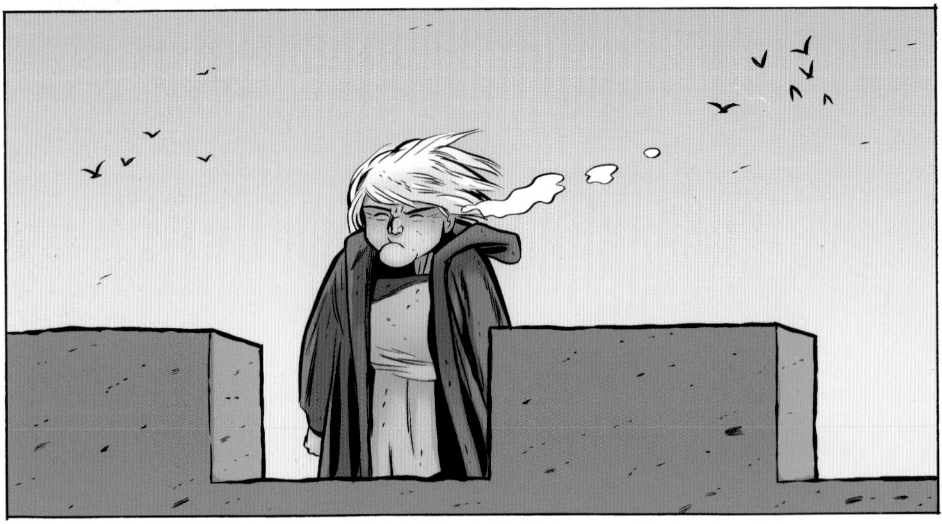

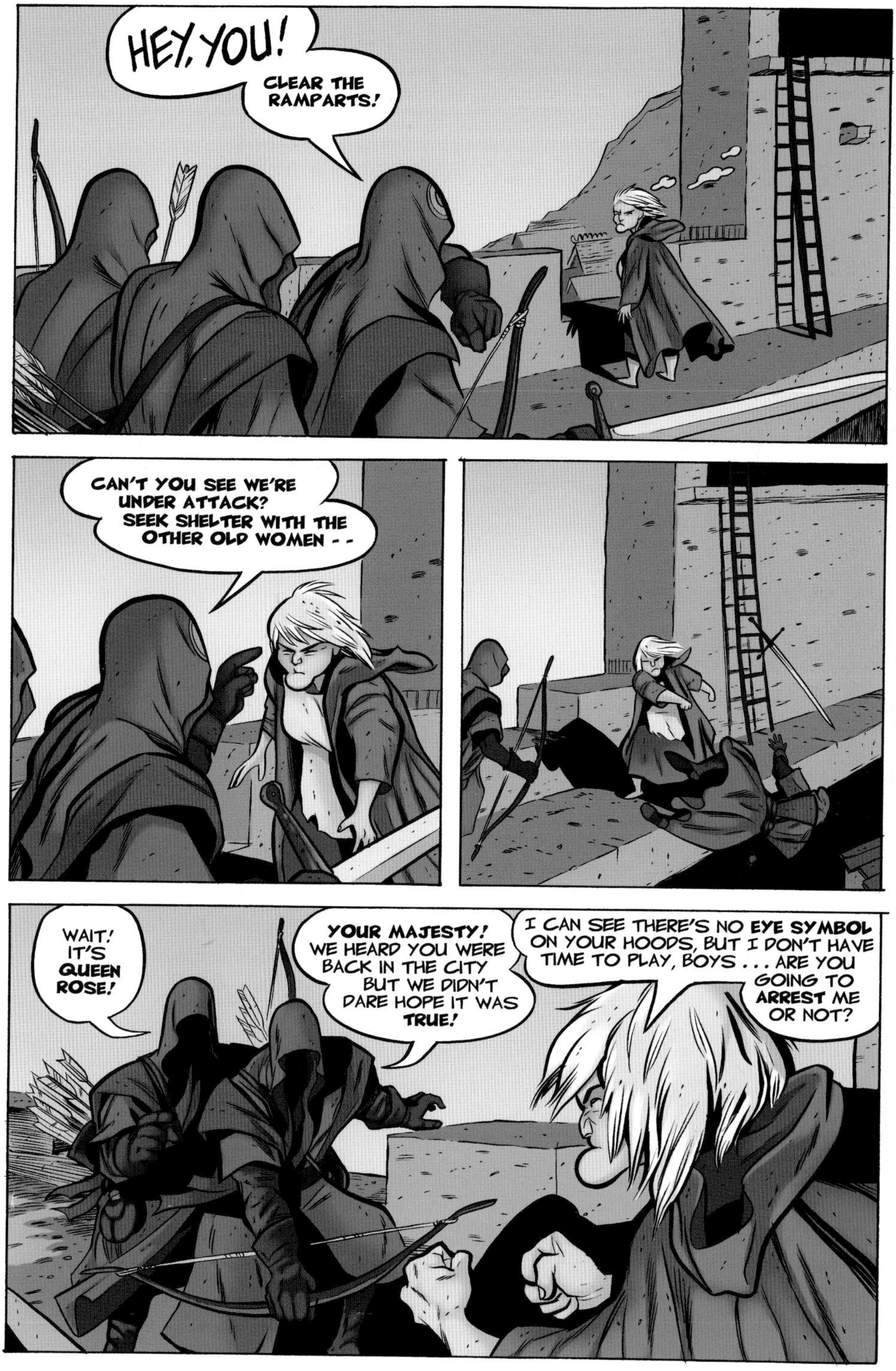
HEY, YOU!
CLEAR THE RAMPARTS!
CAN'T YOU SEE WE'RE UNDER ATTACK? SEEK SHELTER WITH THE OTHER OLD WOMEN - -
WAIT! IT'S QUEEN ROSE!
YOUR MAJESTY! WE HEARD YOU WERE BACK IN THE CITY BUT WE DIDN'T DARE HOPE IT WAS TRUE!
I CAN SEE THERE'S NO EYE SYMBOL ON YOUR HOODS, BUT I DON'T HAVE TIME TO PLAY, BOYS . . . ARE YOU GOING TO ARREST ME OR NOT?

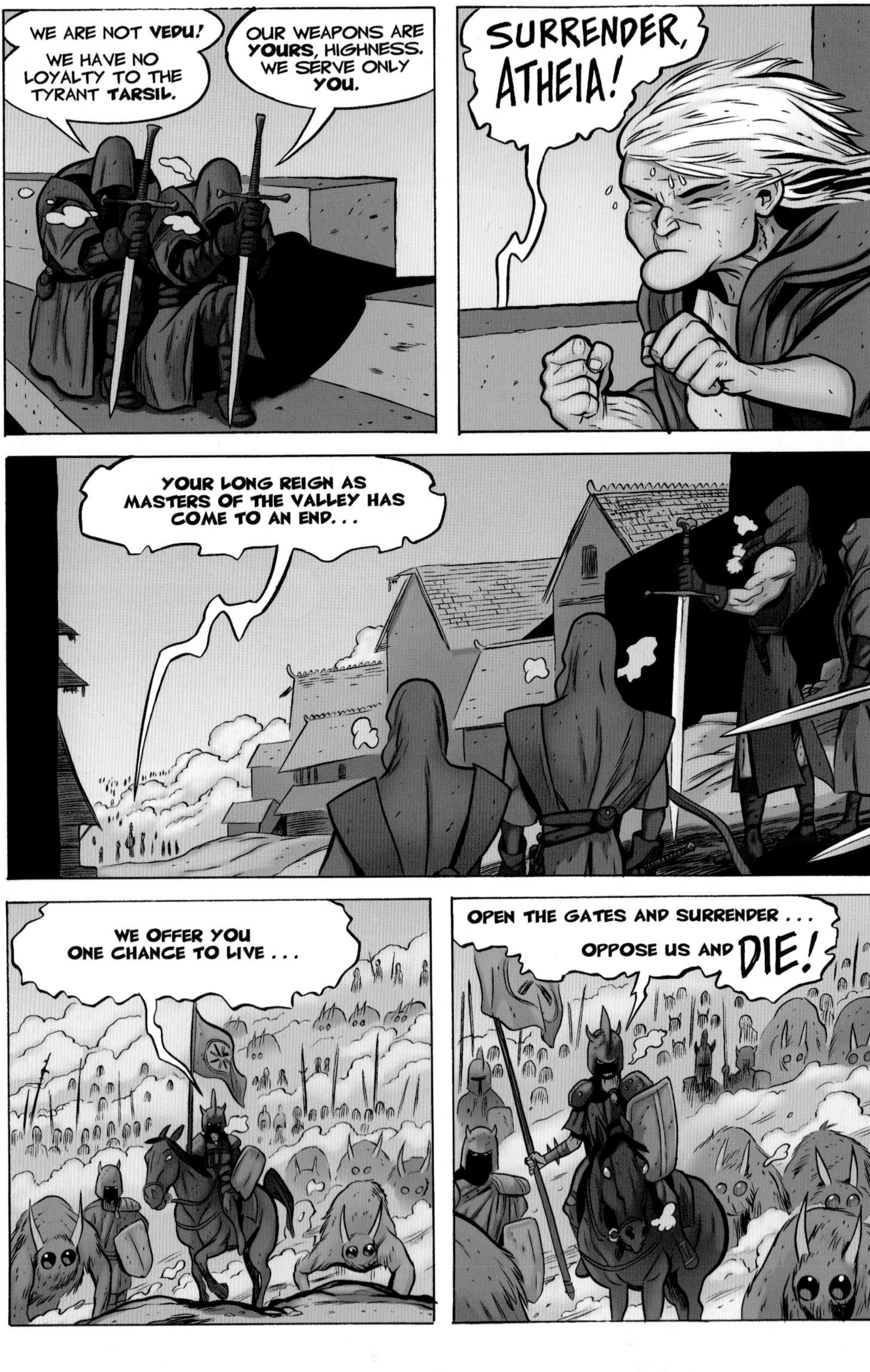
WE ARE NOT VEDU! WE HAVE NO LOYALTY TO THE TYRANT TARSIL.
OUR WEAPONS ARE YOURS, HIGHNESS. WE SERVE ONLY YOU.
SURRENDER, ATHEIA!
YOUR LONG REIGN AS MASTERS OF THE VALLEY HAS COME TO AN END...
WE OFFER YOU ONE CHANCE TO LIVE...
OPEN THE GATES AND SURRENDER...
OPPOSE US AND DIE!

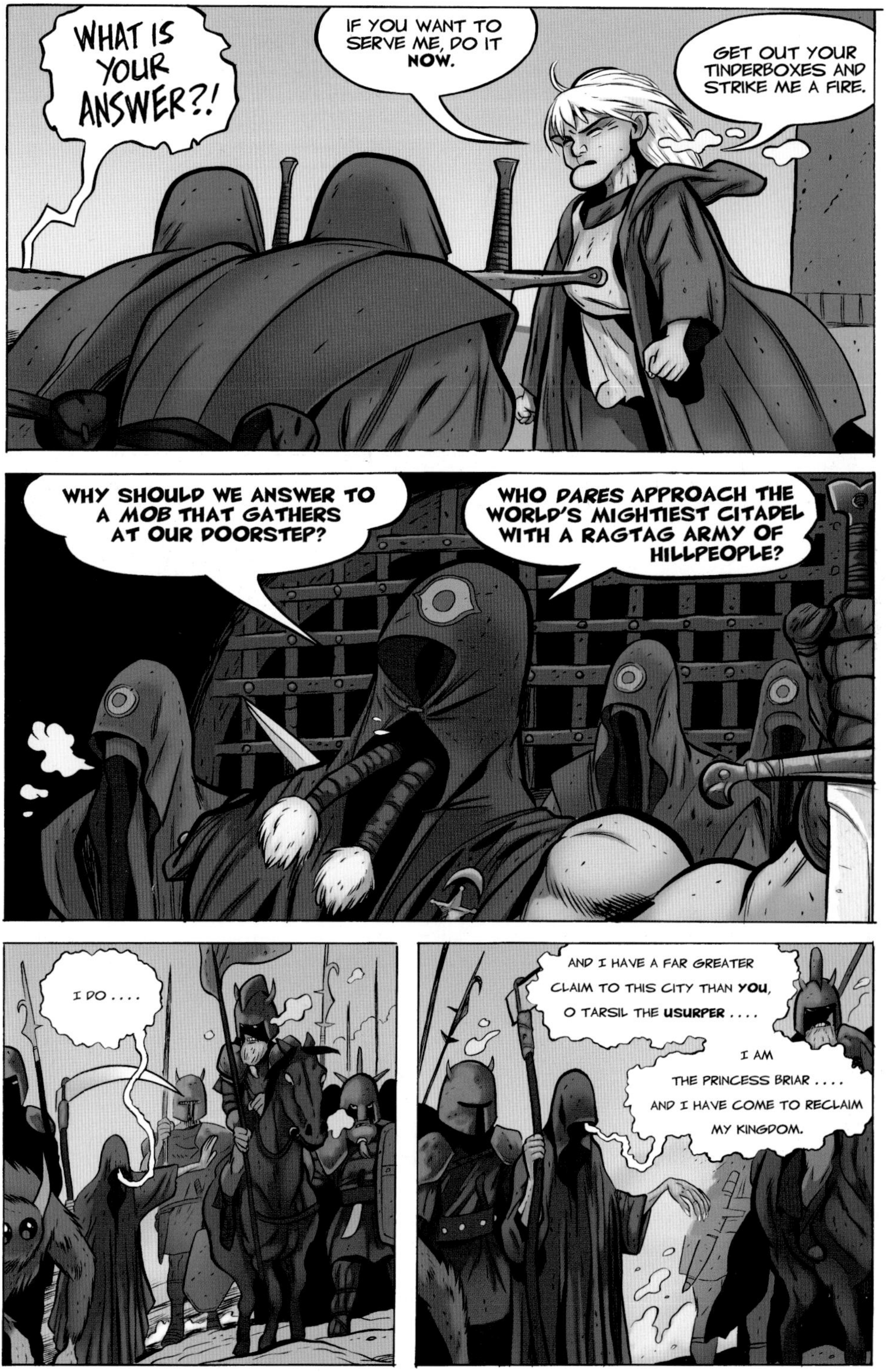
WHAT IS YOUR ANSWER?!
IF YOU WANT TO SERVE ME, DO IT NOW.
GET OUT YOUR TINDERBOXES AND STRIKE ME A FIRE.
WHY SHOULD WE ANSWER TO A MOB THAT GATHERS AT OUR DOORSTEP?
WHO DARES APPROACH THE WORLD'S MIGHTIEST CITADEL WITH A RAGTAG ARMY OF HILLPEOPLE?
I DO . . . .
AND I HAVE A FAR GREATER CLAIM TO THIS CITY THAN YOU, O TARSIL THE USURPER . . . .
I AM THE PRINCESS BRIAR . . . . AND I HAVE COME TO RECLAIM MY KINGDOM.

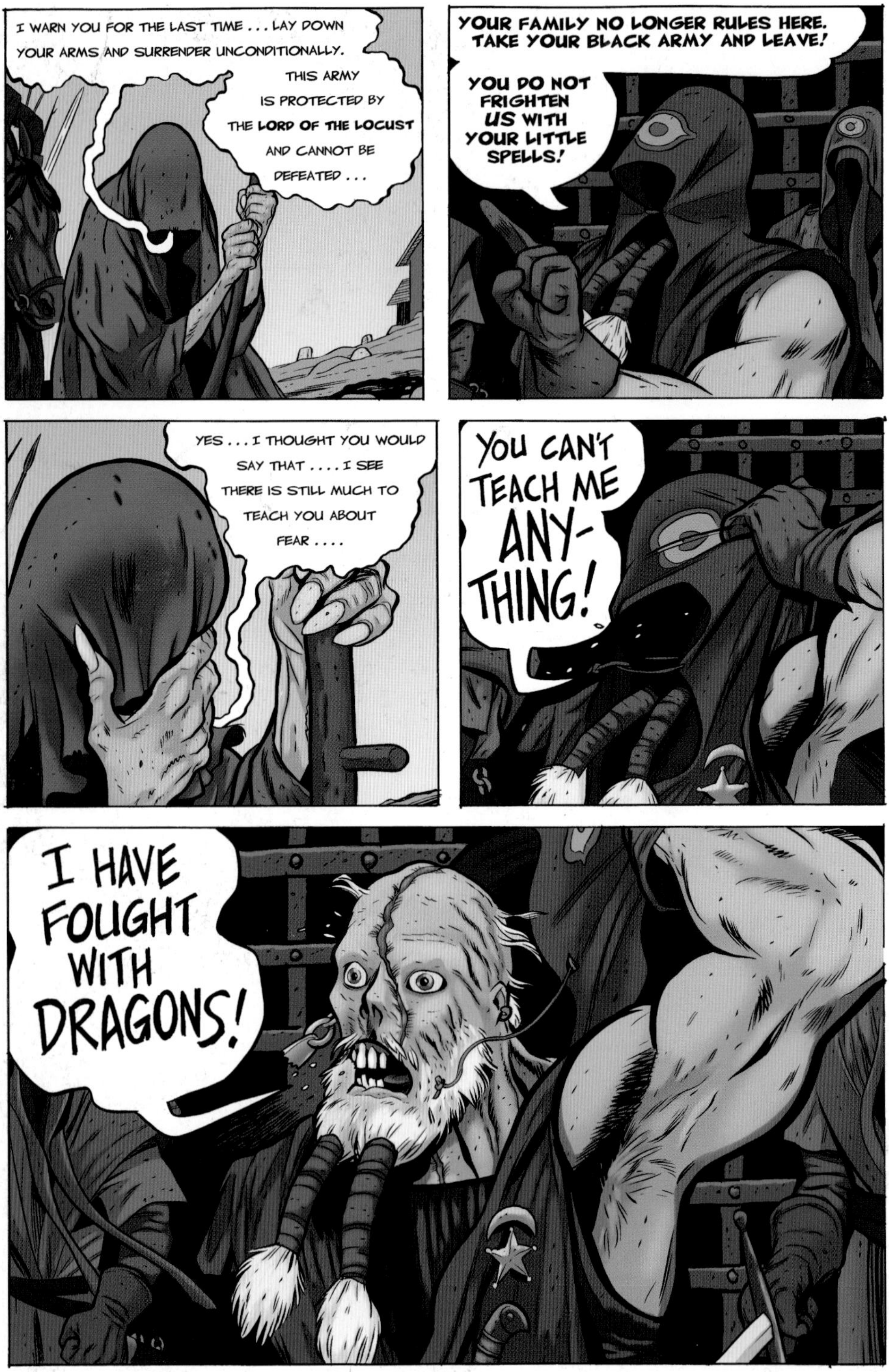
I WARN YOU FOR THE LAST TIME . . . LAY DOWN YOUR ARMS AND SURRENDER UNCONDITIONALLY.
THIS ARMY IS PROTECTED BY THE LORD OF THE LOCUST AND CANNOT BE DEFEATED . . .
YOUR FAMILY NO LONGER RULES HERE. TAKE YOUR BLACK ARMY AND LEAVE!
YOU DO NOT FRIGHTEN US WITH YOUR LITTLE SPELLS!
YES . . . I THOUGHT YOU WOULD SAY THAT . . . . I SEE THERE IS STILL MUCH TO TEACH YOU ABOUT FEAR . . . .
YOU CAN'T TEACH ME ANY-THING!
I HAVE FOUGHT WITH DRAGONS!

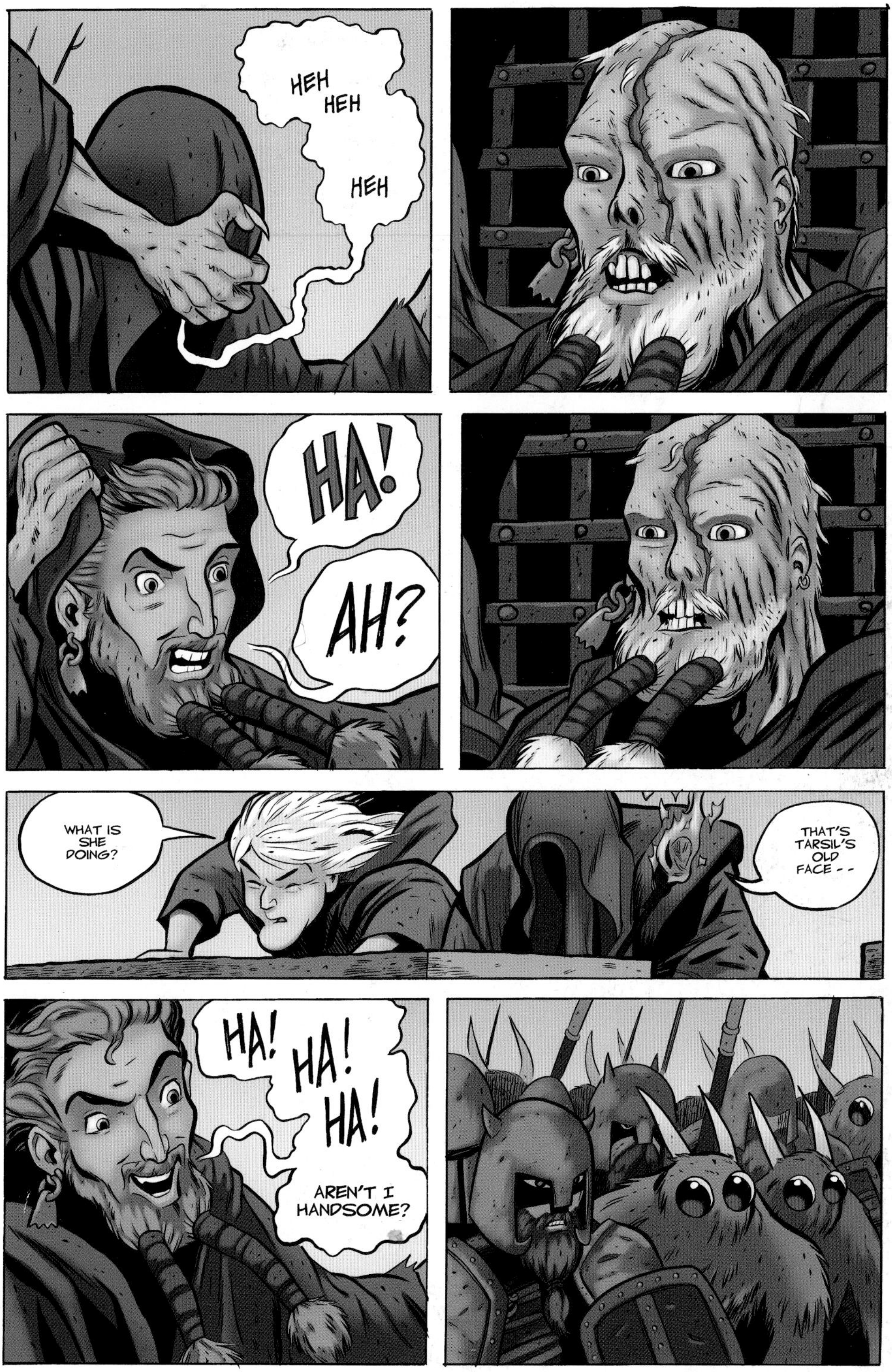
HEH
HEH
HEH
HA!
AH?
WHAT IS SHE DOING?
THAT'S TARSIL'S OLD FACE - -
HA!
HA!
HA!
AREN'T I HANDSOME?

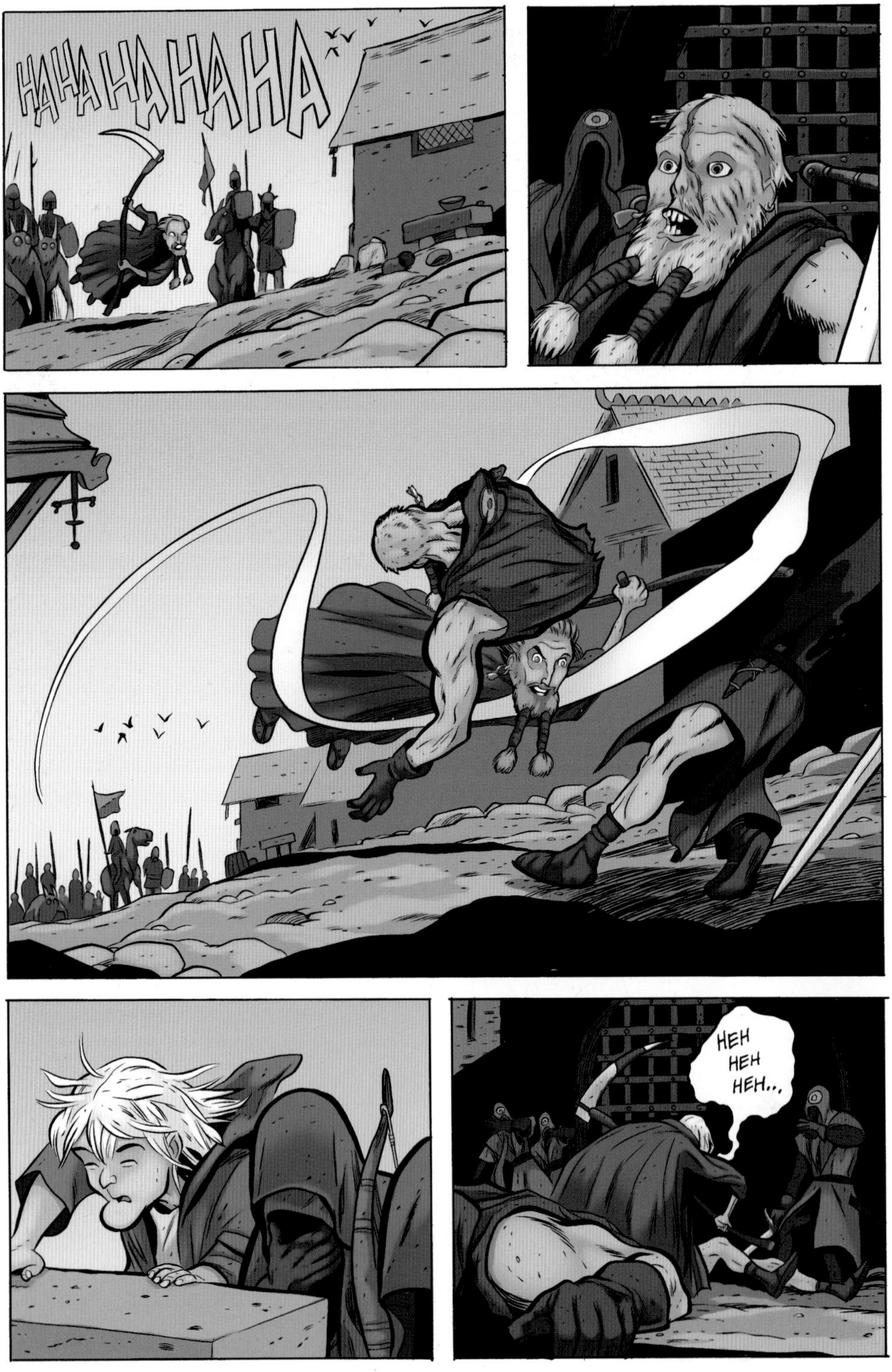
HAHAHAHAHAHA
HEH HEH HEH...

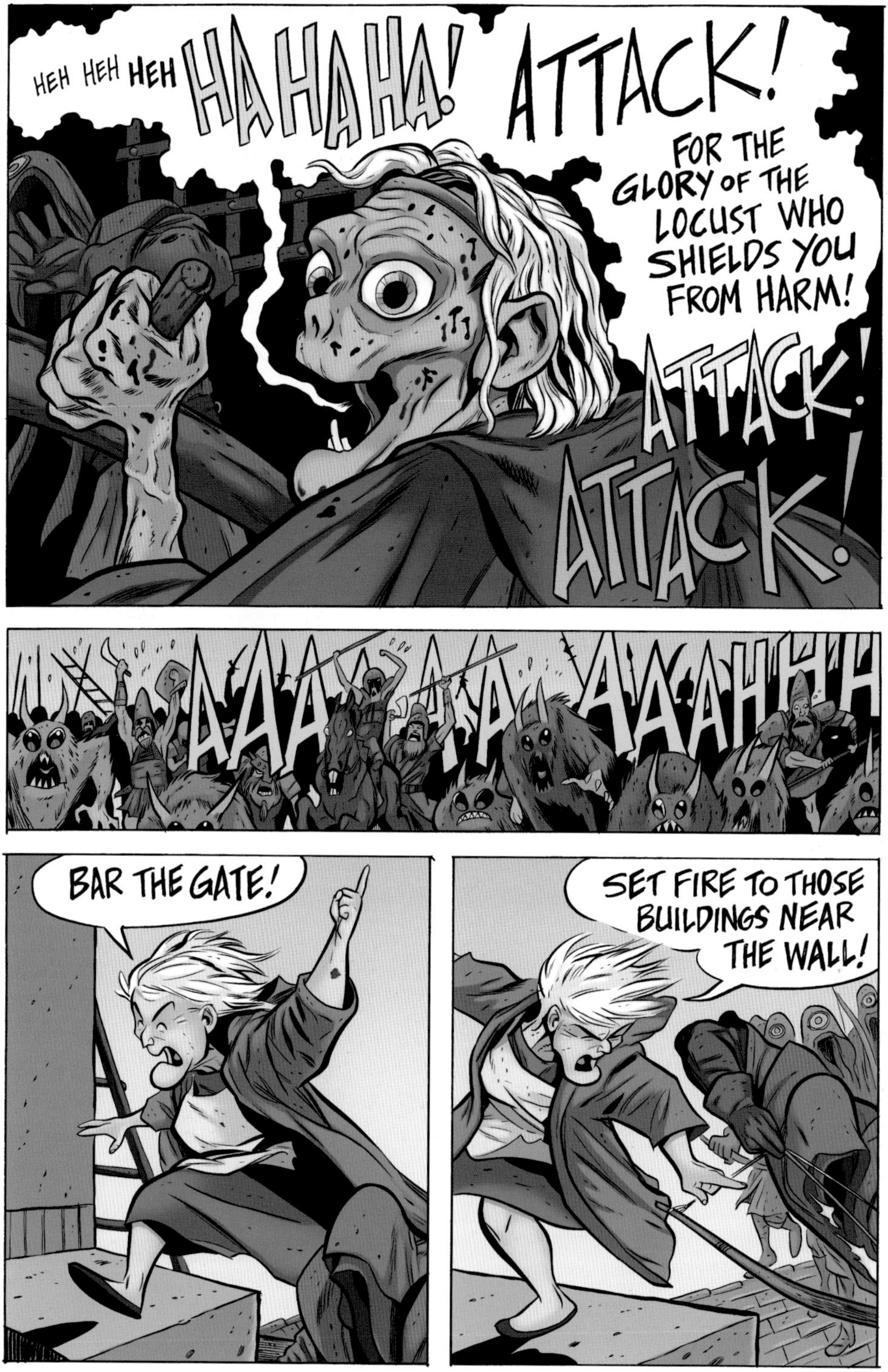
HEH HEH HEH HAHAHA! ATTACK!
FOR THE GLORY OF THE LOCUST WHO SHIELDS YOU FROM HARM!
ATTACK! ATTACK!
AAAAAAAAAAHHHH
BAR THE GATE!
SET FIRE TO THOSE BUILDINGS NEAR THE WALL!

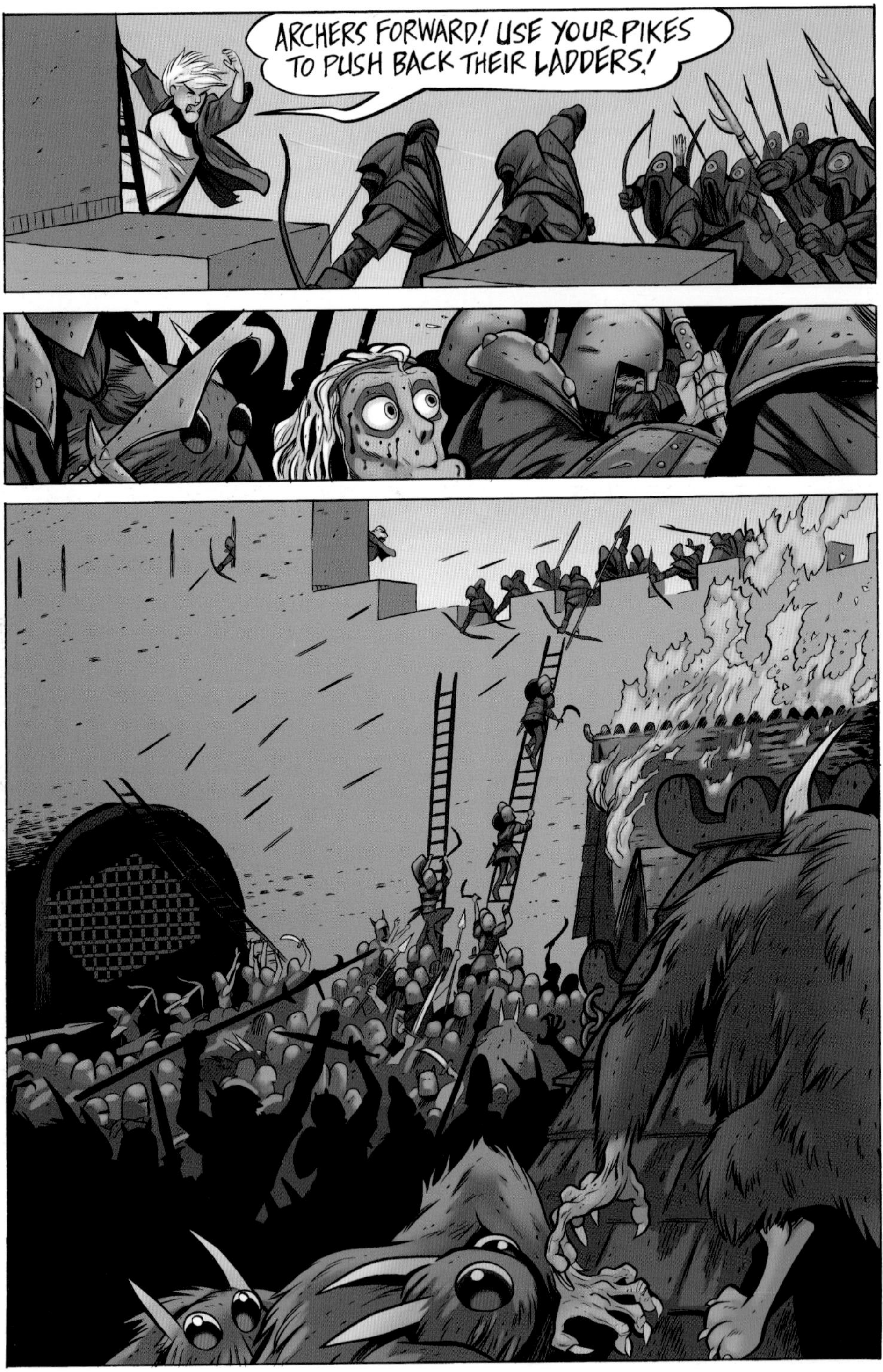
ARCHERS FORWARD! USE YOUR PIKES TO PUSH BACK THEIR LADDERS!

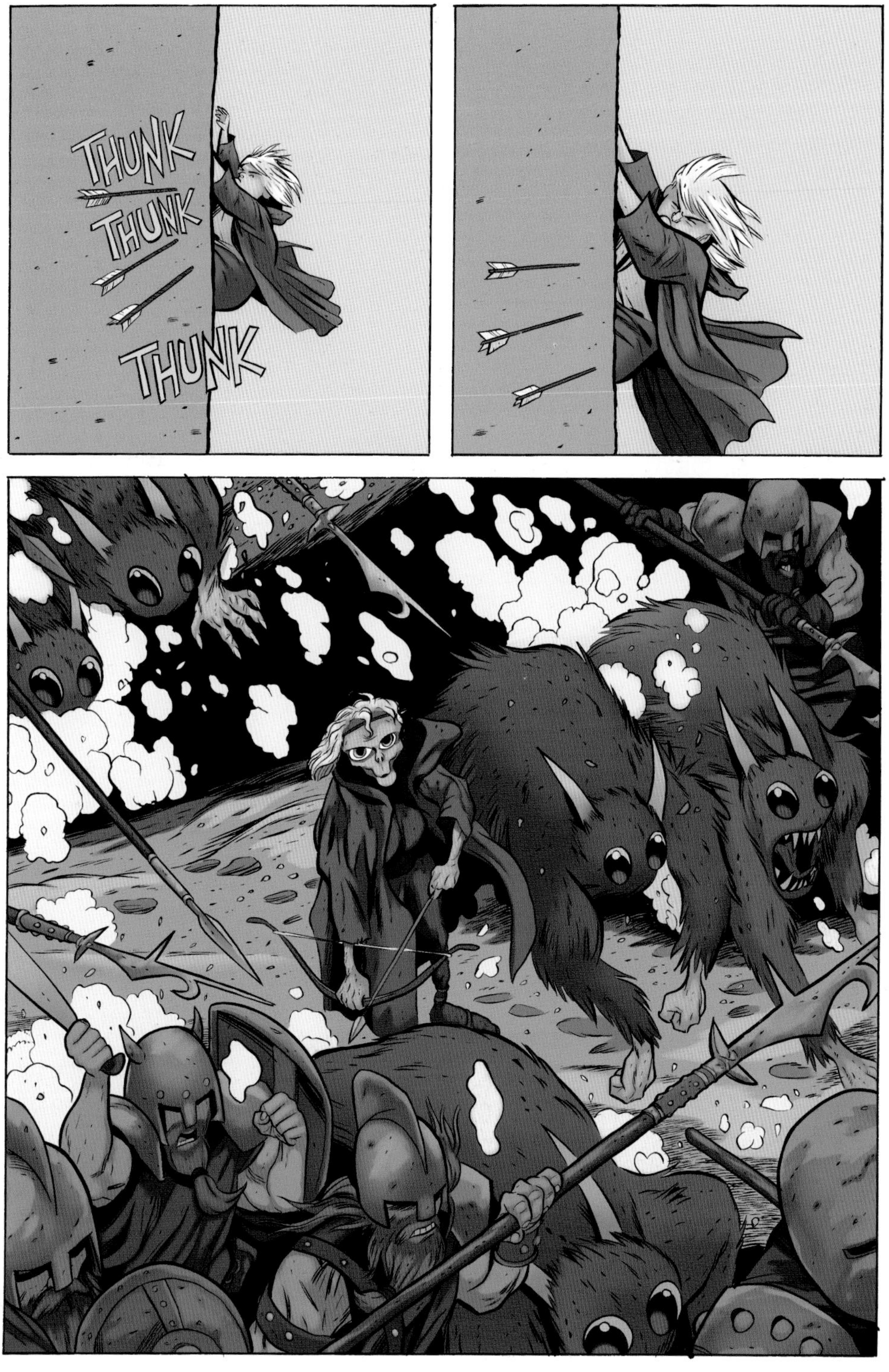
THUNK
THUNK
THUNK

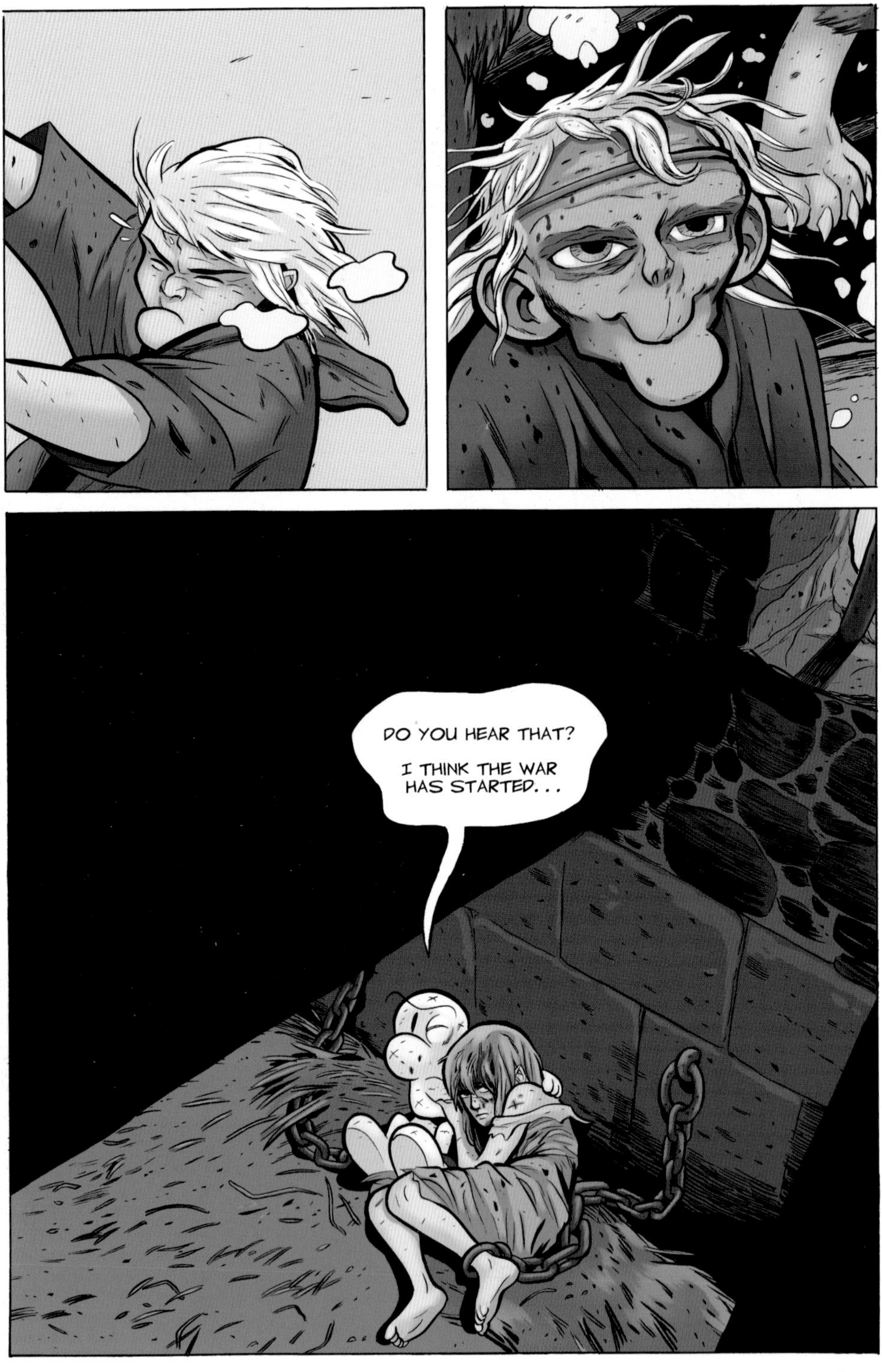
DO YOU HEAR THAT?
I THINK THE WAR HAS STARTED...

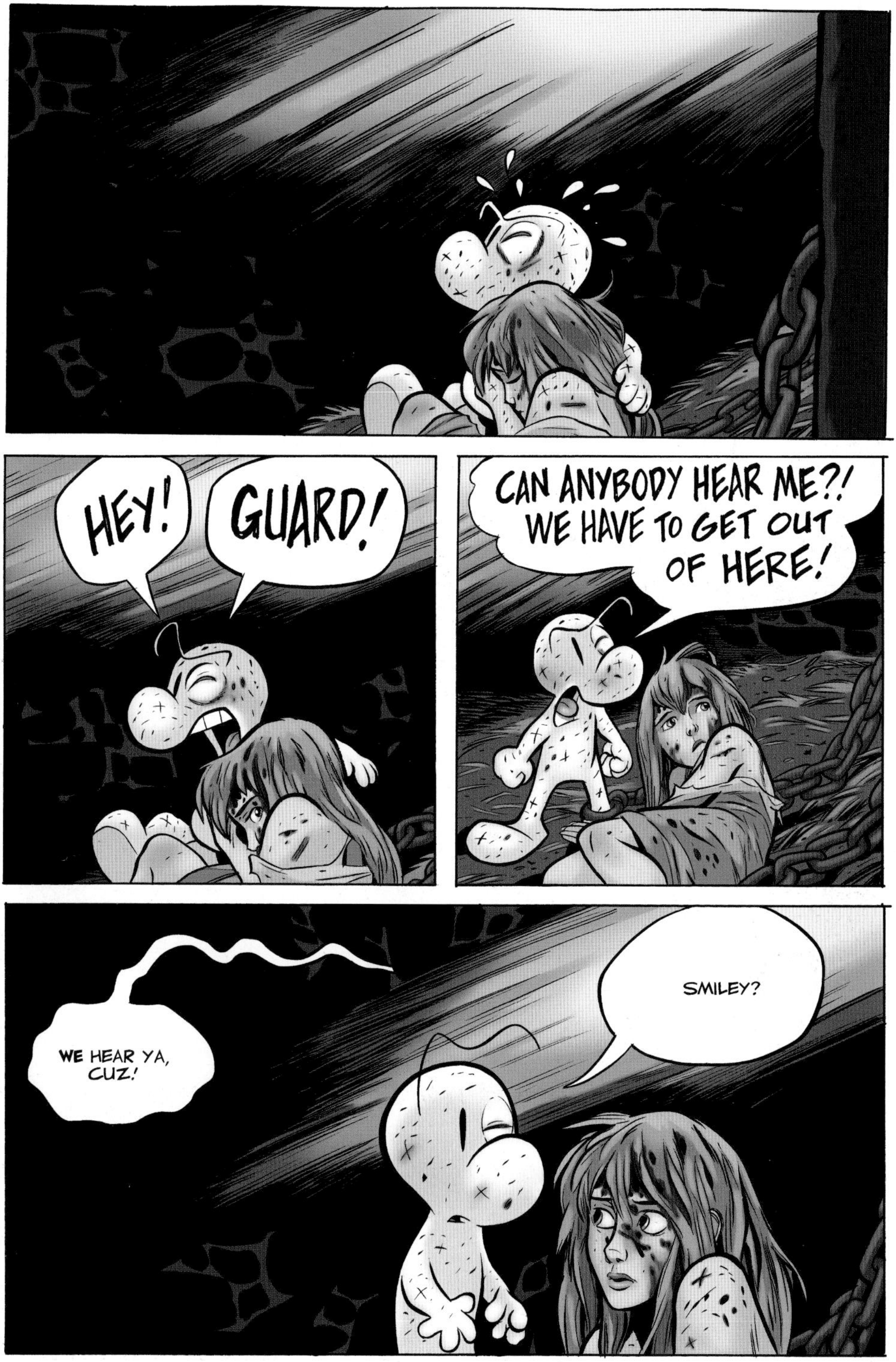
HEY!
GUARD!
CAN ANYBODY HEAR ME?! WE HAVE TO GET OUT OF HERE!
WE HEAR YA, CUZ!
SMILEY?

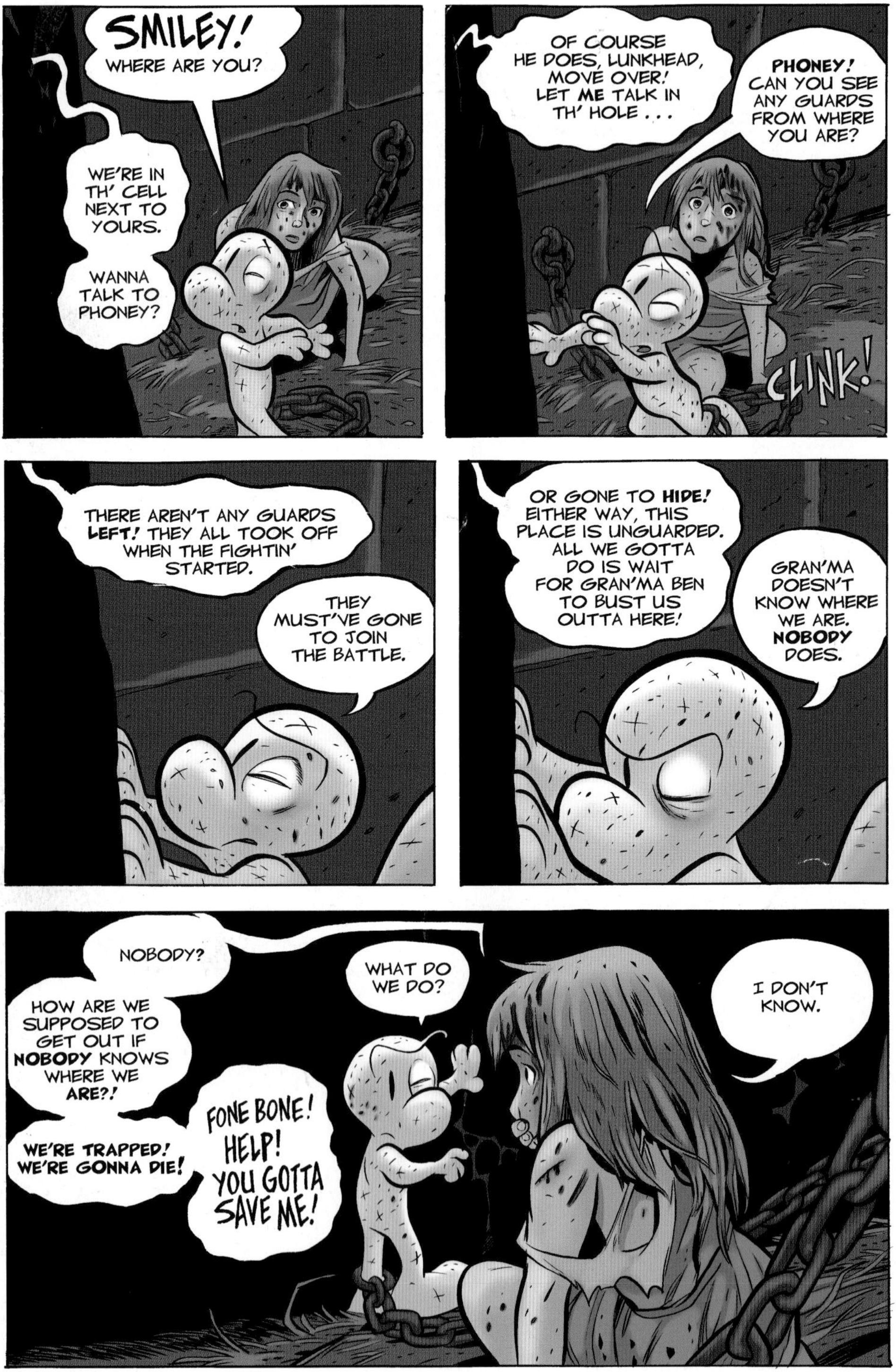
SMILEY! WHERE ARE YOU?
WE'RE IN TH' CELL NEXT TO YOURS.
WANNA TALK TO PHONEY?
OF COURSE HE DOES, LUNKHEAD, MOVE OVER! LET ME TALK IN TH' HOLE . . .
PHONEY! CAN YOU SEE ANY GUARDS FROM WHERE YOU ARE?
CLINK!
THERE AREN'T ANY GUARDS LEFT! THEY ALL TOOK OFF WHEN THE FIGHTIN' STARTED.
THEY MUST'VE GONE TO JOIN THE BATTLE.
OR GONE TO HIDE! EITHER WAY, THIS PLACE IS UNGUARDED. ALL WE GOTTA DO IS WAIT FOR GRAN'MA BEN TO BUST US OUTTA HERE!
GRAN'MA DOESN'T KNOW WHERE WE ARE. NOBODY DOES.
NOBODY?
HOW ARE WE SUPPOSED TO GET OUT IF NOBODY KNOWS WHERE WE ARE?!
WE'RE TRAPPED! WE'RE GONNA DIE!
FONE BONE! HELP! YOU GOTTA SAVE ME!
WHAT DO WE DO?
I DON'T KNOW.

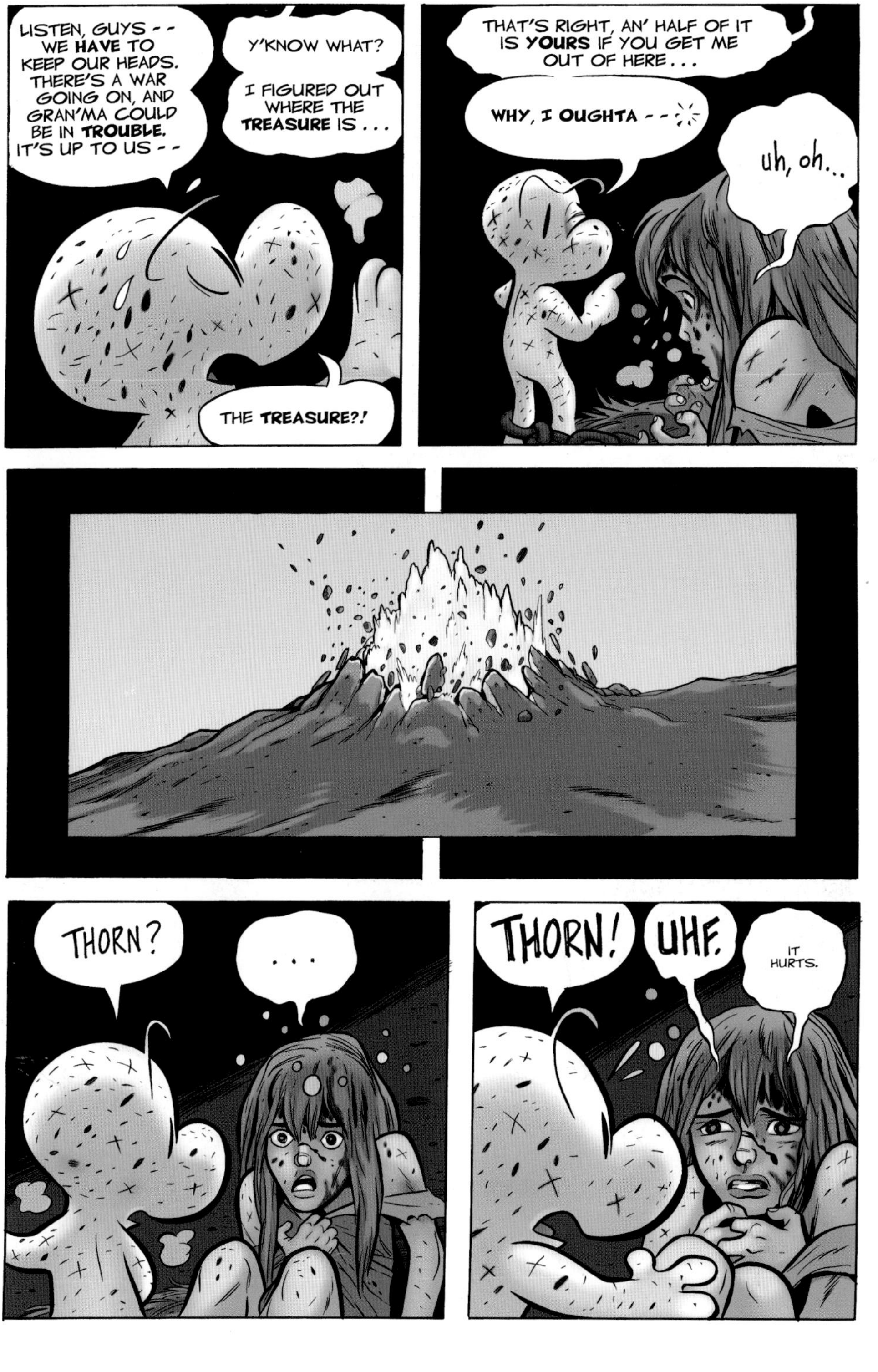
LISTEN, GUYS -- WE HAVE TO KEEP OUR HEADS. THERE'S A WAR GOING ON, AND GRAN'MA COULD BE IN TROUBLE. IT'S UP TO US --
Y'KNOW WHAT?
I FIGURED OUT WHERE THE TREASURE IS...
THE TREASURE?!
THAT'S RIGHT, AN' HALF OF IT IS YOURS IF YOU GET ME OUT OF HERE...
WHY, I OUGHTA --
uh, oh...
THORN?
...
THORN!
UHF.
IT HURTS.

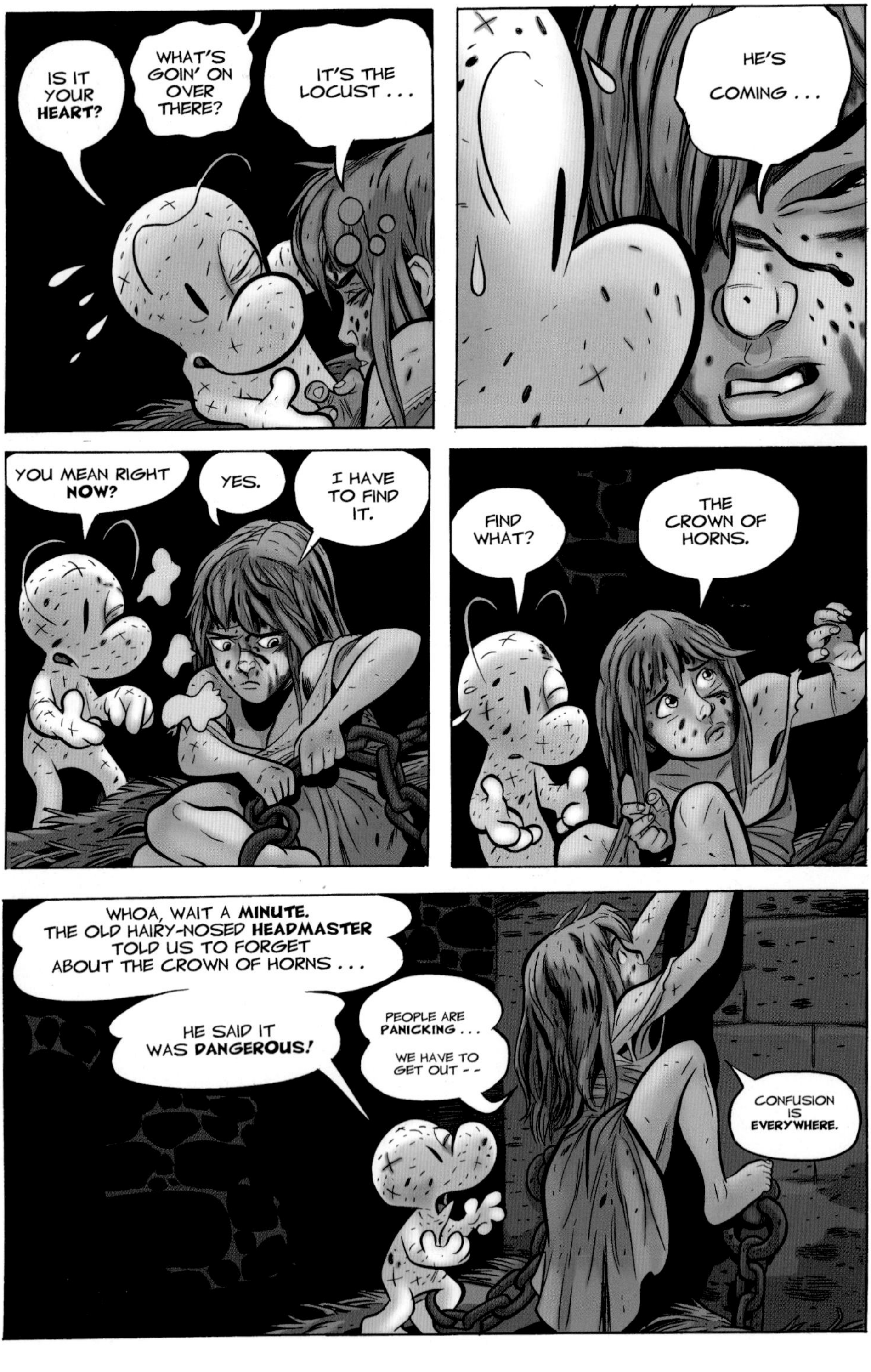
IS IT YOUR **HEART?**
WHAT'S GOIN' ON OVER THERE?
IT'S THE LOCUST . . .
HE'S COMING . . .
YOU MEAN RIGHT **NOW?**
YES.
I HAVE TO FIND IT.
FIND WHAT?
THE CROWN OF HORNS.
WHOA, WAIT A **MINUTE.** THE OLD HAIRY-NOSED **HEADMASTER** TOLD US TO FORGET ABOUT THE CROWN OF HORNS . . .
HE SAID IT WAS **DANGEROUS!**
PEOPLE ARE **PANICKING** . . .
WE HAVE TO GET OUT - -
CONFUSION IS **EVERYWHERE.**

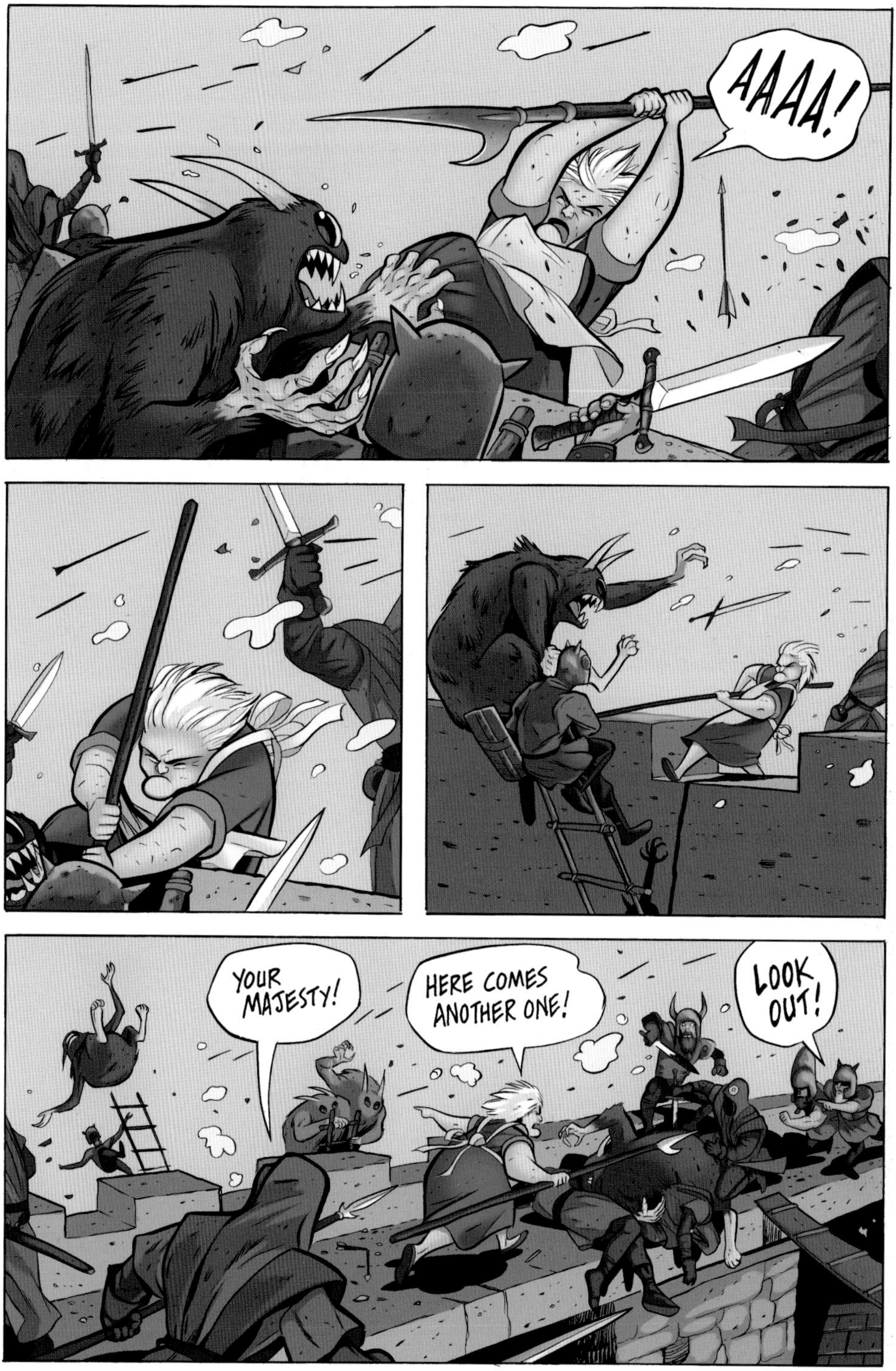
AAAA!
YOUR MAJESTY!
HERE COMES ANOTHER ONE!
LOOK OUT!

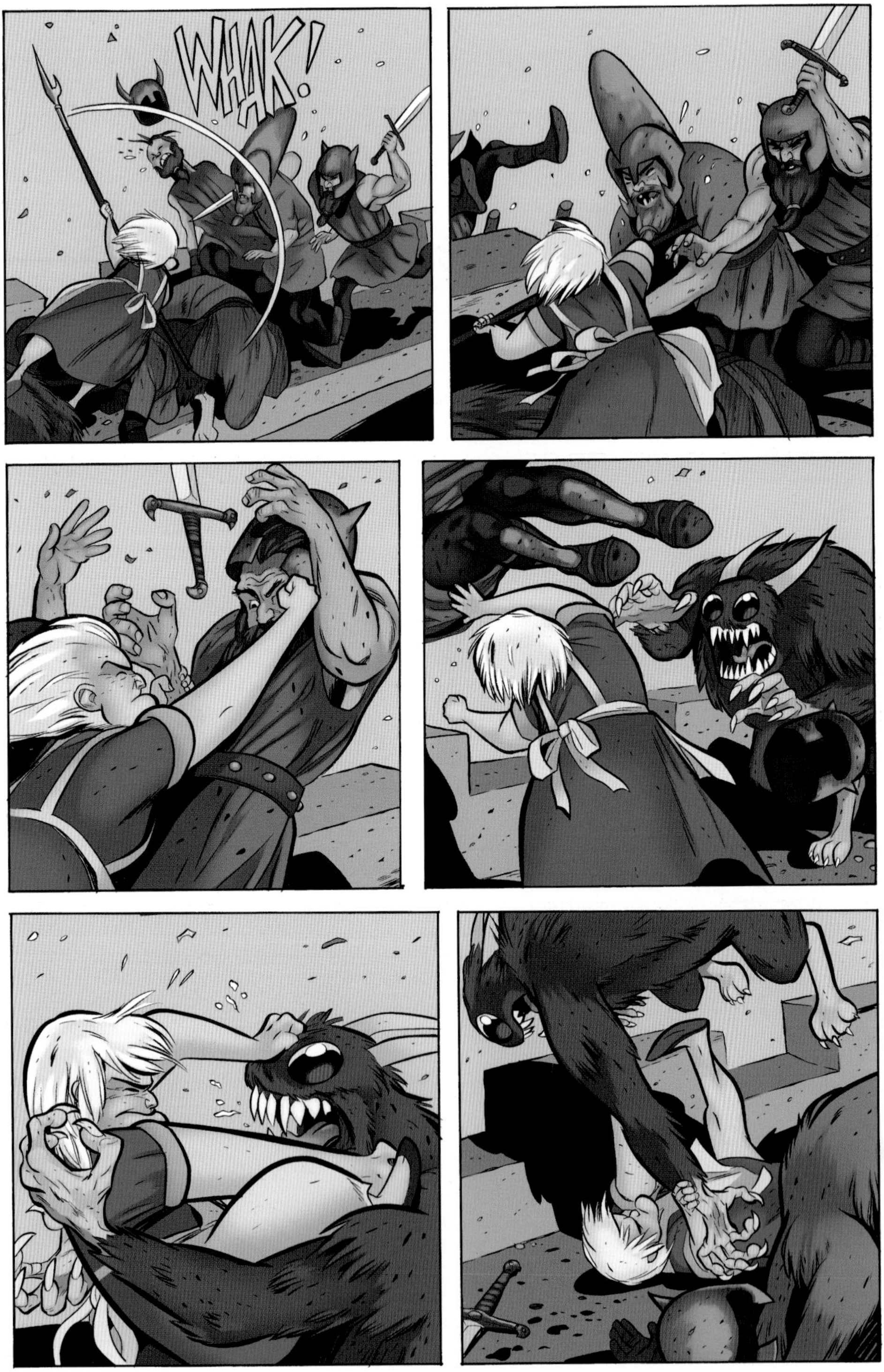
WHAK!

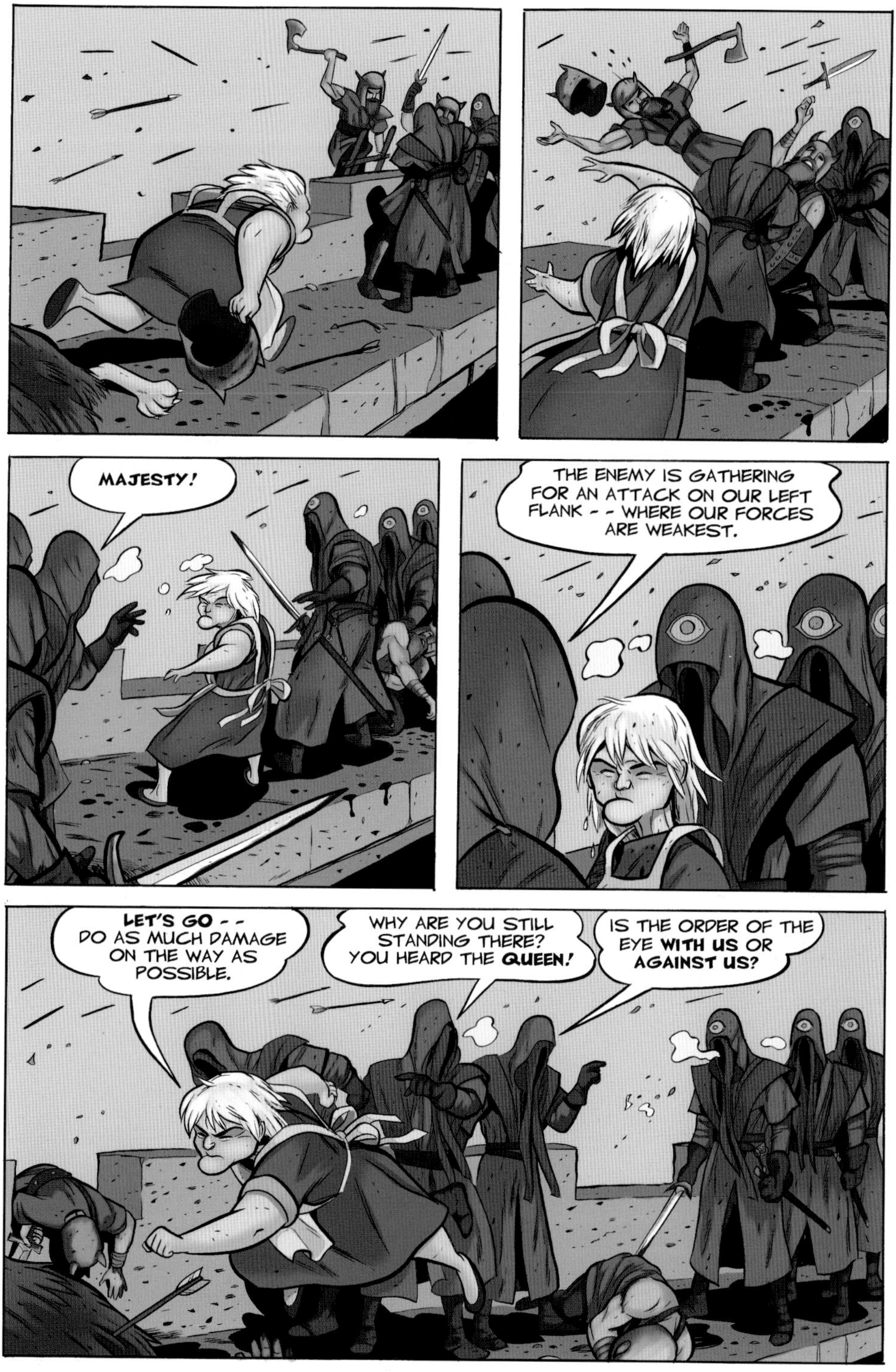
MAJESTY!
THE ENEMY IS GATHERING FOR AN ATTACK ON OUR LEFT FLANK - - WHERE OUR FORCES ARE WEAKEST.
LET'S GO - - DO AS MUCH DAMAGE ON THE WAY AS POSSIBLE.
WHY ARE YOU STILL STANDING THERE? YOU HEARD THE QUEEN!
IS THE ORDER OF THE EYE WITH US OR AGAINST US?

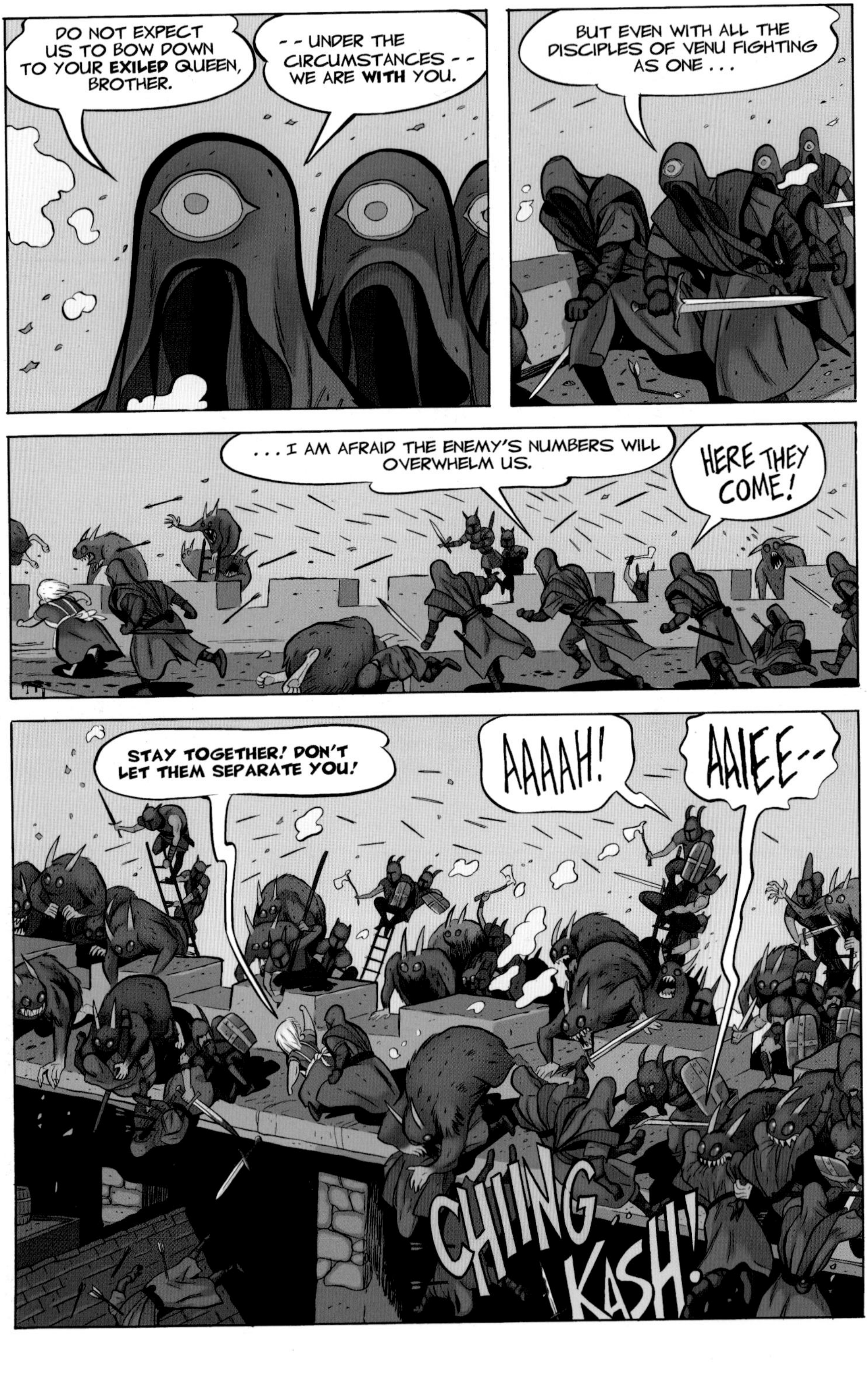
DO NOT EXPECT US TO BOW DOWN TO YOUR EXILED QUEEN, BROTHER.
- - UNDER THE CIRCUMSTANCES - - WE ARE WITH YOU.
BUT EVEN WITH ALL THE DISCIPLES OF VENU FIGHTING AS ONE . . .
. . . I AM AFRAID THE ENEMY'S NUMBERS WILL OVERWHELM US.
HERE THEY COME!
STAY TOGETHER! DON'T LET THEM SEPARATE YOU!
AAAAH!
AAIEE- -
CHING KASH!

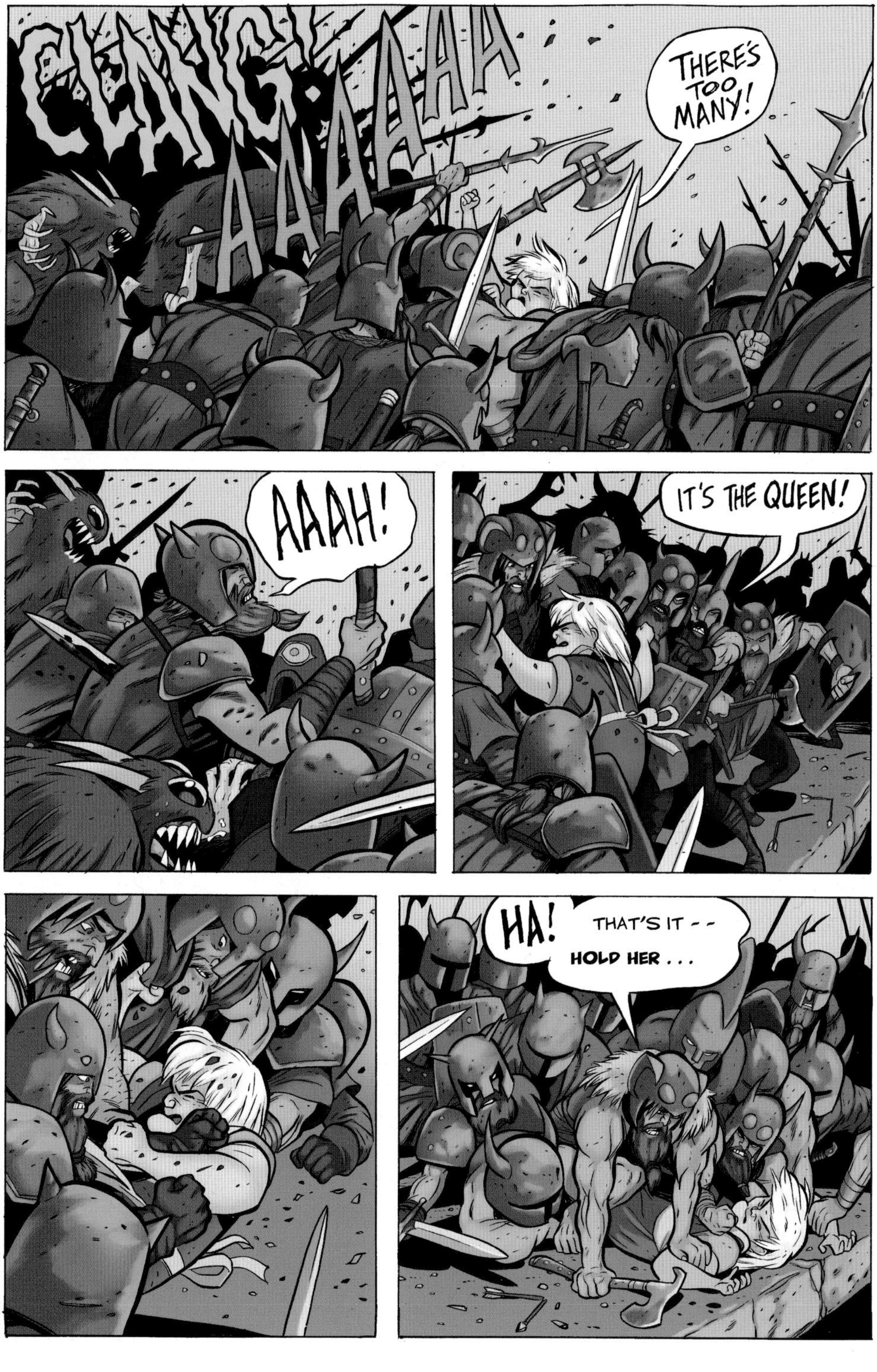
CLANG!
AAAAAAAA
THERE'S TOO MANY!
AAAH!
IT'S THE QUEEN!
HA!
THAT'S IT - -
HOLD HER . . .

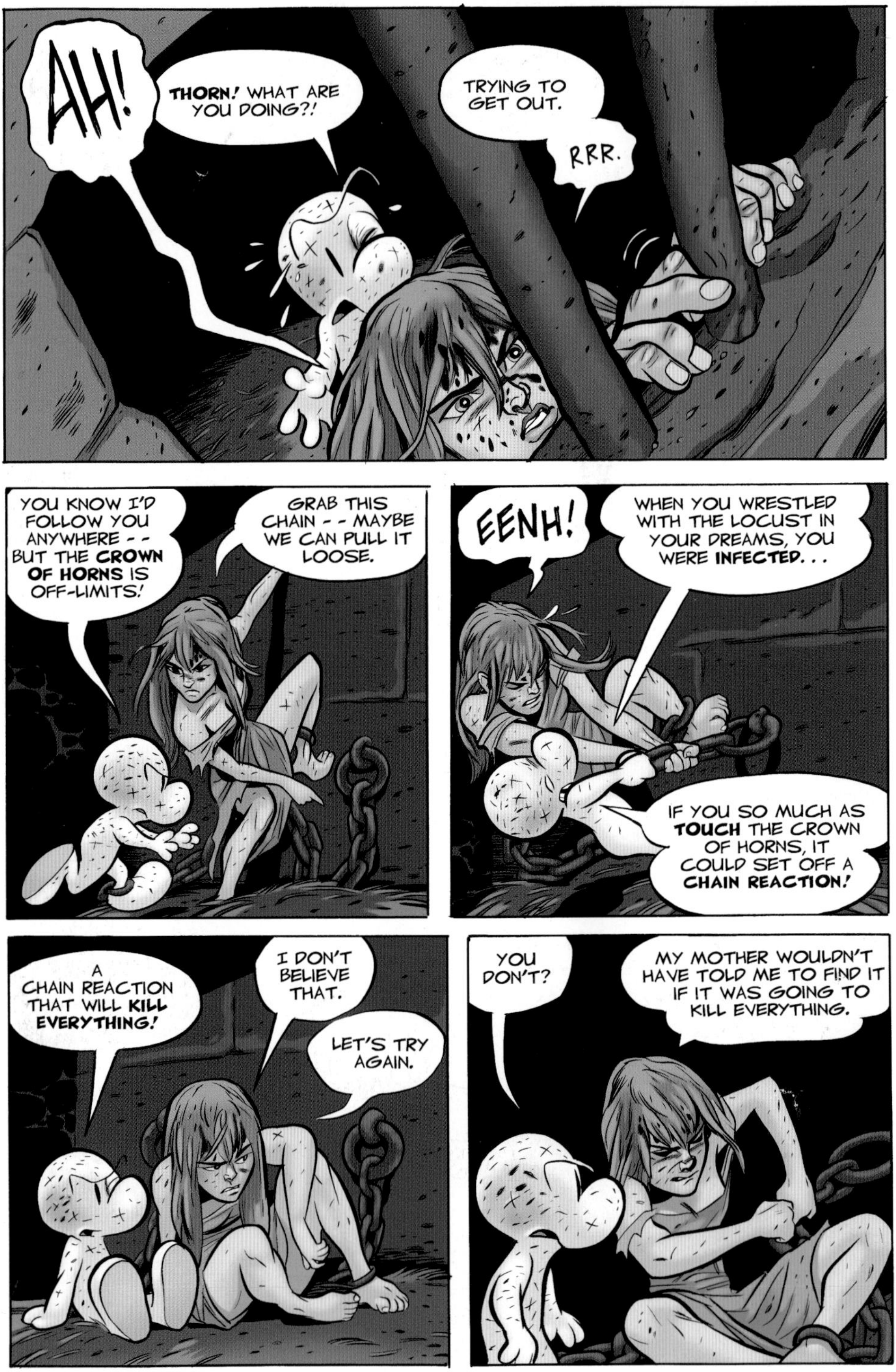
AH!
THORN! WHAT ARE YOU DOING?!
TRYING TO GET OUT.
RRR.
YOU KNOW I'D FOLLOW YOU ANYWHERE - - BUT THE CROWN OF HORNS IS OFF-LIMITS!
GRAB THIS CHAIN - - MAYBE WE CAN PULL IT LOOSE.
EENH!
WHEN YOU WRESTLED WITH THE LOCUST IN YOUR DREAMS, YOU WERE INFECTED. . .
IF YOU SO MUCH AS TOUCH THE CROWN OF HORNS, IT COULD SET OFF A CHAIN REACTION!
A CHAIN REACTION THAT WILL KILL EVERYTHING!
I DON'T BELIEVE THAT.
LET'S TRY AGAIN.
YOU DON'T?
MY MOTHER WOULDN'T HAVE TOLD ME TO FIND IT IF IT WAS GOING TO KILL EVERYTHING.

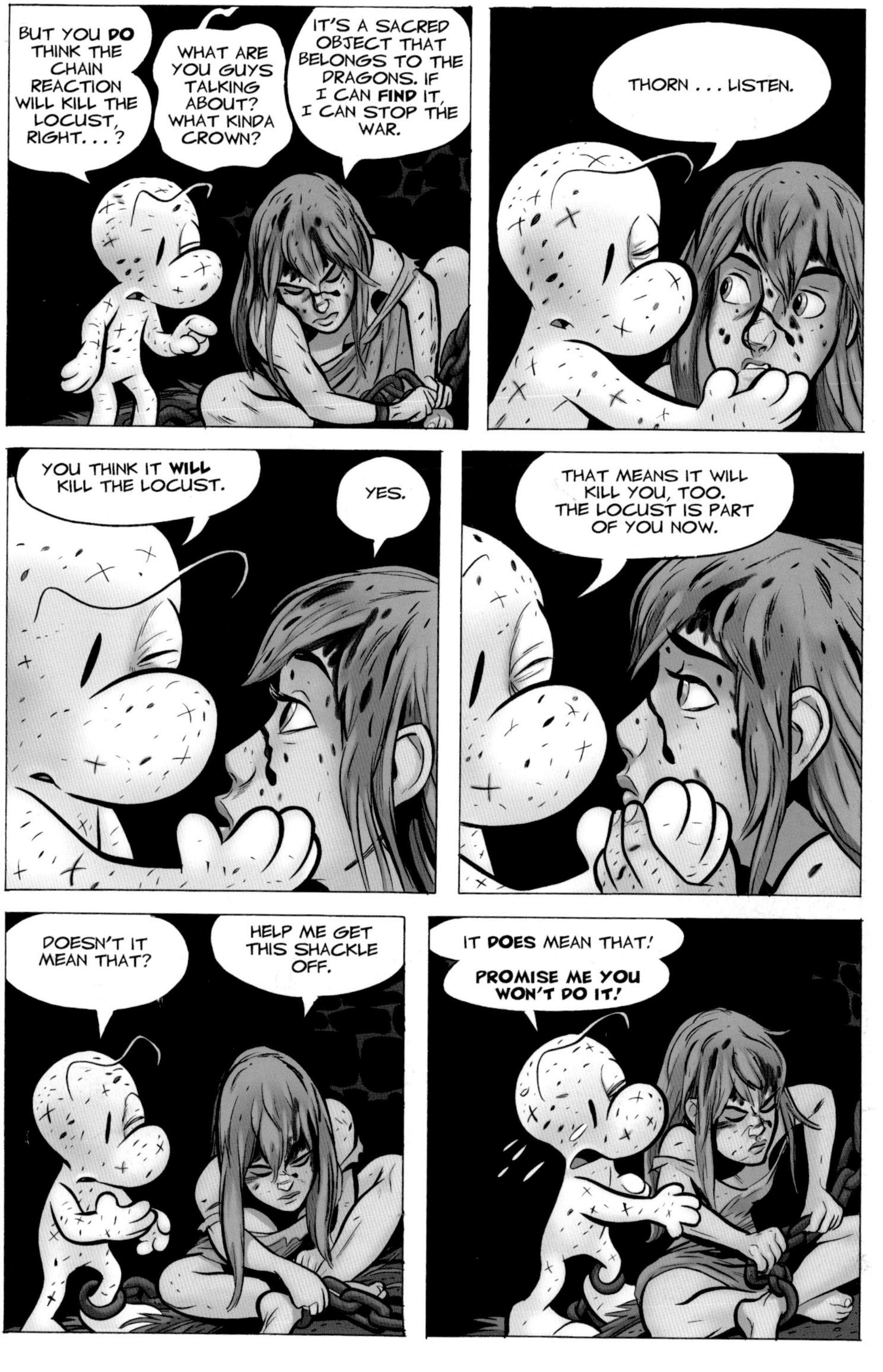
BUT YOU **DO** THINK THE CHAIN REACTION WILL KILL THE LOCUST, RIGHT. . . ?
WHAT ARE YOU GUYS TALKING ABOUT? WHAT KINDA CROWN?
IT'S A SACRED OBJECT THAT BELONGS TO THE DRAGONS. IF I CAN **FIND** IT, I CAN STOP THE WAR.
THORN . . . LISTEN.
YOU THINK IT **WILL** KILL THE LOCUST.
YES.
THAT MEANS IT WILL KILL YOU, TOO. THE LOCUST IS PART OF YOU NOW.
DOESN'T IT MEAN THAT?
HELP ME GET THIS SHACKLE OFF.
IT **DOES** MEAN THAT!
PROMISE ME YOU WON'T DO IT!

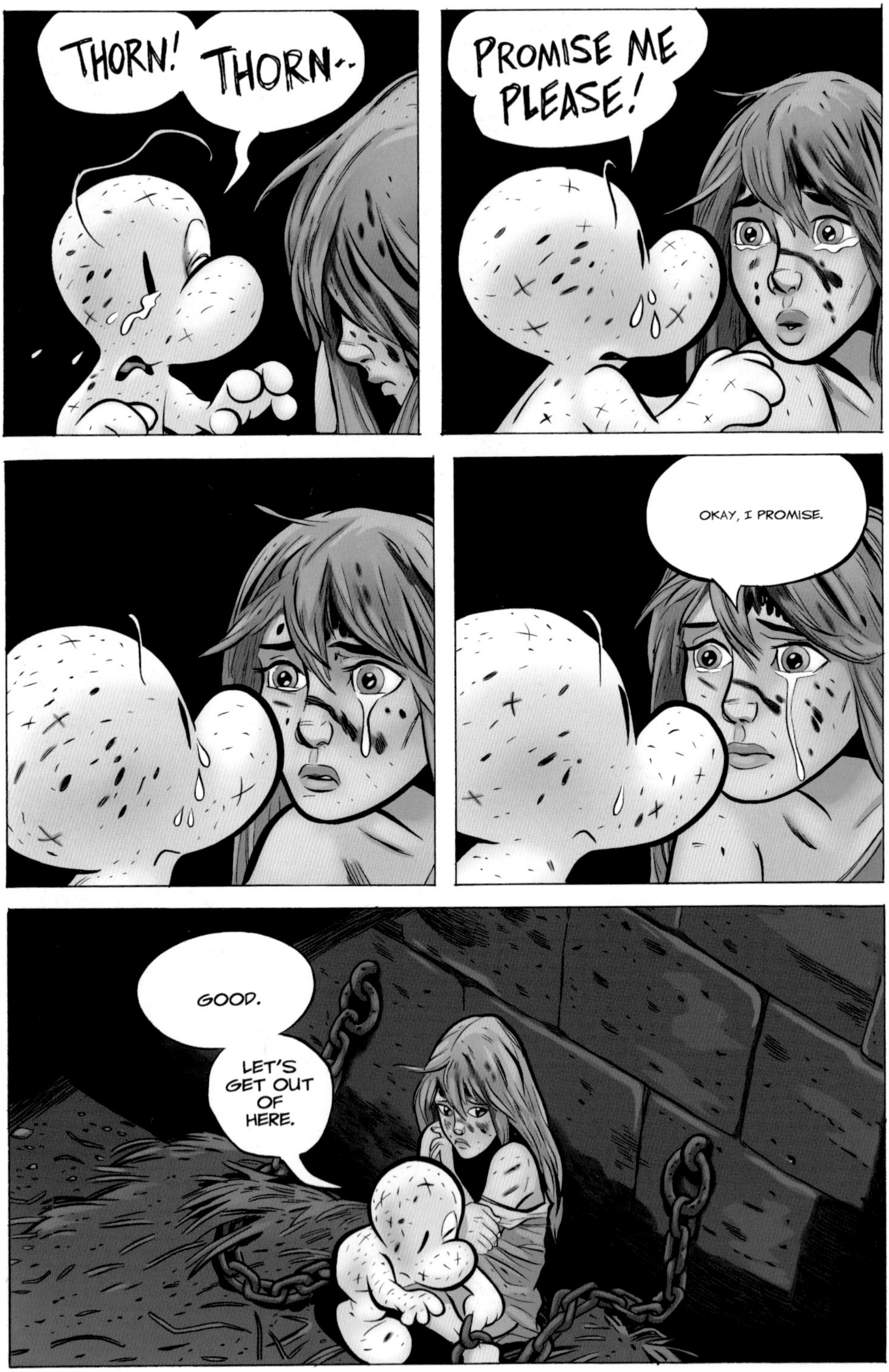
THORN!
THORN..
PROMISE ME PLEASE!
OKAY, I PROMISE.
GOOD.
LET'S GET OUT OF HERE.

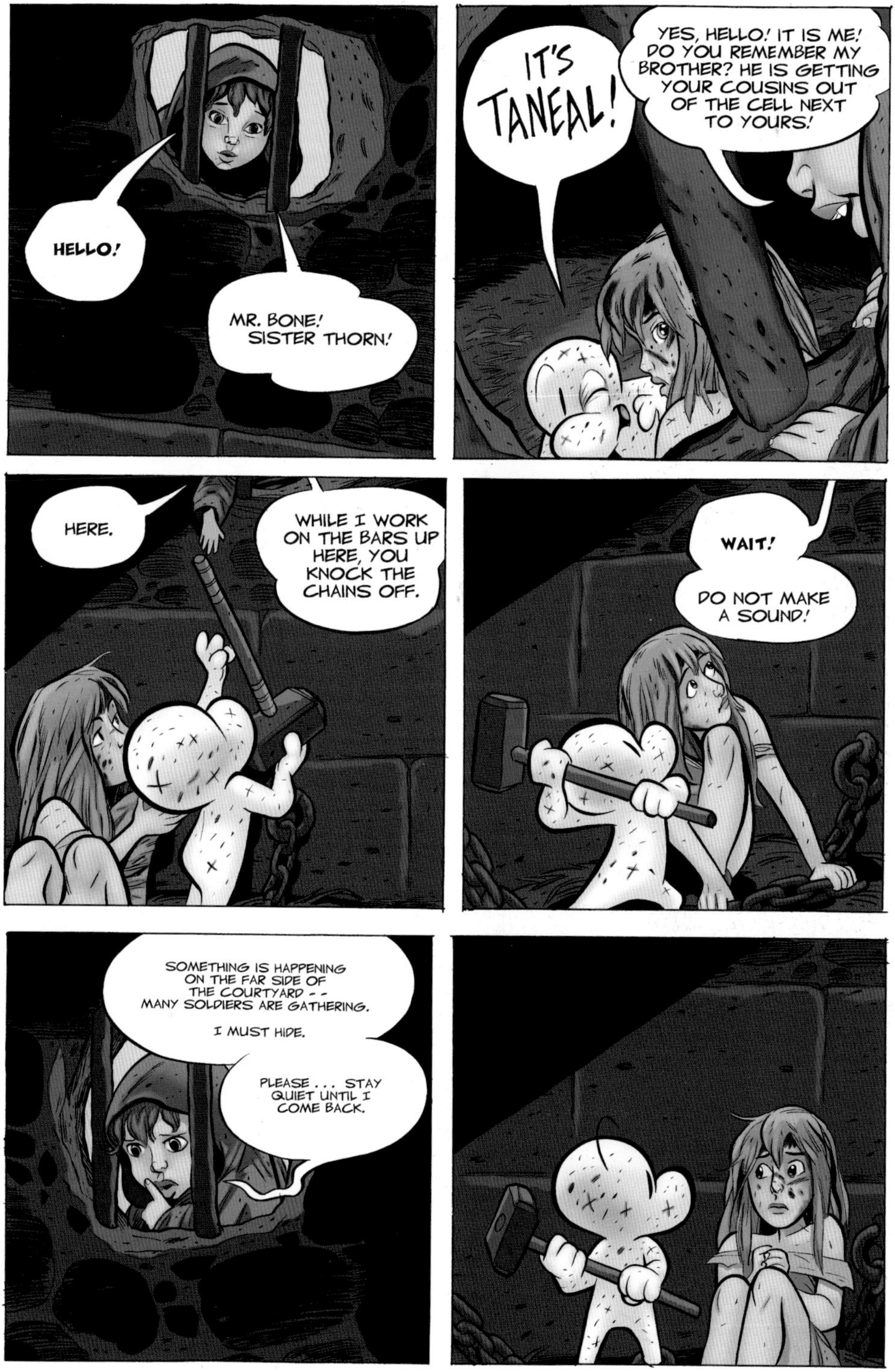
HELLO!
MR. BONE! SISTER THORN!
IT'S TANEAL!
YES, HELLO! IT IS ME! DO YOU REMEMBER MY BROTHER? HE IS GETTING YOUR COUSINS OUT OF THE CELL NEXT TO YOURS!
HERE.
WHILE I WORK ON THE BARS UP HERE, YOU KNOCK THE CHAINS OFF.
WAIT!
DO NOT MAKE A SOUND!
SOMETHING IS HAPPENING ON THE FAR SIDE OF THE COURTYARD -- MANY SOLDIERS ARE GATHERING.
I MUST HIDE.
PLEASE . . . STAY QUIET UNTIL I COME BACK.

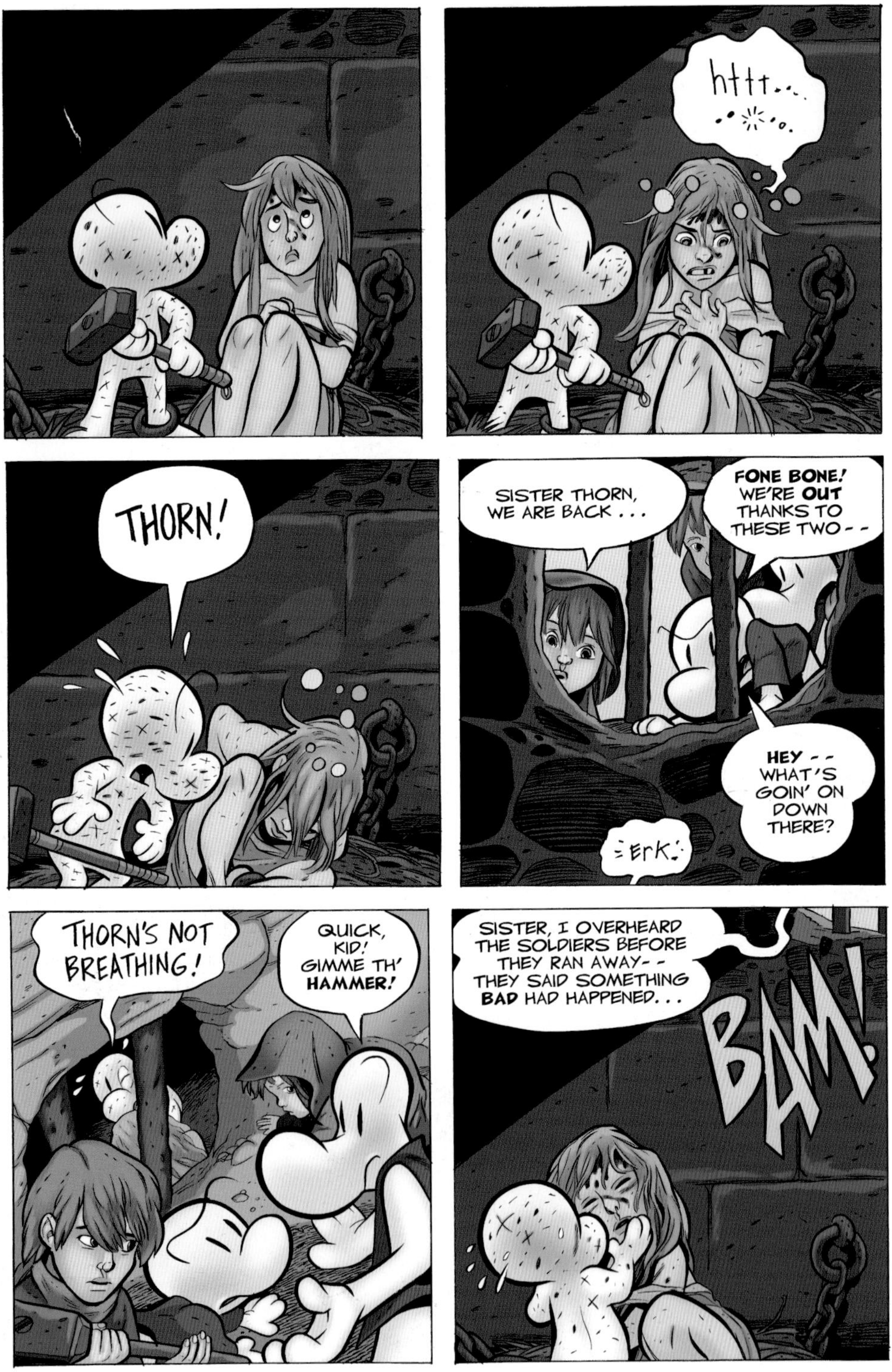
httt...
THORN!
SISTER THORN, WE ARE BACK . . .
FONE BONE! WE'RE OUT THANKS TO THESE TWO - -
HEY - - WHAT'S GOIN' ON DOWN THERE?
Erk
THORN'S NOT BREATHING!
QUICK, KID! GIMME TH' HAMMER!
SISTER, I OVERHEARD THE SOLDIERS BEFORE THEY RAN AWAY- - THEY SAID SOMETHING BAD HAD HAPPENED. . .
BAM!

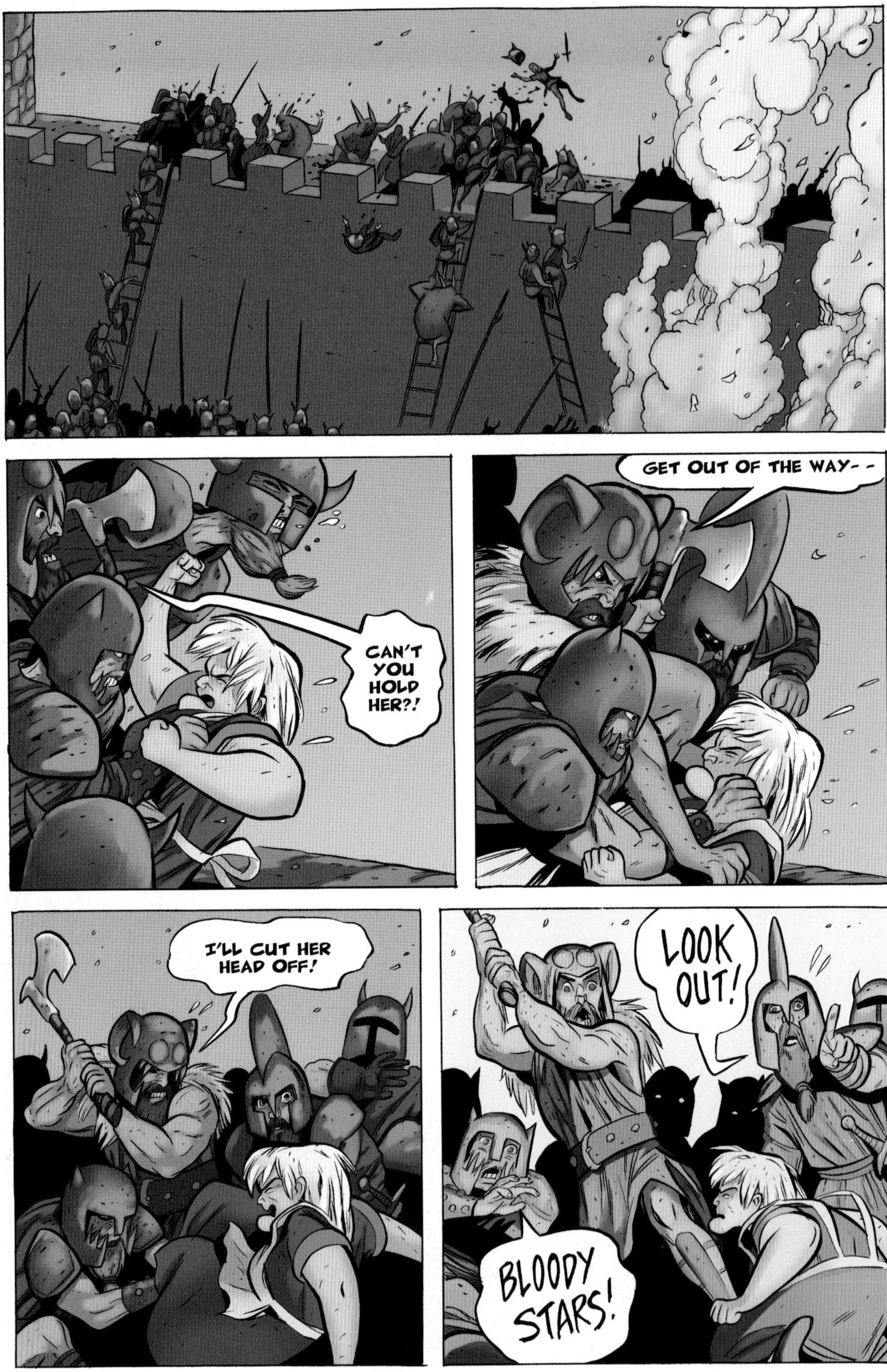
CAN'T YOU HOLD HER?!
GET OUT OF THE WAY- -
I'LL CUT HER HEAD OFF!
LOOK OUT!
BLOODY STARS!

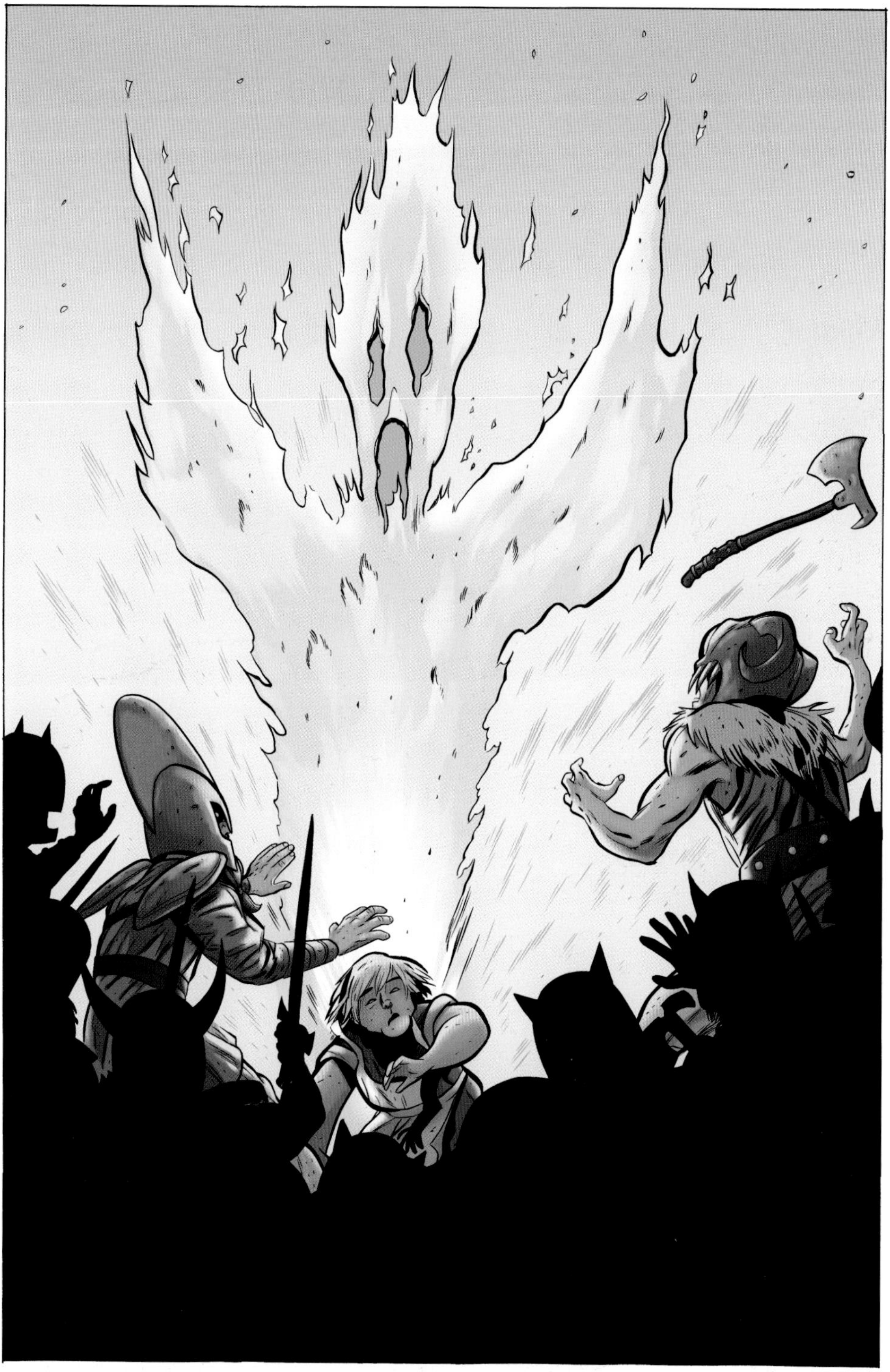

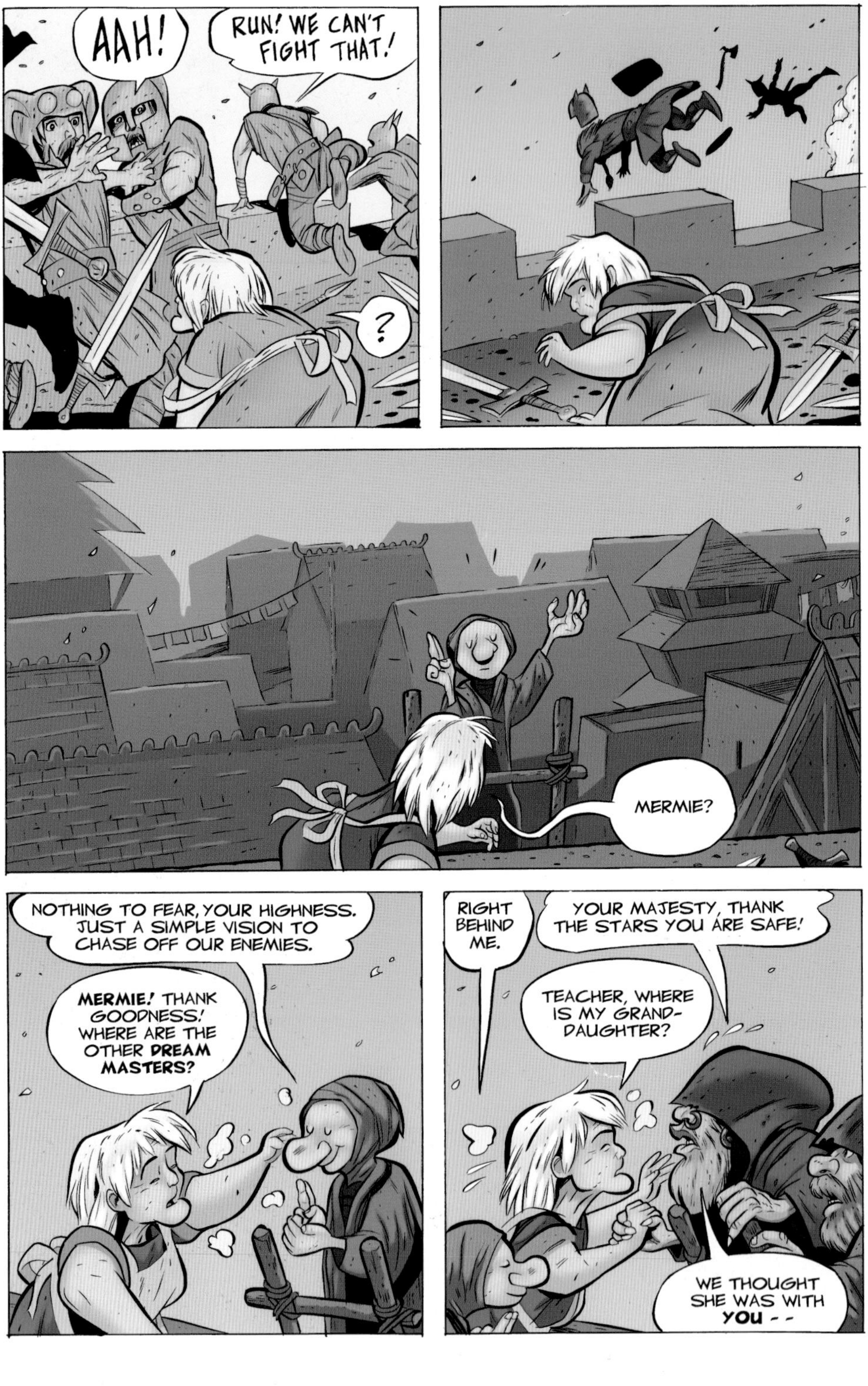
AAH!
RUN! WE CAN'T FIGHT THAT!
?
MERMIE?
NOTHING TO FEAR, YOUR HIGHNESS. JUST A SIMPLE VISION TO CHASE OFF OUR ENEMIES.
MERMIE! THANK GOODNESS! WHERE ARE THE OTHER DREAM MASTERS?
RIGHT BEHIND ME.
YOUR MAJESTY, THANK THE STARS YOU ARE SAFE!
TEACHER, WHERE IS MY GRAND-DAUGHTER?
WE THOUGHT SHE WAS WITH YOU - -

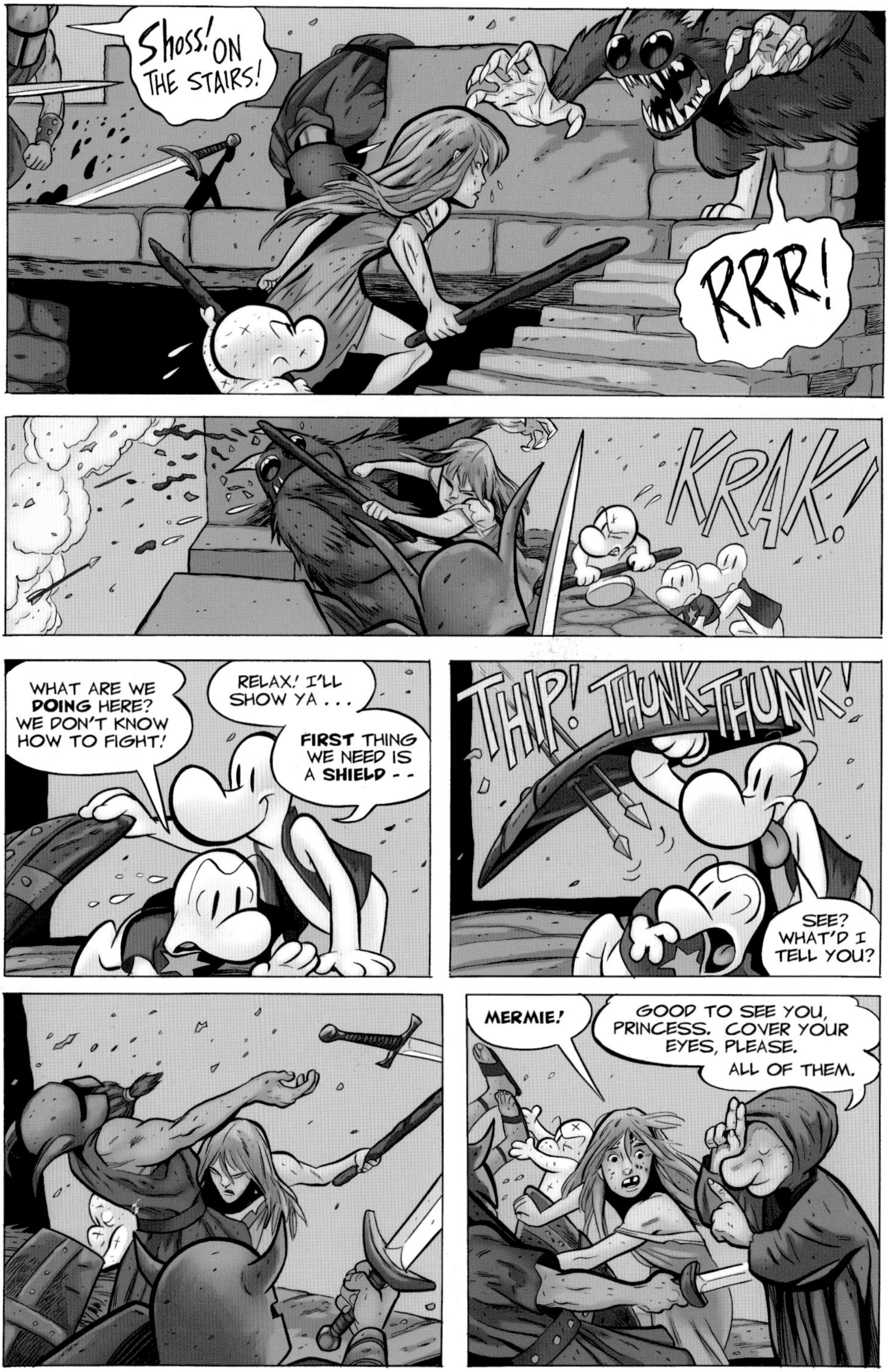
Shoss! ON THE STAIRS!
RRR!
KRAK!
WHAT ARE WE DOING HERE? WE DON'T KNOW HOW TO FIGHT!
RELAX! I'LL SHOW YA . . .
FIRST THING WE NEED IS A SHIELD - -
THIP! THUNK THUNK!
SEE? WHAT'D I TELL YOU?
MERMIE!
GOOD TO SEE YOU, PRINCESS. COVER YOUR EYES, PLEASE.
ALL OF THEM.

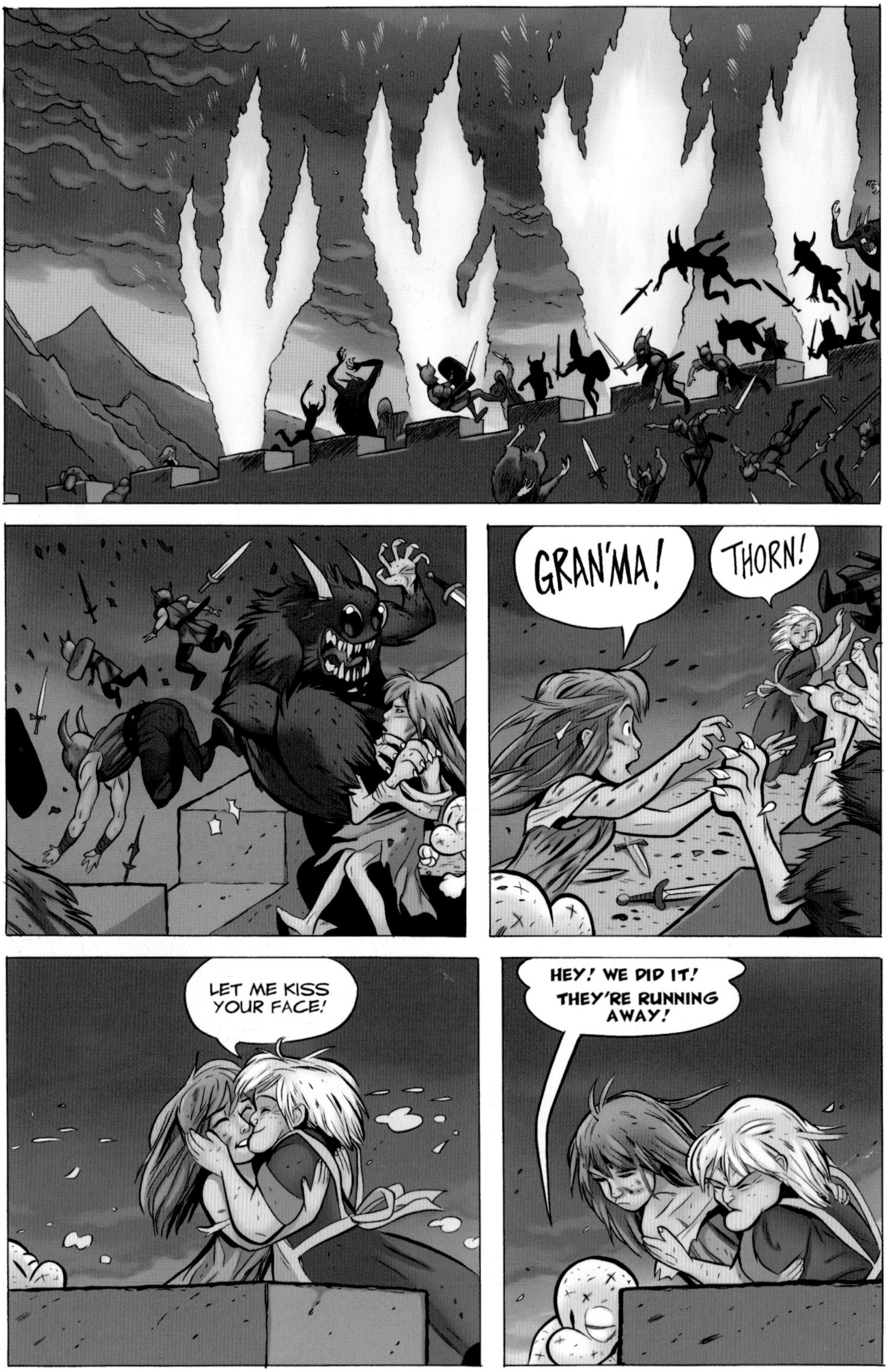
GRAN'MA!
THORN!
LET ME KISS YOUR FACE!
HEY! WE DID IT! THEY'RE RUNNING AWAY!

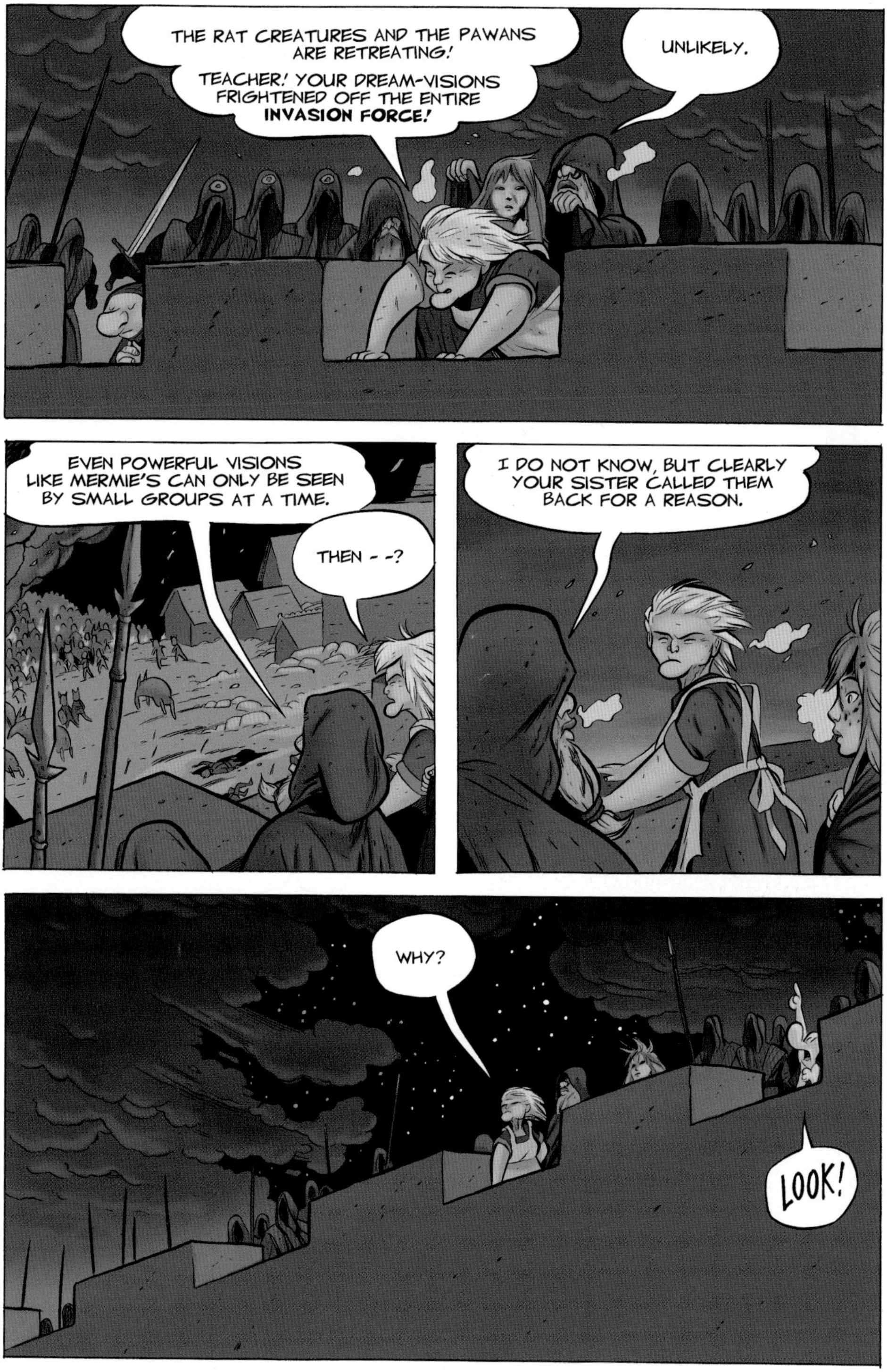
THE RAT CREATURES AND THE PAWANS ARE RETREATING!
TEACHER! YOUR DREAM-VISIONS FRIGHTENED OFF THE ENTIRE **INVASION FORCE!**
UNLIKELY.
EVEN POWERFUL VISIONS LIKE MERMIE'S CAN ONLY BE SEEN BY SMALL GROUPS AT A TIME.
THEN - -?
I DO NOT KNOW, BUT CLEARLY YOUR SISTER CALLED THEM BACK FOR A REASON.
WHY?
LOOK!

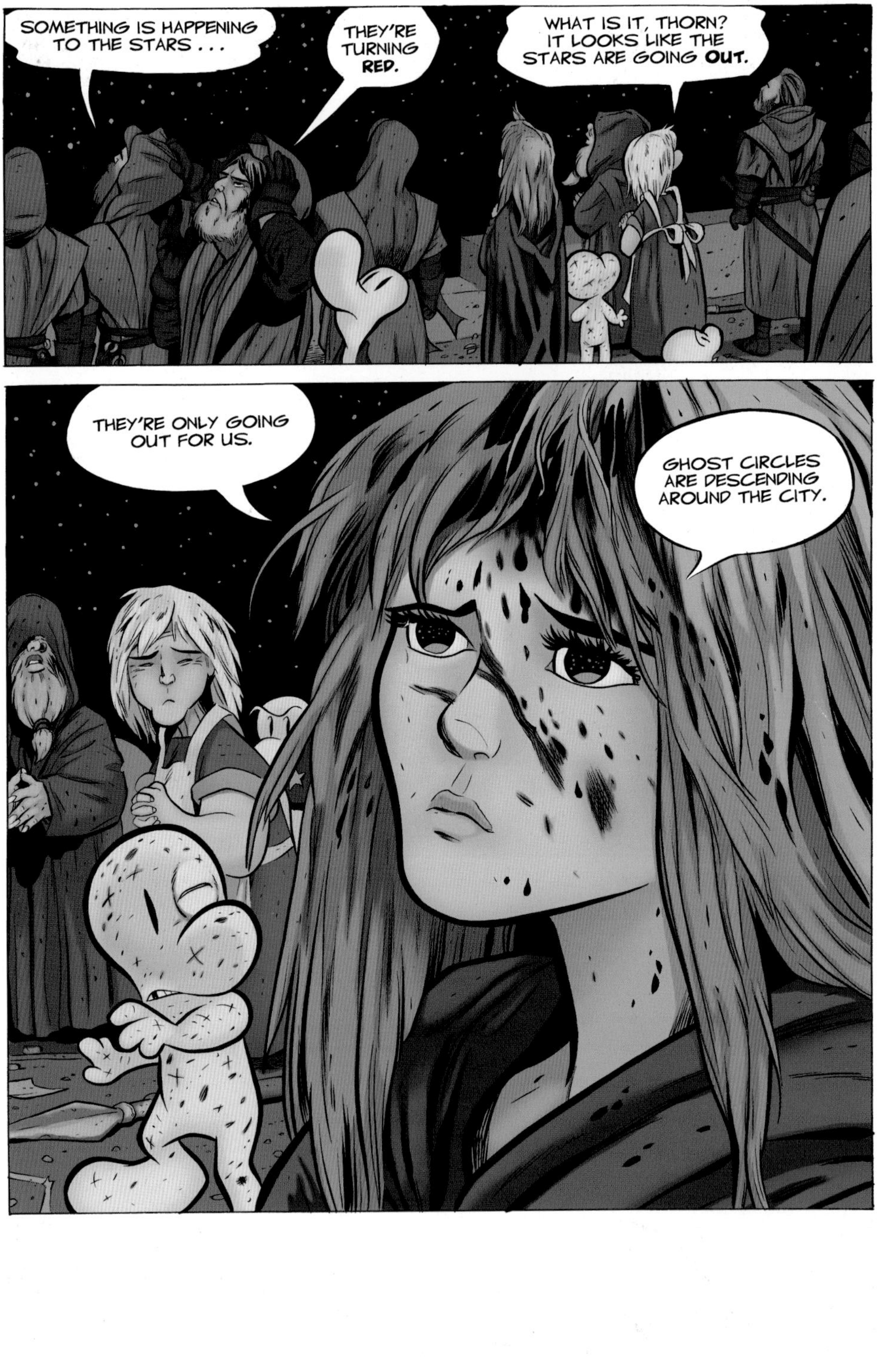
SOMETHING IS HAPPENING TO THE STARS . . .
THEY'RE TURNING **RED.**
WHAT IS IT, THORN? IT LOOKS LIKE THE STARS ARE GOING **OUT.**
THEY'RE ONLY GOING OUT FOR US.
GHOST CIRCLES ARE DESCENDING AROUND THE CITY.

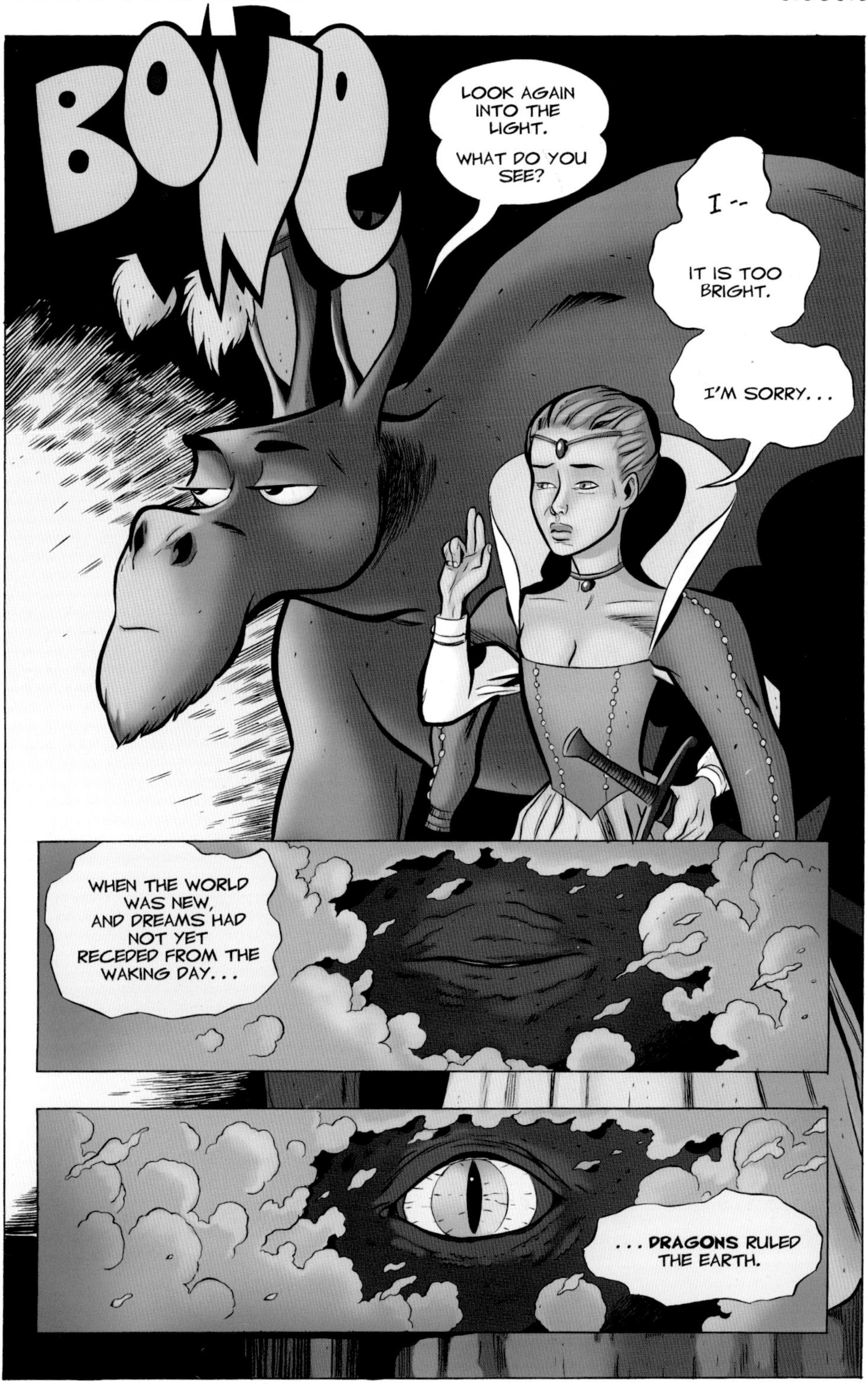
BONE
LOOK AGAIN INTO THE LIGHT.
WHAT DO YOU SEE?
I --
IT IS TOO BRIGHT.
I'M SORRY...
WHEN THE WORLD WAS NEW, AND DREAMS HAD NOT YET RECEDED FROM THE WAKING DAY...
...DRAGONS RULED THE EARTH.

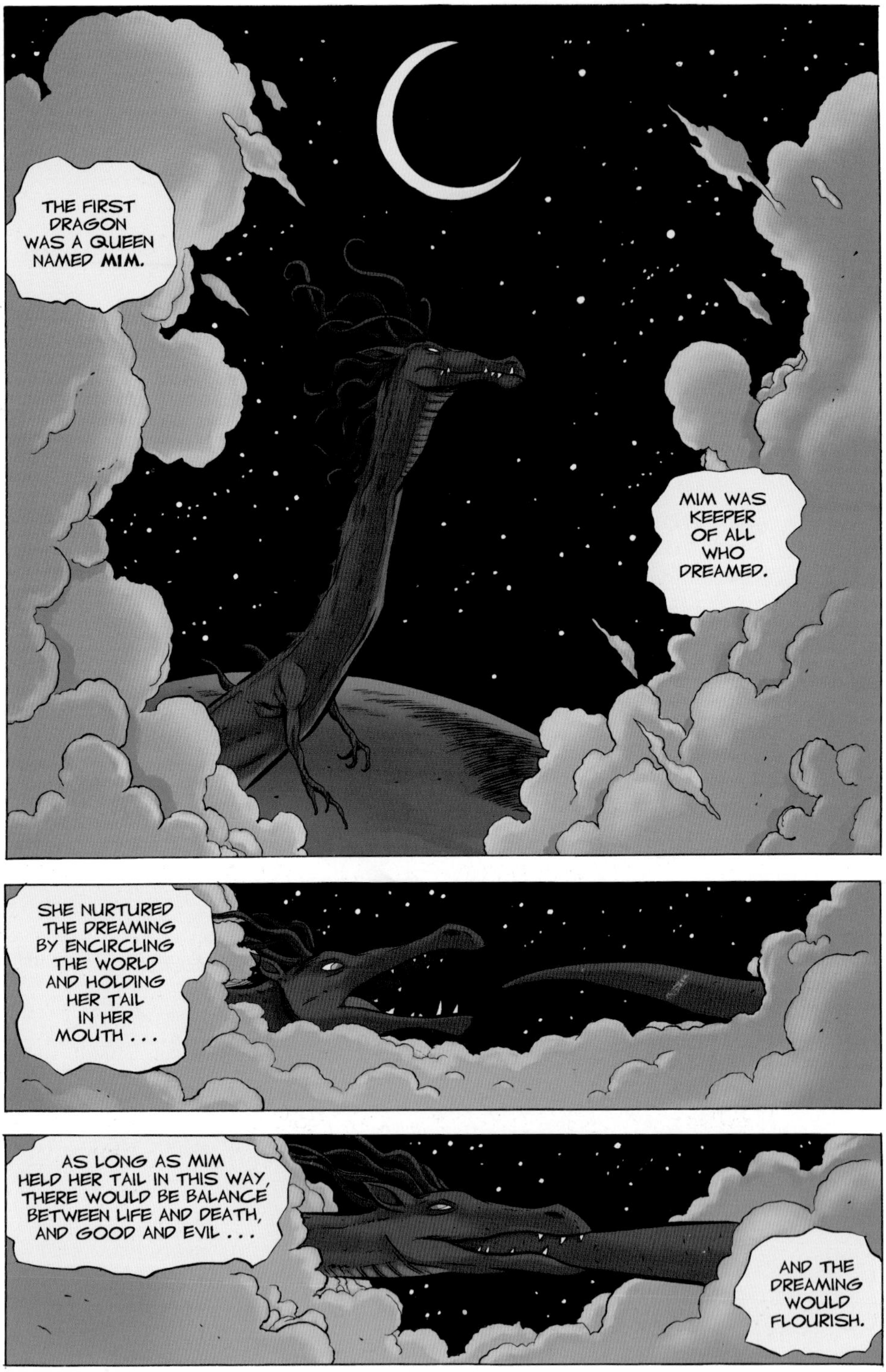
THE FIRST DRAGON WAS A QUEEN NAMED **MIM.**
MIM WAS KEEPER OF ALL WHO DREAMED.
SHE NURTURED THE DREAMING BY ENCIRCLING THE WORLD AND HOLDING HER TAIL IN HER MOUTH . . .
AS LONG AS MIM HELD HER TAIL IN THIS WAY, THERE WOULD BE BALANCE BETWEEN LIFE AND DEATH, AND GOOD AND EVIL . . .
AND THE DREAMING WOULD FLOURISH.

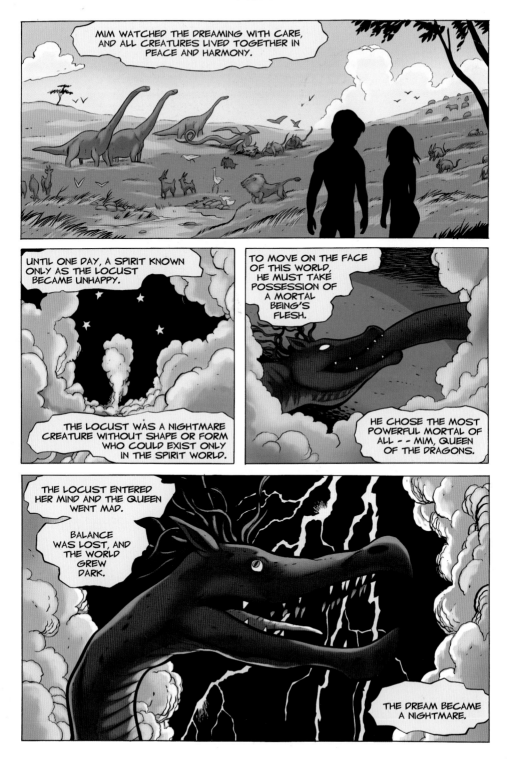

MIM WATCHED THE DREAMING WITH CARE, AND ALL CREATURES LIVED TOGETHER IN PEACE AND HARMONY.

UNTIL ONE DAY, A SPIRIT KNOWN ONLY AS THE LOCUST BECAME UNHAPPY.

THE LOCUST WAS A NIGHTMARE CREATURE WITHOUT SHAPE OR FORM WHO COULD EXIST ONLY IN THE SPIRIT WORLD.

TO MOVE ON THE FACE OF THIS WORLD, HE MUST TAKE POSSESSION OF A MORTAL BEING'S FLESH.

HE CHOSE THE MOST POWERFUL MORTAL OF ALL -- MIM, QUEEN OF THE DRAGONS.

THE LOCUST ENTERED HER MIND AND THE QUEEN WENT MAD.

BALANCE WAS LOST, AND THE WORLD GREW DARK.

THE DREAM BECAME A NIGHTMARE.

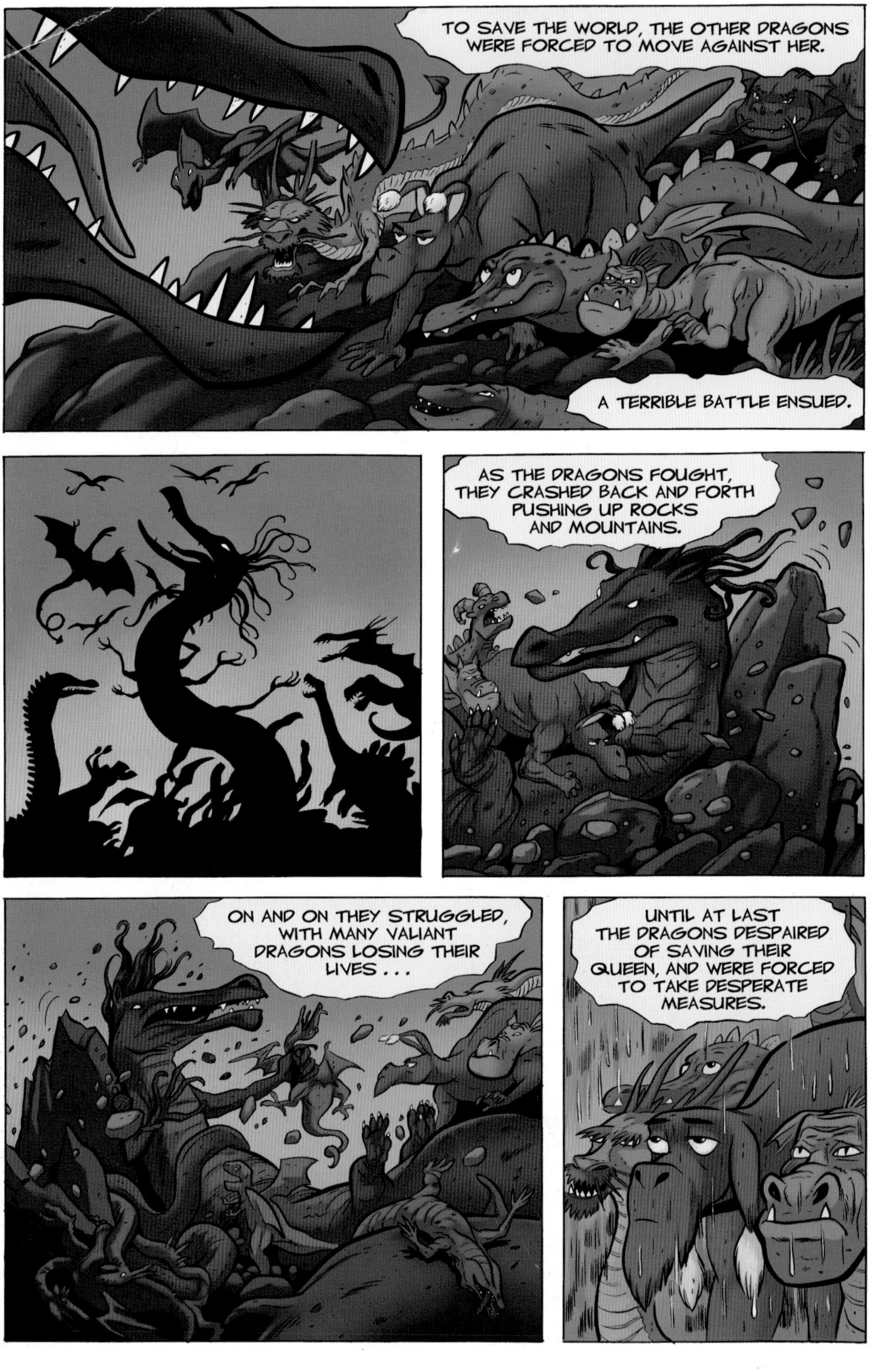
TO SAVE THE WORLD, THE OTHER DRAGONS WERE FORCED TO MOVE AGAINST HER.
A TERRIBLE BATTLE ENSUED.
AS THE DRAGONS FOUGHT, THEY CRASHED BACK AND FORTH PUSHING UP ROCKS AND MOUNTAINS.
ON AND ON THEY STRUGGLED, WITH MANY VALIANT DRAGONS LOSING THEIR LIVES . . .
UNTIL AT LAST THE DRAGONS DESPAIRED OF SAVING THEIR QUEEN, AND WERE FORCED TO TAKE DESPERATE MEASURES.

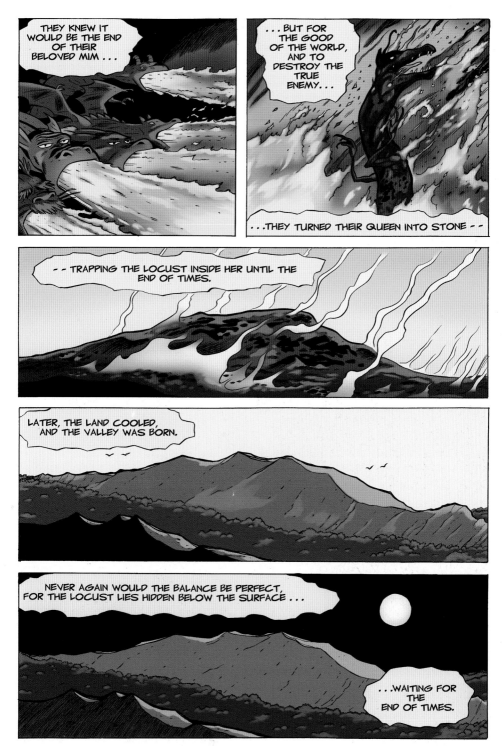

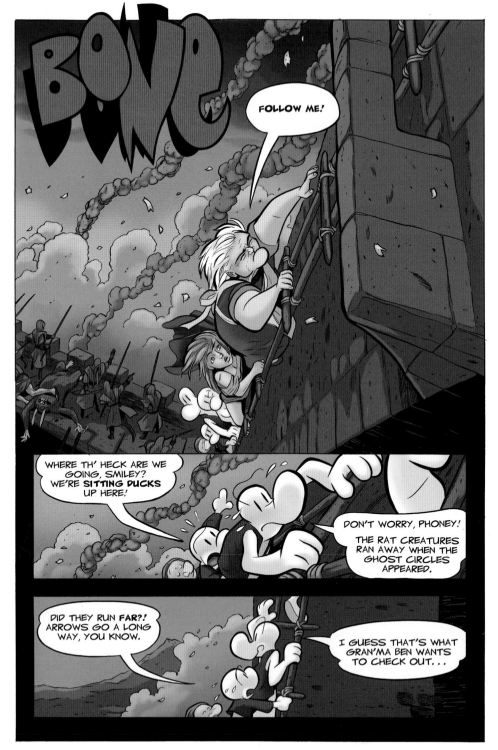

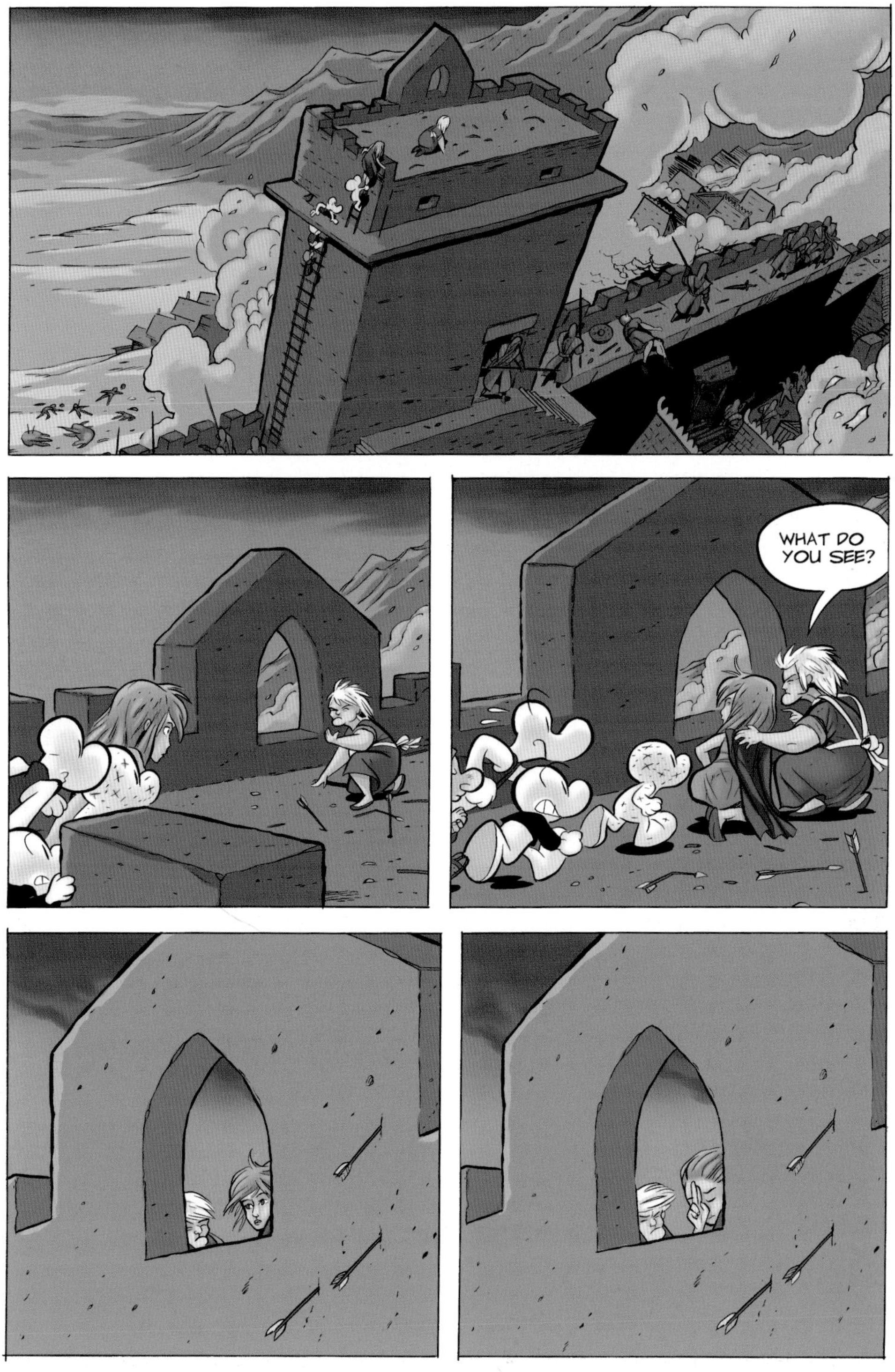
WHAT DO YOU SEE?

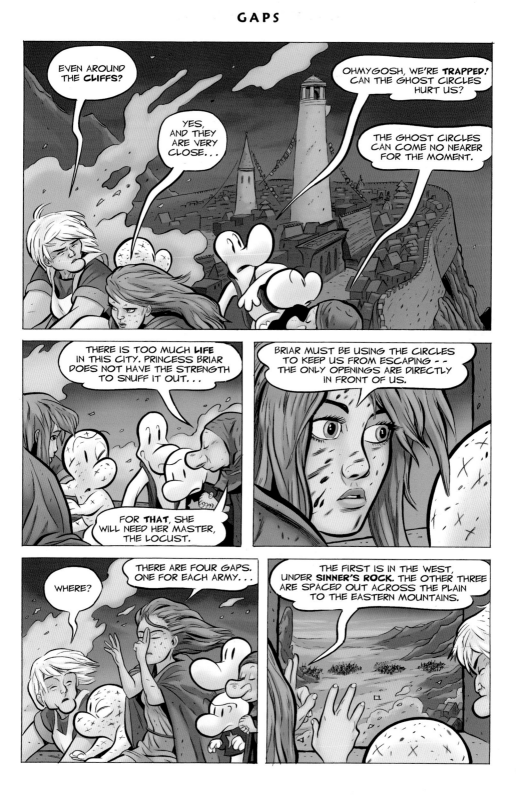

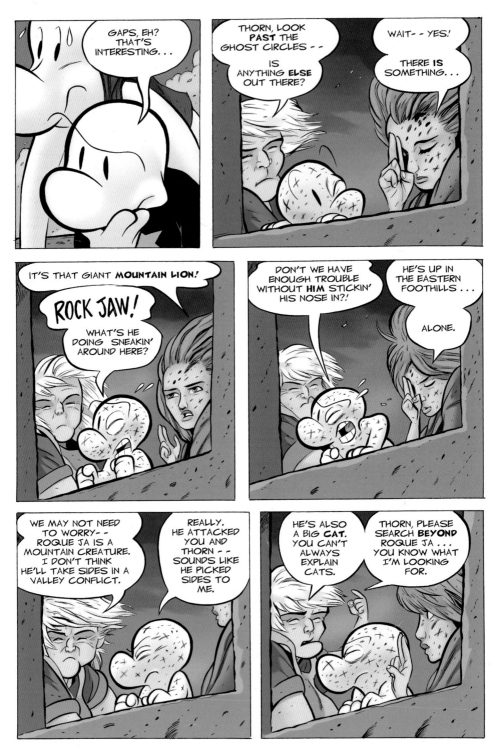

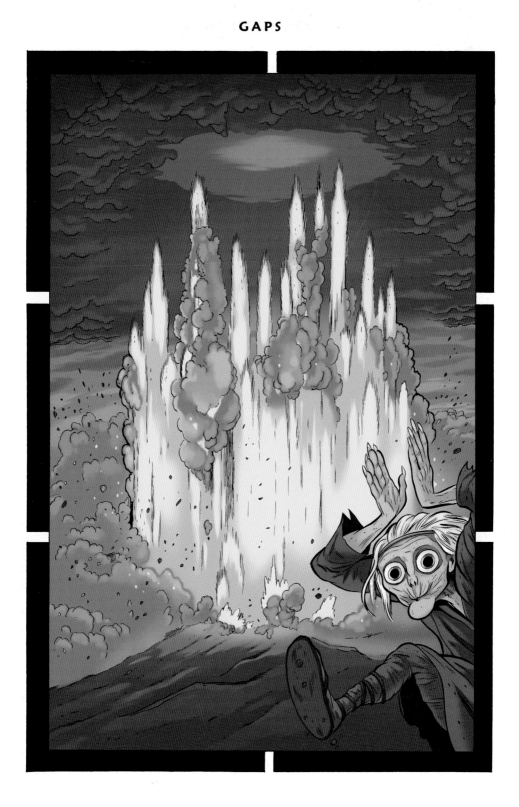

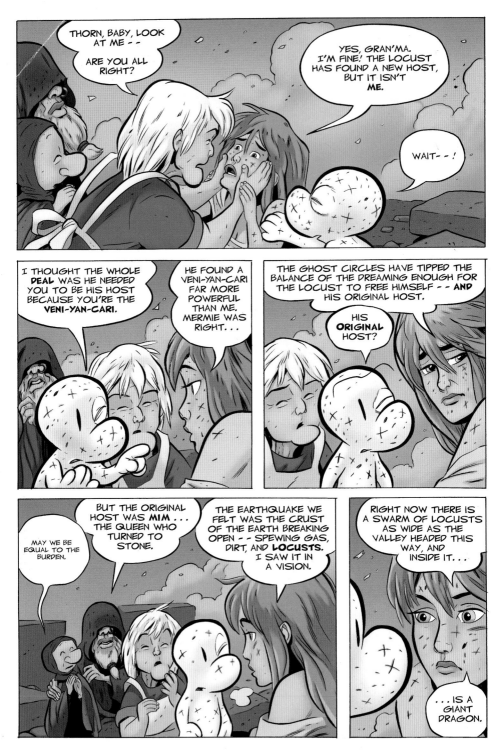

GAPS

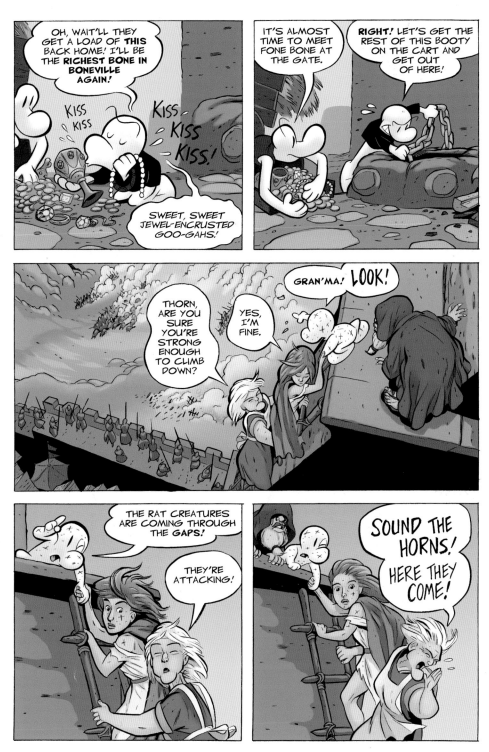

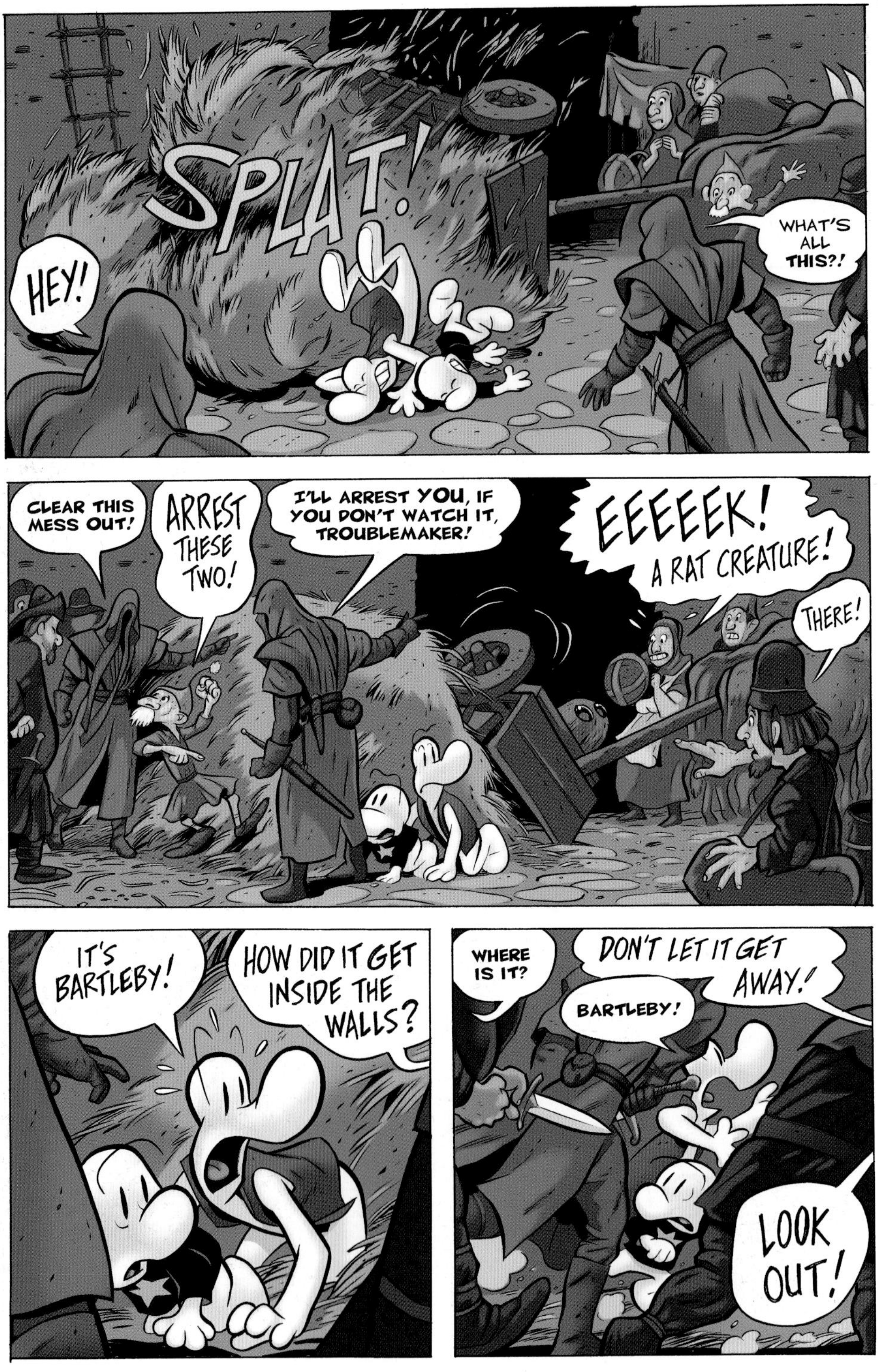
SPLAT!
HEY!
WHAT'S ALL THIS?!
CLEAR THIS MESS OUT!
ARREST THESE TWO!
I'LL ARREST YOU, IF YOU DON'T WATCH IT, TROUBLEMAKER!
EEEEEK! A RAT CREATURE!
THERE!
IT'S BARTLEBY!
HOW DID IT GET INSIDE THE WALLS?
WHERE IS IT?
DON'T LET IT GET AWAY!
BARTLEBY!
LOOK OUT!

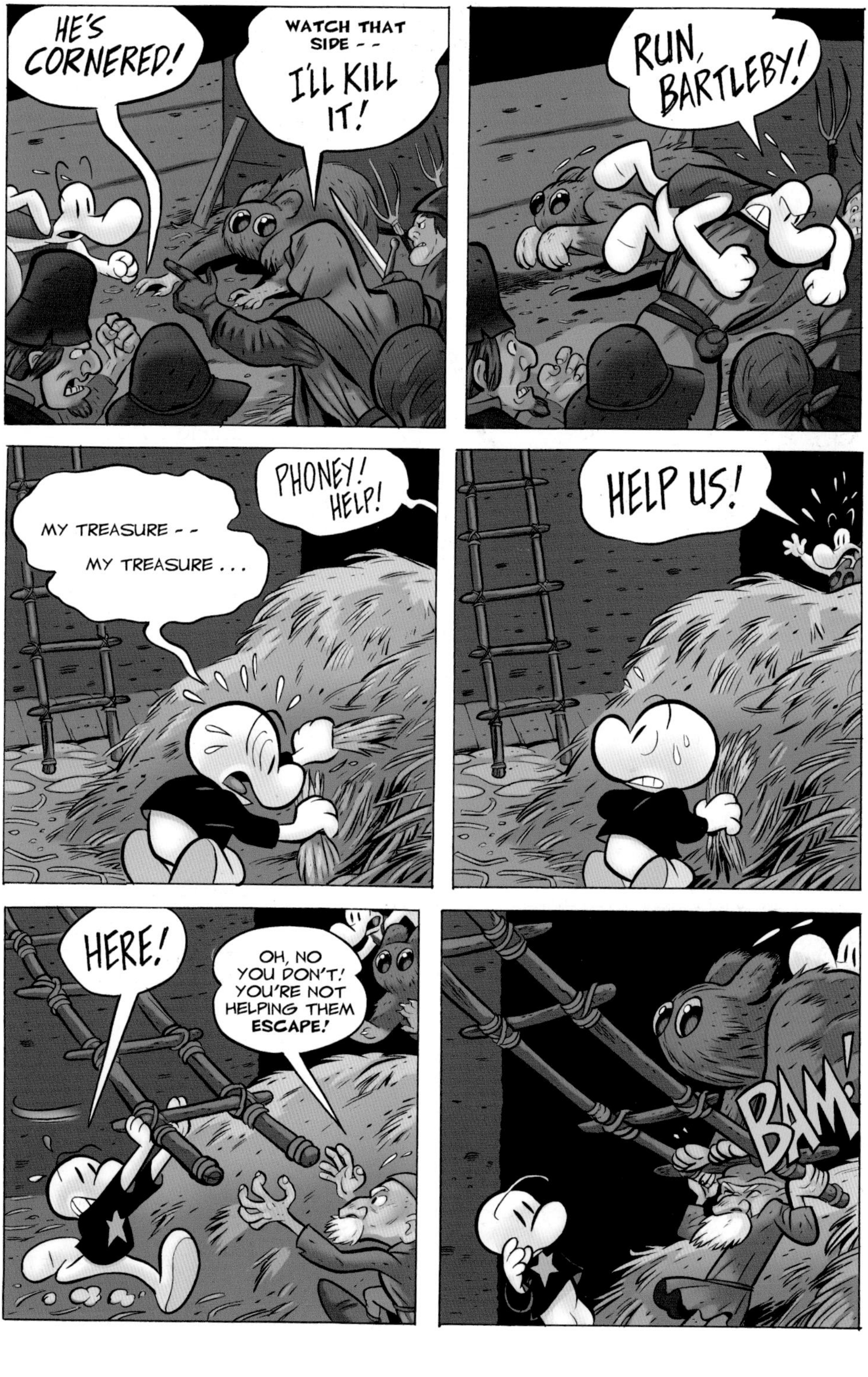
HE'S CORNERED!
WATCH THAT SIDE -- I'LL KILL IT!
RUN, BARTLEBY!
MY TREASURE -- MY TREASURE ...
PHONEY! HELP!
HELP US!
HERE!
OH, NO YOU DON'T! YOU'RE NOT HELPING THEM ESCAPE!
BAM!

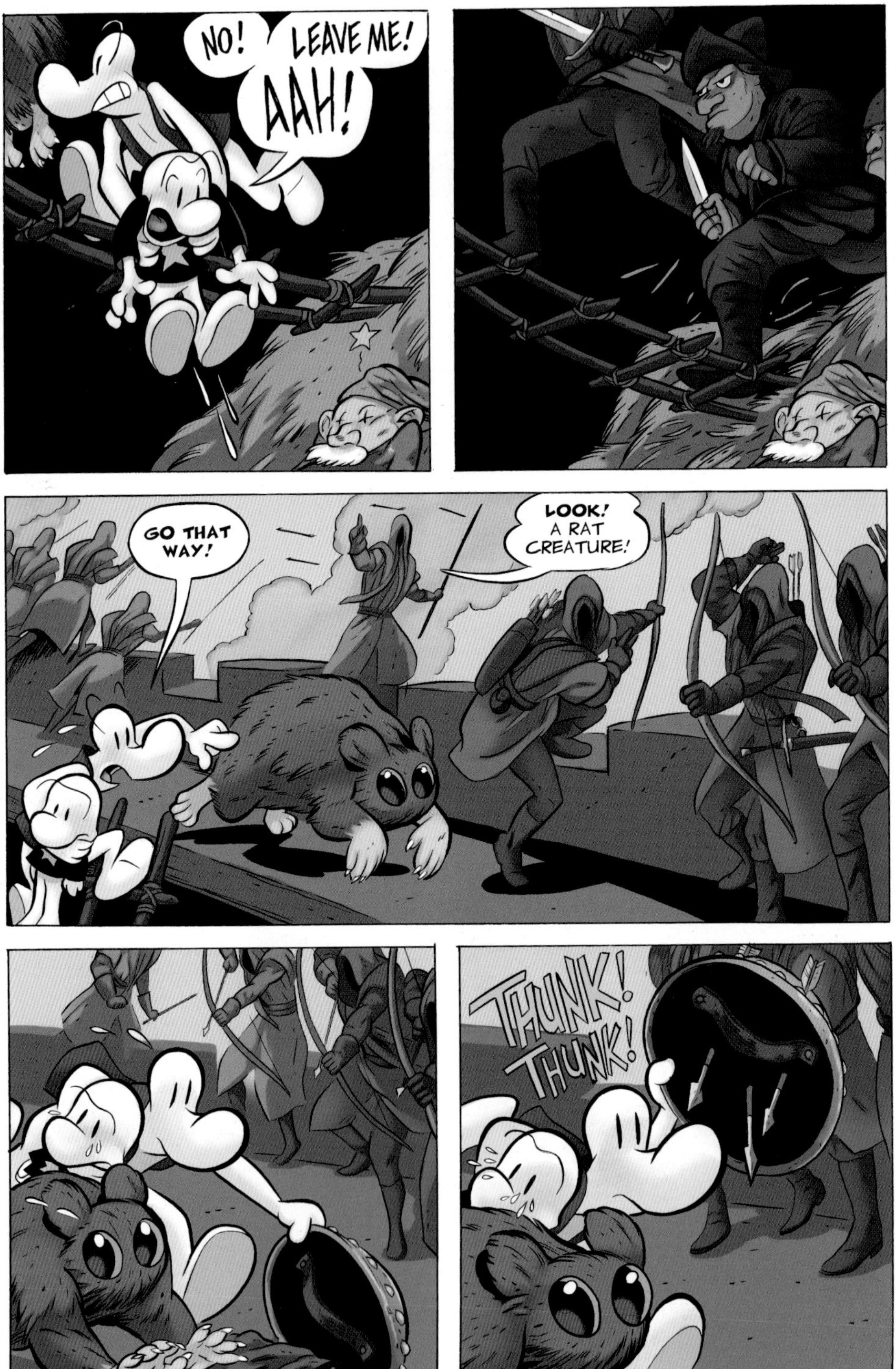
NO!
LEAVE ME!
AAH!
GO THAT WAY!
LOOK! A RAT CREATURE!
THUNK! THUNK!

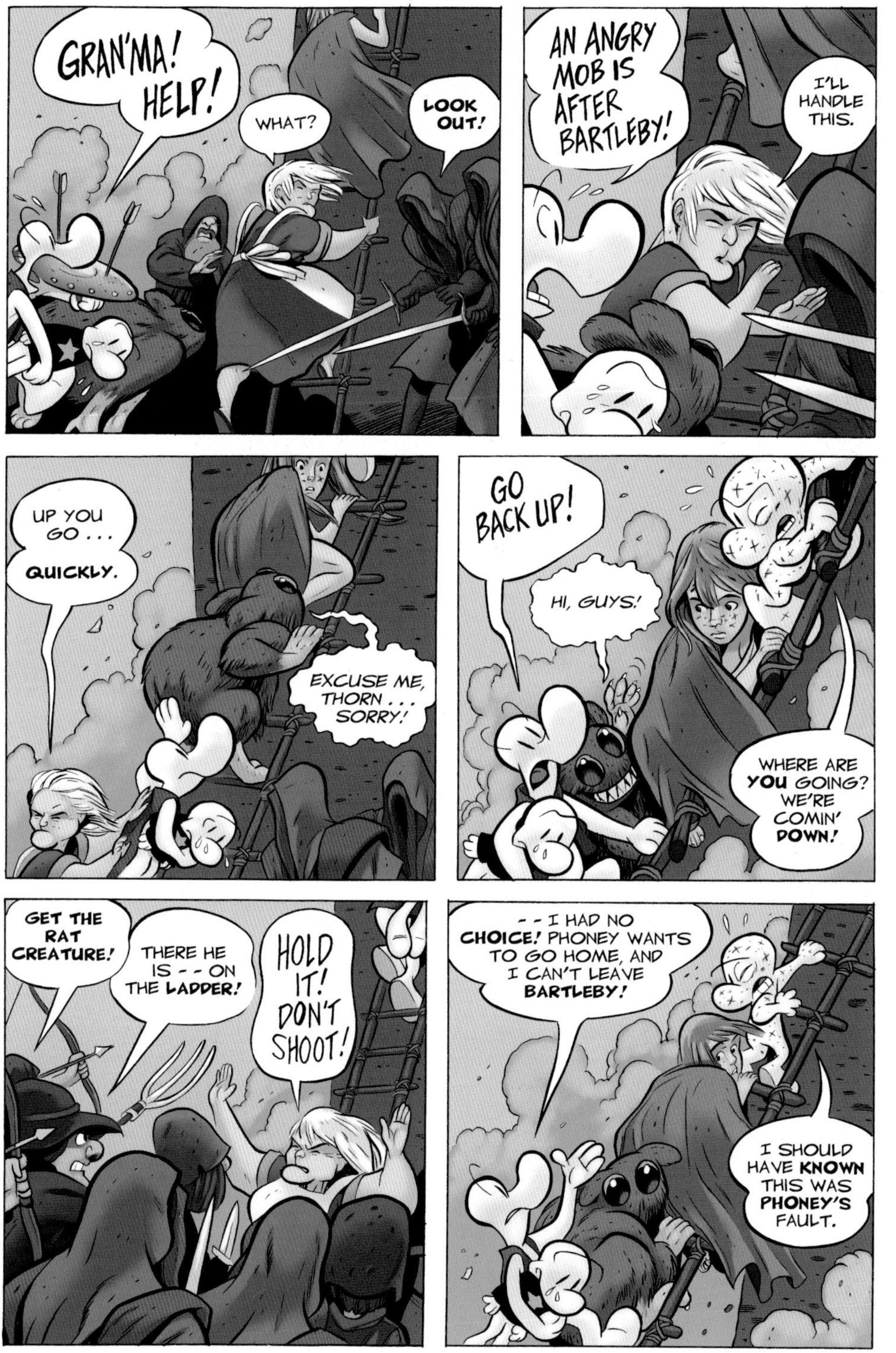
GRAN'MA! HELP!
WHAT?
LOOK OUT!
AN ANGRY MOB IS AFTER BARTLEBY!
I'LL HANDLE THIS.
UP YOU GO . . .
QUICKLY.
EXCUSE ME, THORN . . . SORRY!
GO BACK UP!
HI, GUYS!
WHERE ARE YOU GOING? WE'RE COMIN' DOWN!
GET THE RAT CREATURE!
THERE HE IS - - ON THE LADDER!
HOLD IT! DON'T SHOOT!
- - I HAD NO CHOICE! PHONEY WANTS TO GO HOME, AND I CAN'T LEAVE BARTLEBY!
I SHOULD HAVE KNOWN THIS WAS PHONEY'S FAULT.

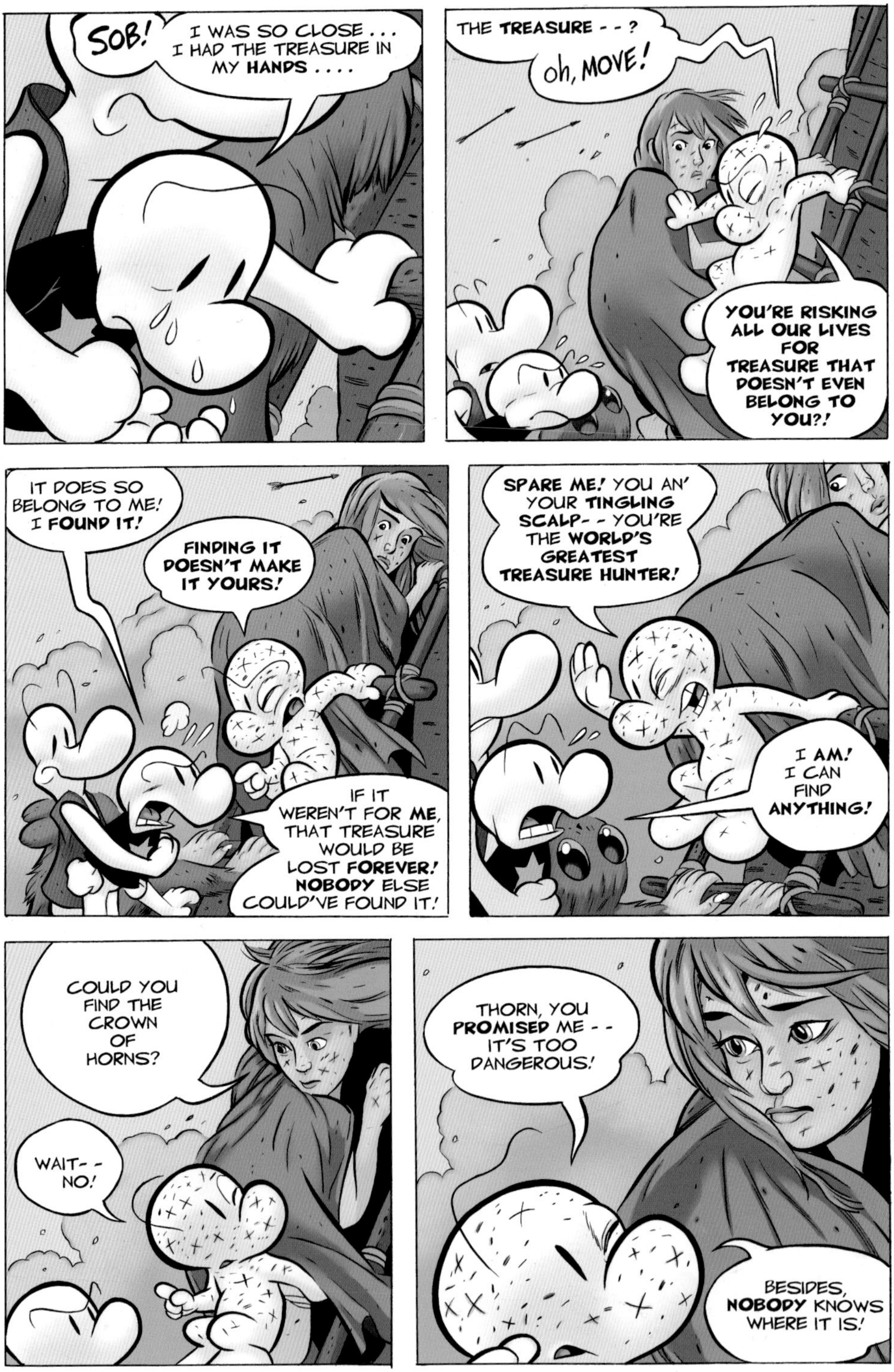
SOB!
I WAS SO CLOSE . . . I HAD THE TREASURE IN MY HANDS . . . .
THE TREASURE - - ?
oh, MOVE!
YOU'RE RISKING ALL OUR LIVES FOR TREASURE THAT DOESN'T EVEN BELONG TO YOU?!
IT DOES SO BELONG TO ME! I FOUND IT!
FINDING IT DOESN'T MAKE IT YOURS!
IF IT WEREN'T FOR ME, THAT TREASURE WOULD BE LOST FOREVER! NOBODY ELSE COULD'VE FOUND IT!
SPARE ME! YOU AN' YOUR TINGLING SCALP- - YOU'RE THE WORLD'S GREATEST TREASURE HUNTER!
I AM! I CAN FIND ANYTHING!
COULD YOU FIND THE CROWN OF HORNS?
WAIT- - NO!
THORN, YOU PROMISED ME - - IT'S TOO DANGEROUS!
BESIDES, NOBODY KNOWS WHERE IT IS!

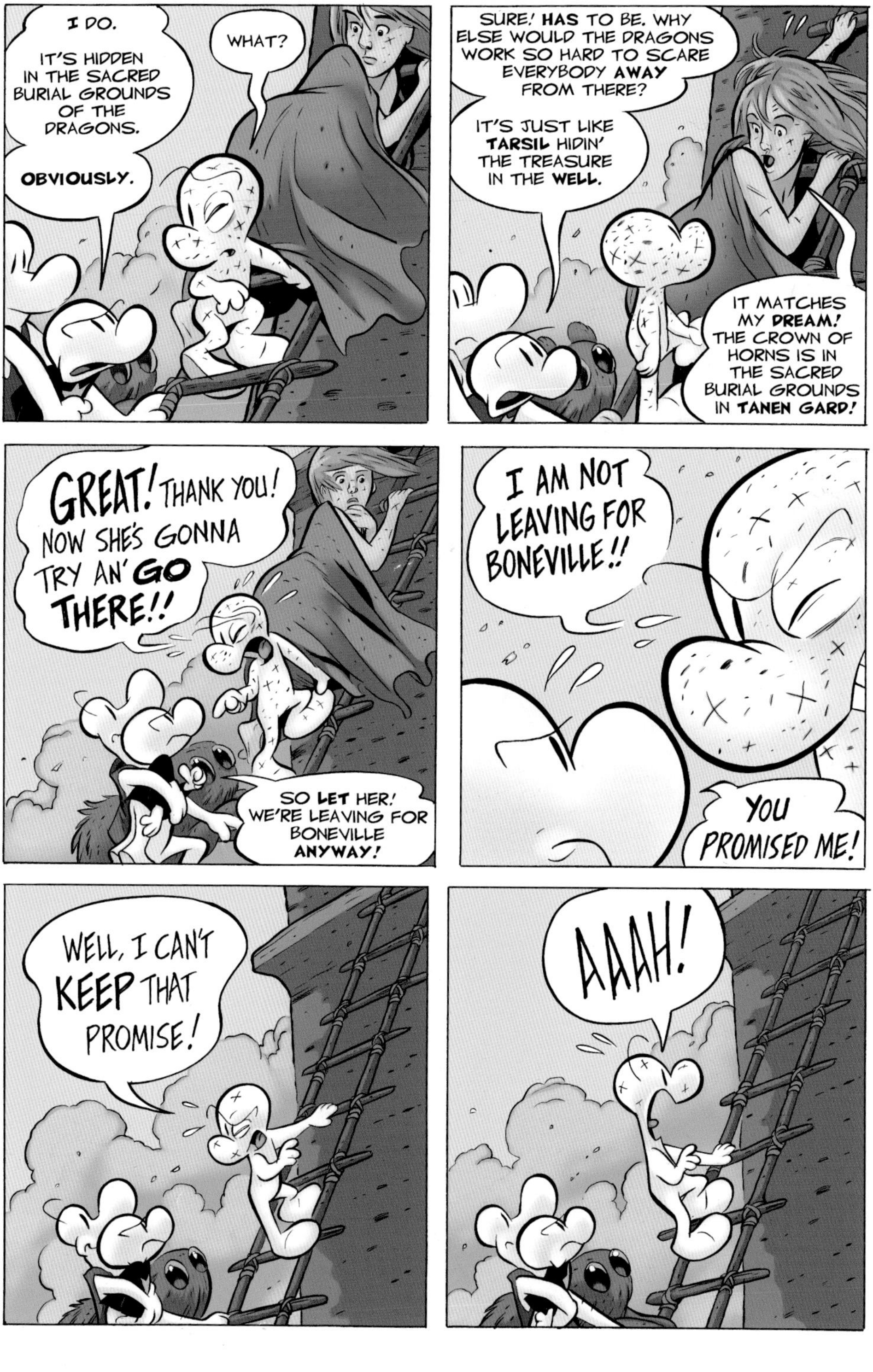
I DO.
IT'S HIDDEN IN THE SACRED BURIAL GROUNDS OF THE DRAGONS.
OBVIOUSLY.
WHAT?
SURE! HAS TO BE. WHY ELSE WOULD THE DRAGONS WORK SO HARD TO SCARE EVERYBODY AWAY FROM THERE?
IT'S JUST LIKE TARSIL HIDIN' THE TREASURE IN THE WELL.
IT MATCHES MY DREAM! THE CROWN OF HORNS IS IN THE SACRED BURIAL GROUNDS IN TANEN GARD!
GREAT! THANK YOU! NOW SHE'S GONNA TRY AN' GO THERE!!
SO LET HER! WE'RE LEAVING FOR BONEVILLE ANYWAY!
I AM NOT LEAVING FOR BONEVILLE!!
YOU PROMISED ME!
WELL, I CAN'T KEEP THAT PROMISE!
AAAH!

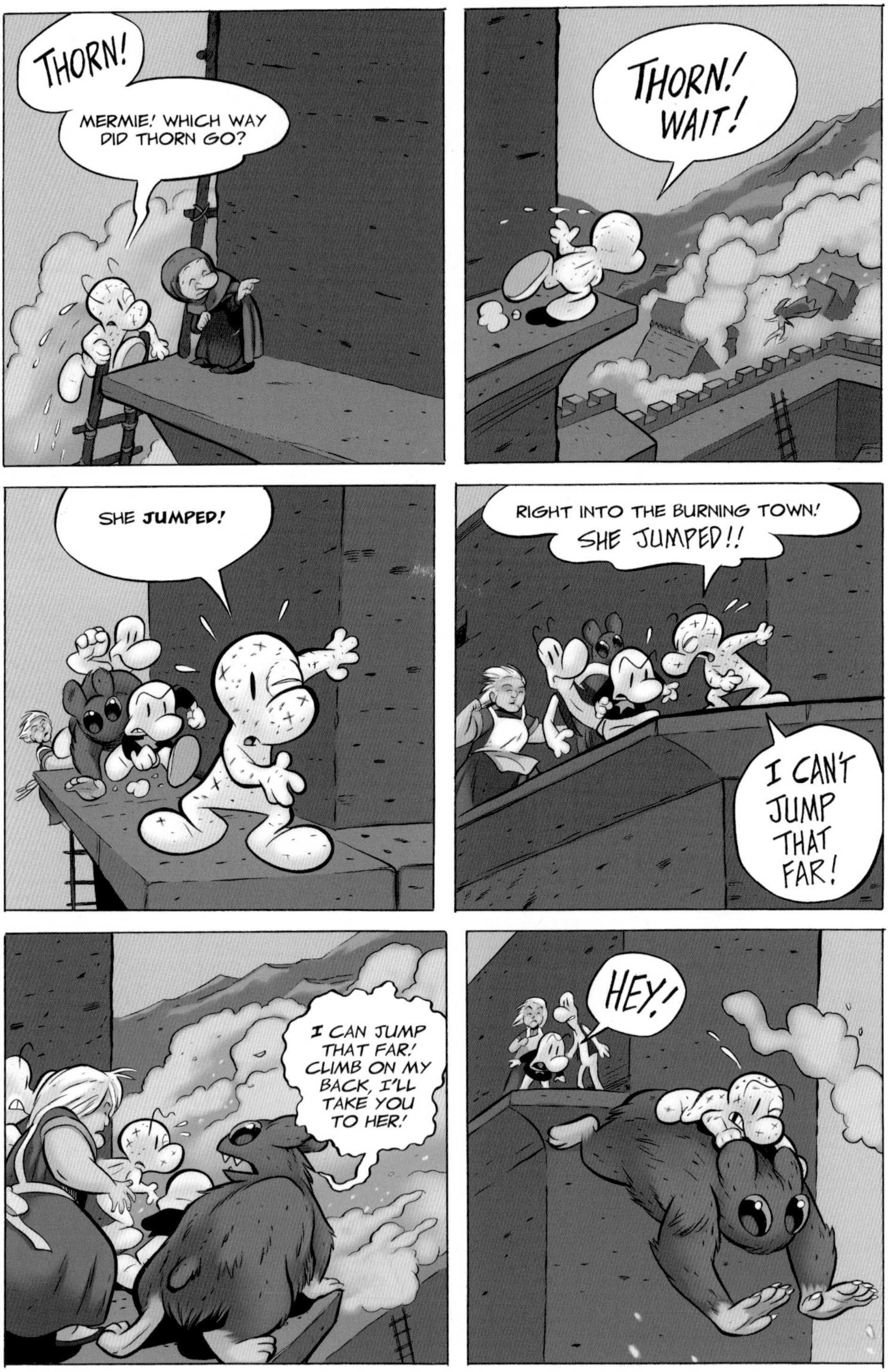
THORN!
MERMIE! WHICH WAY DID THORN GO?
THORN! WAIT!
SHE **JUMPED!**
RIGHT INTO THE BURNING TOWN! SHE JUMPED!!
I CAN'T JUMP THAT FAR!
I CAN JUMP THAT FAR! CLIMB ON MY BACK, I'LL TAKE YOU TO HER!
HEY!

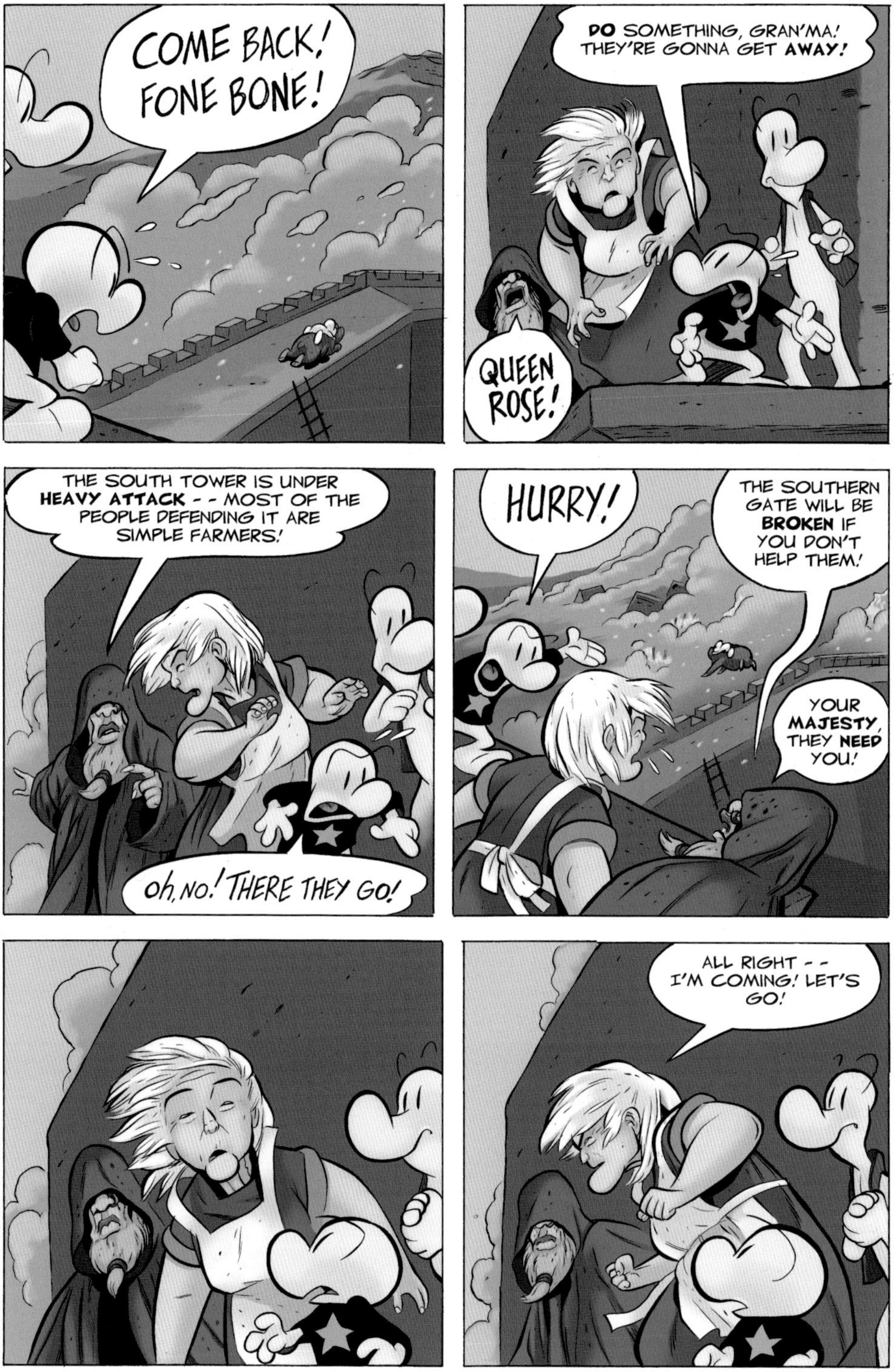
COME BACK! FONE BONE!
DO SOMETHING, GRAN'MA! THEY'RE GONNA GET AWAY!
QUEEN ROSE!
THE SOUTH TOWER IS UNDER HEAVY ATTACK - - MOST OF THE PEOPLE DEFENDING IT ARE SIMPLE FARMERS!
OH, NO! THERE THEY GO!
HURRY!
THE SOUTHERN GATE WILL BE BROKEN IF YOU DON'T HELP THEM!
YOUR MAJESTY, THEY NEED YOU!
ALL RIGHT - - I'M COMING! LET'S GO!

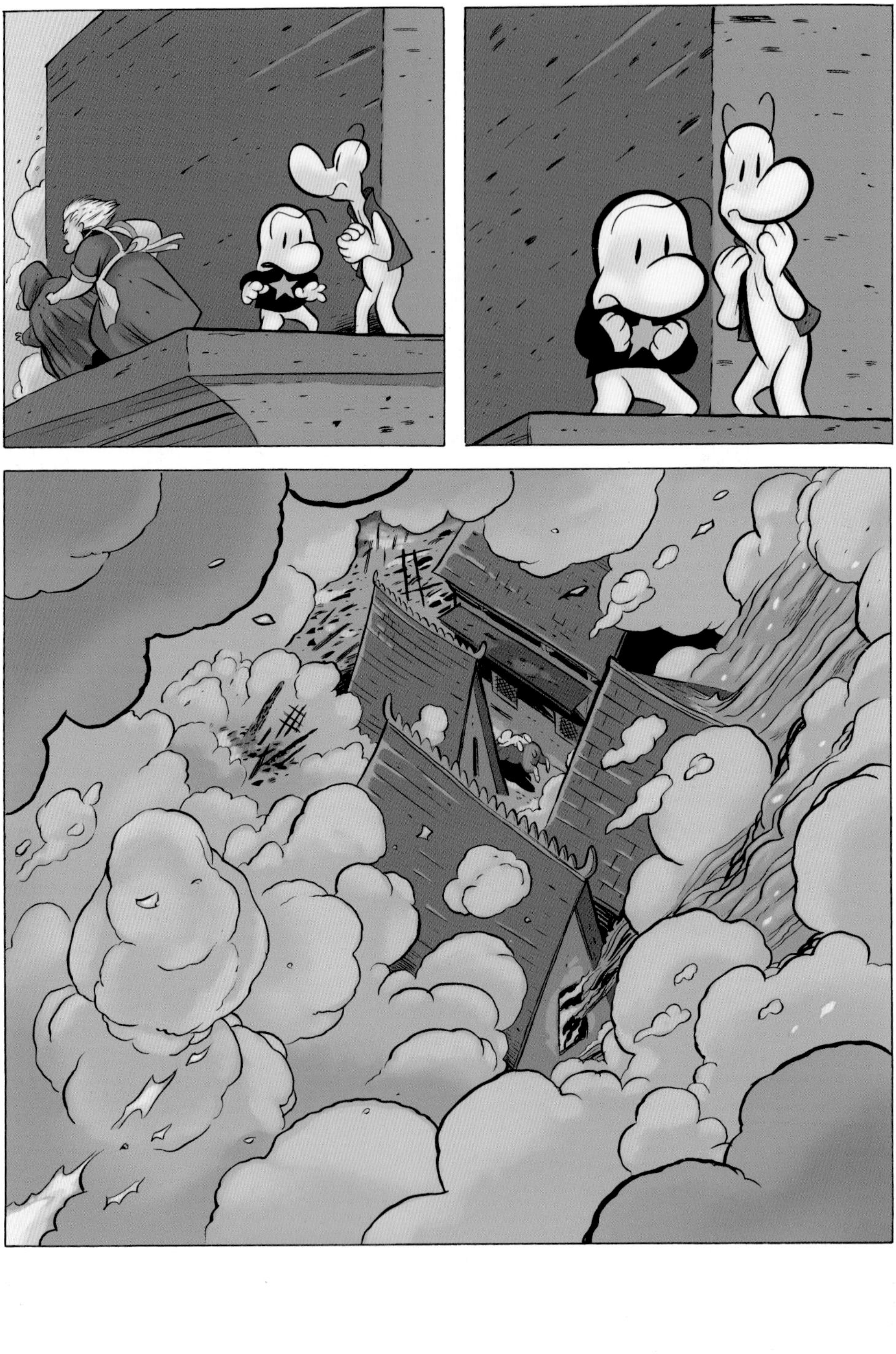

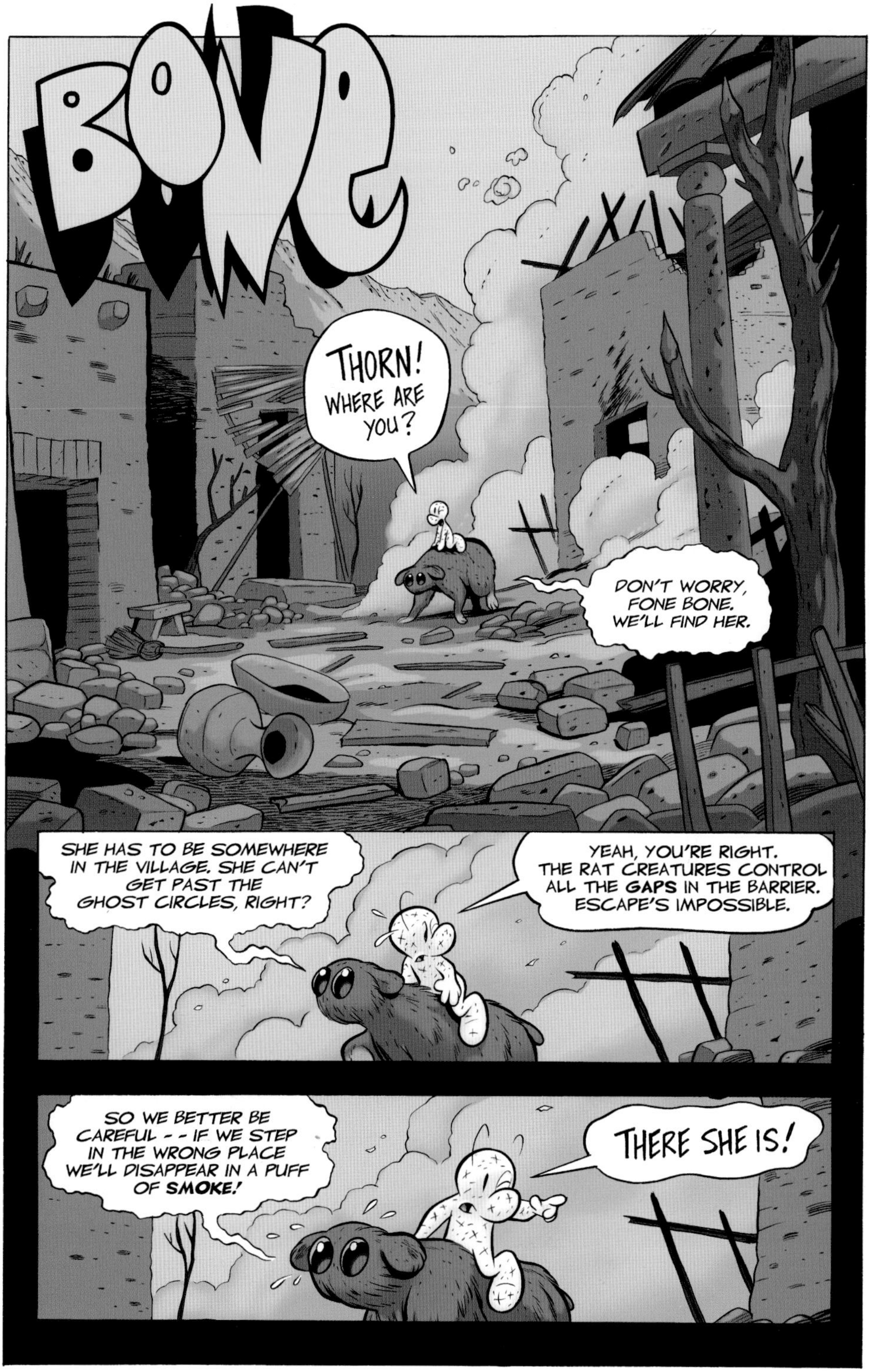
BONE
THORN! WHERE ARE YOU?
DON'T WORRY, FONE BONE. WE'LL FIND HER.
SHE HAS TO BE SOMEWHERE IN THE VILLAGE. SHE CAN'T GET PAST THE GHOST CIRCLES, RIGHT?
YEAH, YOU'RE RIGHT. THE RAT CREATURES CONTROL ALL THE GAPS IN THE BARRIER. ESCAPE'S IMPOSSIBLE.
SO WE BETTER BE CAREFUL - - IF WE STEP IN THE WRONG PLACE WE'LL DISAPPEAR IN A PUFF OF SMOKE!
THERE SHE IS!

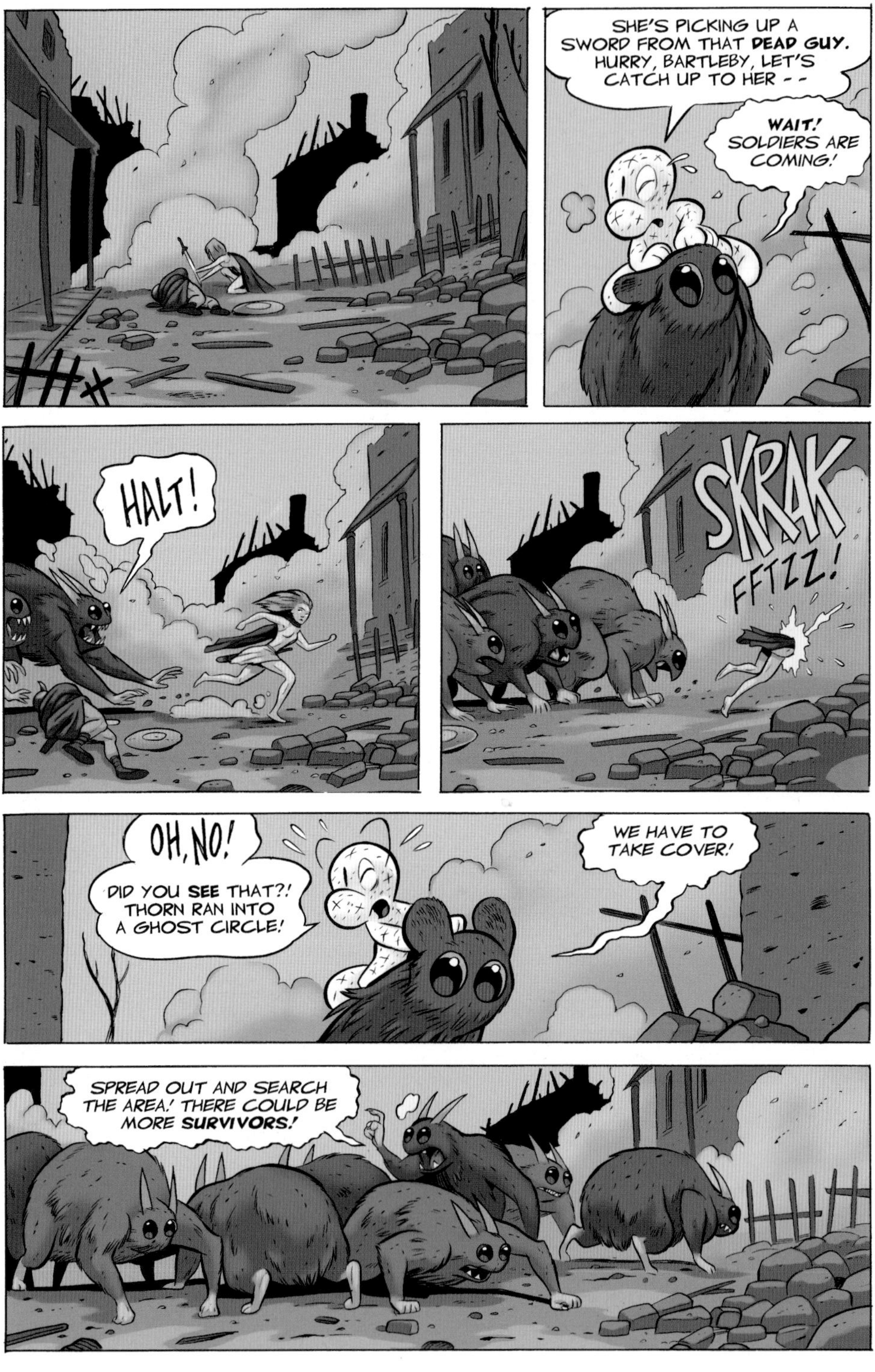
SHE'S PICKING UP A SWORD FROM THAT **DEAD GUY.** HURRY, BARTLEBY, LET'S CATCH UP TO HER - -
WAIT! SOLDIERS ARE COMING!
HALT!
SKRAK
FFTZZ!
OH, NO!
DID YOU **SEE** THAT?! THORN RAN INTO A GHOST CIRCLE!
WE HAVE TO TAKE COVER!
SPREAD OUT AND SEARCH THE AREA! THERE COULD BE MORE **SURVIVORS!**

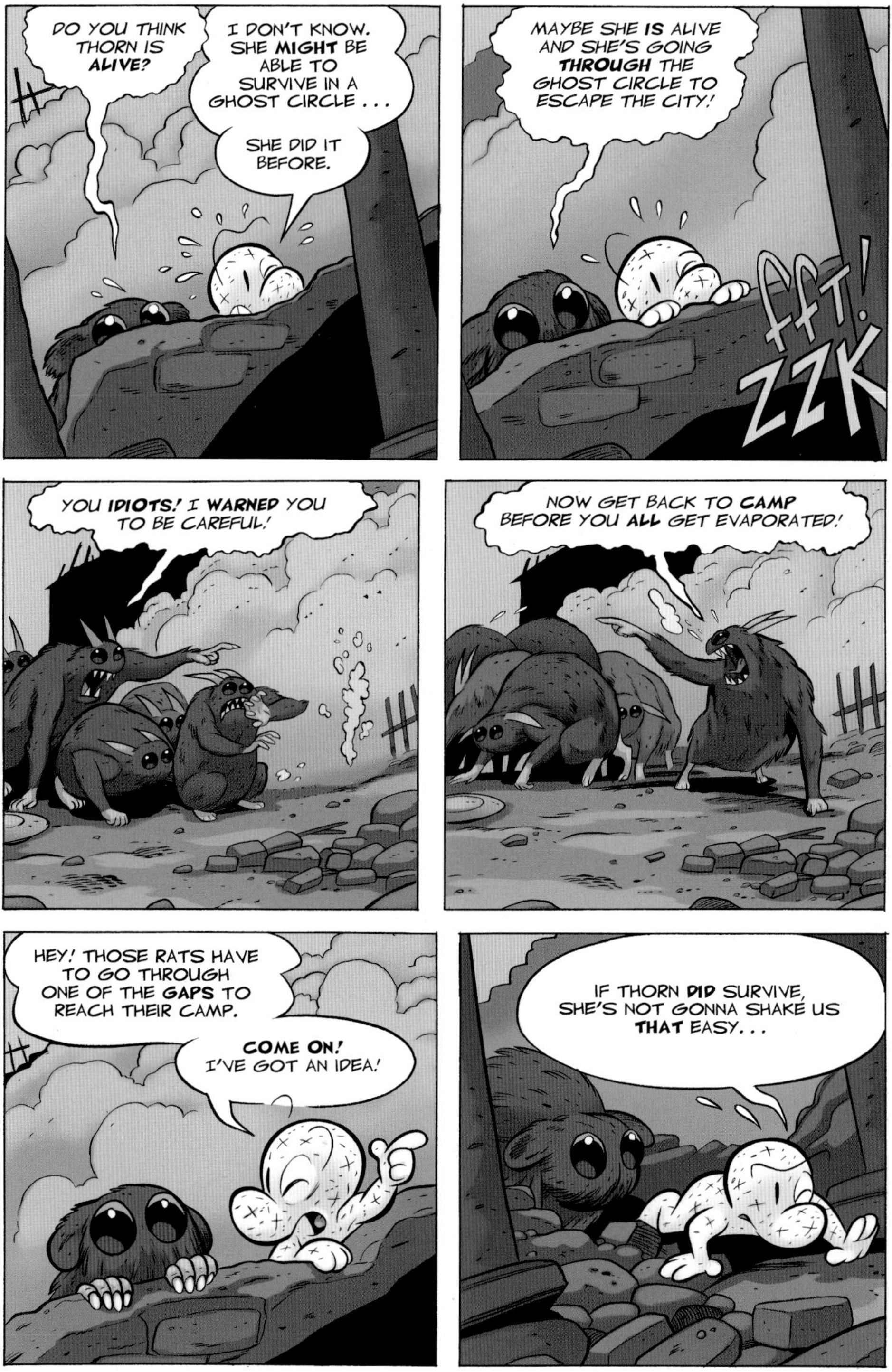
DO YOU THINK THORN IS ALIVE?
I DON'T KNOW. SHE MIGHT BE ABLE TO SURVIVE IN A GHOST CIRCLE . . .
SHE DID IT BEFORE.
MAYBE SHE IS ALIVE AND SHE'S GOING THROUGH THE GHOST CIRCLE TO ESCAPE THE CITY!
FFT! ZZK
YOU IDIOTS! I WARNED YOU TO BE CAREFUL!
NOW GET BACK TO CAMP BEFORE YOU ALL GET EVAPORATED!
HEY! THOSE RATS HAVE TO GO THROUGH ONE OF THE GAPS TO REACH THEIR CAMP.
COME ON! I'VE GOT AN IDEA!
IF THORN DID SURVIVE, SHE'S NOT GONNA SHAKE US THAT EASY. . .

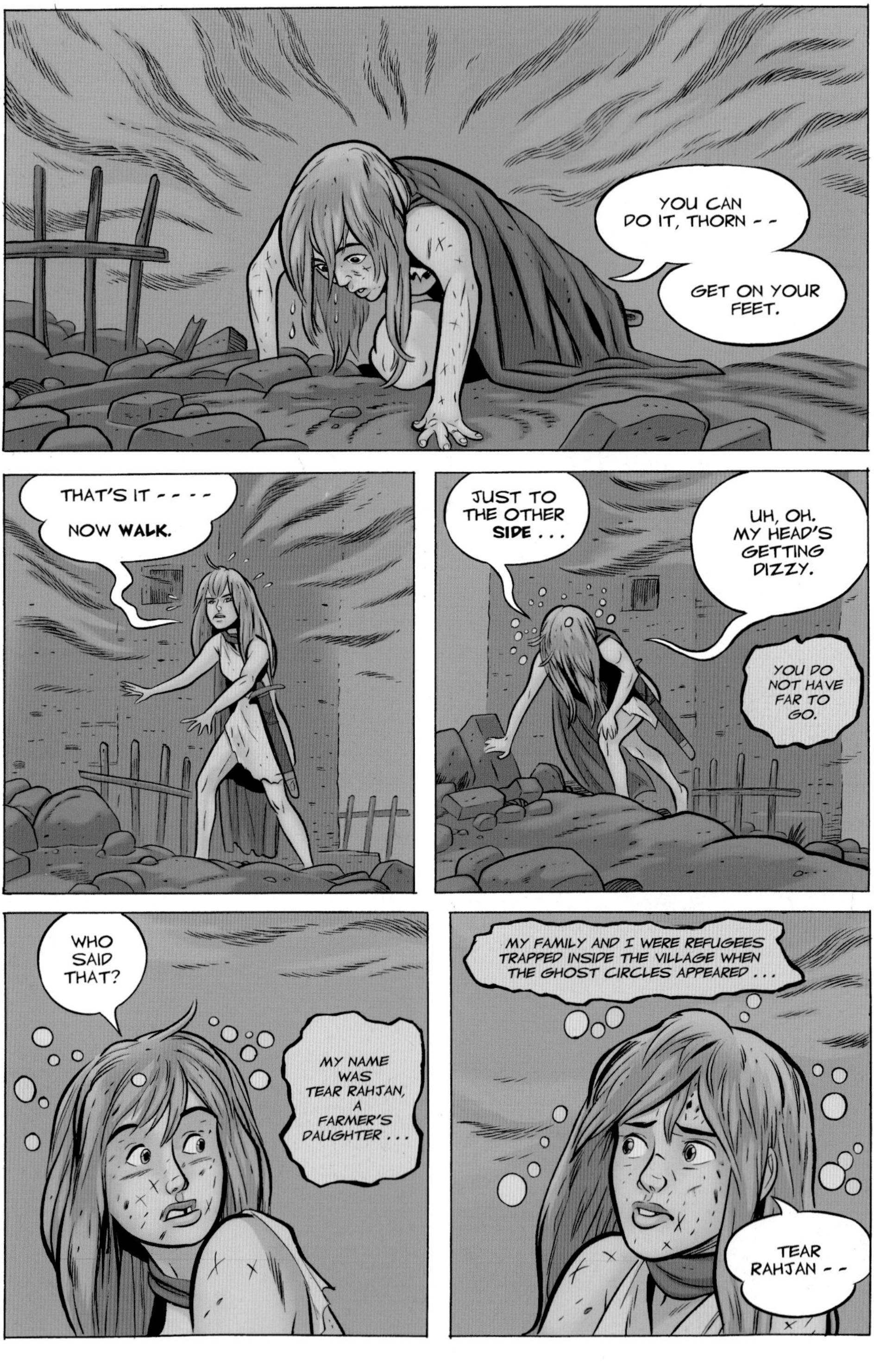
YOU CAN DO IT, THORN - -
GET ON YOUR FEET.
THAT'S IT - - - -
NOW **WALK.**
JUST TO THE OTHER **SIDE** . . .
UH, OH. MY HEAD'S GETTING DIZZY.
YOU DO NOT HAVE FAR TO GO.
WHO SAID THAT?
MY NAME WAS TEAR RAHJAN, A FARMER'S DAUGHTER . . .
MY FAMILY AND I WERE REFUGEES TRAPPED INSIDE THE VILLAGE WHEN THE GHOST CIRCLES APPEARED . . .
TEAR RAHJAN - -

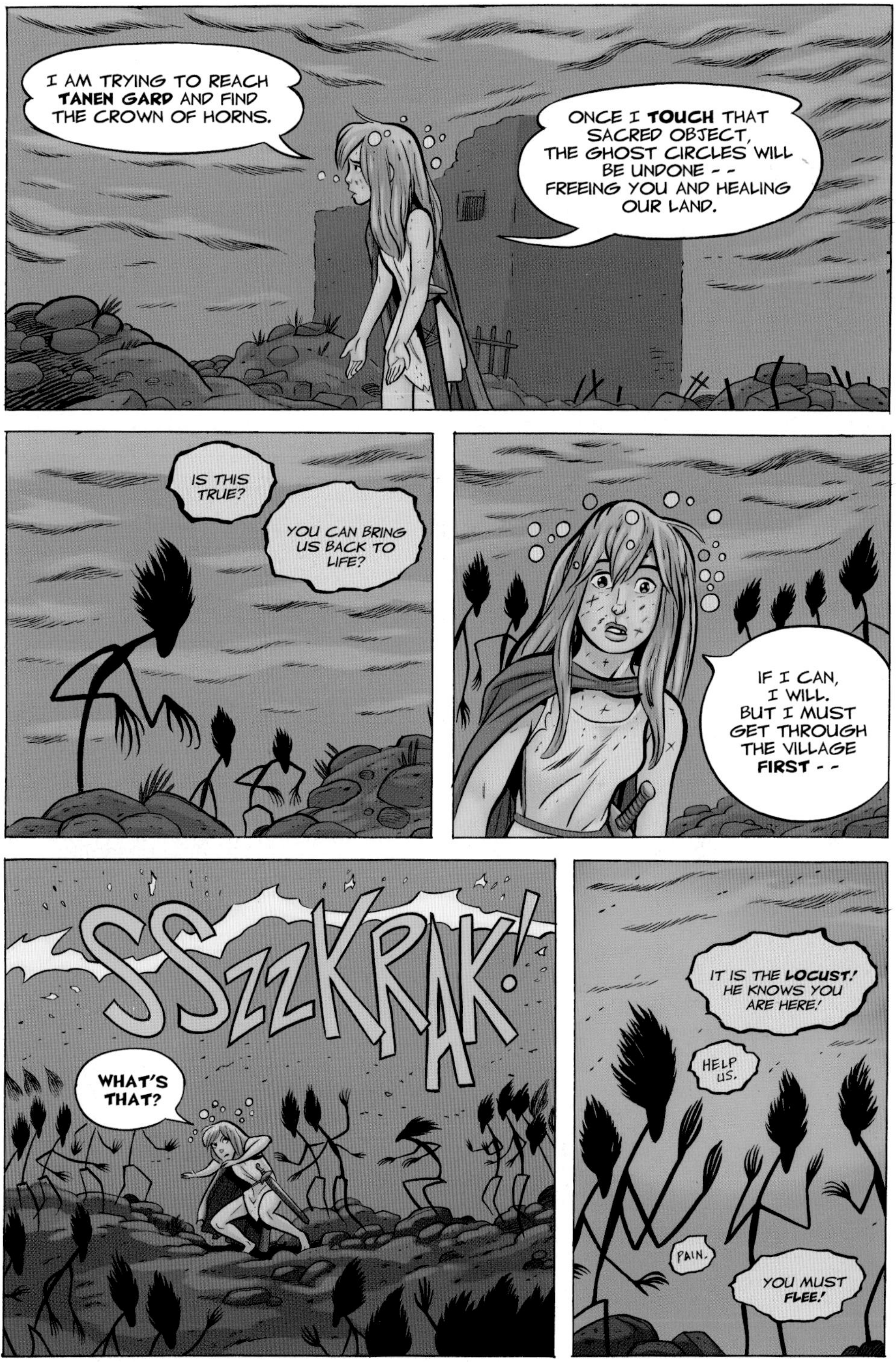
I AM TRYING TO REACH TANEN GARD AND FIND THE CROWN OF HORNS.
ONCE I TOUCH THAT SACRED OBJECT, THE GHOST CIRCLES WILL BE UNDONE - - FREEING YOU AND HEALING OUR LAND.
IS THIS TRUE?
YOU CAN BRING US BACK TO LIFE?
IF I CAN, I WILL. BUT I MUST GET THROUGH THE VILLAGE FIRST - -
SSzzKRAK!
WHAT'S THAT?
IT IS THE LOCUST! HE KNOWS YOU ARE HERE!
HELP US.
PAIN.
YOU MUST FLEE!

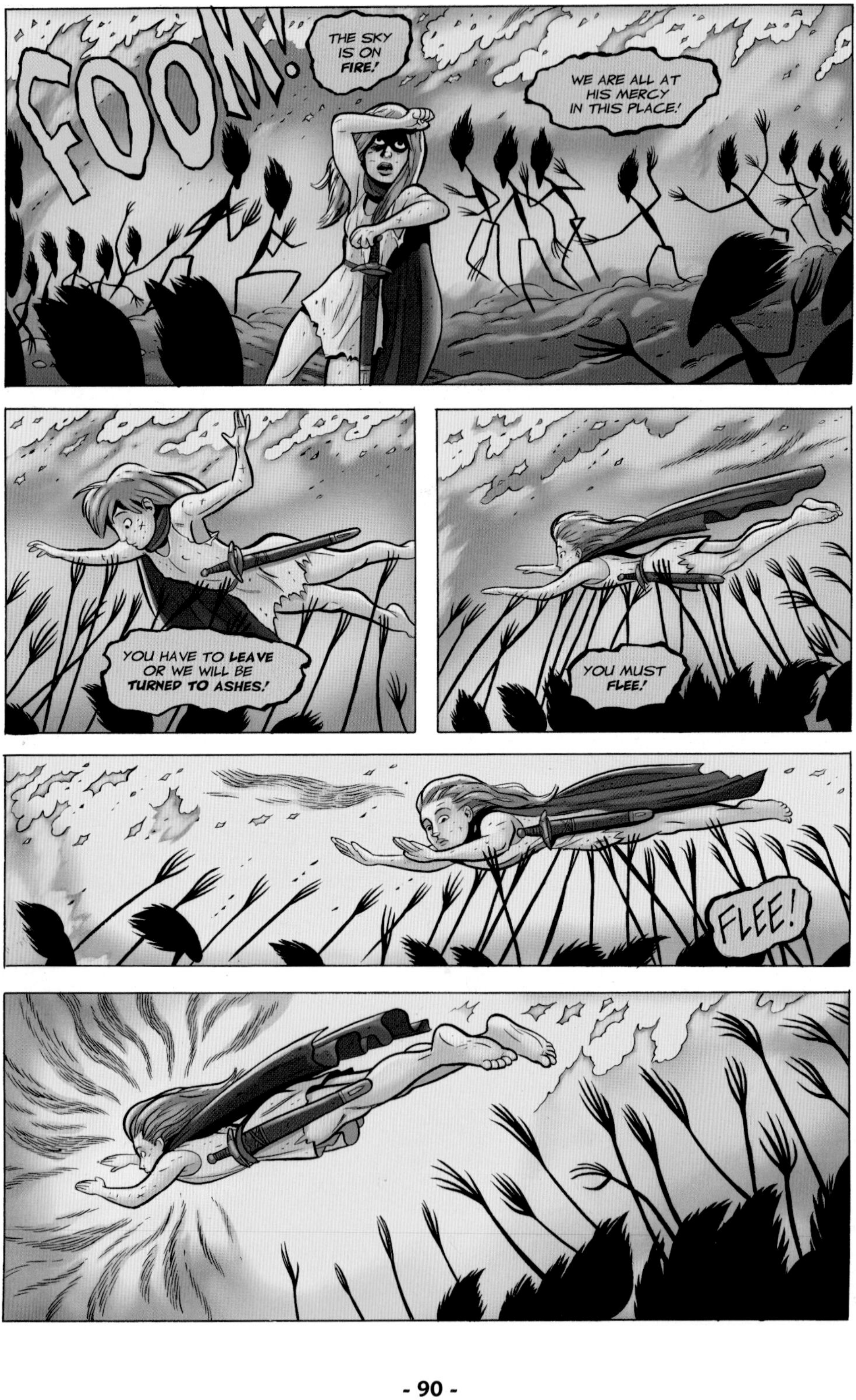
FOOM!
THE SKY IS ON FIRE!
WE ARE ALL AT HIS MERCY IN THIS PLACE!
YOU HAVE TO LEAVE OR WE WILL BE TURNED TO ASHES!
YOU MUST FLEE!
FLEE!

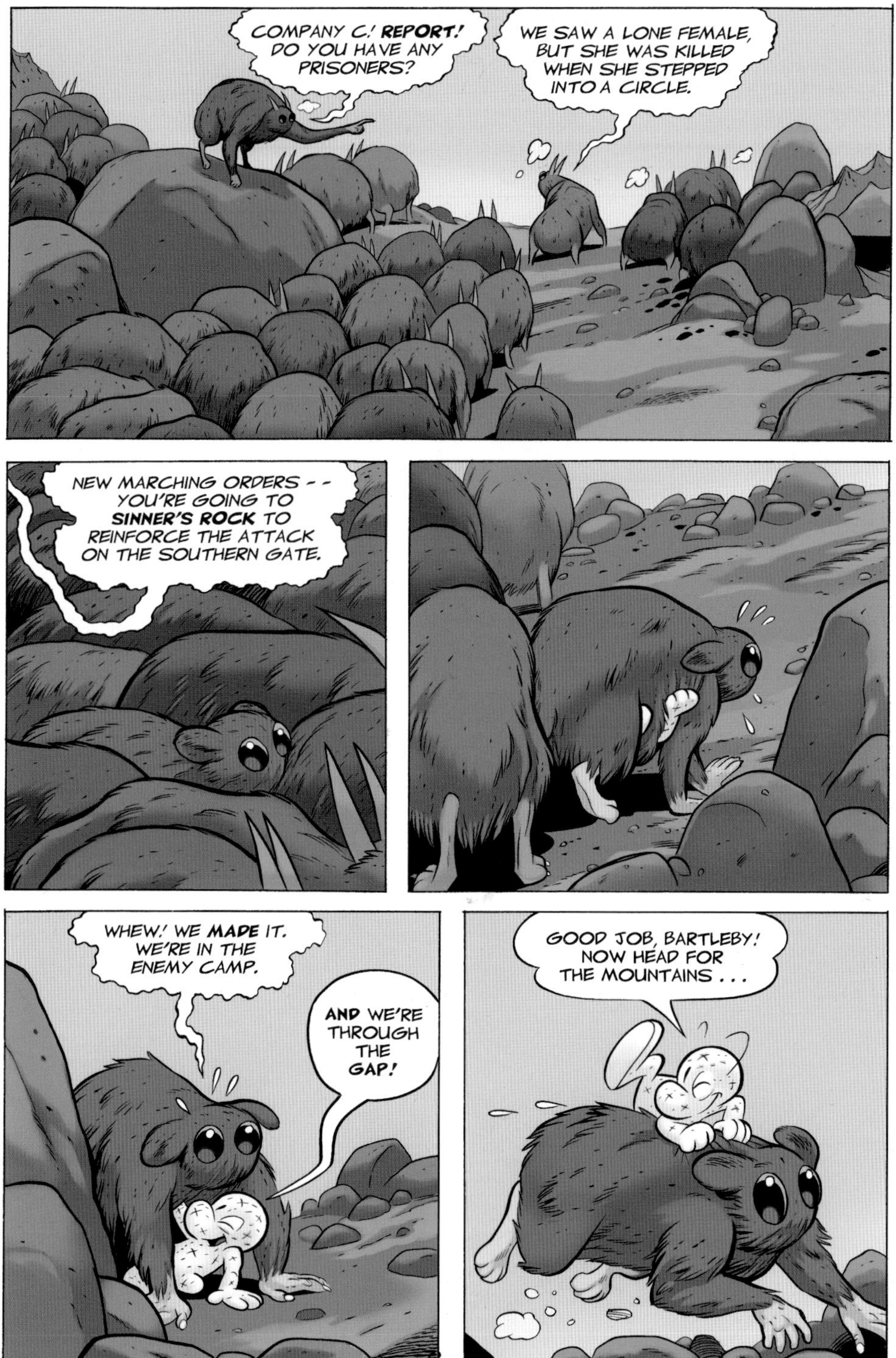
COMPANY C! REPORT! DO YOU HAVE ANY PRISONERS?
WE SAW A LONE FEMALE, BUT SHE WAS KILLED WHEN SHE STEPPED INTO A CIRCLE.
NEW MARCHING ORDERS - - YOU'RE GOING TO SINNER'S ROCK TO REINFORCE THE ATTACK ON THE SOUTHERN GATE.
WHEW! WE MADE IT. WE'RE IN THE ENEMY CAMP.
AND WE'RE THROUGH THE GAP!
GOOD JOB, BARTLEBY! NOW HEAD FOR THE MOUNTAINS . . .

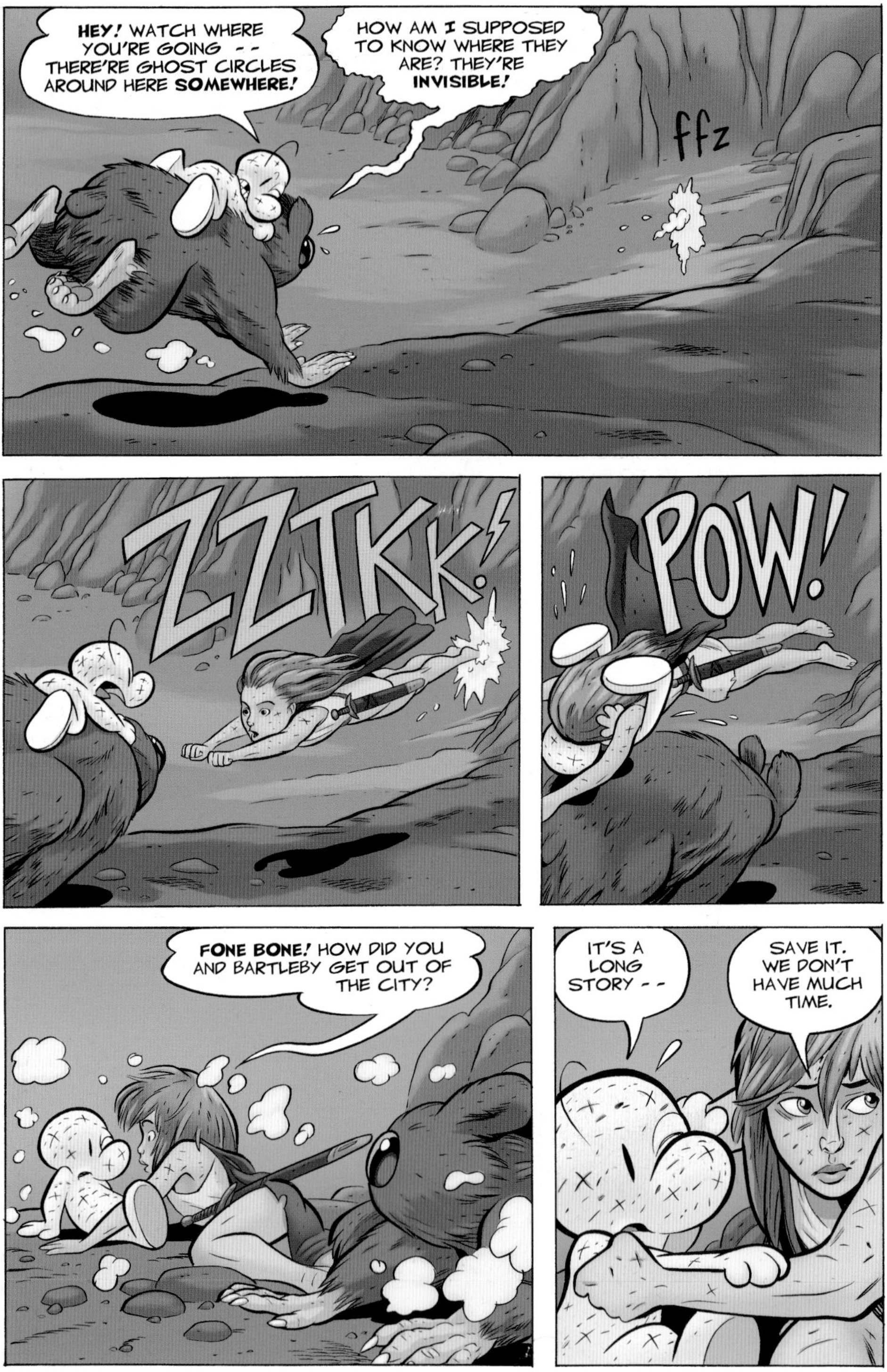
HEY! WATCH WHERE YOU'RE GOING -- THERE'RE GHOST CIRCLES AROUND HERE SOMEWHERE!
HOW AM I SUPPOSED TO KNOW WHERE THEY ARE? THEY'RE INVISIBLE!
ffz
ZZTKK!
POW!
FONE BONE! HOW DID YOU AND BARTLEBY GET OUT OF THE CITY?
IT'S A LONG STORY --
SAVE IT. WE DON'T HAVE MUCH TIME.

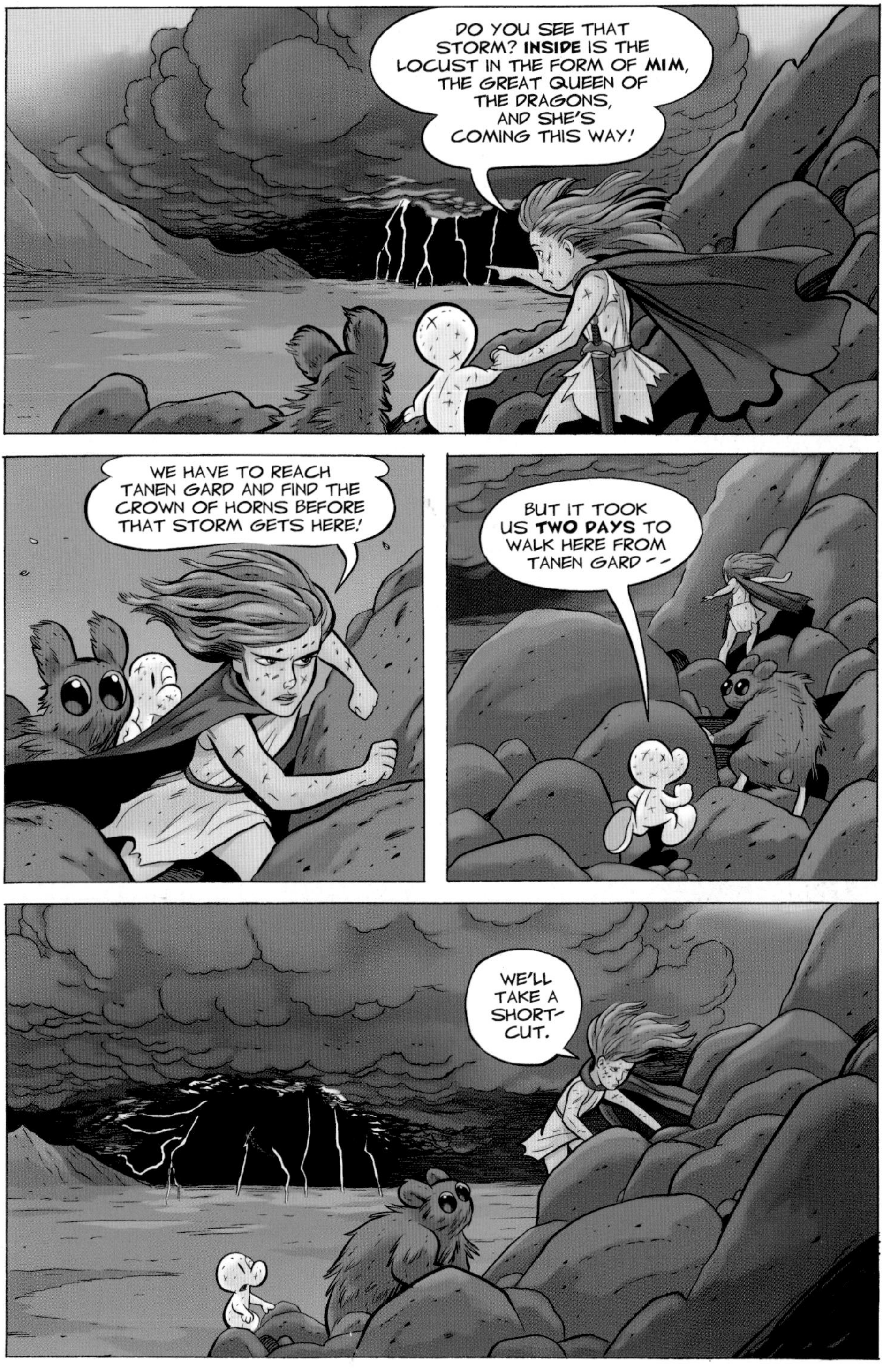
DO YOU SEE THAT STORM? INSIDE IS THE LOCUST IN THE FORM OF MIM, THE GREAT QUEEN OF THE DRAGONS, AND SHE'S COMING THIS WAY!
WE HAVE TO REACH TANEN GARD AND FIND THE CROWN OF HORNS BEFORE THAT STORM GETS HERE!
BUT IT TOOK US TWO DAYS TO WALK HERE FROM TANEN GARD --
WE'LL TAKE A SHORT-CUT.

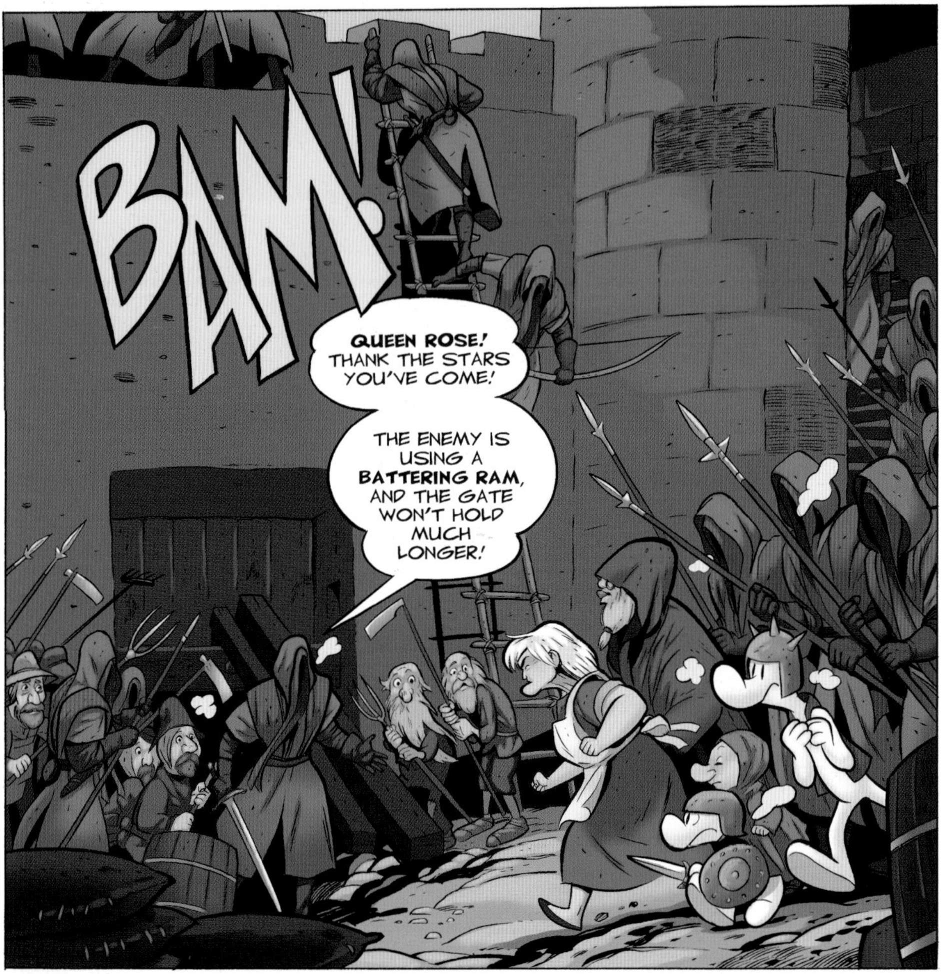
BAM!
QUEEN ROSE! THANK THE STARS YOU'VE COME!
THE ENEMY IS USING A BATTERING RAM, AND THE GATE WON'T HOLD MUCH LONGER!

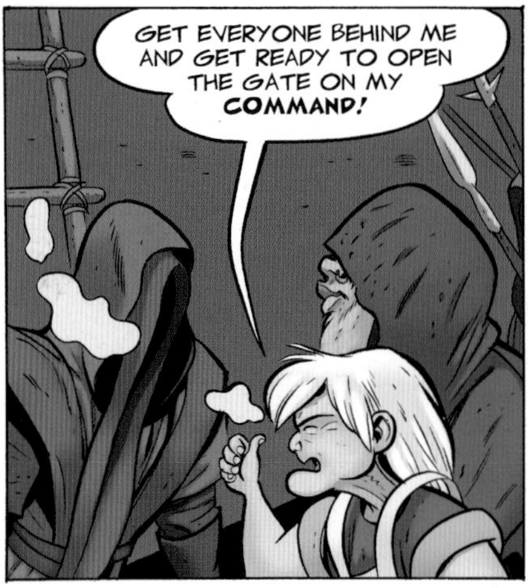
GET EVERYONE BEHIND ME AND GET READY TO OPEN THE GATE ON MY COMMAND!

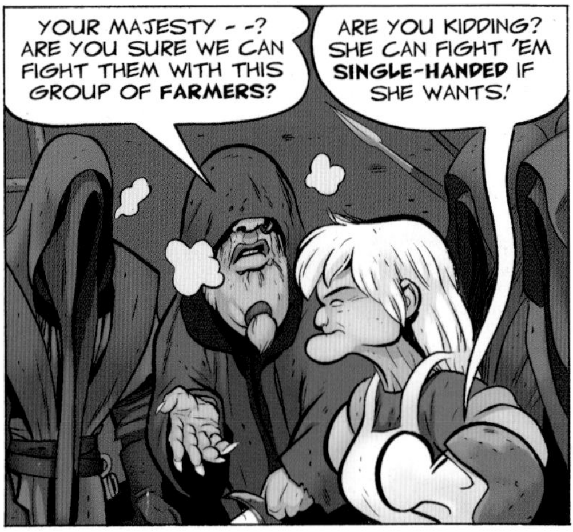
YOUR MAJESTY - -? ARE YOU SURE WE CAN FIGHT THEM WITH THIS GROUP OF FARMERS?
ARE YOU KIDDING? SHE CAN FIGHT 'EM SINGLE-HANDED IF SHE WANTS!

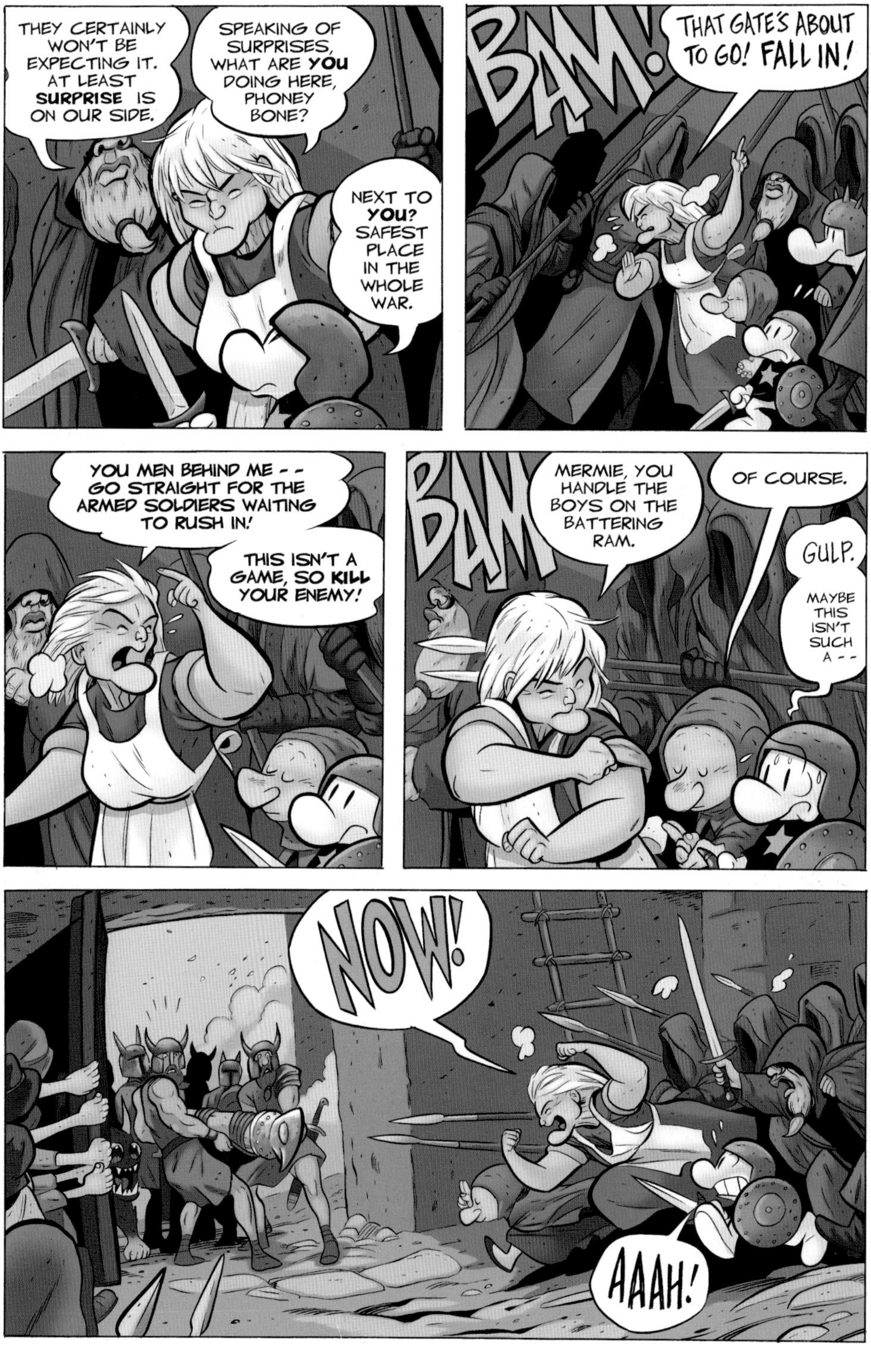
THEY CERTAINLY WON'T BE EXPECTING IT. AT LEAST SURPRISE IS ON OUR SIDE.
SPEAKING OF SURPRISES, WHAT ARE YOU DOING HERE, PHONEY BONE?
NEXT TO YOU? SAFEST PLACE IN THE WHOLE WAR.
BAM!
THAT GATE'S ABOUT TO GO! FALL IN!
YOU MEN BEHIND ME - - GO STRAIGHT FOR THE ARMED SOLDIERS WAITING TO RUSH IN!
THIS ISN'T A GAME, SO KILL YOUR ENEMY!
BAM
MERMIE, YOU HANDLE THE BOYS ON THE BATTERING RAM.
OF COURSE.
GULP.
MAYBE THIS ISN'T SUCH A - -
NOW!
AAAH!

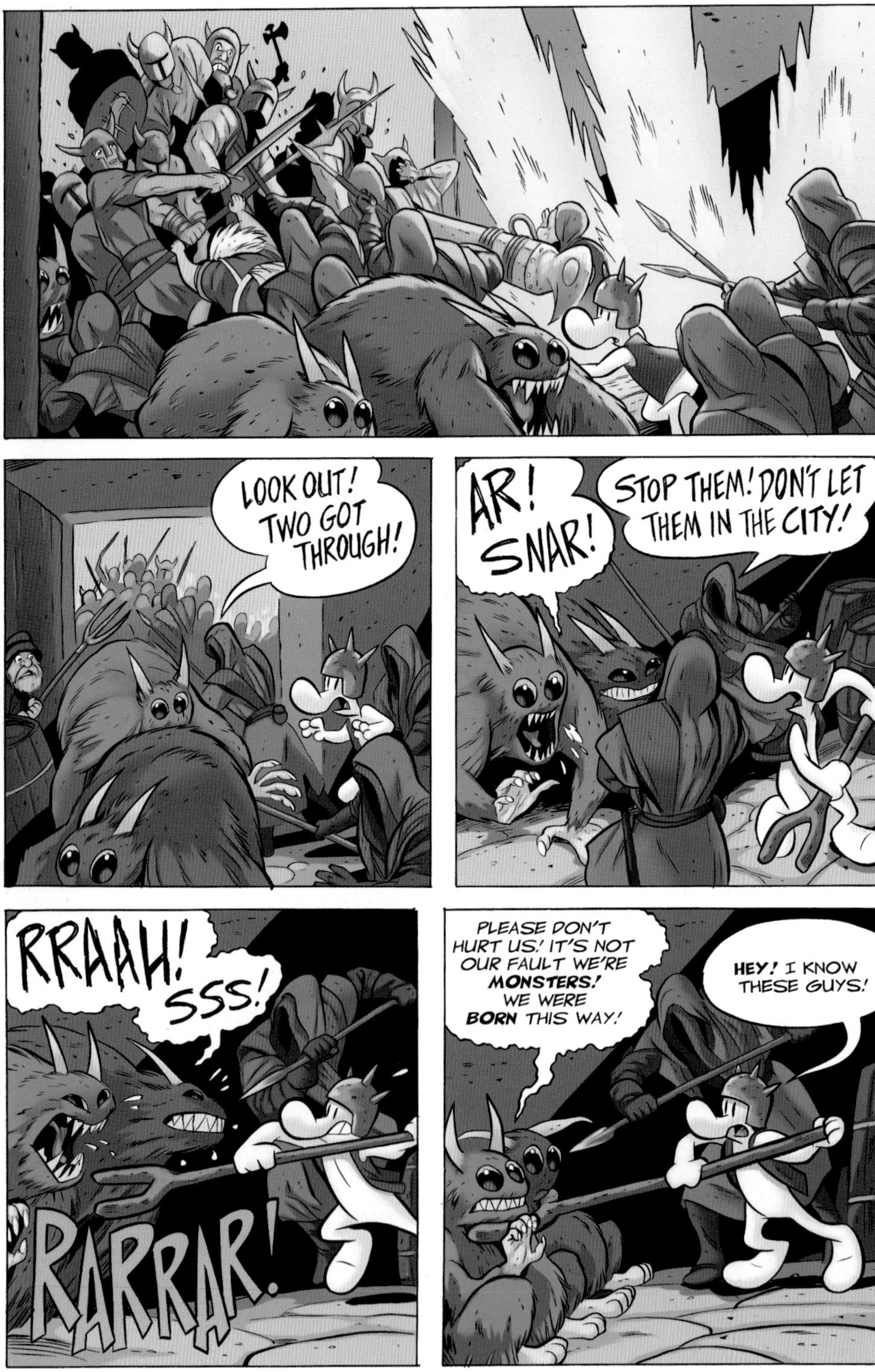
LOOK OUT! TWO GOT THROUGH!
AR! SNAR!
STOP THEM! DON'T LET THEM IN THE CITY!
RRAAH! SSS!
RARRAR!
PLEASE DON'T HURT US! IT'S NOT OUR FAULT WE'RE **MONSTERS!** WE WERE **BORN** THIS WAY!
HEY! I KNOW THESE GUYS!

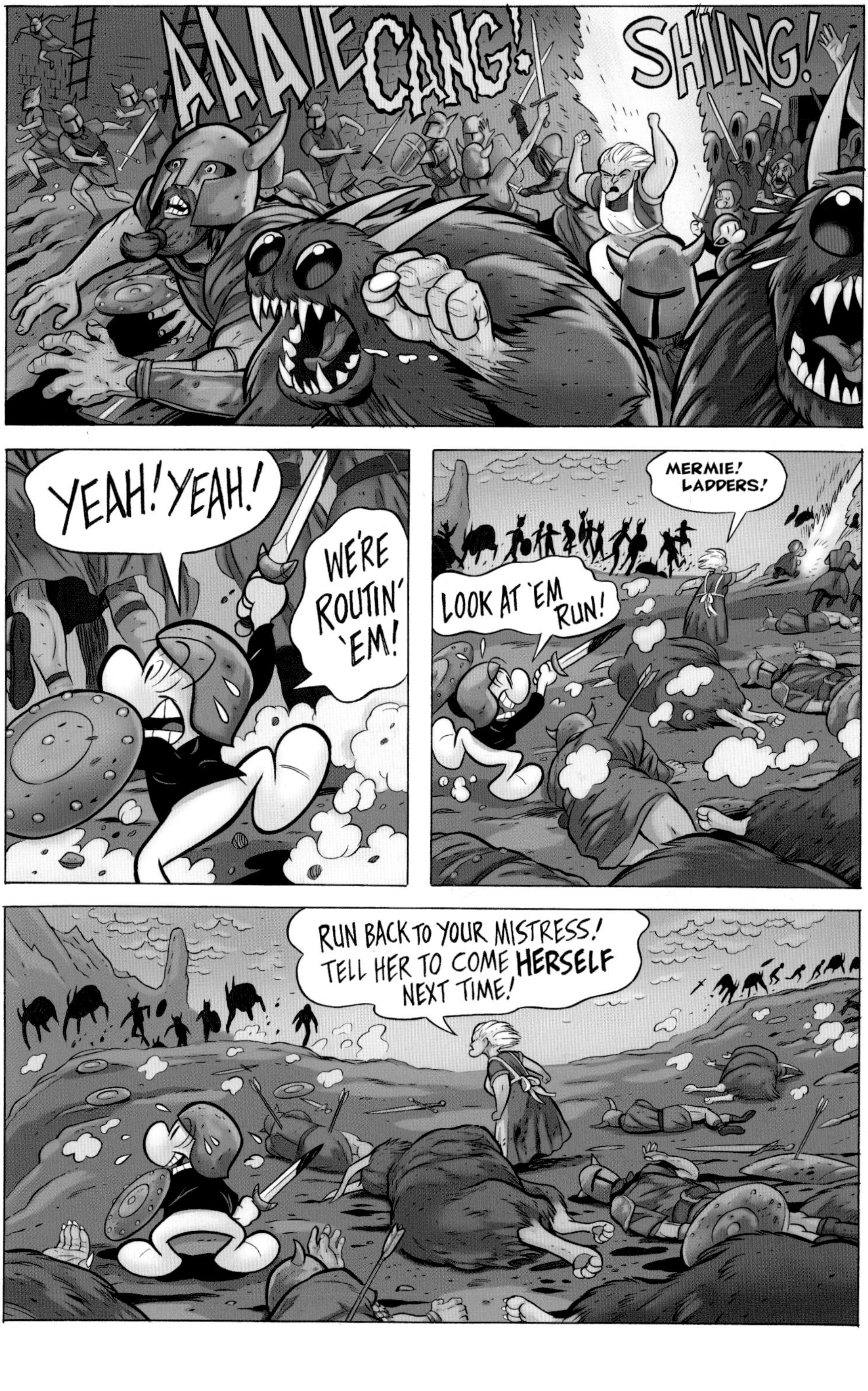
AAAIE
CANG!
SHING!
YEAH! YEAH!
WE'RE ROUTIN' 'EM!
MERMIE! LADDERS!
LOOK AT 'EM RUN!
RUN BACK TO YOUR MISTRESS! TELL HER TO COME **HERSELF** NEXT TIME!

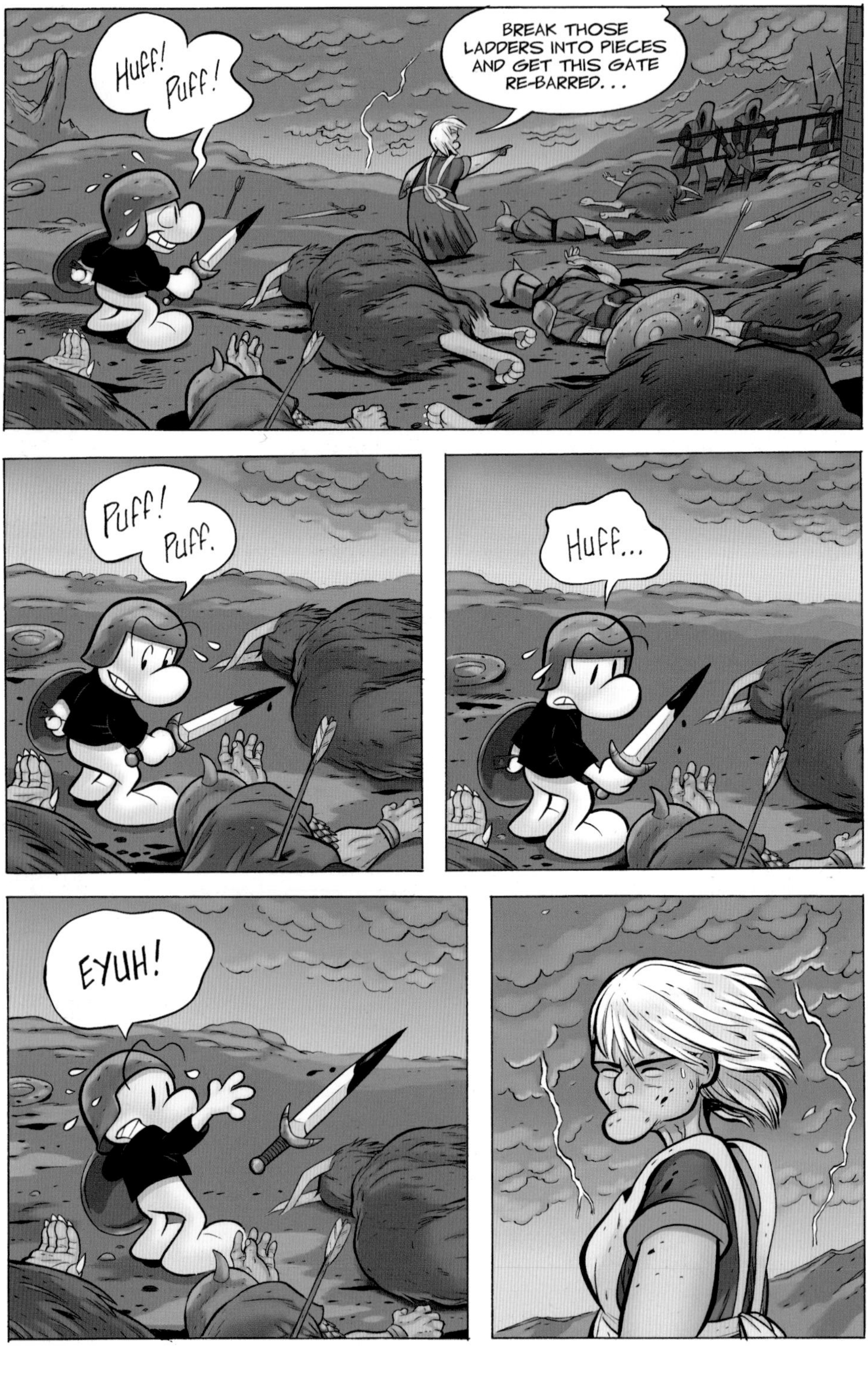
Huff! Puff!
BREAK THOSE LADDERS INTO PIECES AND GET THIS GATE RE-BARRED...
Puff! Puff.
Huff...
EYUH!

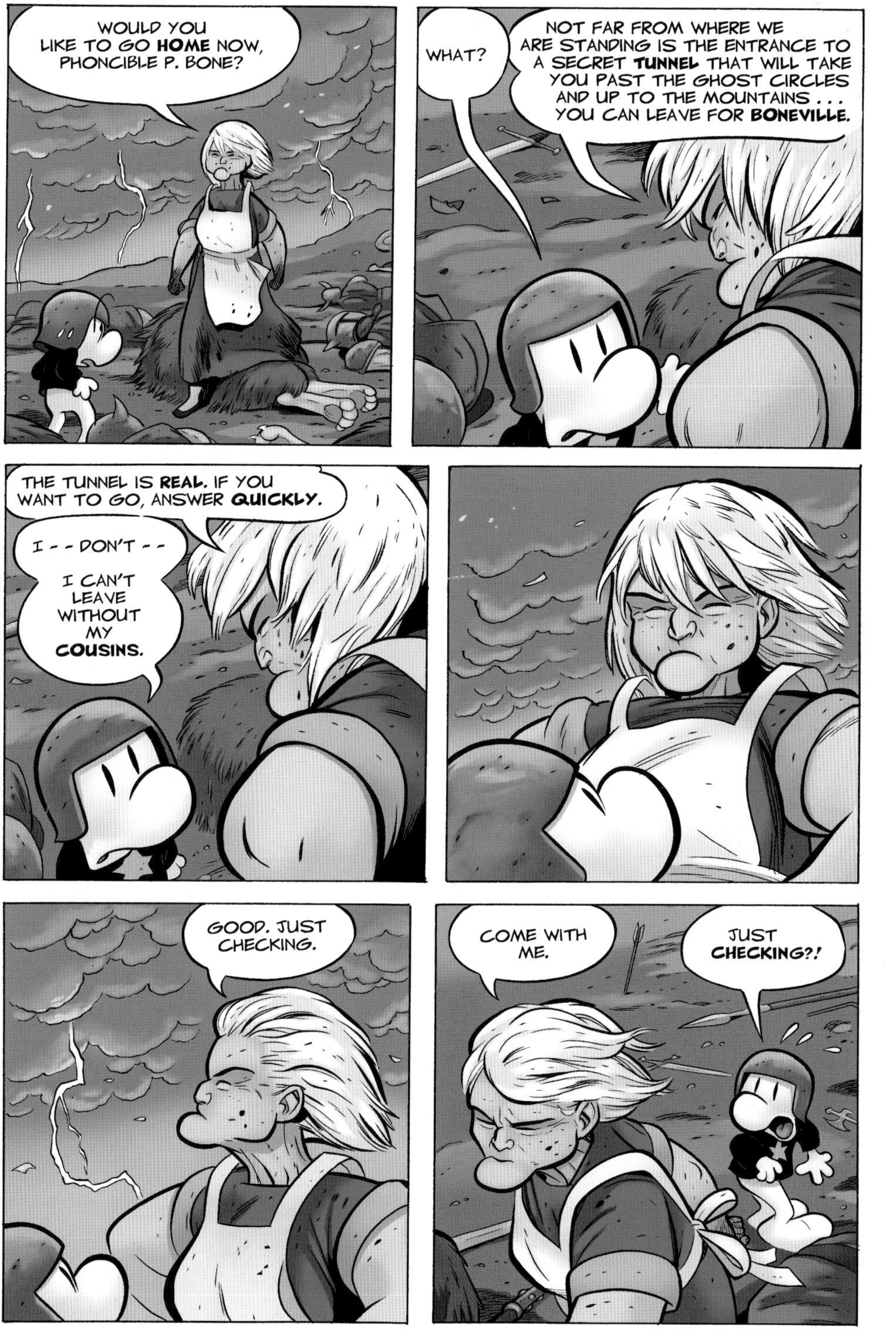
WOULD YOU LIKE TO GO **HOME** NOW, PHONCIBLE P. BONE?
WHAT?
NOT FAR FROM WHERE WE ARE STANDING IS THE ENTRANCE TO A SECRET **TUNNEL** THAT WILL TAKE YOU PAST THE GHOST CIRCLES AND UP TO THE MOUNTAINS . . . YOU CAN LEAVE FOR **BONEVILLE.**
THE TUNNEL IS **REAL.** IF YOU WANT TO GO, ANSWER **QUICKLY.**
I - - DON'T - -
I CAN'T LEAVE WITHOUT MY **COUSINS.**
GOOD. JUST CHECKING.
COME WITH ME.
JUST **CHECKING?!**

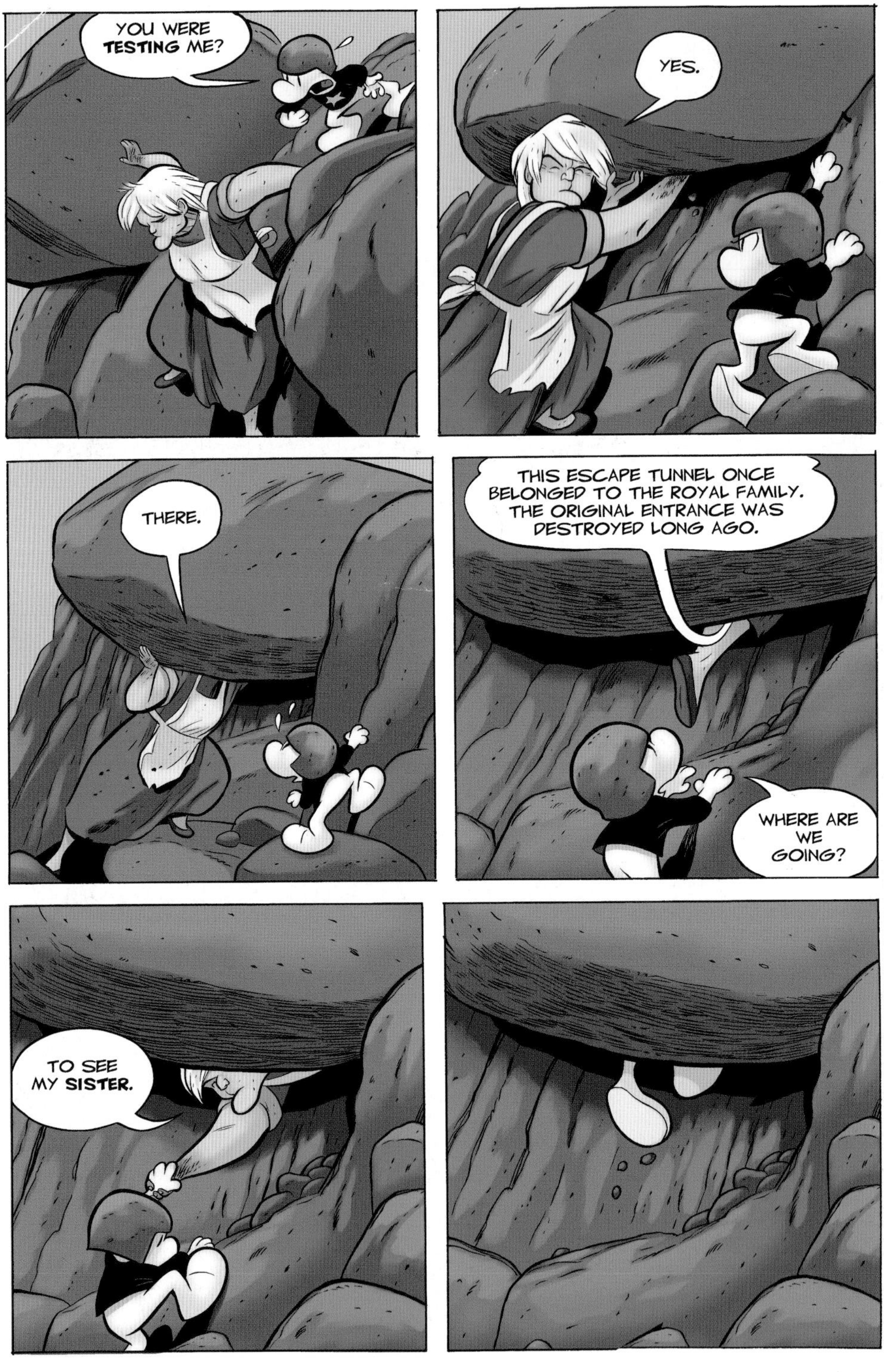
YOU WERE TESTING ME?
YES.
THERE.
THIS ESCAPE TUNNEL ONCE BELONGED TO THE ROYAL FAMILY. THE ORIGINAL ENTRANCE WAS DESTROYED LONG AGO.
WHERE ARE WE GOING?
TO SEE MY SISTER.

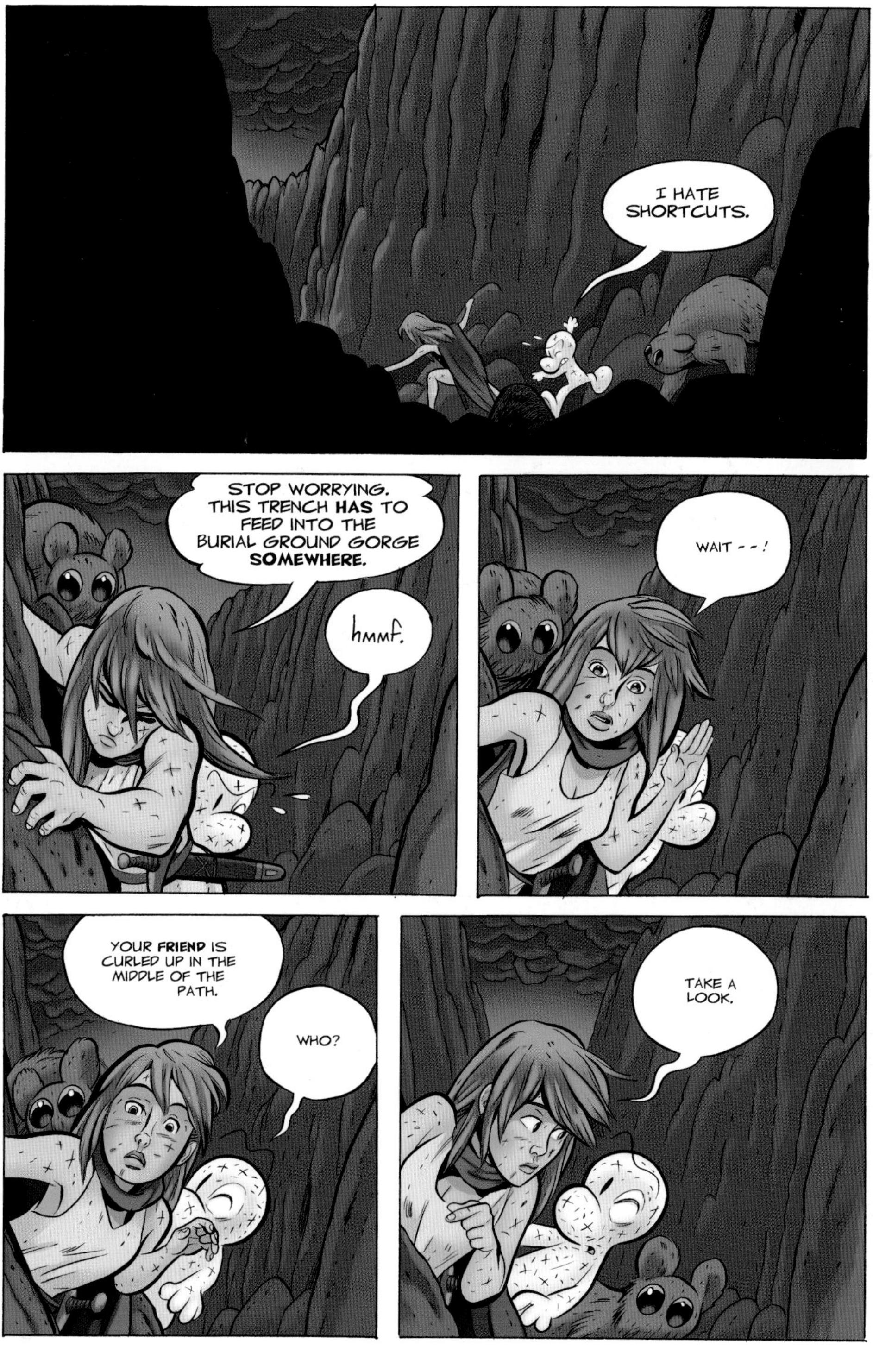
I HATE SHORTCUTS.
STOP WORRYING. THIS TRENCH HAS TO FEED INTO THE BURIAL GROUND GORGE SOMEWHERE.
hmmf.
WAIT - - !
YOUR FRIEND IS CURLED UP IN THE MIDDLE OF THE PATH.
WHO?
TAKE A LOOK.

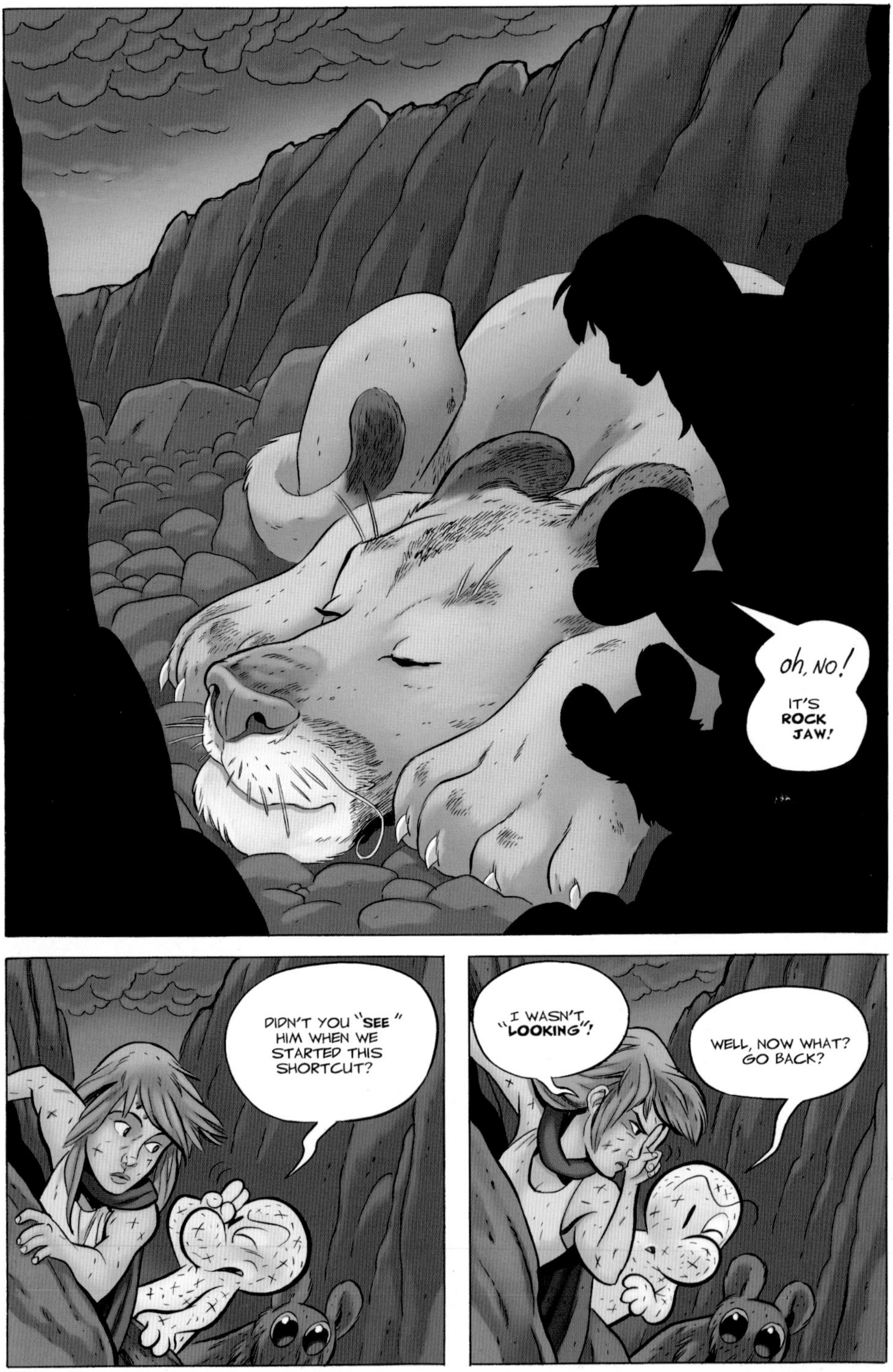
oh, NO!
IT'S ROCK JAW!
DIDN'T YOU "SEE" HIM WHEN WE STARTED THIS SHORTCUT?
"I WASN'T "LOOKING"!
WELL, NOW WHAT? GO BACK?

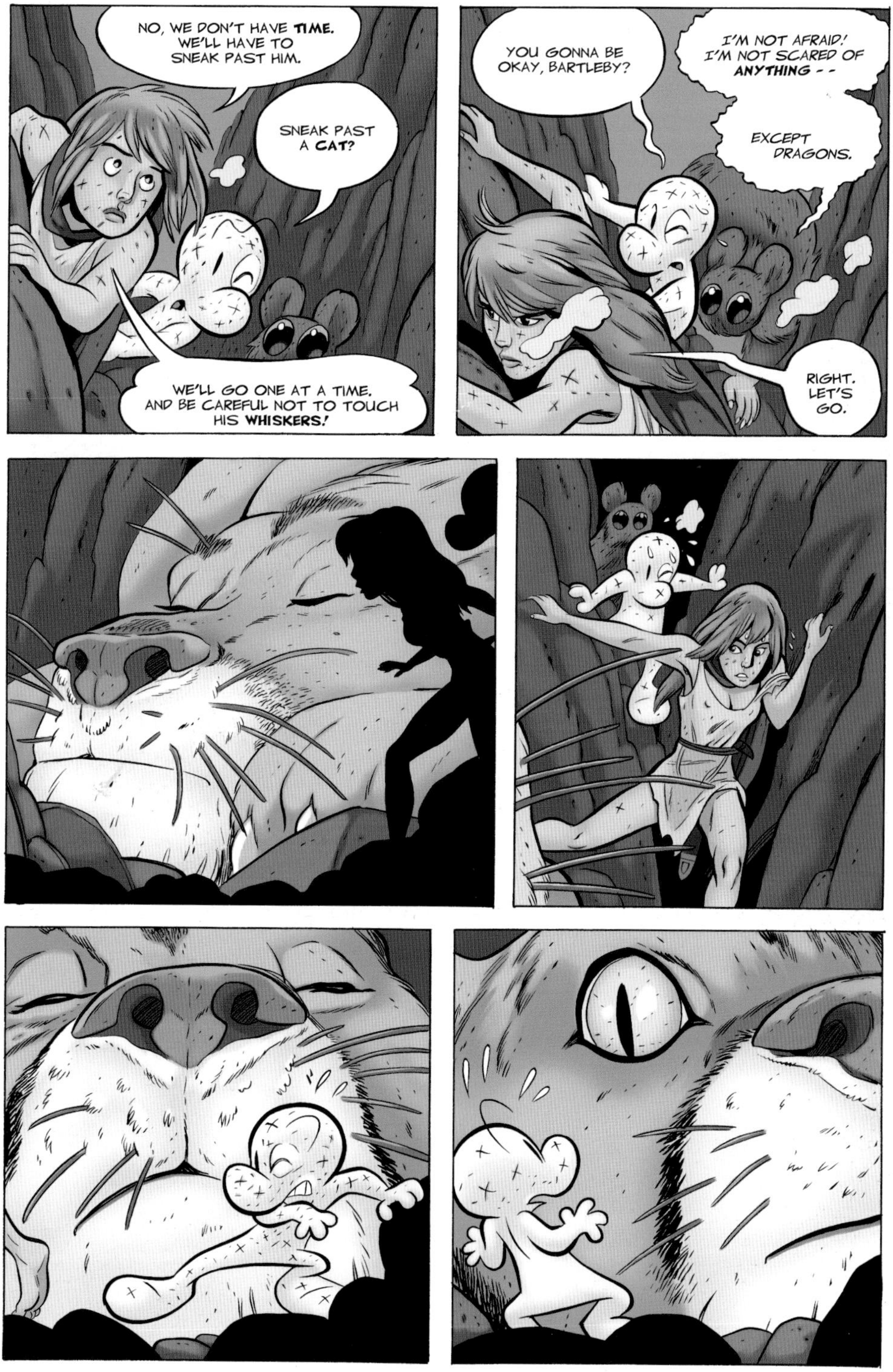
NO, WE DON'T HAVE TIME. WE'LL HAVE TO SNEAK PAST HIM.
SNEAK PAST A CAT?
WE'LL GO ONE AT A TIME. AND BE CAREFUL NOT TO TOUCH HIS WHISKERS!
YOU GONNA BE OKAY, BARTLEBY?
I'M NOT AFRAID! I'M NOT SCARED OF ANYTHING - -
EXCEPT DRAGONS.
RIGHT. LET'S GO.

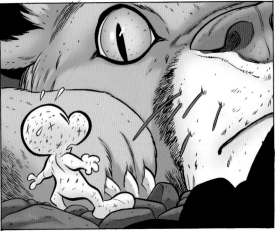

RUN, FONE BONE!

WAIT!

PUT YOUR SWORD AWAY.

BARTLEBY... COME OVER TO US...

SLOWLY...

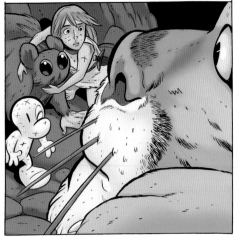

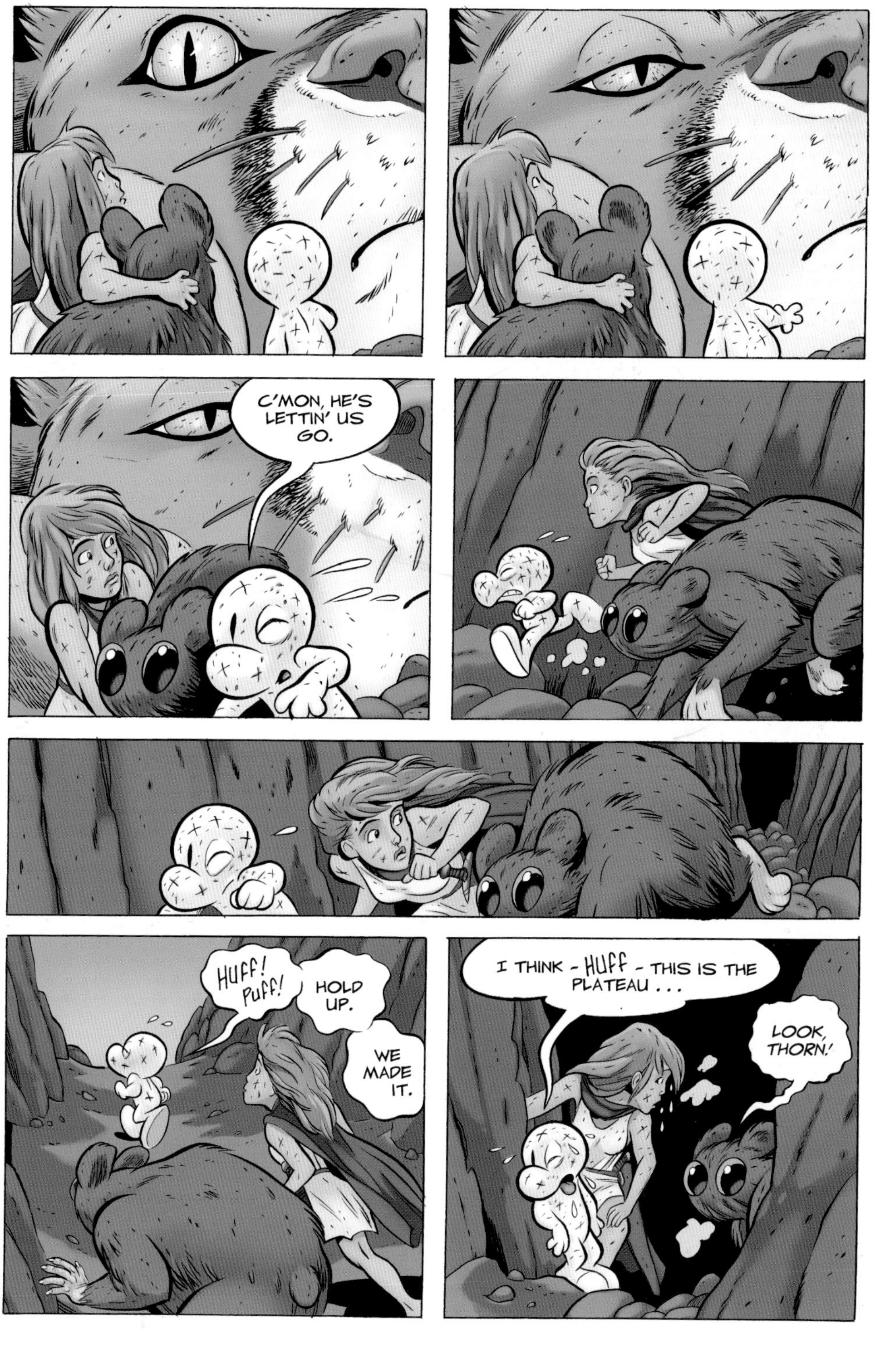
C'MON, HE'S LETTIN' US GO.
HUFF! PUFF!
HOLD UP.
WE MADE IT.
I THINK - HUFF - THIS IS THE PLATEAU . . .
LOOK, THORN!

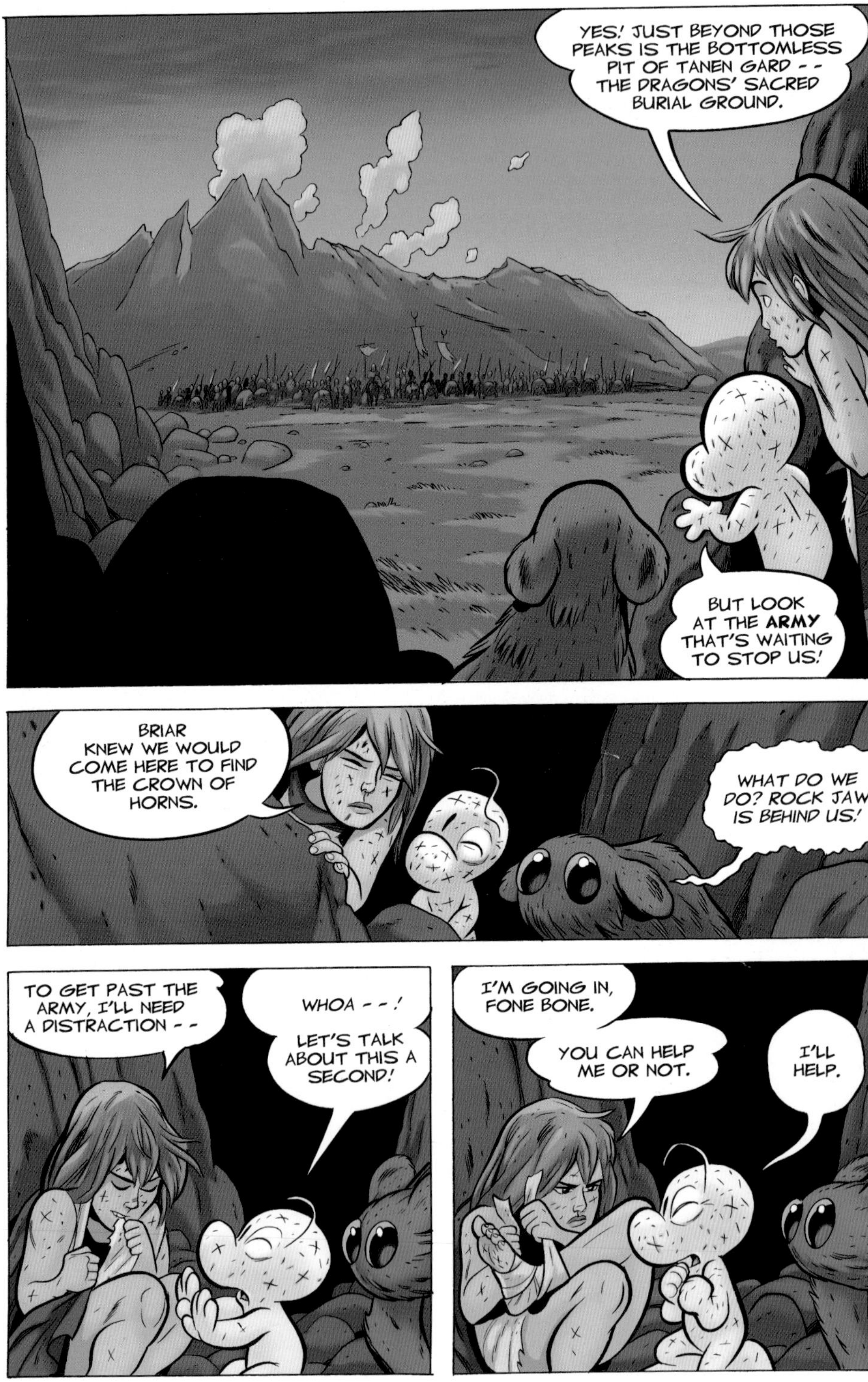
YES! JUST BEYOND THOSE PEAKS IS THE BOTTOMLESS PIT OF TANEN GARD -- THE DRAGONS' SACRED BURIAL GROUND.
BUT LOOK AT THE **ARMY** THAT'S WAITING TO STOP US!
BRIAR KNEW WE WOULD COME HERE TO FIND THE CROWN OF HORNS.
WHAT DO WE DO? ROCK JAW IS BEHIND US!
TO GET PAST THE ARMY, I'LL NEED A DISTRACTION --
WHOA --!
LET'S TALK ABOUT THIS A SECOND!
I'M GOING IN, FONE BONE.
YOU CAN HELP ME OR NOT.
I'LL HELP.

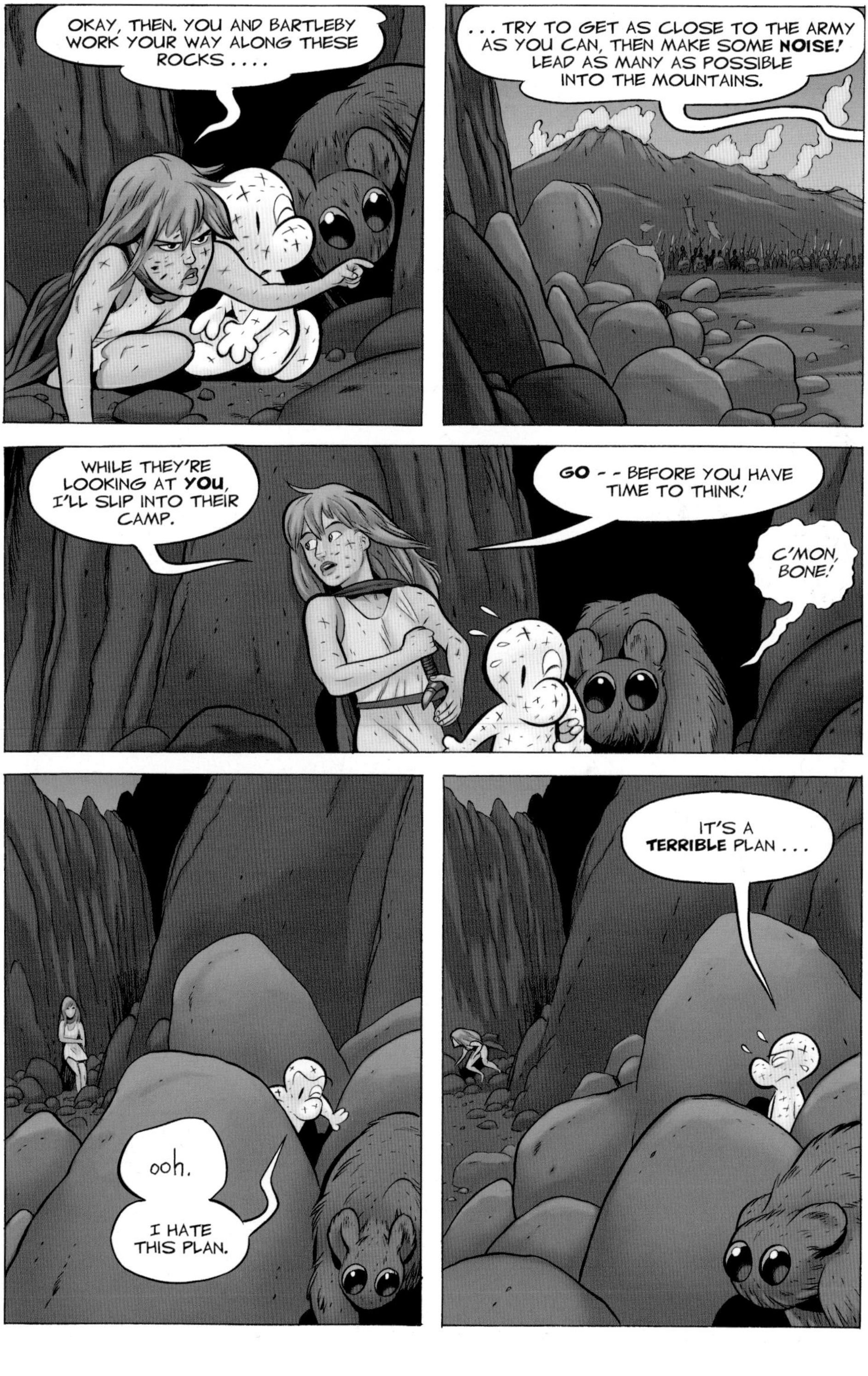
OKAY, THEN. YOU AND BARTLEBY WORK YOUR WAY ALONG THESE ROCKS . . . .
. . . TRY TO GET AS CLOSE TO THE ARMY AS YOU CAN, THEN MAKE SOME NOISE! LEAD AS MANY AS POSSIBLE INTO THE MOUNTAINS.
WHILE THEY'RE LOOKING AT YOU, I'LL SLIP INTO THEIR CAMP.
GO - - BEFORE YOU HAVE TIME TO THINK!
C'MON, BONE!
ooh.
I HATE THIS PLAN.
IT'S A TERRIBLE PLAN . . .

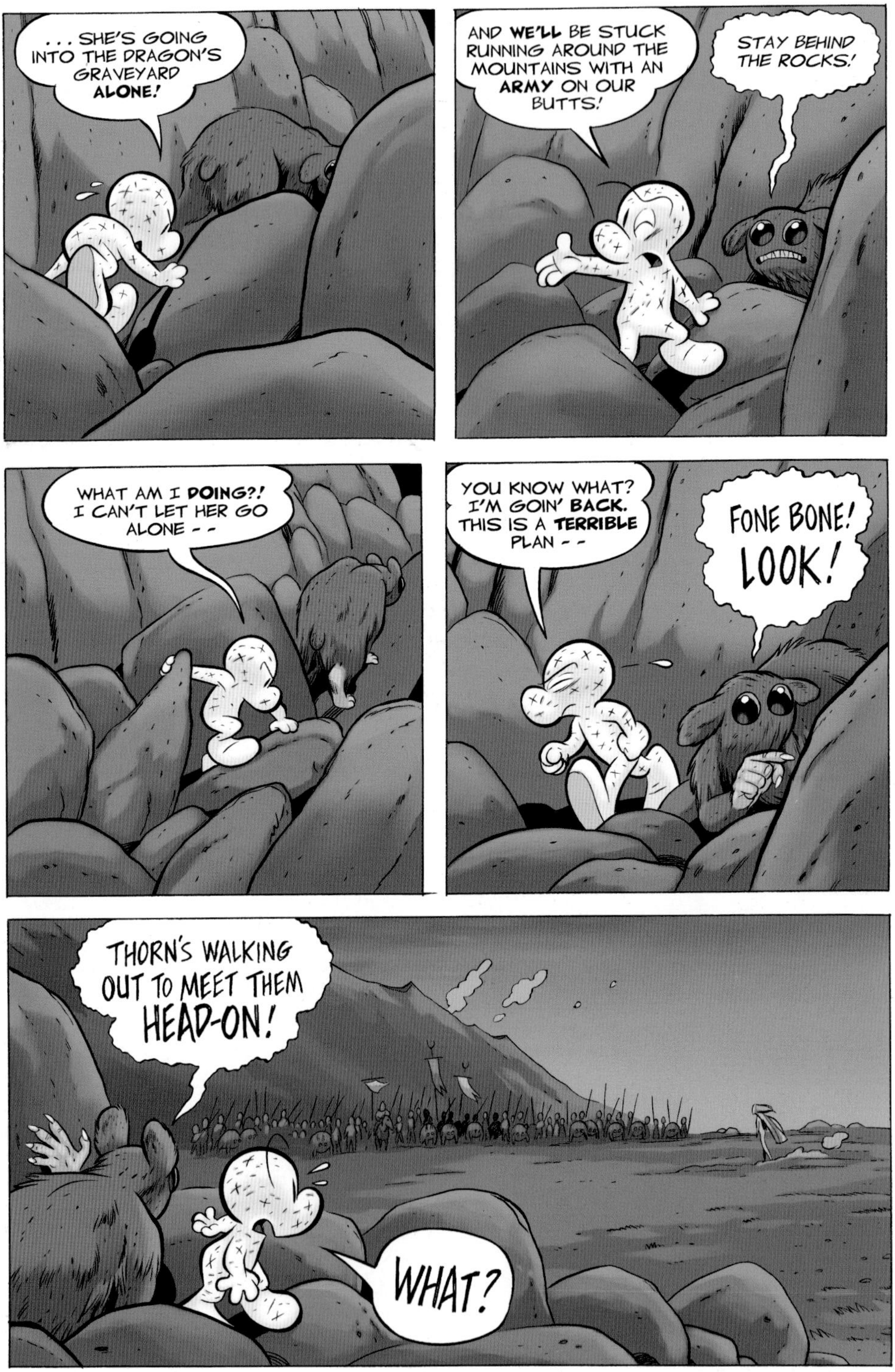
. . . SHE'S GOING INTO THE DRAGON'S GRAVEYARD ALONE!
AND WE'LL BE STUCK RUNNING AROUND THE MOUNTAINS WITH AN ARMY ON OUR BUTTS!
STAY BEHIND THE ROCKS!
WHAT AM I DOING?! I CAN'T LET HER GO ALONE - -
YOU KNOW WHAT? I'M GOIN' BACK. THIS IS A TERRIBLE PLAN - -
FONE BONE! LOOK!
THORN'S WALKING OUT TO MEET THEM HEAD-ON!
WHAT?

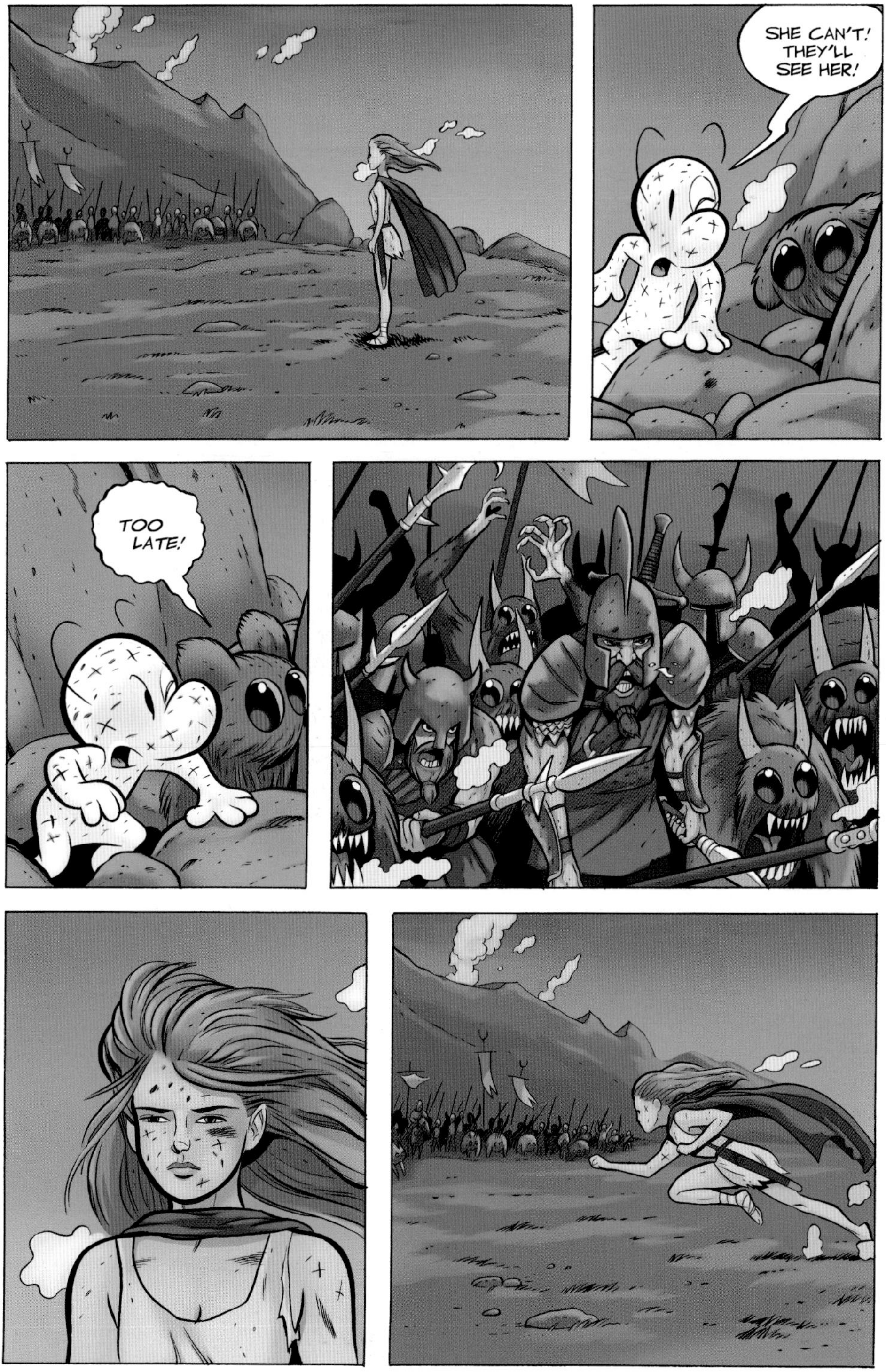
SHE CAN'T! THEY'LL SEE HER!
TOO LATE!

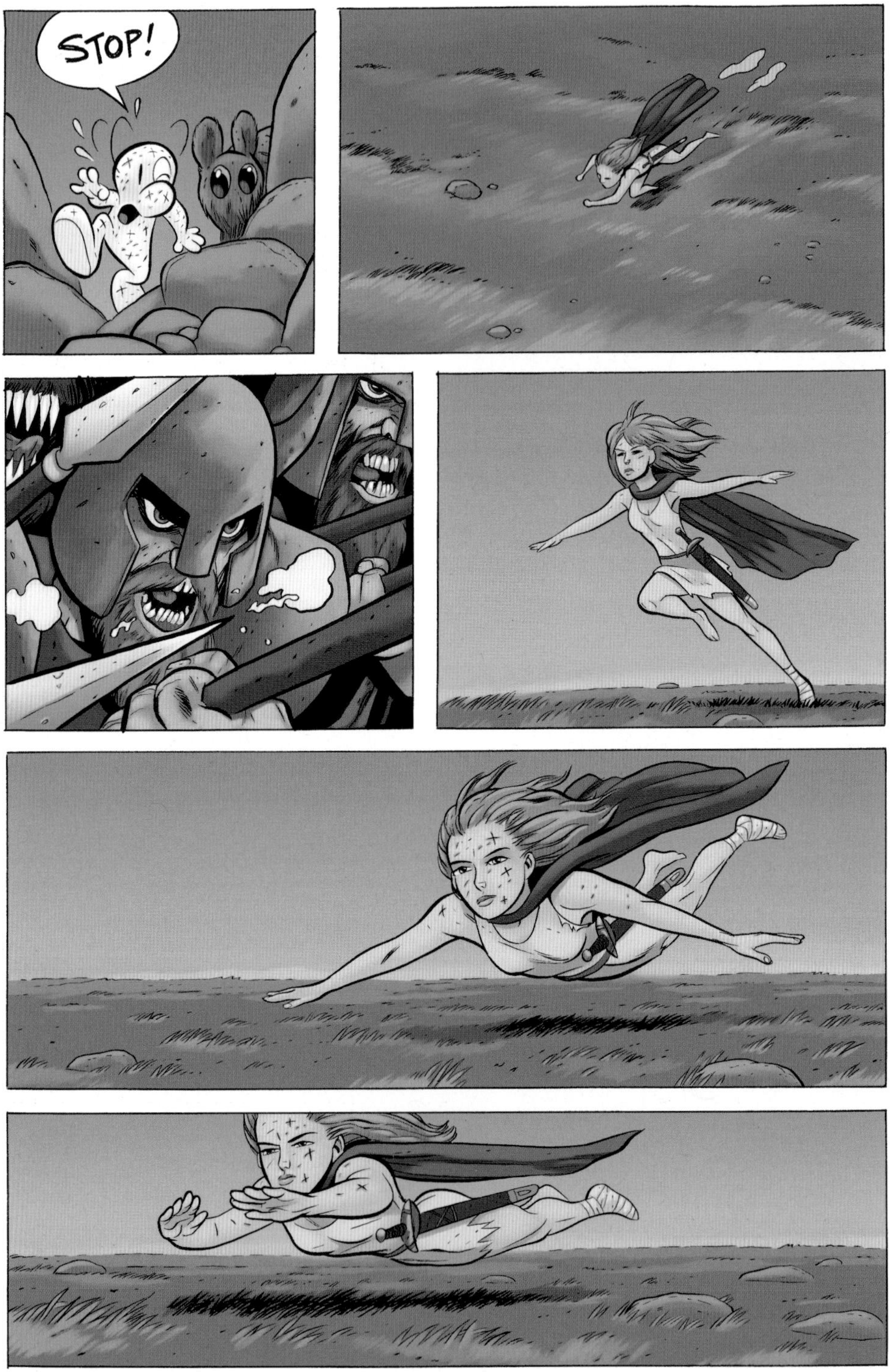
STOP!

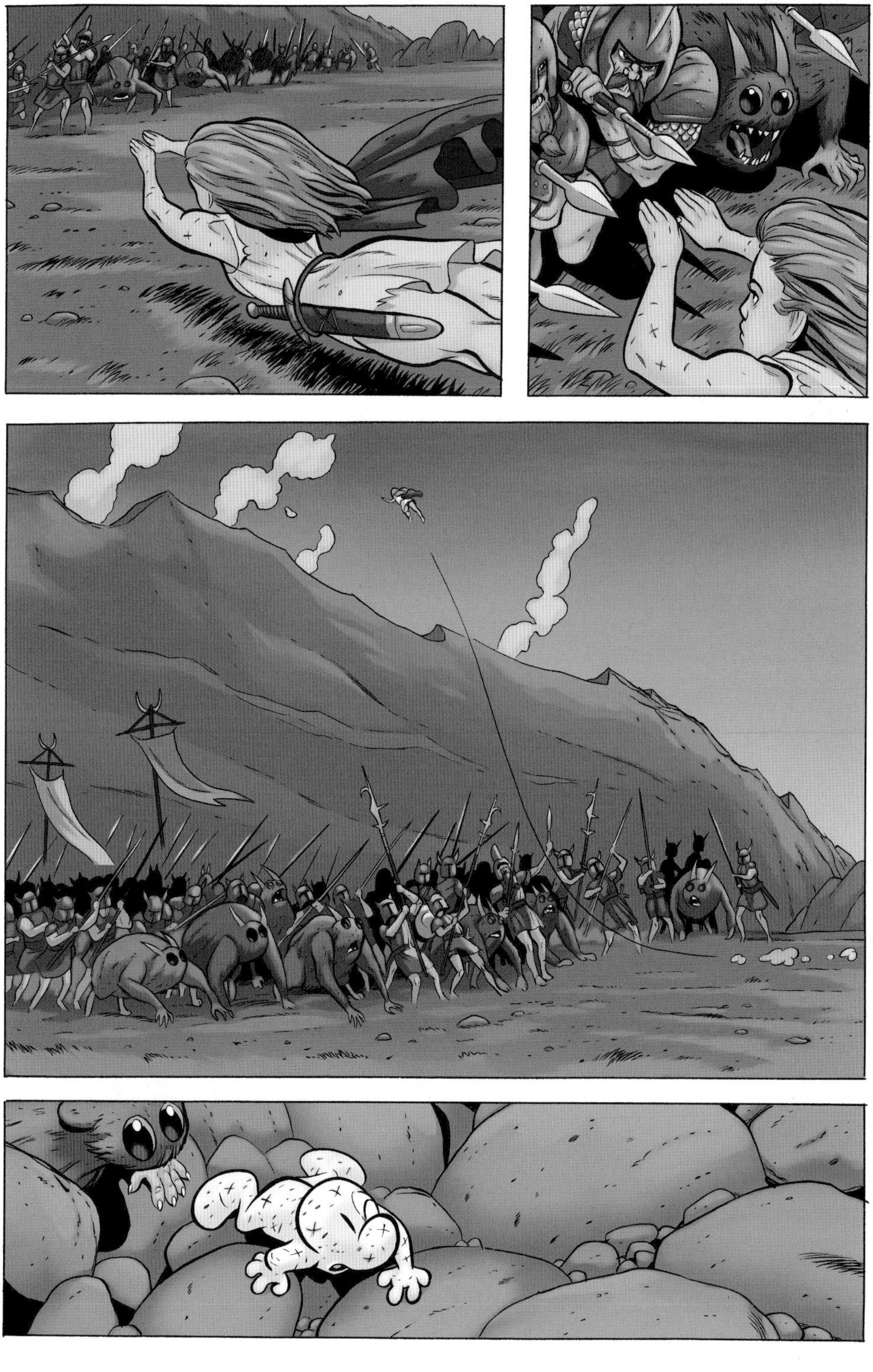

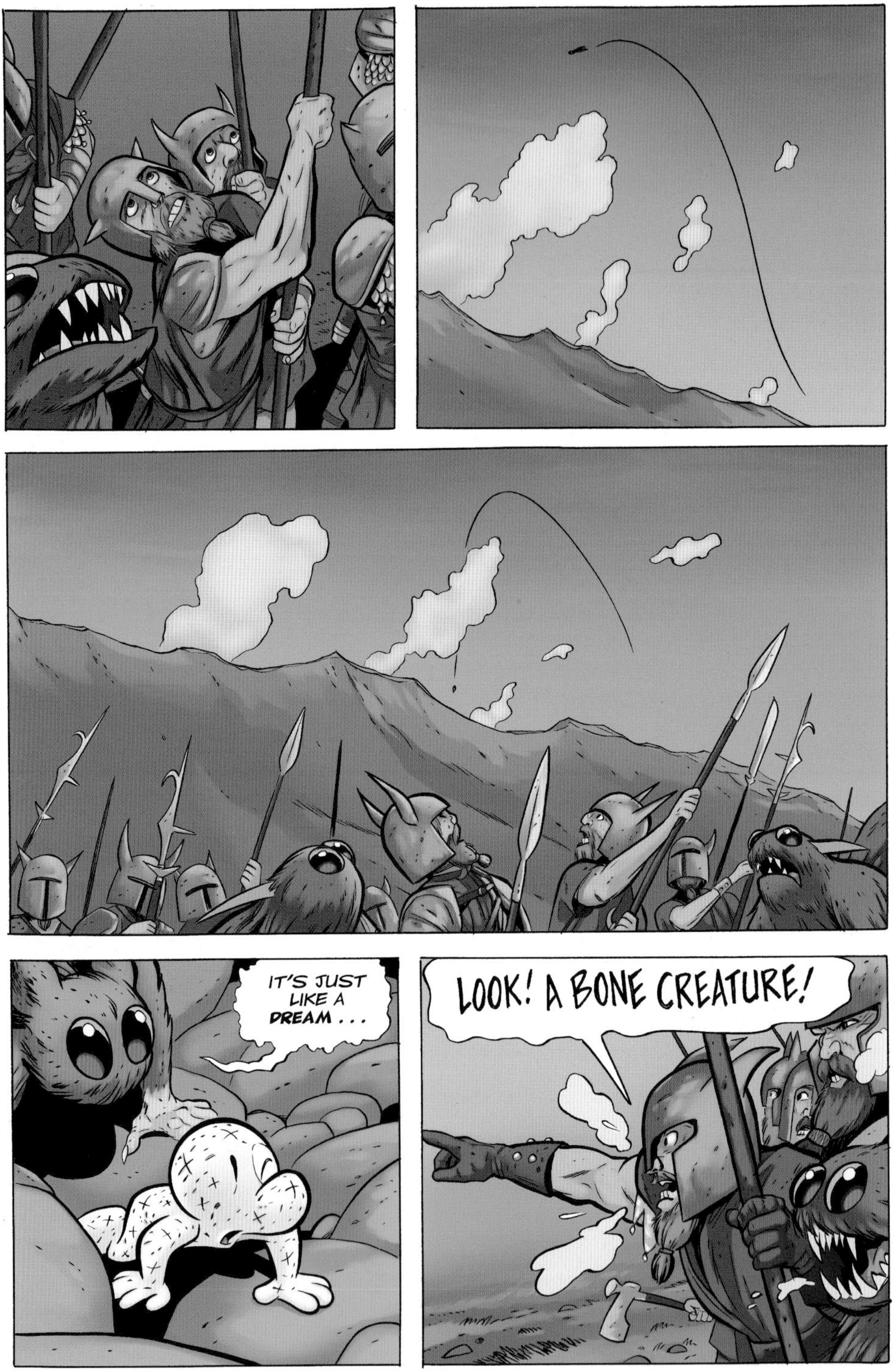
IT'S JUST LIKE A DREAM . . .
LOOK! A BONE CREATURE!

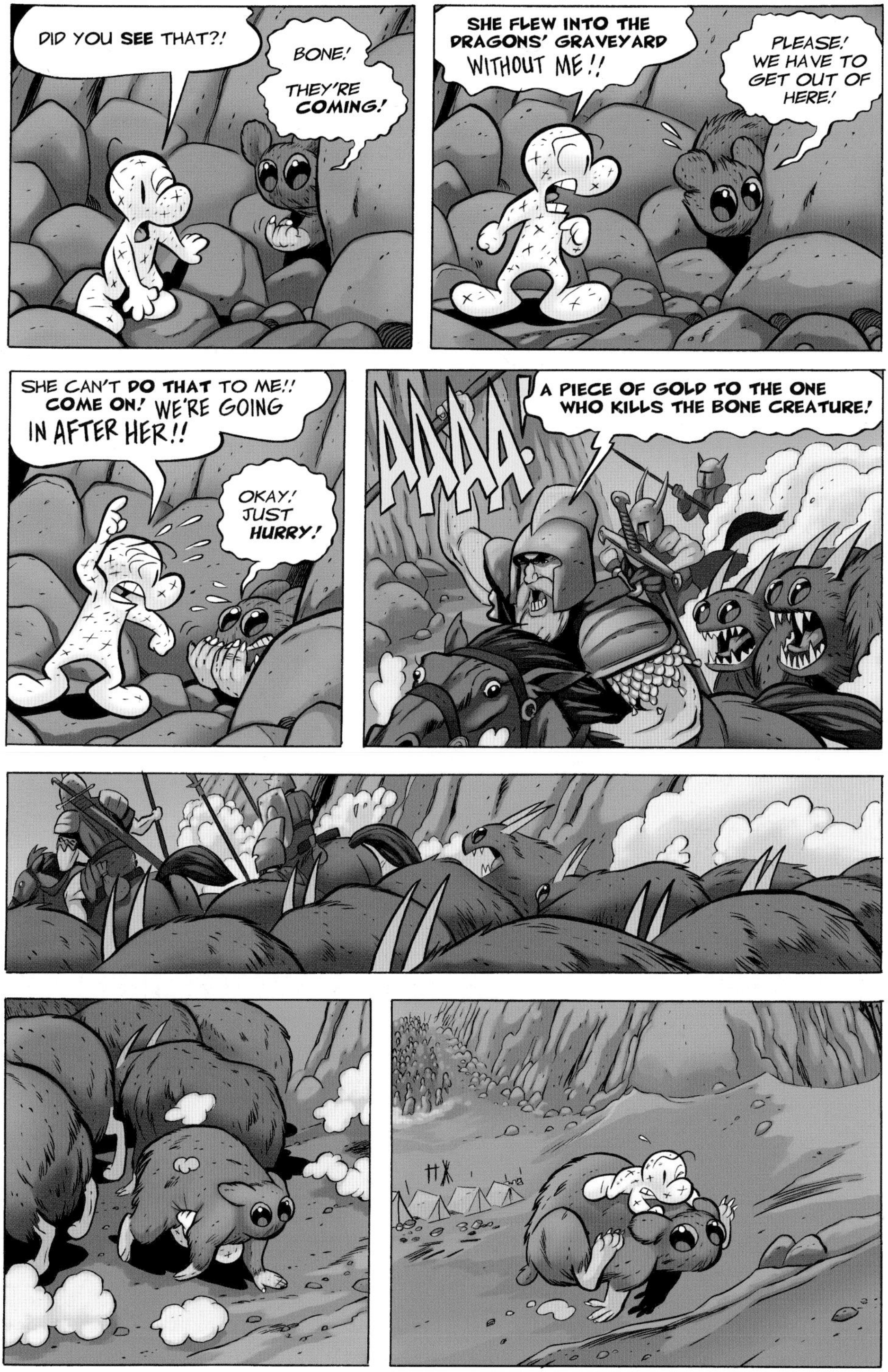
DID YOU SEE THAT?!
BONE! THEY'RE COMING!
SHE FLEW INTO THE DRAGONS' GRAVEYARD WITHOUT ME!!
PLEASE! WE HAVE TO GET OUT OF HERE!
SHE CAN'T DO THAT TO ME!! COME ON! WE'RE GOING IN AFTER HER!!
OKAY! JUST HURRY!
AAAA!
A PIECE OF GOLD TO THE ONE WHO KILLS THE BONE CREATURE!

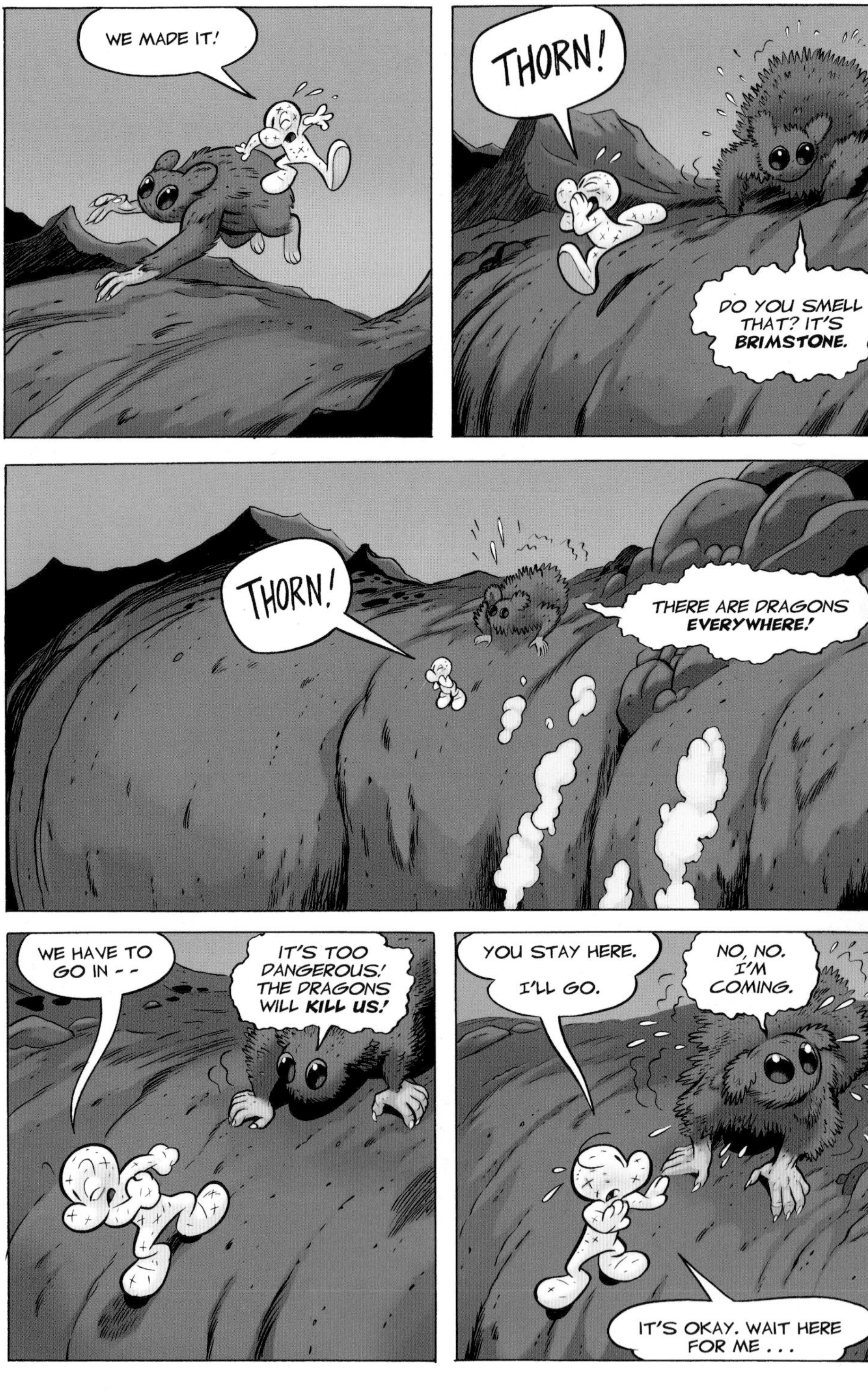
WE MADE IT!
THORN!
DO YOU SMELL THAT? IT'S **BRIMSTONE.**
THORN!
THERE ARE DRAGONS **EVERYWHERE!**
WE HAVE TO GO IN - -
IT'S TOO DANGEROUS! THE DRAGONS WILL **KILL US!**
YOU STAY HERE.
I'LL GO.
NO, NO. I'M COMING.
IT'S OKAY. WAIT HERE FOR ME . . .

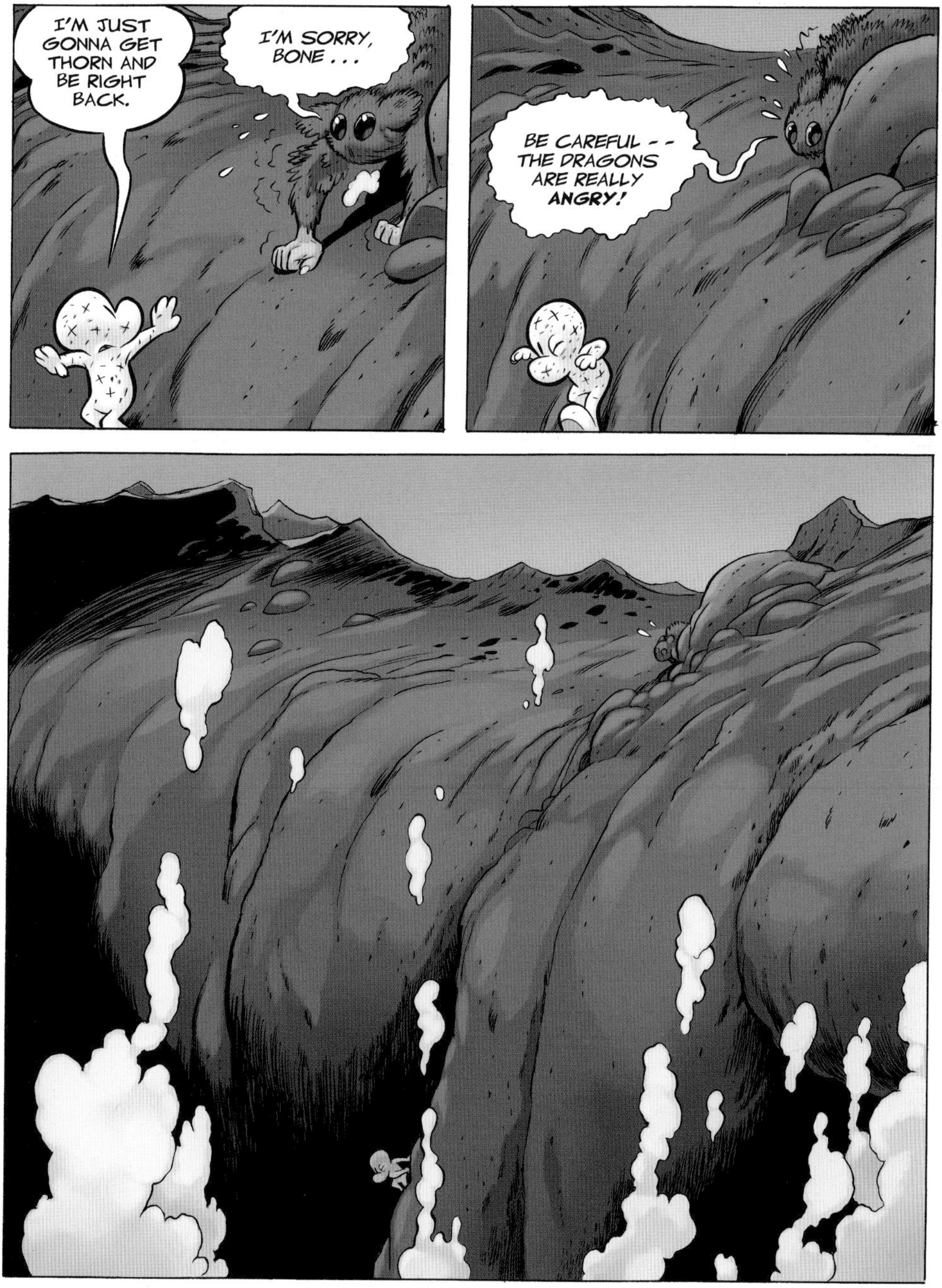
I'M JUST GONNA GET THORN AND BE RIGHT BACK.
I'M SORRY, BONE . . .
BE CAREFUL - - THE DRAGONS ARE REALLY ANGRY!

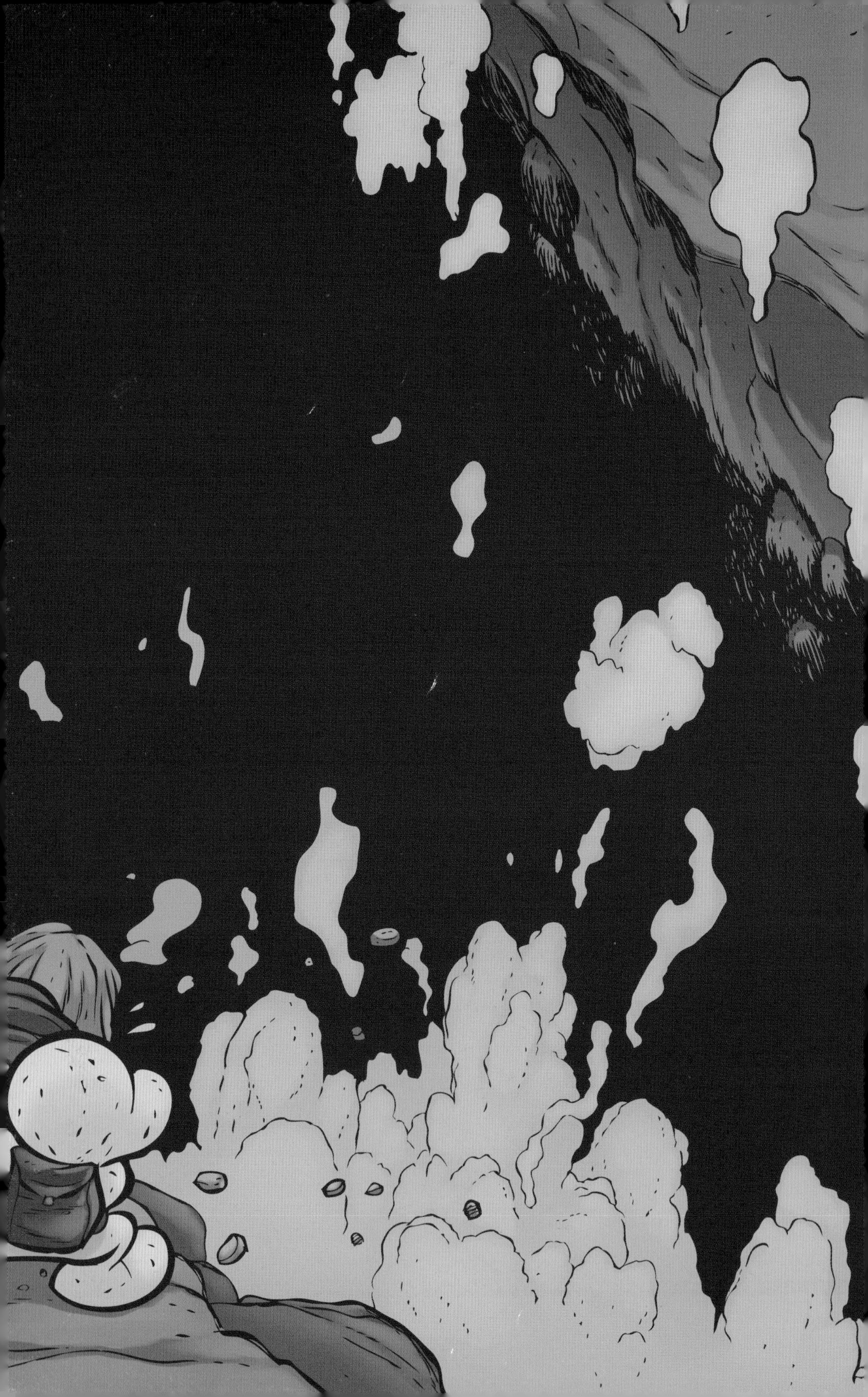

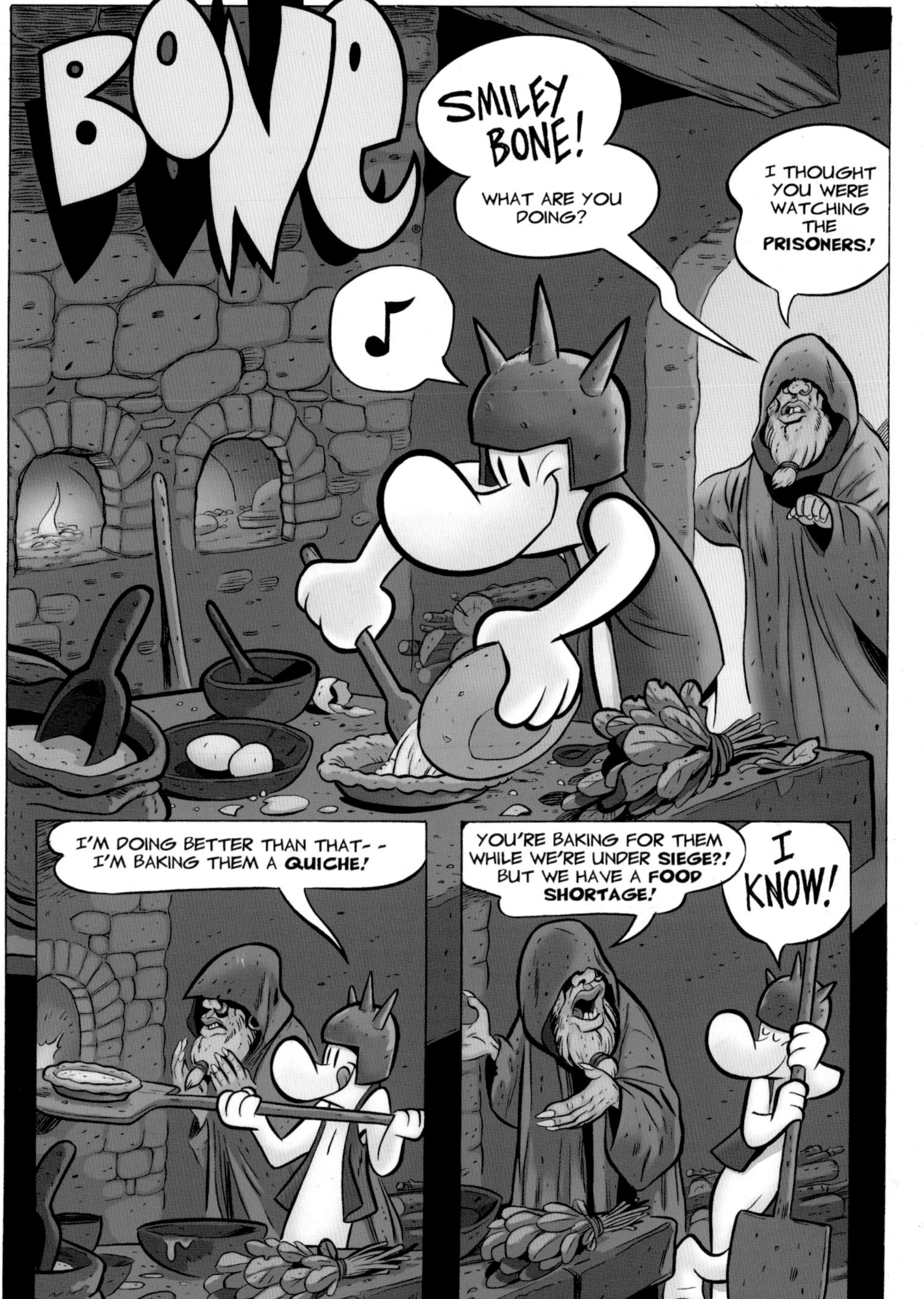
BONE®
SMILEY BONE!
WHAT ARE YOU DOING?
I THOUGHT YOU WERE WATCHING THE PRISONERS!
♪
I'M DOING BETTER THAN THAT- - I'M BAKING THEM A QUICHE!
YOU'RE BAKING FOR THEM WHILE WE'RE UNDER SIEGE?! BUT WE HAVE A FOOD SHORTAGE!
I KNOW!

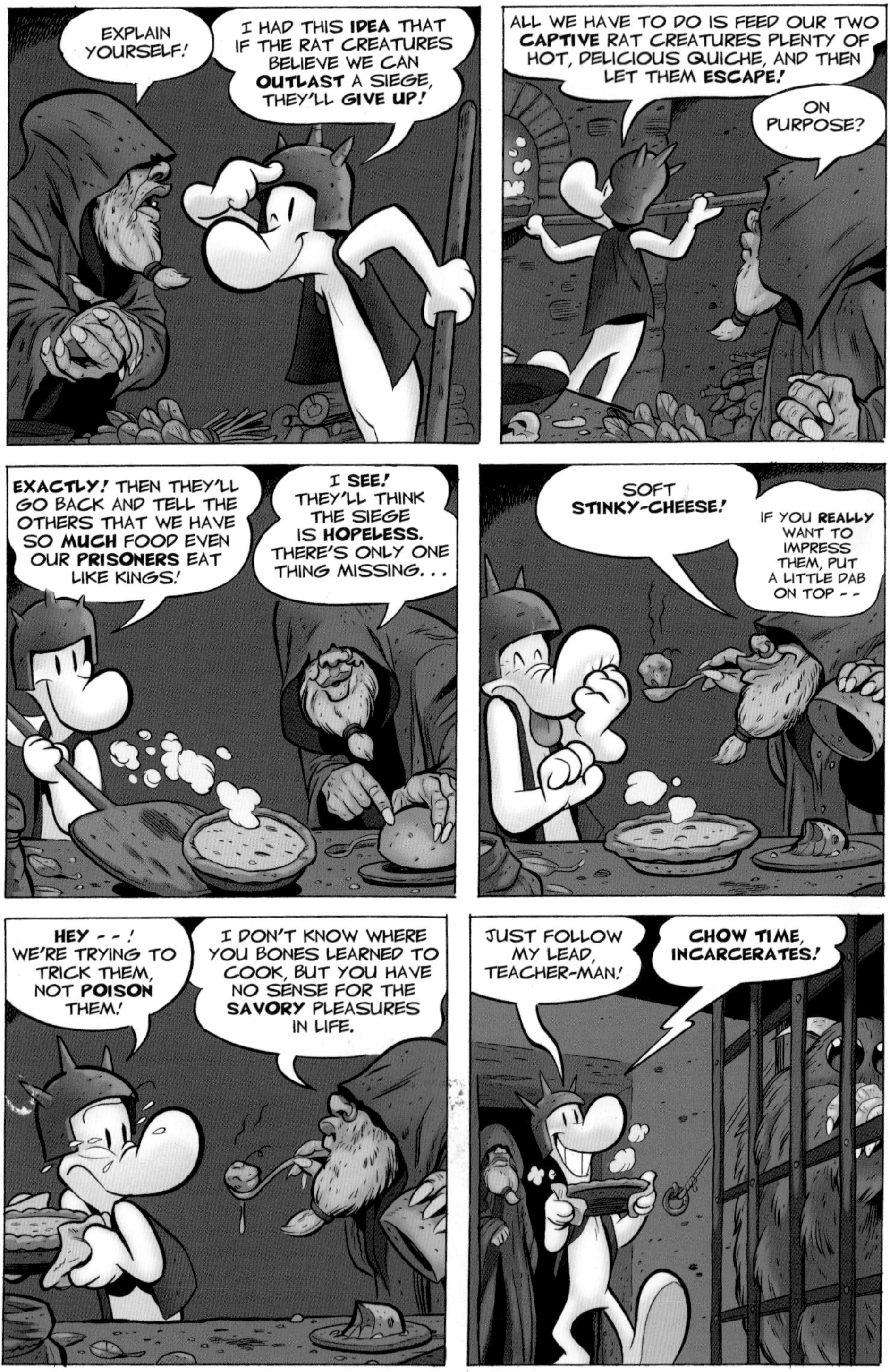
EXPLAIN YOURSELF!
I HAD THIS IDEA THAT IF THE RAT CREATURES BELIEVE WE CAN OUTLAST A SIEGE, THEY'LL GIVE UP!
ALL WE HAVE TO DO IS FEED OUR TWO CAPTIVE RAT CREATURES PLENTY OF HOT, DELICIOUS QUICHE, AND THEN LET THEM ESCAPE!
ON PURPOSE?
EXACTLY! THEN THEY'LL GO BACK AND TELL THE OTHERS THAT WE HAVE SO MUCH FOOD EVEN OUR PRISONERS EAT LIKE KINGS!
I SEE! THEY'LL THINK THE SIEGE IS HOPELESS. THERE'S ONLY ONE THING MISSING. . .
SOFT STINKY-CHEESE!
IF YOU REALLY WANT TO IMPRESS THEM, PUT A LITTLE DAB ON TOP - -
HEY - - ! WE'RE TRYING TO TRICK THEM, NOT POISON THEM!
I DON'T KNOW WHERE YOU BONES LEARNED TO COOK, BUT YOU HAVE NO SENSE FOR THE SAVORY PLEASURES IN LIFE.
JUST FOLLOW MY LEAD, TEACHER-MAN!
CHOW TIME, INCARCERATES!

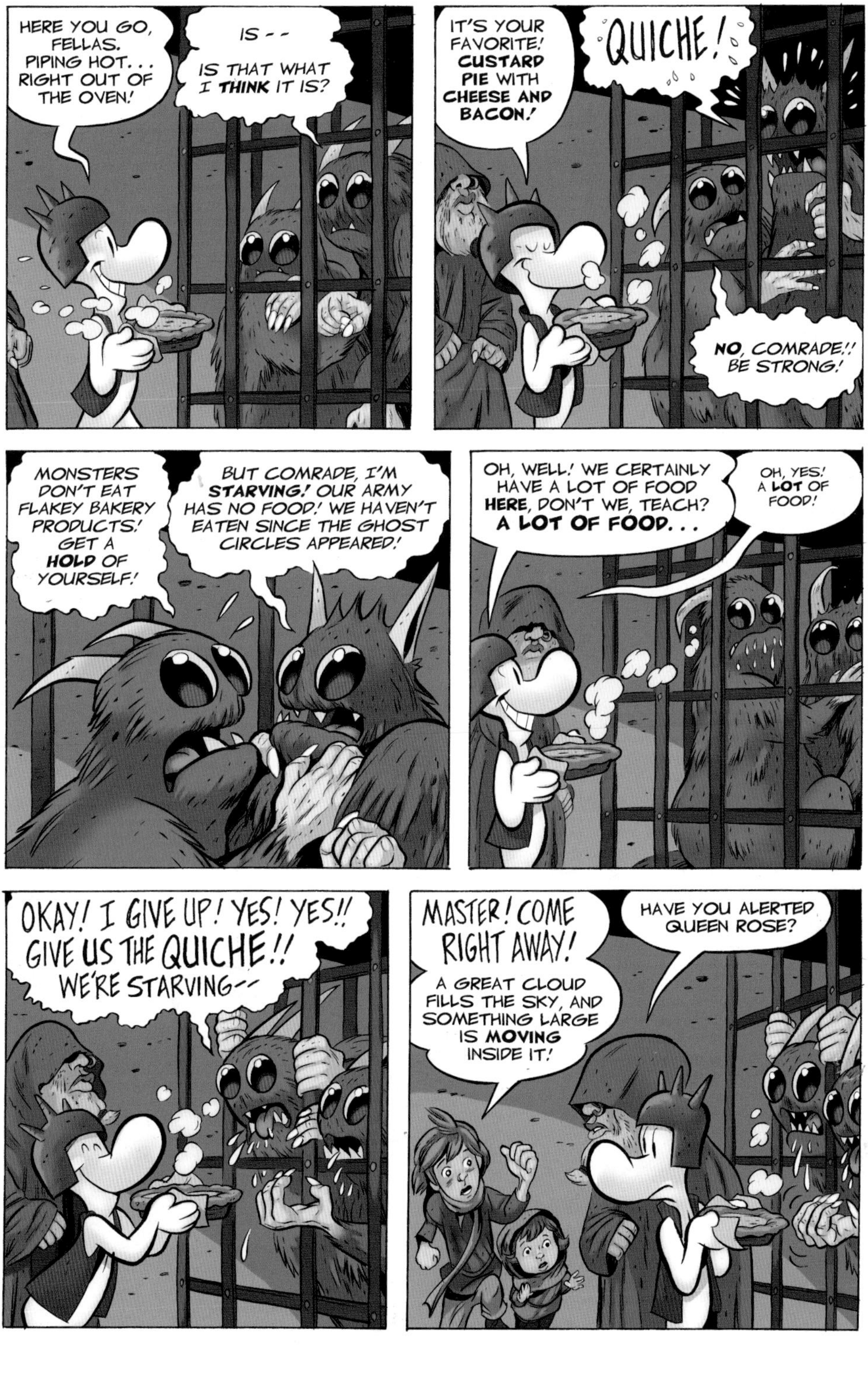
HERE YOU GO, FELLAS. PIPING HOT... RIGHT OUT OF THE OVEN!
IS --
IS THAT WHAT I THINK IT IS?
IT'S YOUR FAVORITE! CUSTARD PIE WITH CHEESE AND BACON!
QUICHE!
NO, COMRADE!! BE STRONG!
MONSTERS DON'T EAT FLAKEY BAKERY PRODUCTS! GET A HOLD OF YOURSELF!
BUT COMRADE, I'M STARVING! OUR ARMY HAS NO FOOD! WE HAVEN'T EATEN SINCE THE GHOST CIRCLES APPEARED!
OH, WELL! WE CERTAINLY HAVE A LOT OF FOOD HERE, DON'T WE, TEACH? A LOT OF FOOD...
OH, YES! A LOT OF FOOD!
OKAY! I GIVE UP! YES! YES!! GIVE US THE QUICHE!! WE'RE STARVING--
MASTER! COME RIGHT AWAY!
A GREAT CLOUD FILLS THE SKY, AND SOMETHING LARGE IS MOVING INSIDE IT!
HAVE YOU ALERTED QUEEN ROSE?

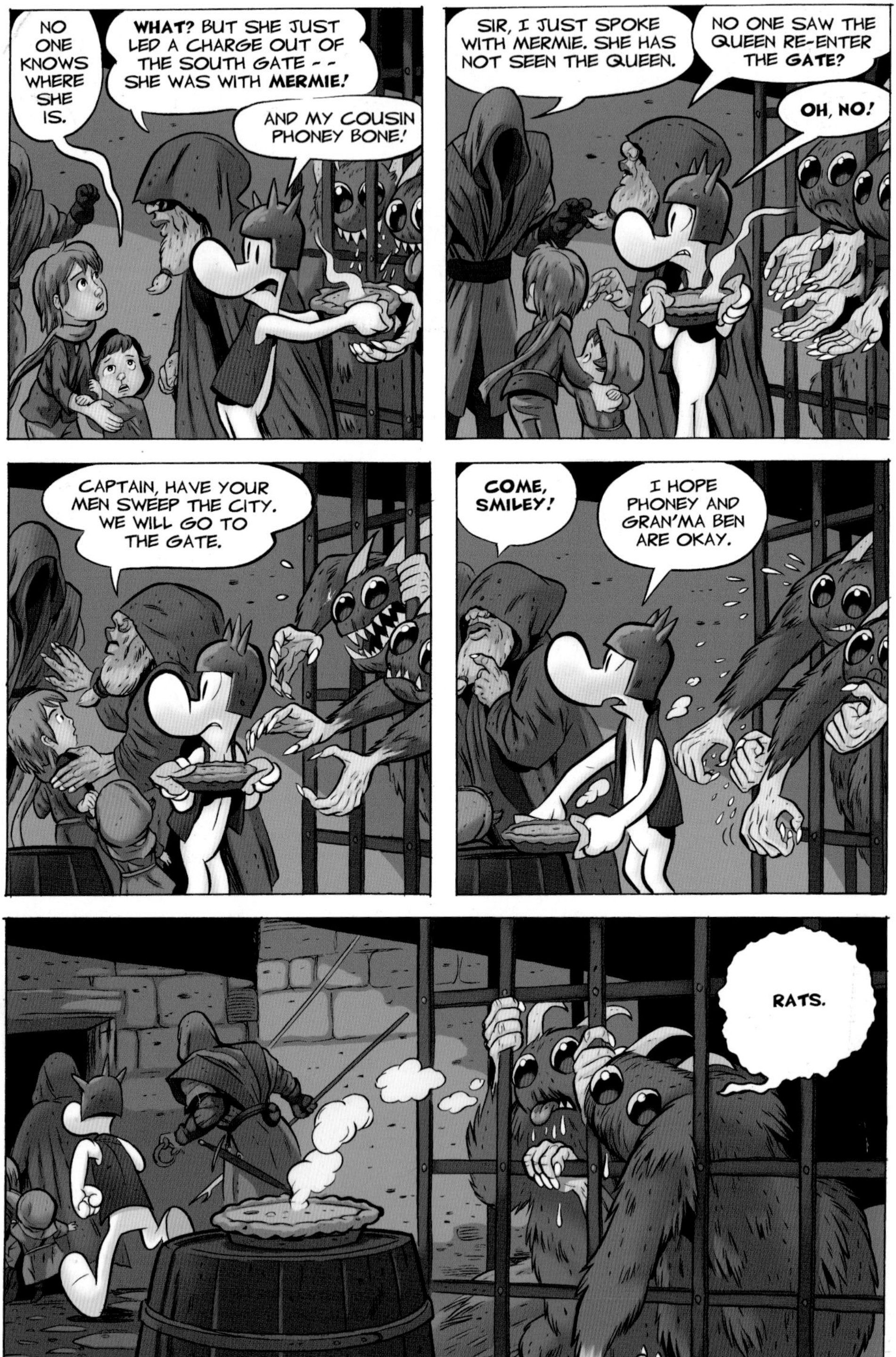

NO ONE KNOWS WHERE SHE IS.
WHAT? BUT SHE JUST LED A CHARGE OUT OF THE SOUTH GATE - - SHE WAS WITH MERMIE!
AND MY COUSIN PHONEY BONE!
SIR, I JUST SPOKE WITH MERMIE. SHE HAS NOT SEEN THE QUEEN.
NO ONE SAW THE QUEEN RE-ENTER THE GATE?
OH, NO!
CAPTAIN, HAVE YOUR MEN SWEEP THE CITY. WE WILL GO TO THE GATE.
COME, SMILEY!
I HOPE PHONEY AND GRAN'MA BEN ARE OKAY.
RATS.

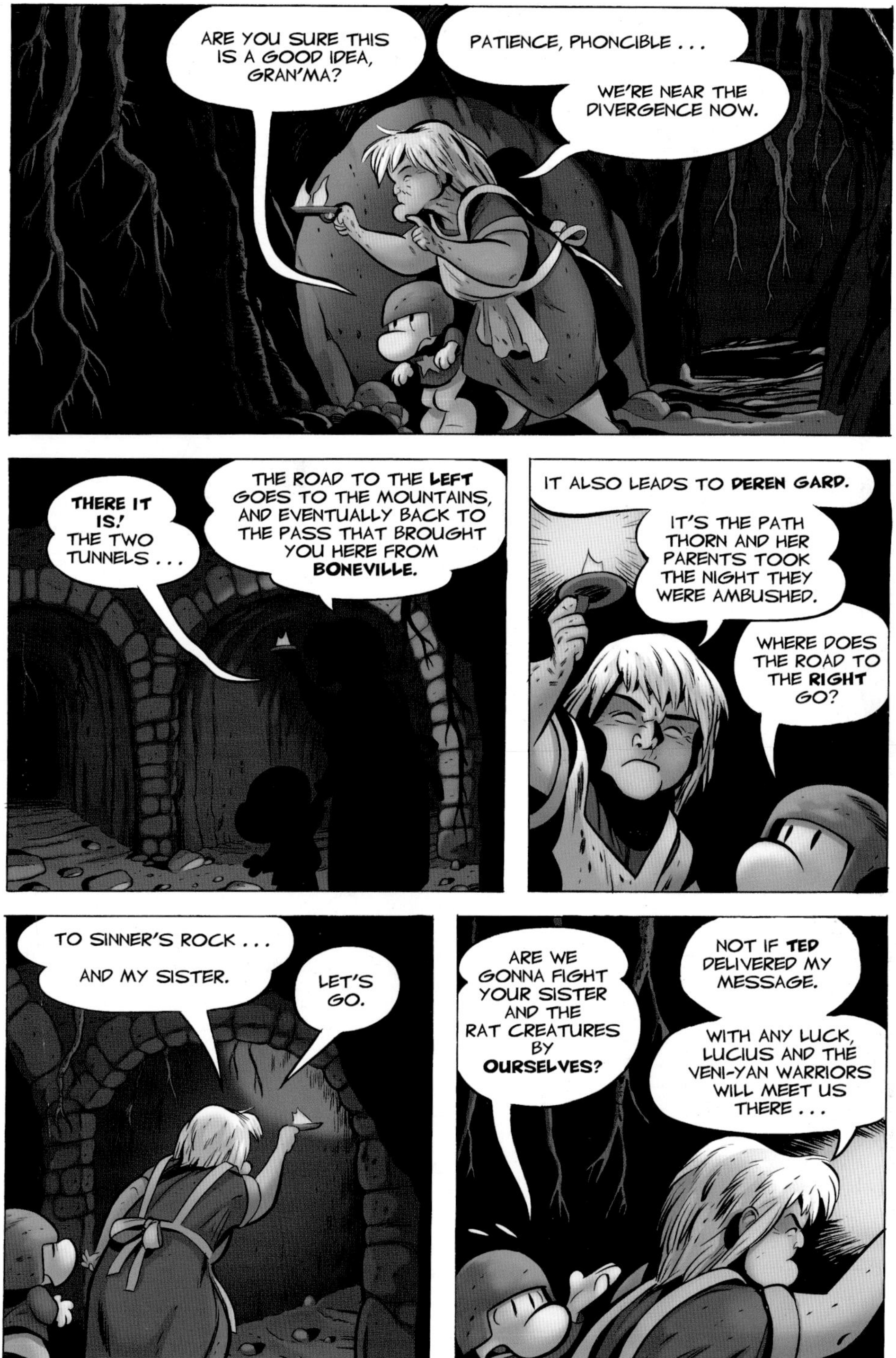
ARE YOU SURE THIS IS A GOOD IDEA, GRAN'MA?
PATIENCE, PHONCIBLE . . .
WE'RE NEAR THE DIVERGENCE NOW.
THERE IT IS! THE TWO TUNNELS . . .
THE ROAD TO THE LEFT GOES TO THE MOUNTAINS, AND EVENTUALLY BACK TO THE PASS THAT BROUGHT YOU HERE FROM BONEVILLE.
IT ALSO LEADS TO DEREN GARD.
IT'S THE PATH THORN AND HER PARENTS TOOK THE NIGHT THEY WERE AMBUSHED.
WHERE DOES THE ROAD TO THE RIGHT GO?
TO SINNER'S ROCK . . .
AND MY SISTER.
LET'S GO.
ARE WE GONNA FIGHT YOUR SISTER AND THE RAT CREATURES BY OURSELVES?
NOT IF TED DELIVERED MY MESSAGE.
WITH ANY LUCK, LUCIUS AND THE VENI-YAN WARRIORS WILL MEET US THERE . . .

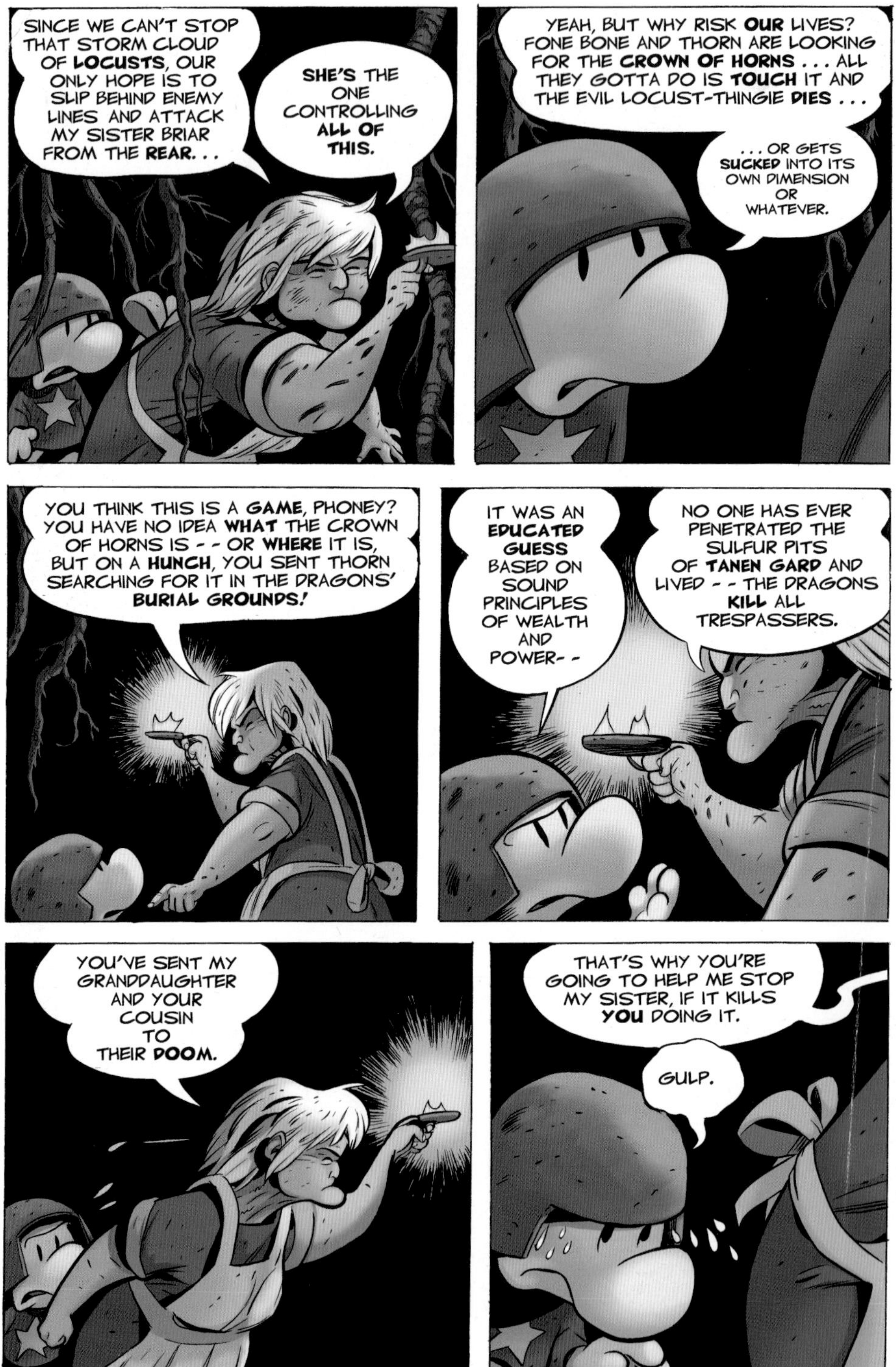
SINCE WE CAN'T STOP THAT STORM CLOUD OF LOCUSTS, OUR ONLY HOPE IS TO SLIP BEHIND ENEMY LINES AND ATTACK MY SISTER BRIAR FROM THE REAR. . .
SHE'S THE ONE CONTROLLING ALL OF THIS.
YEAH, BUT WHY RISK OUR LIVES? FONE BONE AND THORN ARE LOOKING FOR THE CROWN OF HORNS . . . ALL THEY GOTTA DO IS TOUCH IT AND THE EVIL LOCUST-THINGIE DIES . . .
. . . OR GETS SUCKED INTO ITS OWN DIMENSION OR WHATEVER.
YOU THINK THIS IS A GAME, PHONEY? YOU HAVE NO IDEA WHAT THE CROWN OF HORNS IS - - OR WHERE IT IS, BUT ON A HUNCH, YOU SENT THORN SEARCHING FOR IT IN THE DRAGONS' BURIAL GROUNDS!
IT WAS AN EDUCATED GUESS BASED ON SOUND PRINCIPLES OF WEALTH AND POWER- -
NO ONE HAS EVER PENETRATED THE SULFUR PITS OF TANEN GARD AND LIVED - - THE DRAGONS KILL ALL TRESPASSERS.
YOU'VE SENT MY GRANDDAUGHTER AND YOUR COUSIN TO THEIR DOOM.
THAT'S WHY YOU'RE GOING TO HELP ME STOP MY SISTER, IF IT KILLS YOU DOING IT.
GULP.

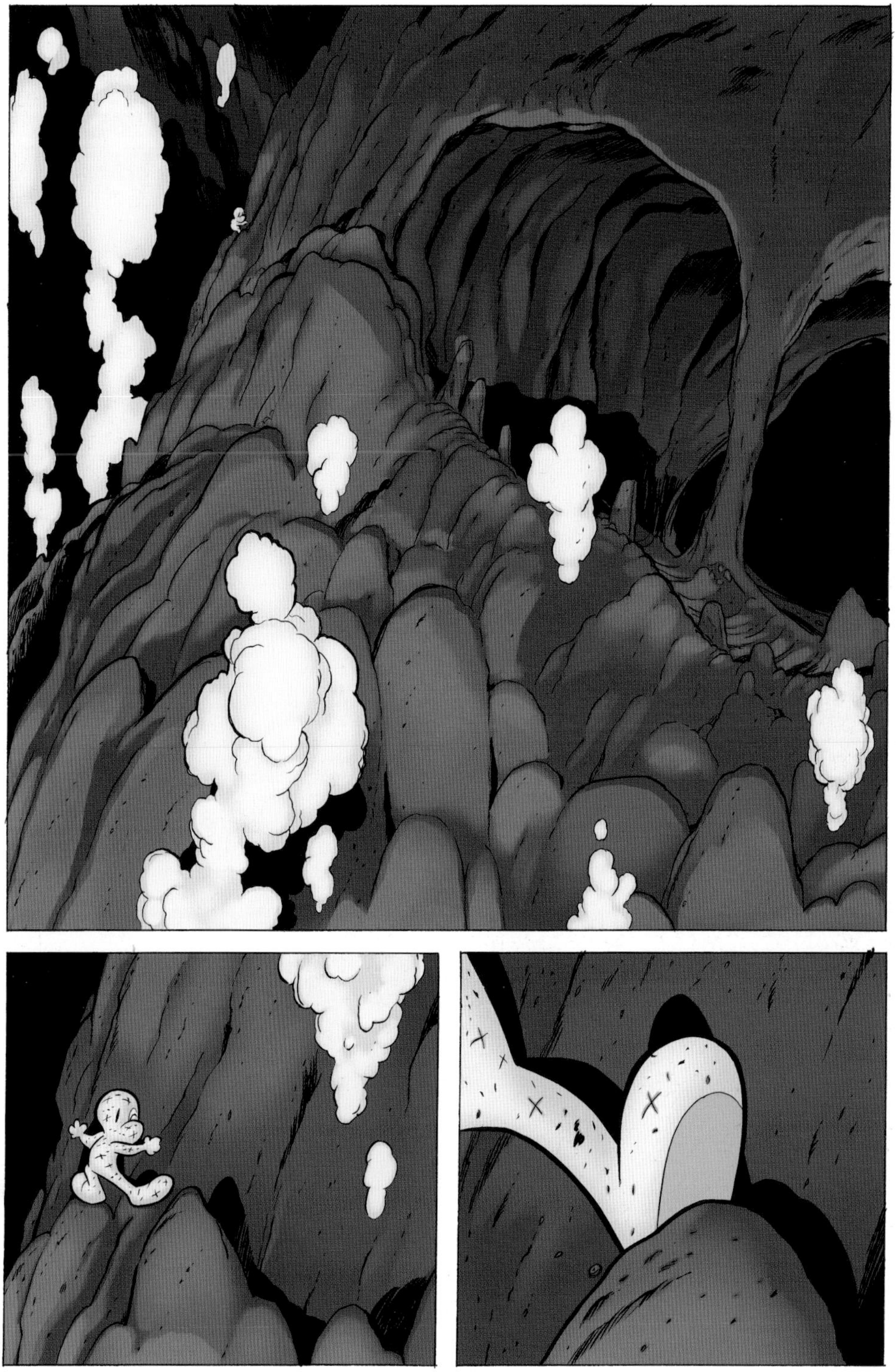

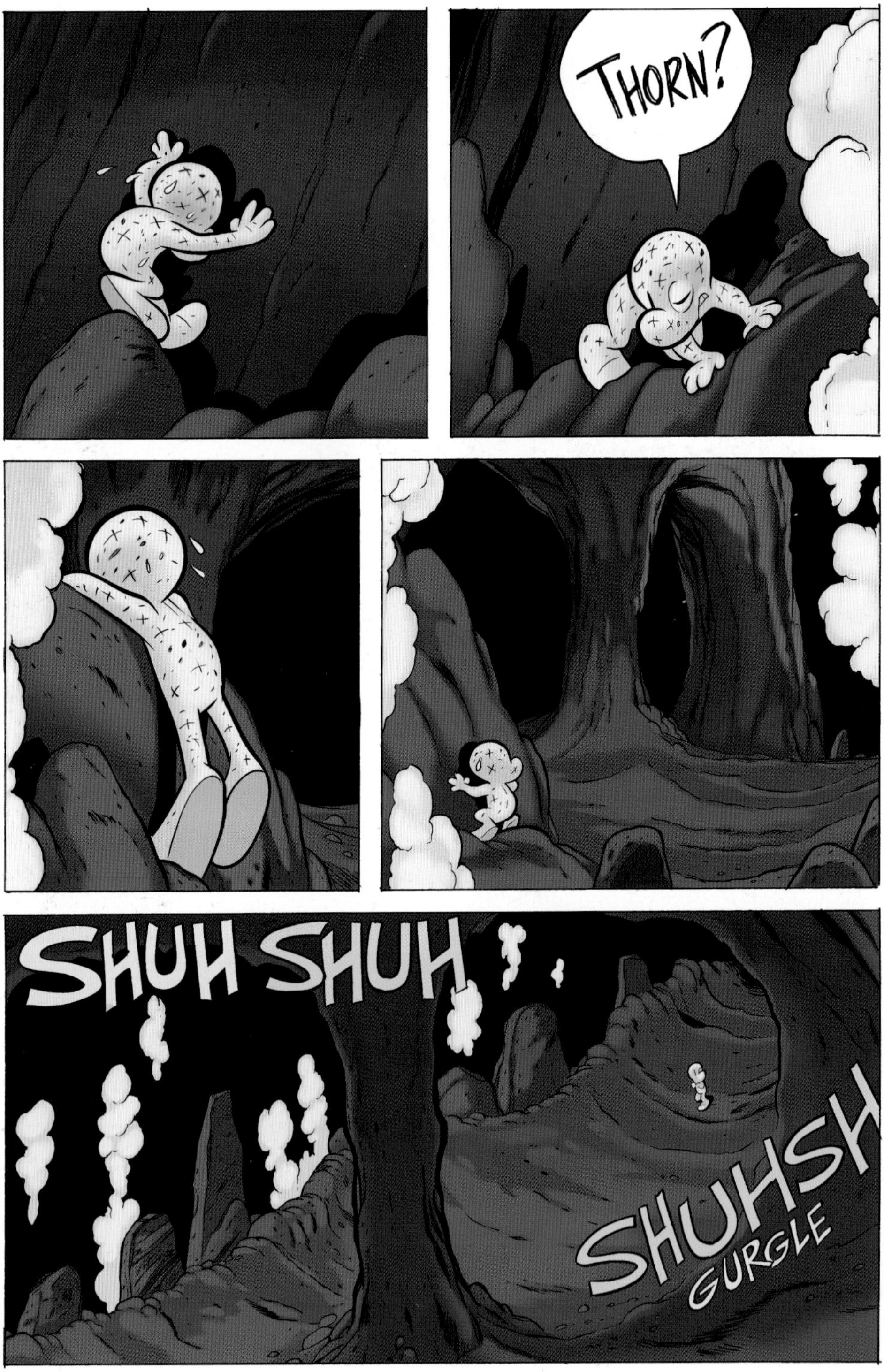
THORN?
SHUH SHUH
SHUHSH
SHUHSH
GURGLE

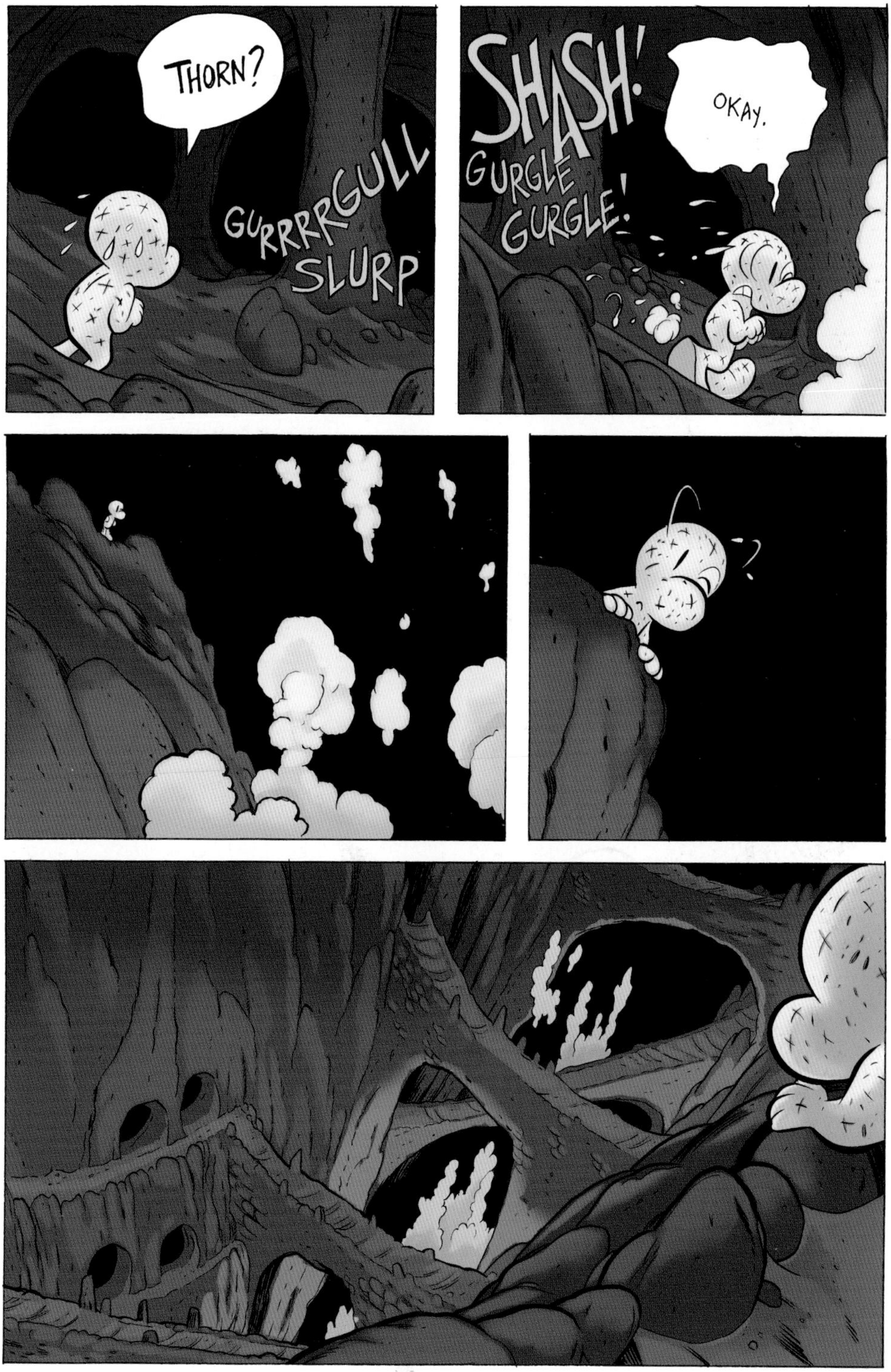
THORN?
GURRRRGULL
SLURP
SHASH!
GURGLE
GURGLE!
OKAY.
?
?

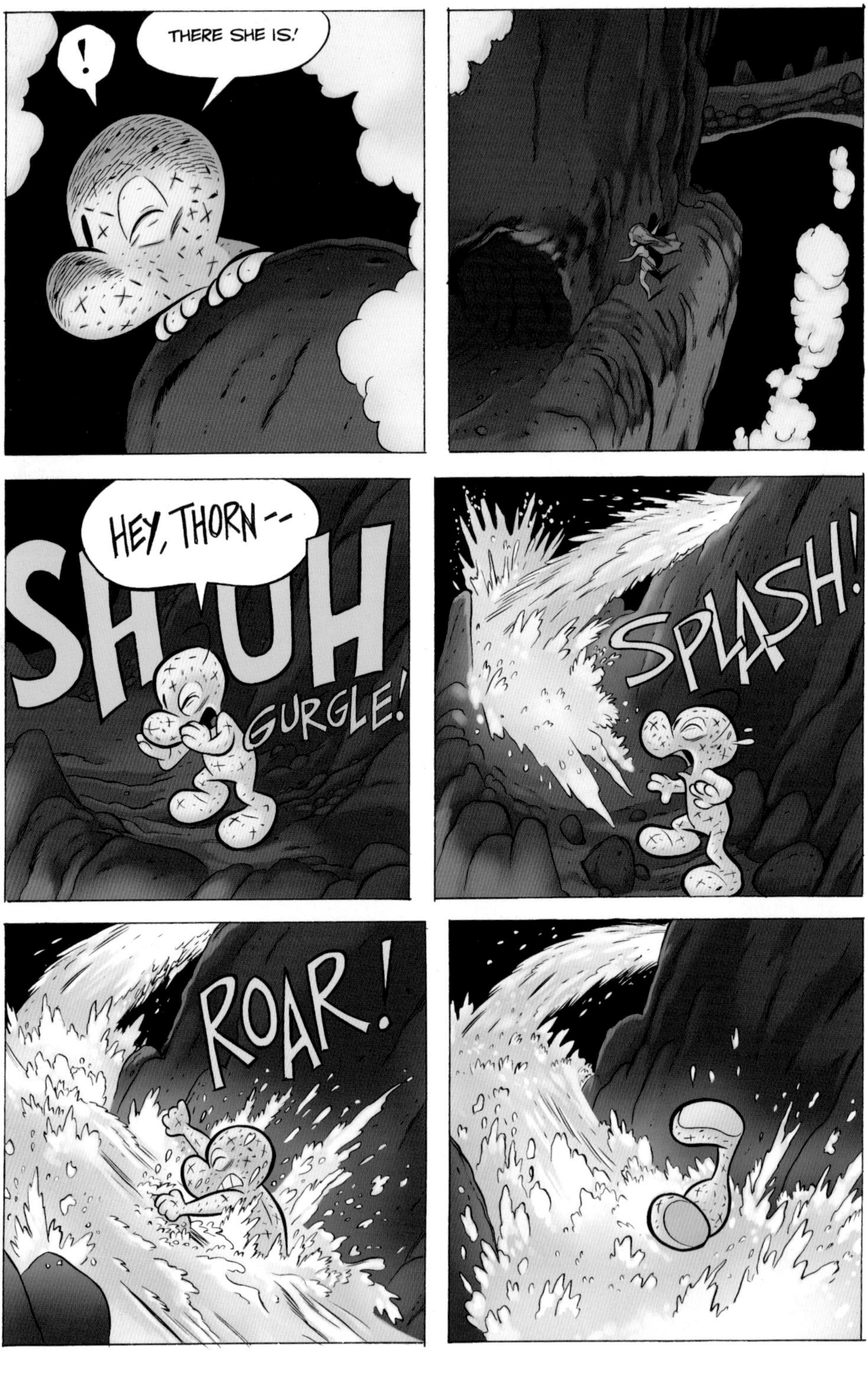
!
THERE SHE IS!
HEY, THORN--
SHUUH
GURGLE!
SPLASH!
ROAR!

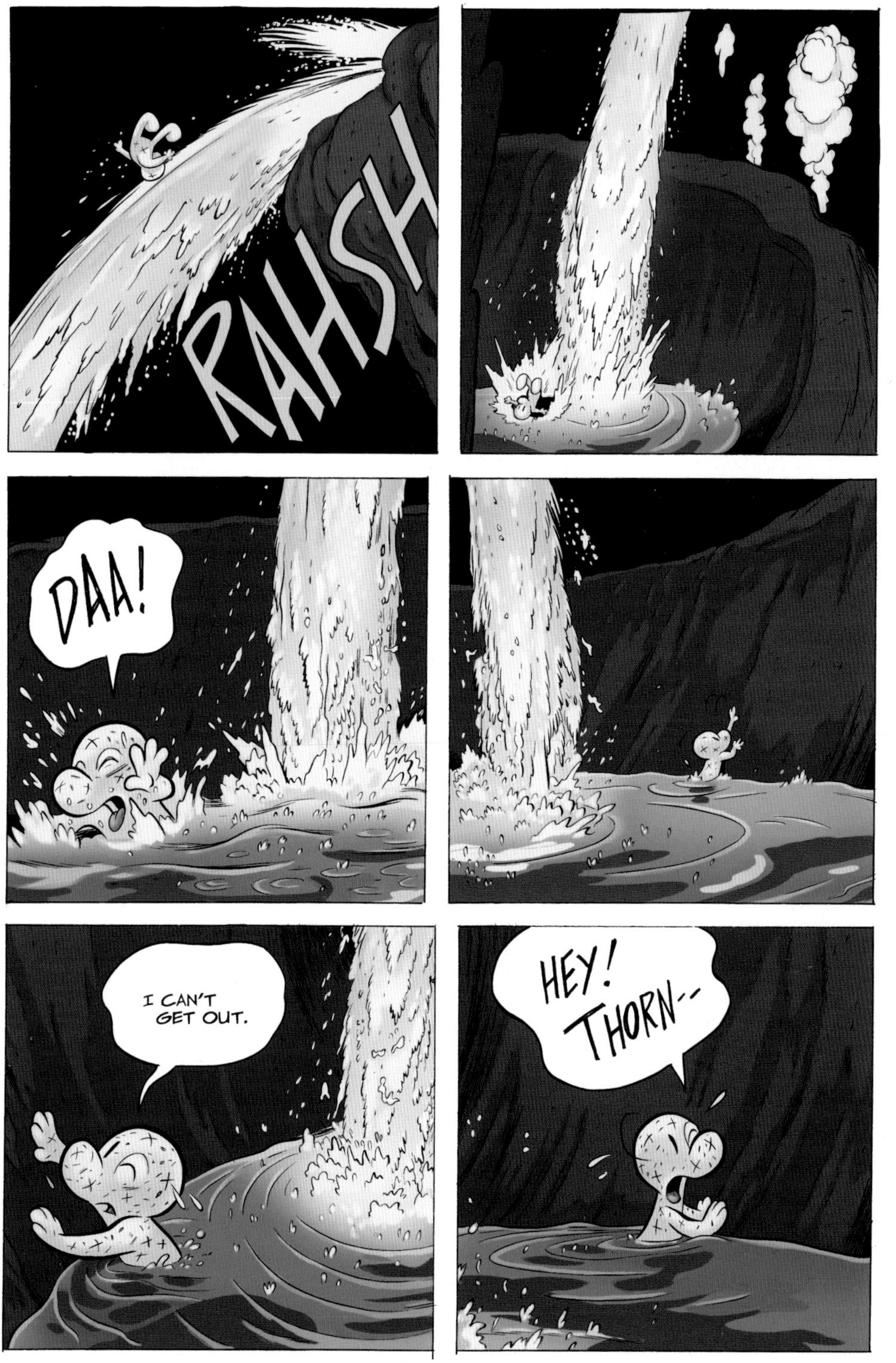
RAHSH
DAA!
I CAN'T GET OUT.
HEY! THORN--

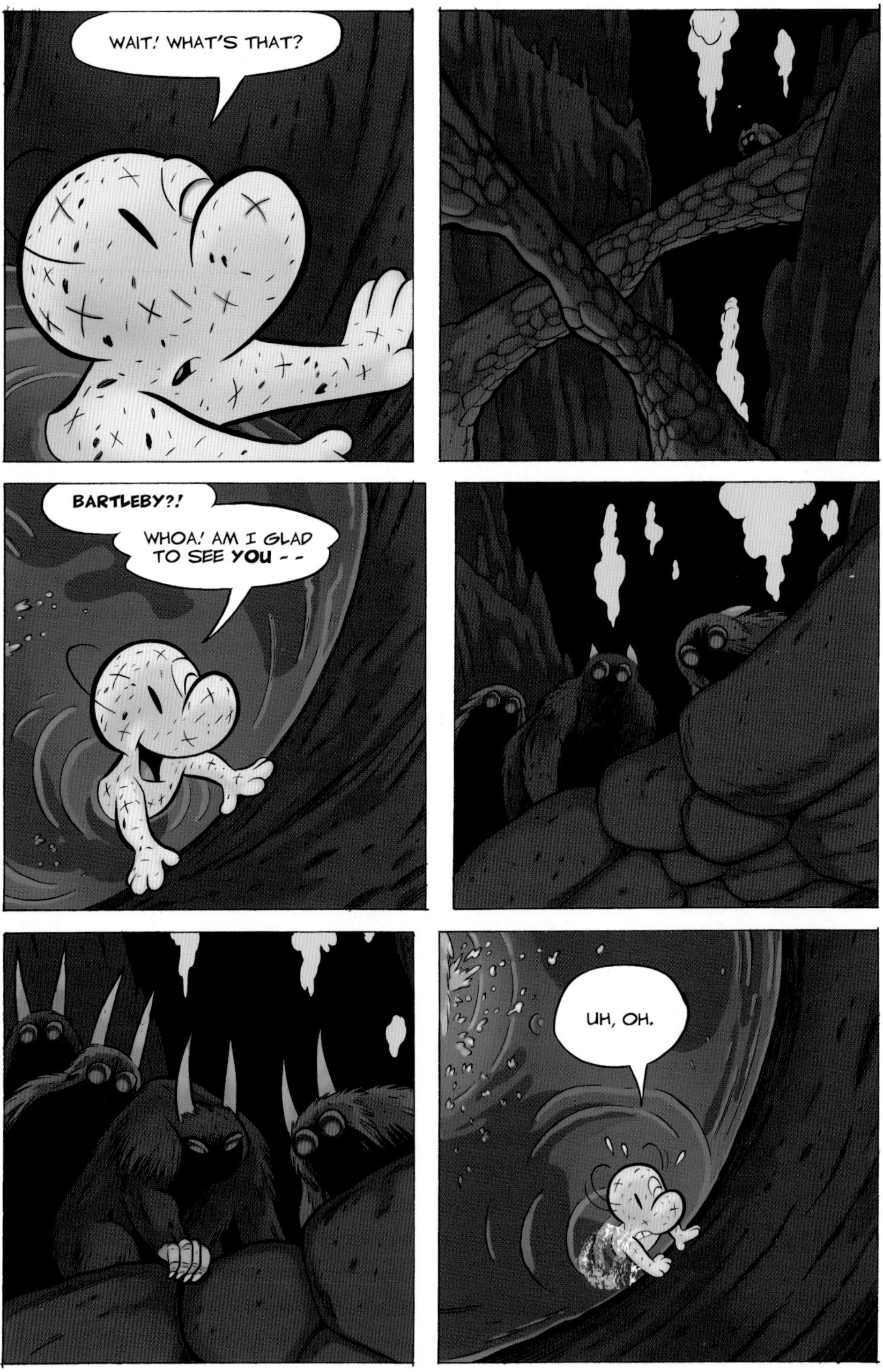
WAIT! WHAT'S THAT?
BARTLEBY?!
WHOA! AM I GLAD TO SEE **YOU** - -
UH, OH.

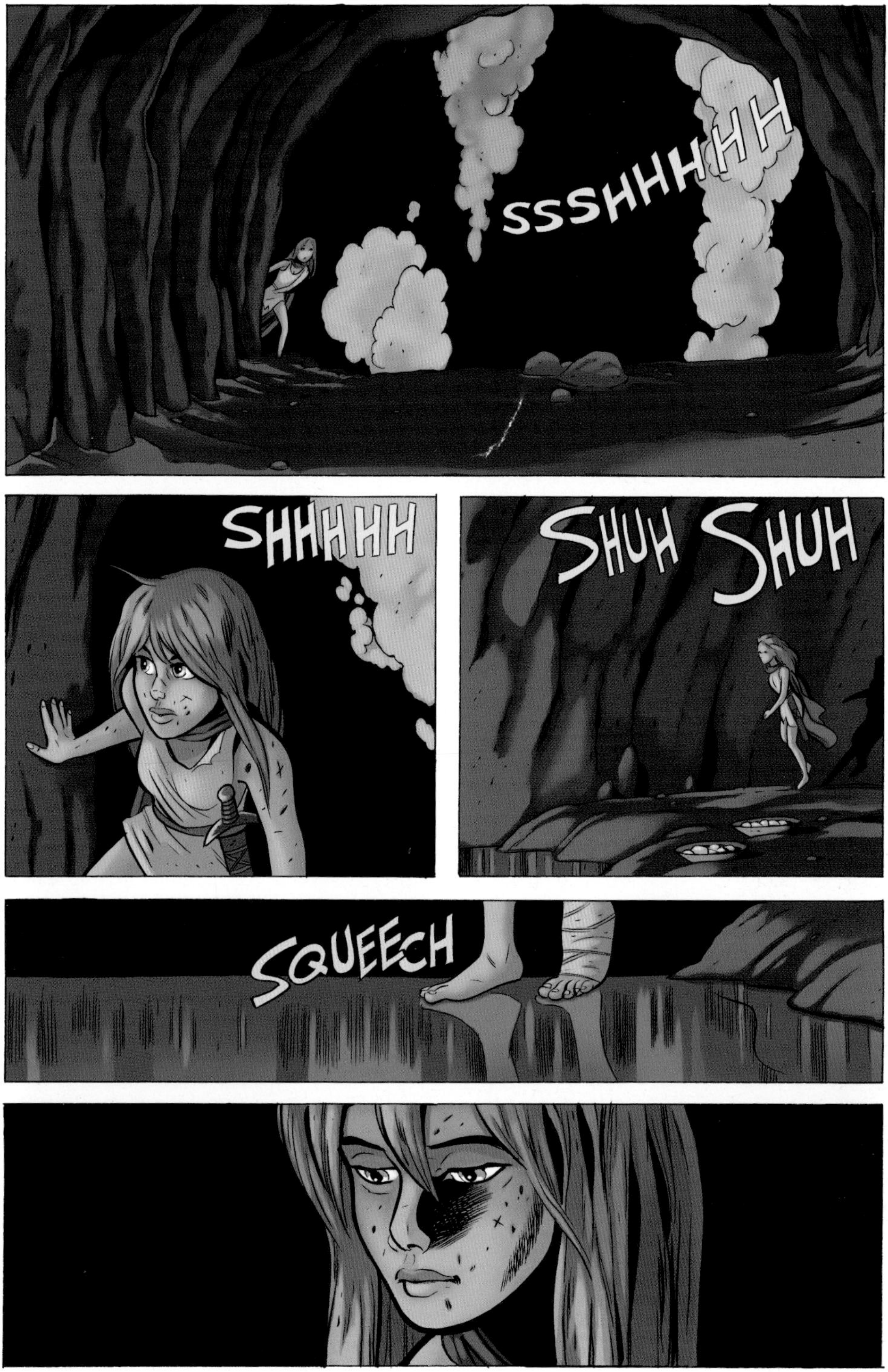
SSSHHHHHH
SHHHHH
SHUH SHUH
SQUEECH

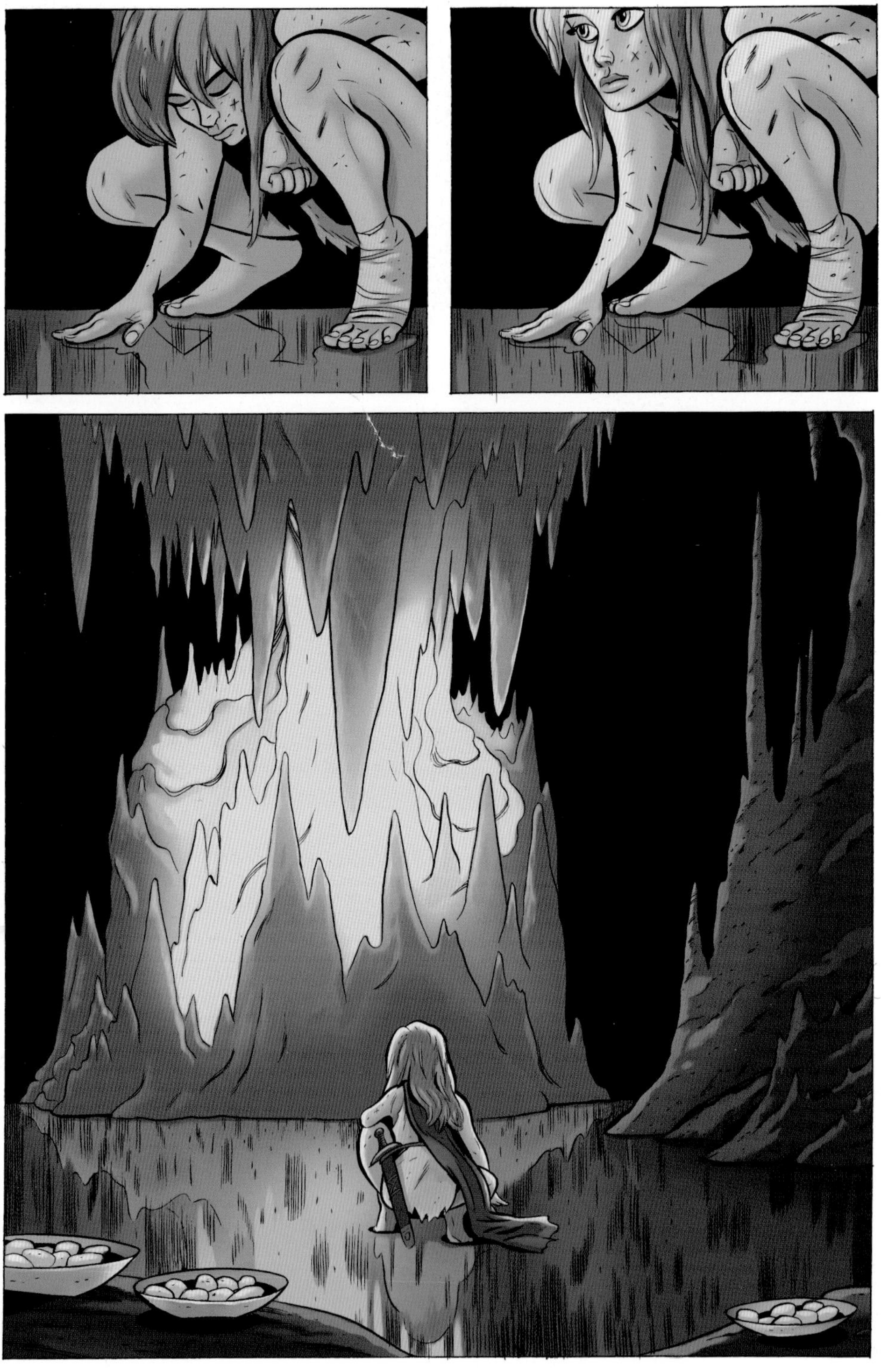

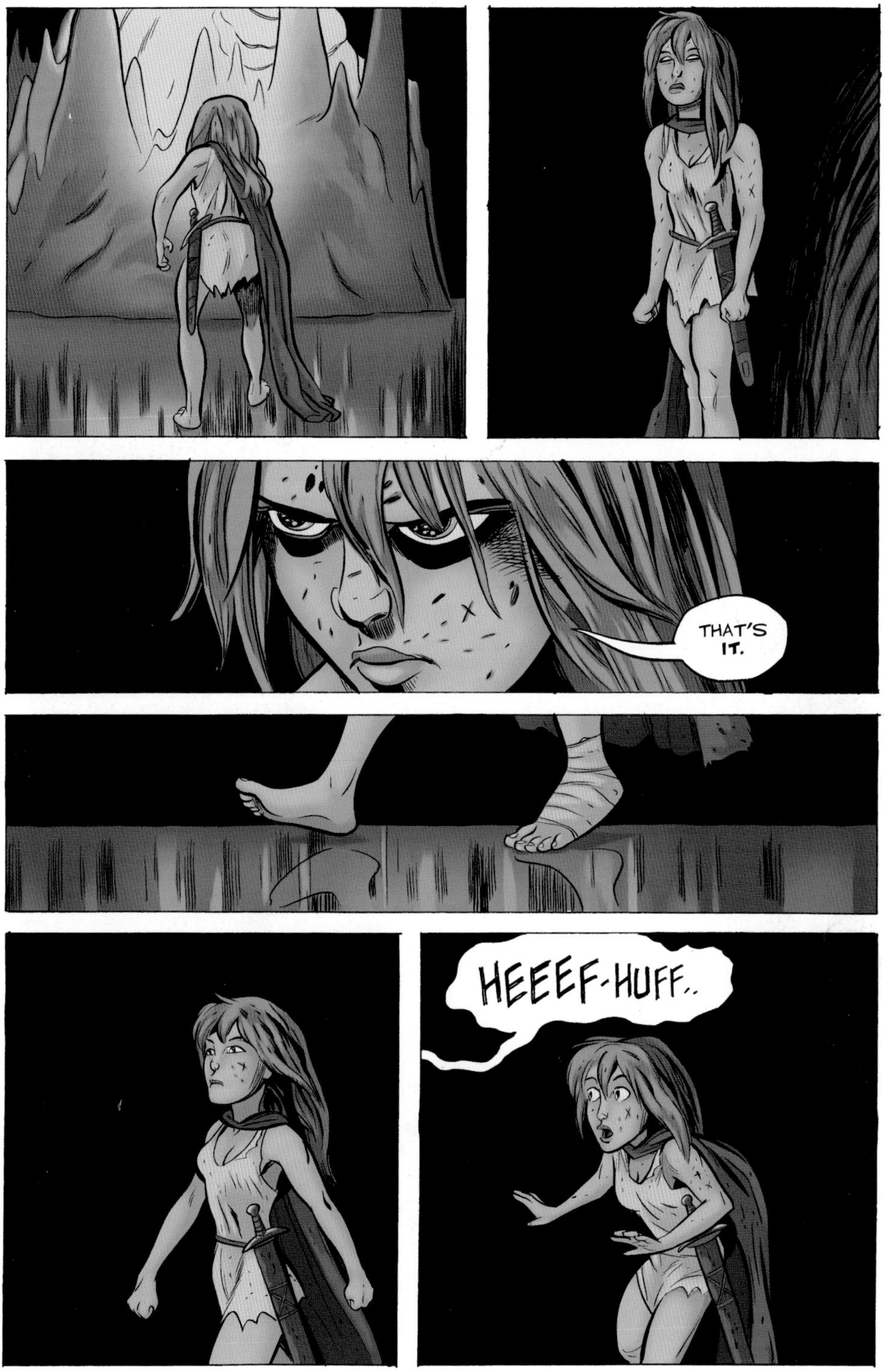
THAT'S IT.
HEEEF-HUFF..

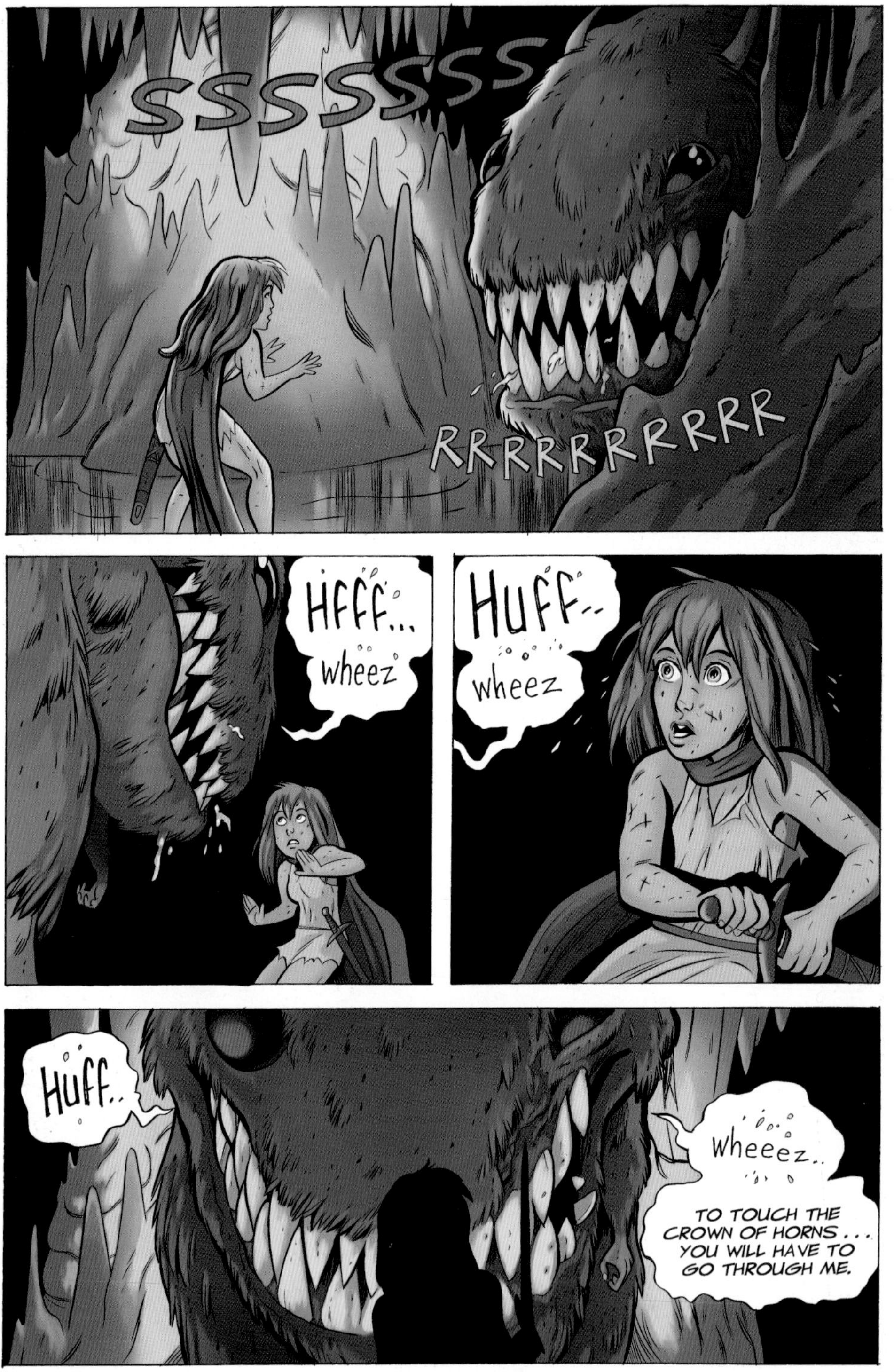
SSSSSSS
RRRRRRRRRR
Hfff...
wheez
Huff..
wheez
Huff..
Wheeez..
TO TOUCH THE CROWN OF HORNS . . . YOU WILL HAVE TO GO THROUGH ME.

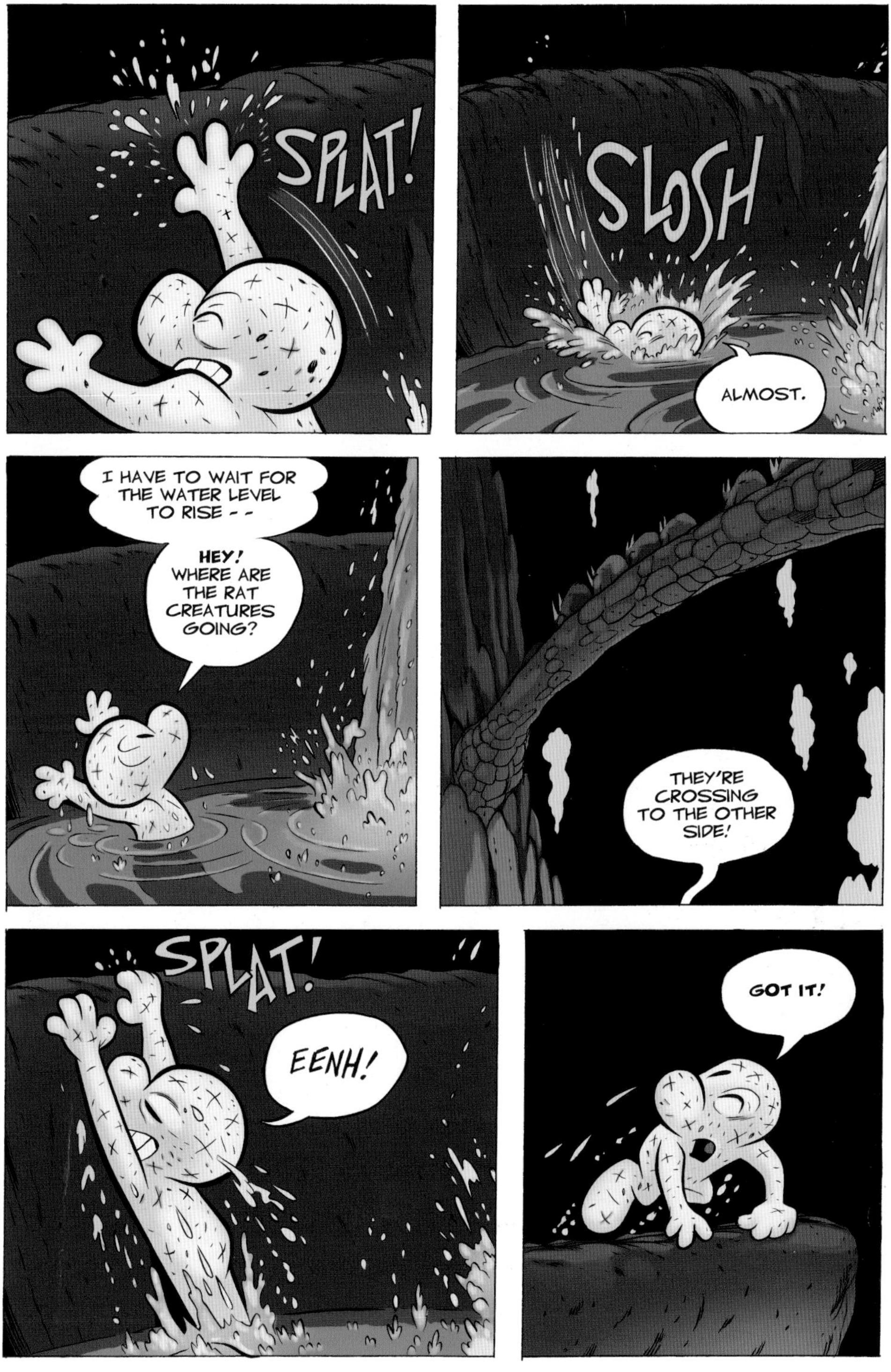
SPLAT!
SLOSH
ALMOST.
I HAVE TO WAIT FOR THE WATER LEVEL TO RISE - -
HEY! WHERE ARE THE RAT CREATURES GOING?
THEY'RE CROSSING TO THE OTHER SIDE!
SPLAT!
EENH!
GOT IT!

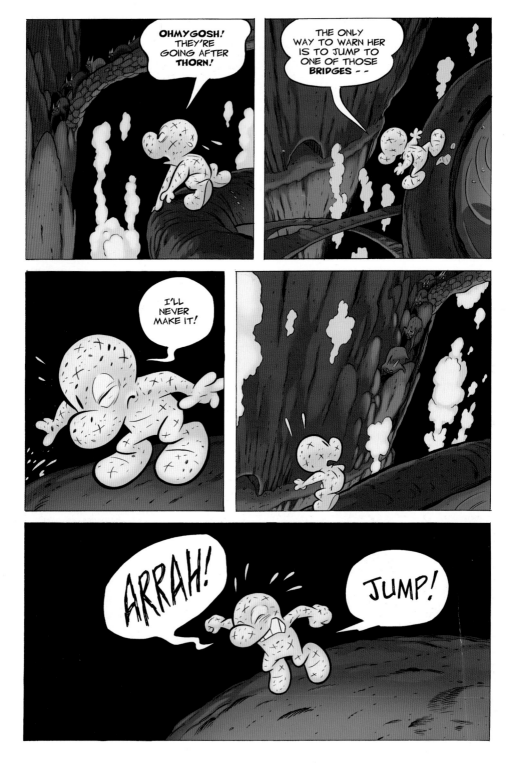

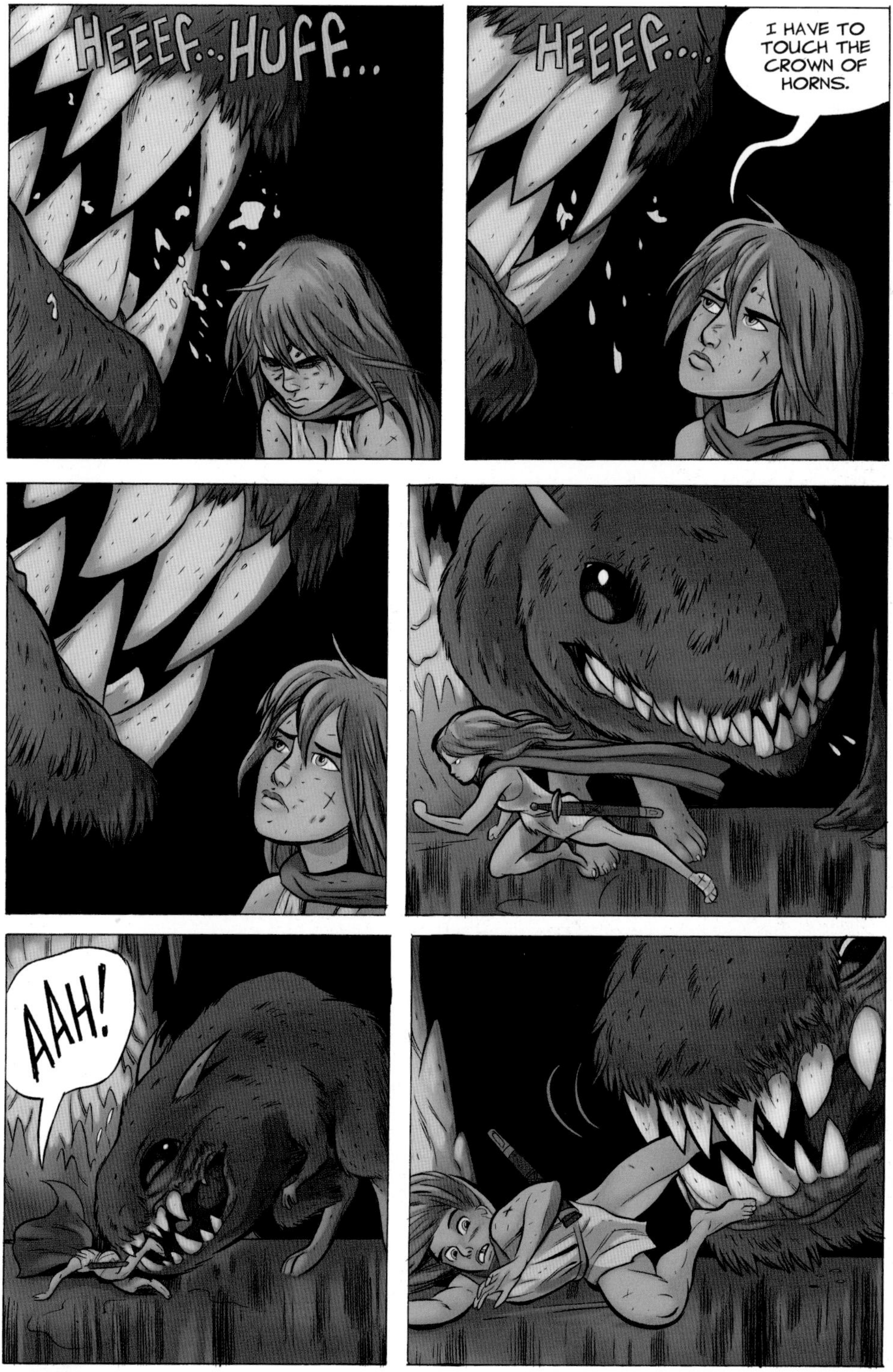
HEEEF...HUFF...
HEEEF...
I HAVE TO TOUCH THE CROWN OF HORNS.
AAH!

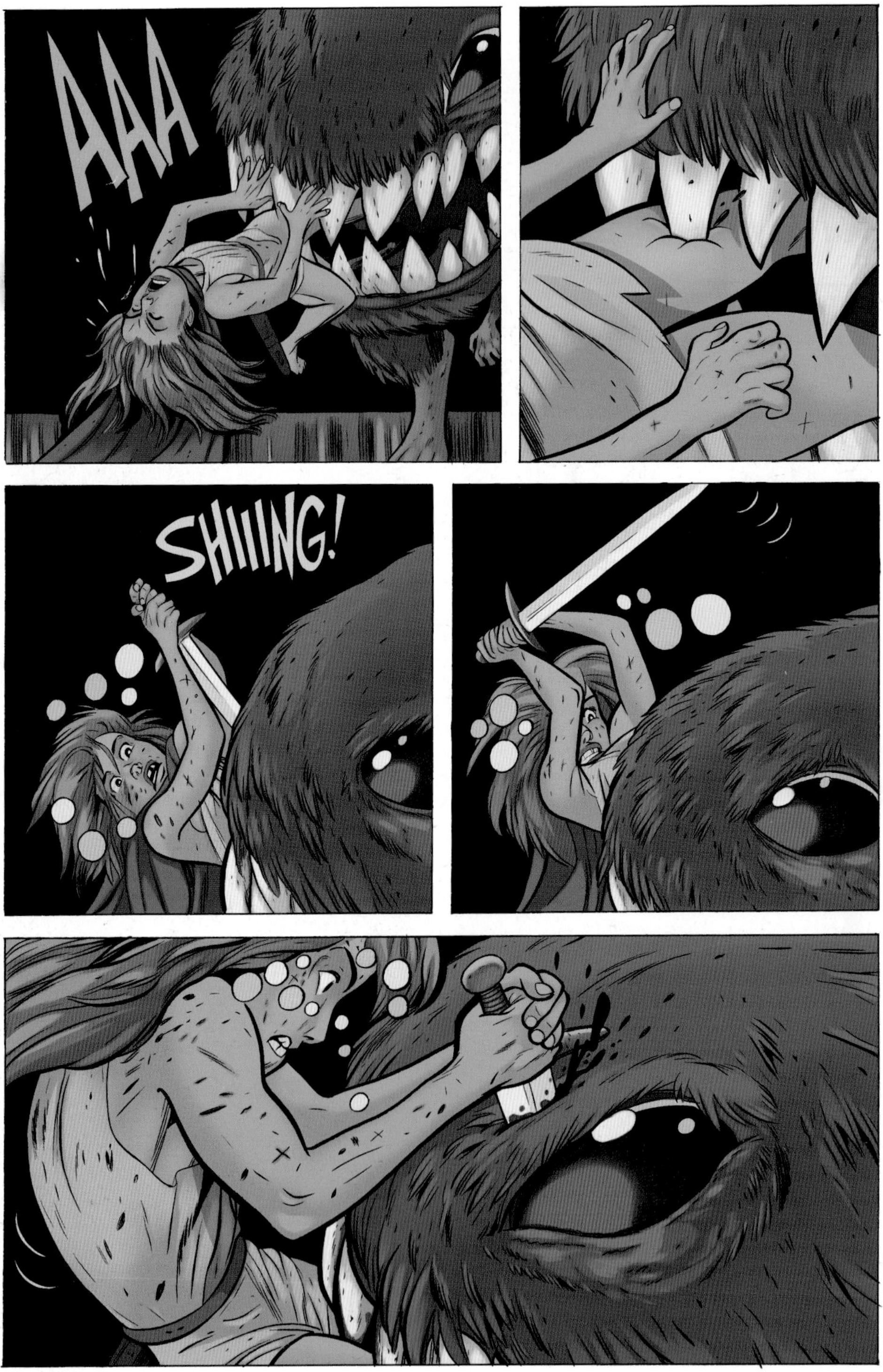
AAA
SHIIING!

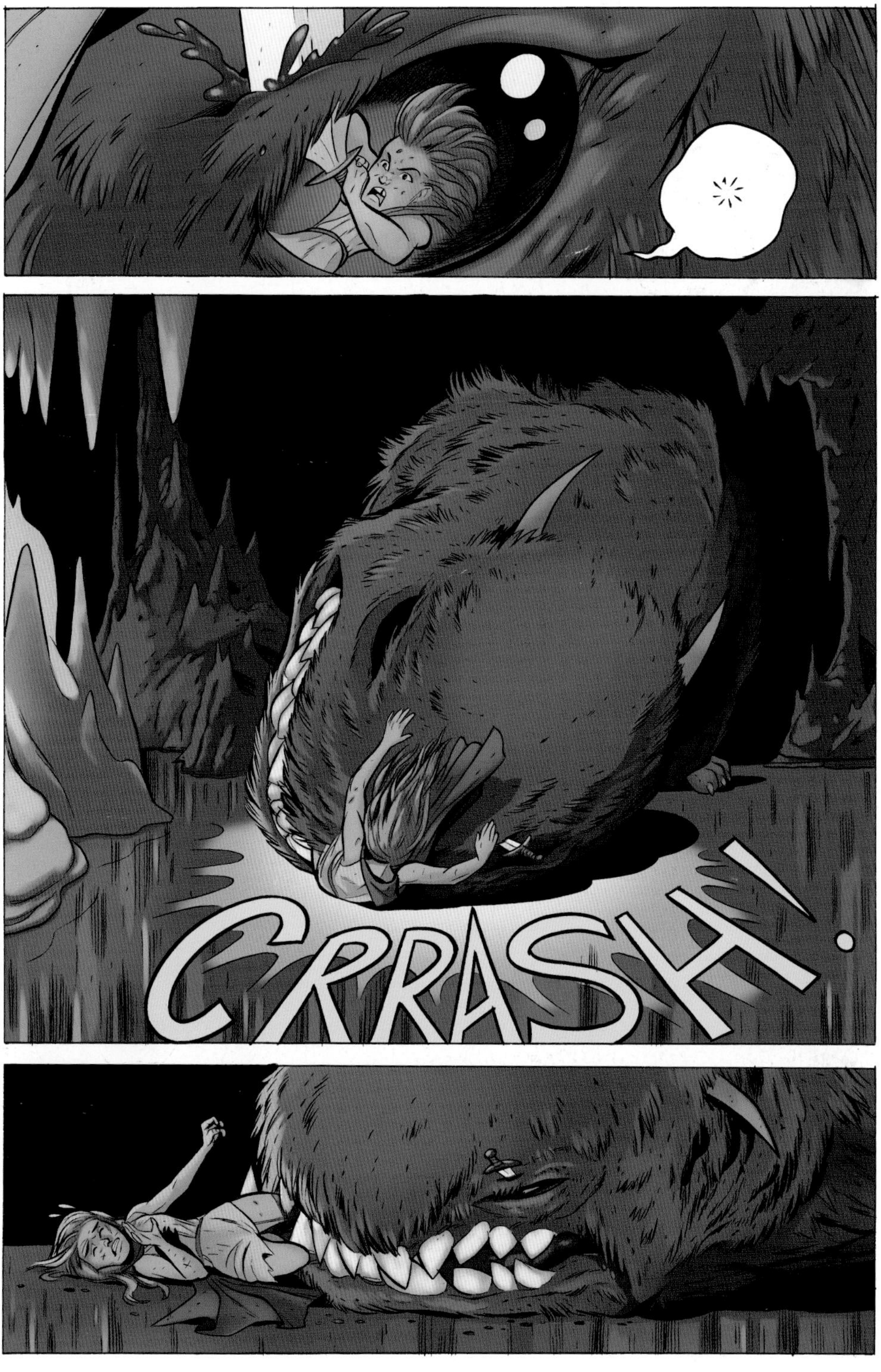
CRRASH!

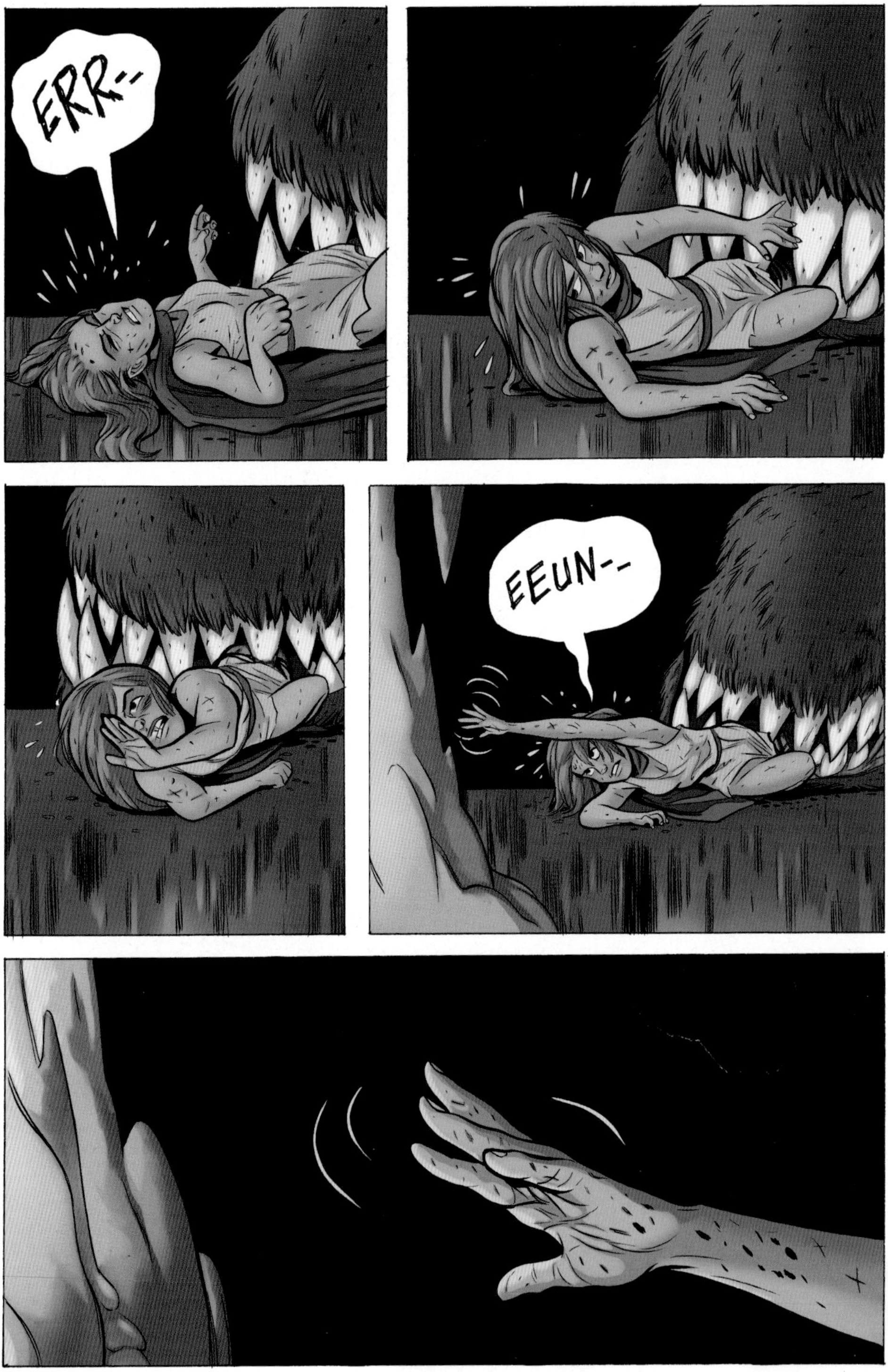
ERR-..
EEUN-_

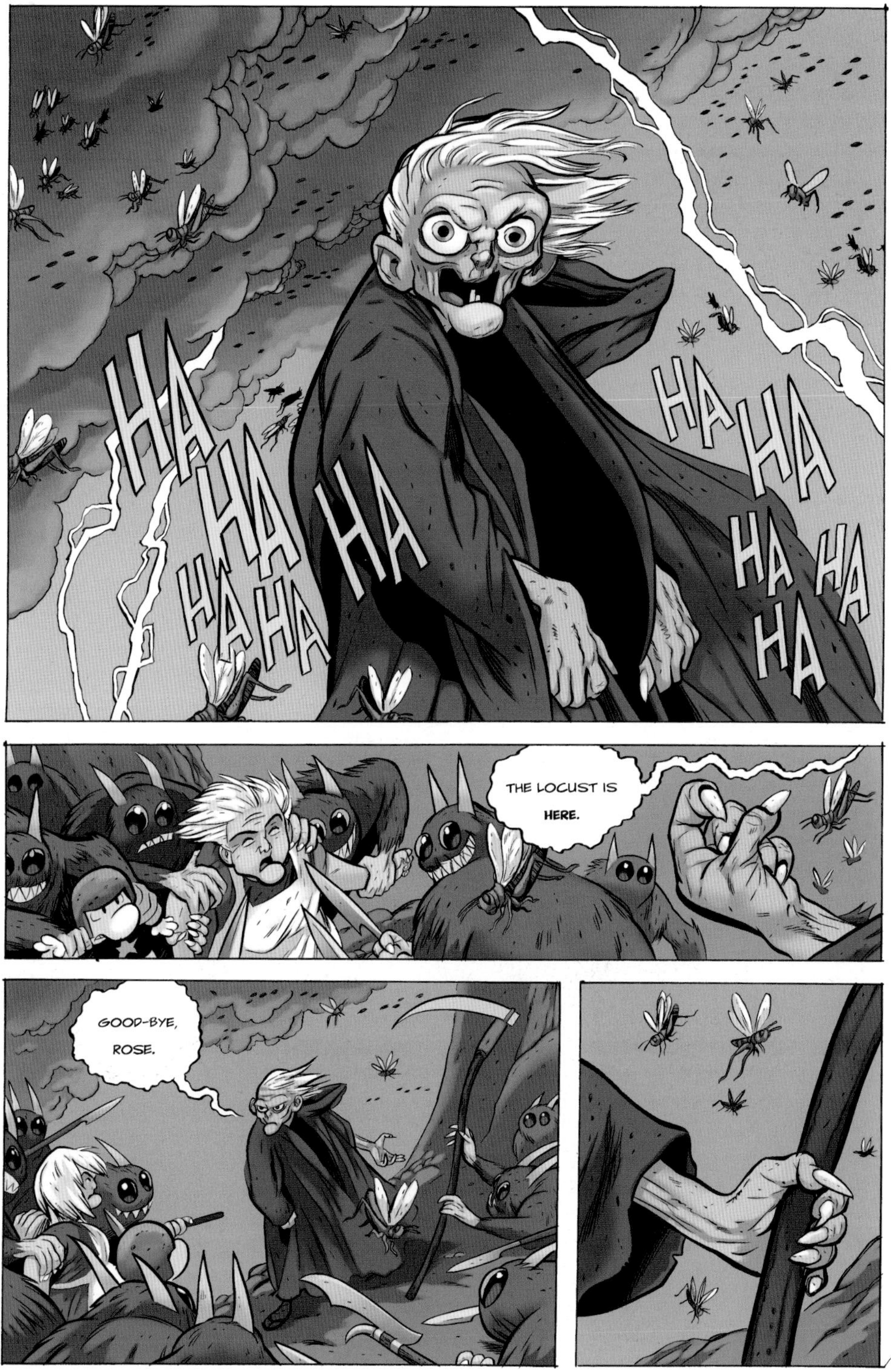
HA HA HA HA HA HA
HA
HA HA HA HA HA HA
THE LOCUST IS HERE.
GOOD-BYE, ROSE.

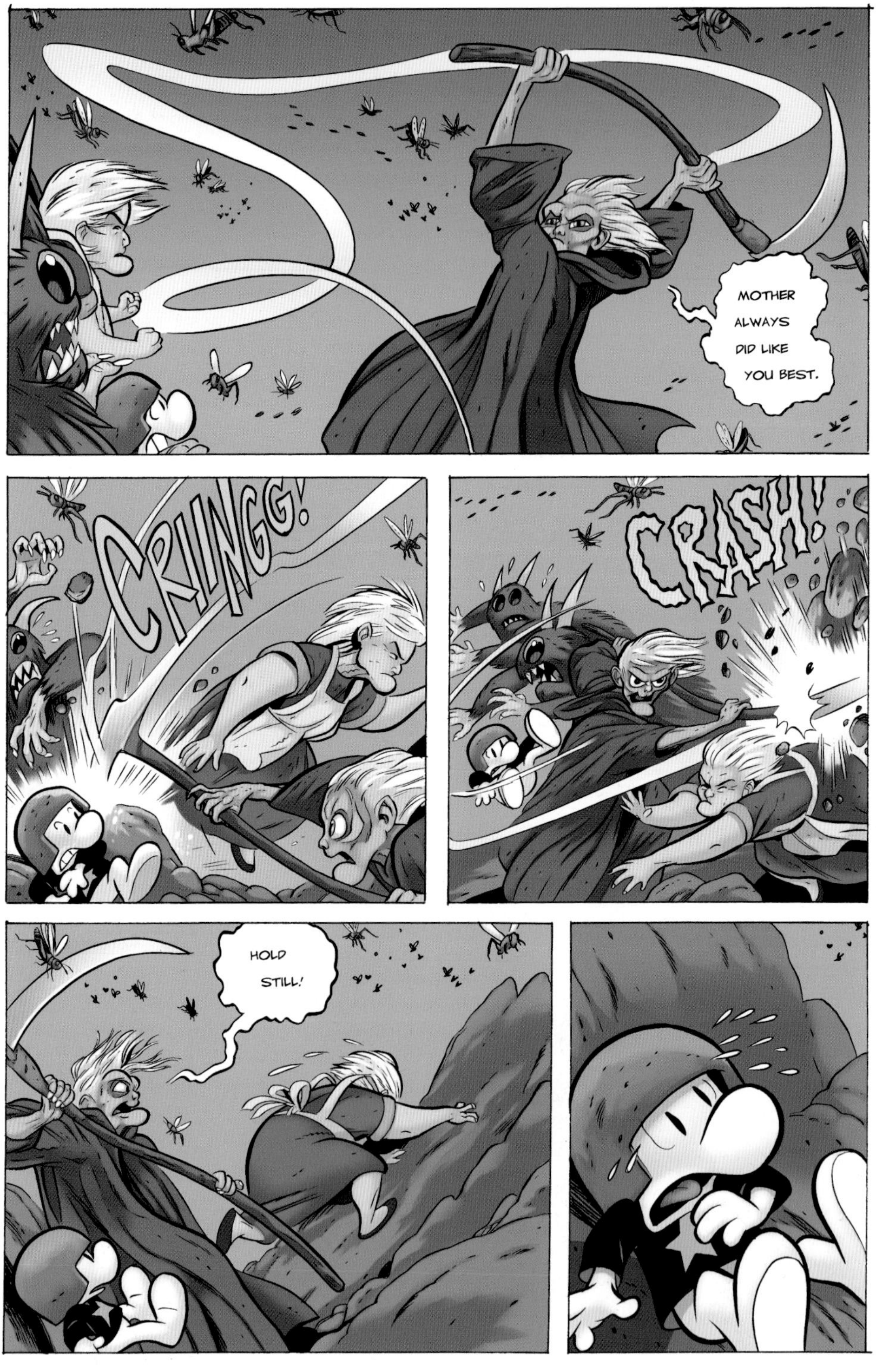
MOTHER ALWAYS DID LIKE YOU BEST.
CRINGG!
CRASH!
HOLD STILL!

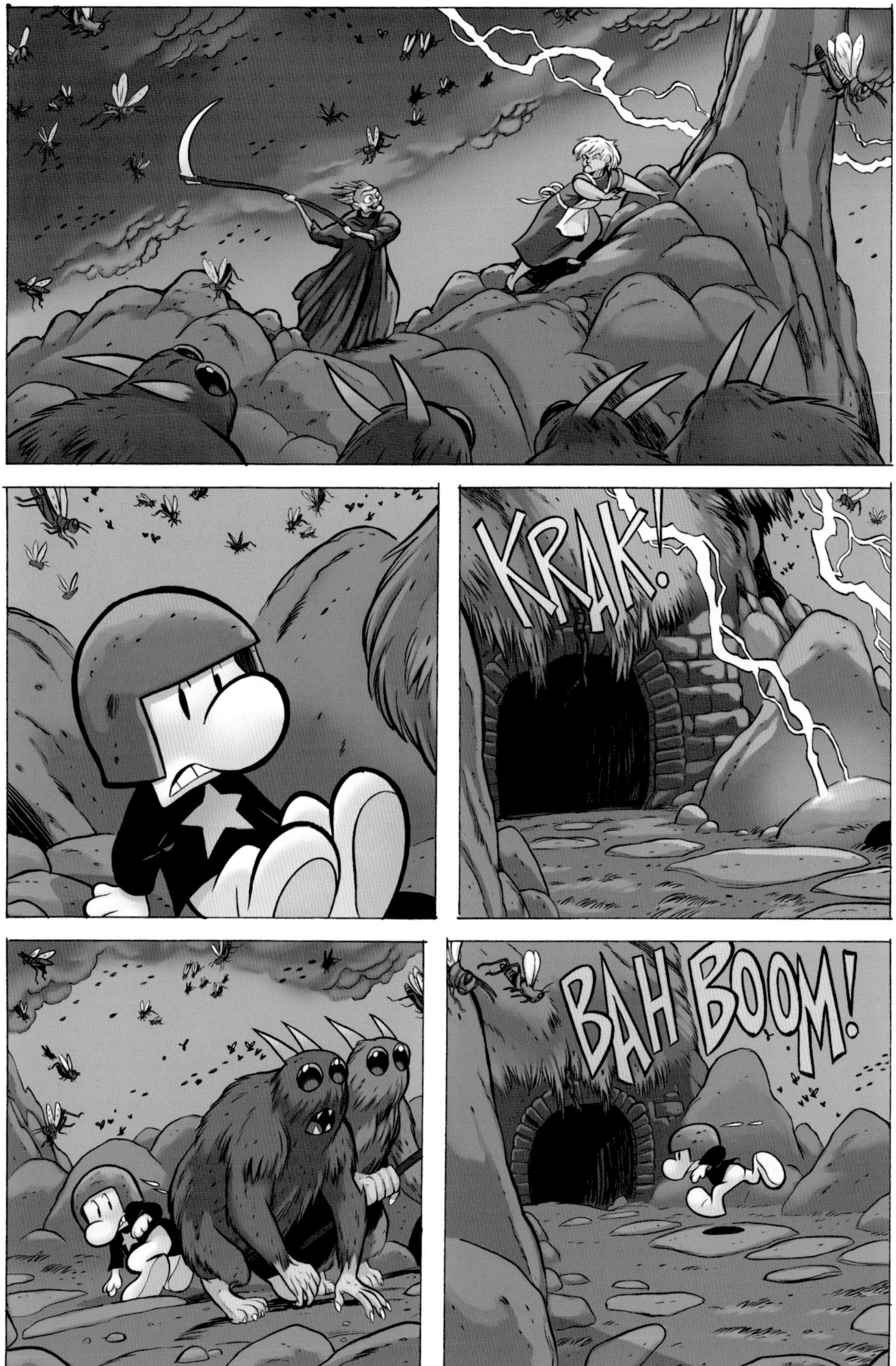
KRAK!
BAH BOOM!

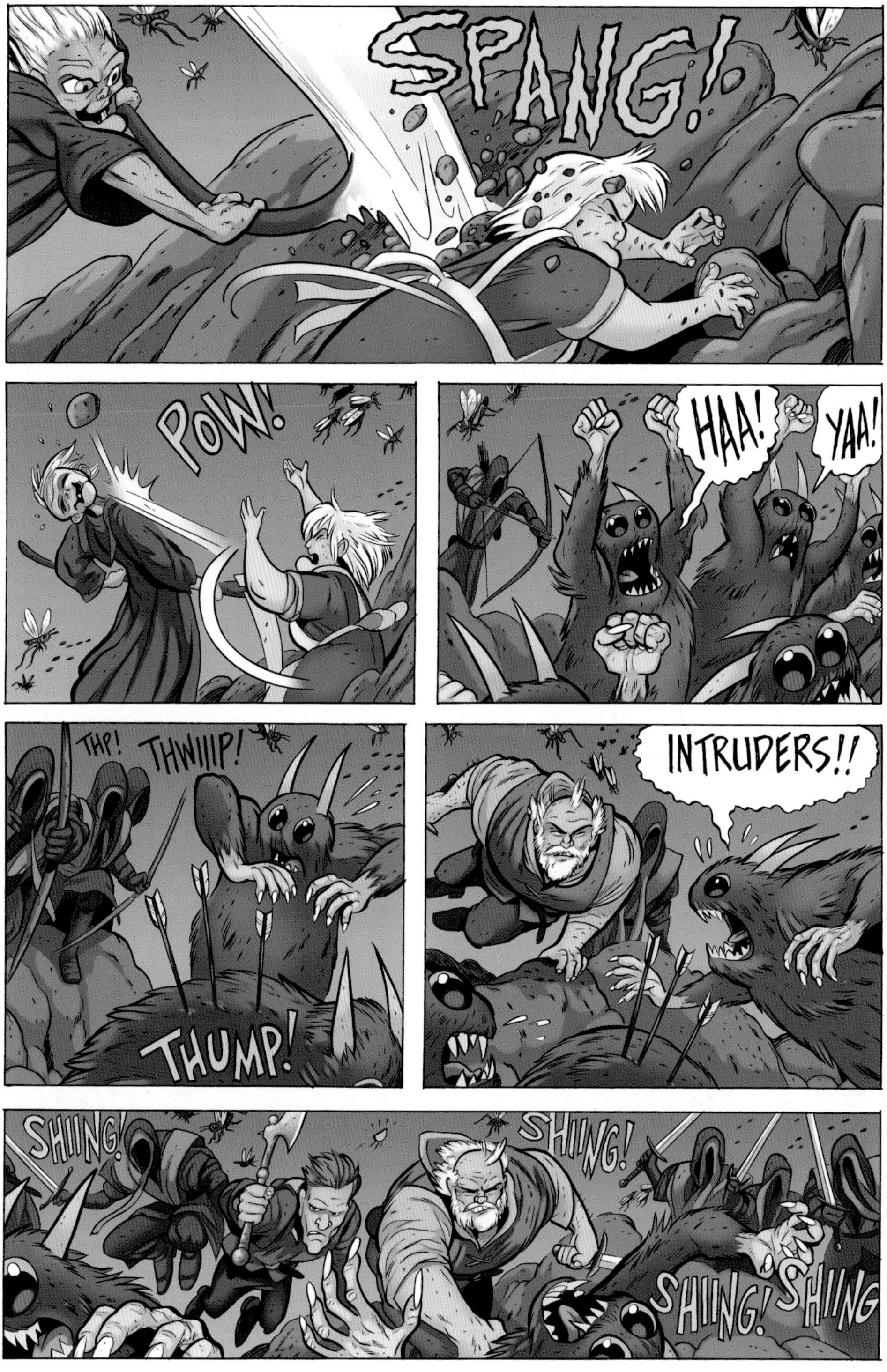
SPANG!
POW!
HAA!
YAA!
THP!
THWIIIP!
THUMP!
INTRUDERS!!
SHIING!
SHIING!
SHIING!
SHIING

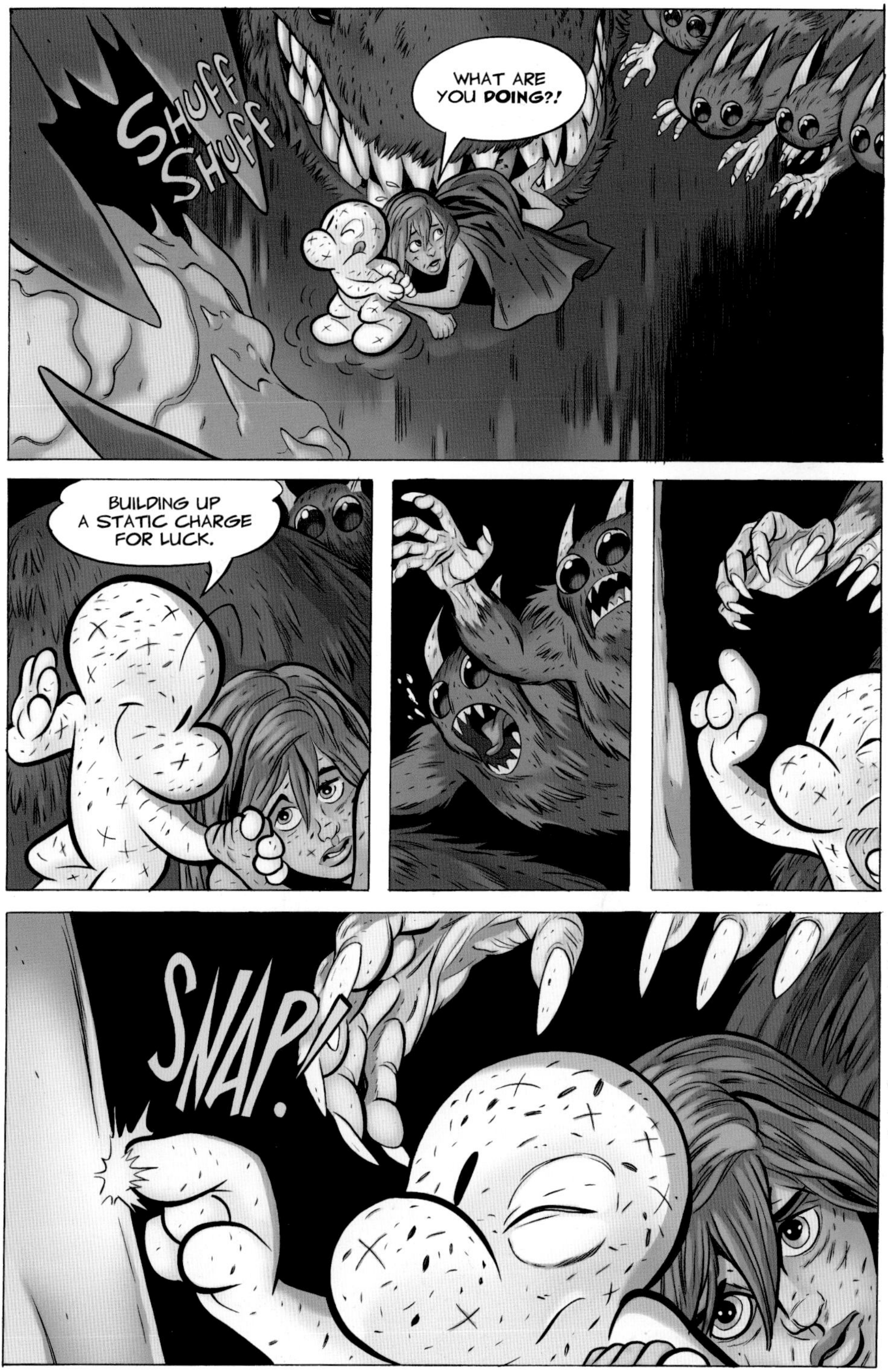
SHUFF SHUFF
WHAT ARE YOU DOING?!
BUILDING UP A STATIC CHARGE FOR LUCK.
SNAP!

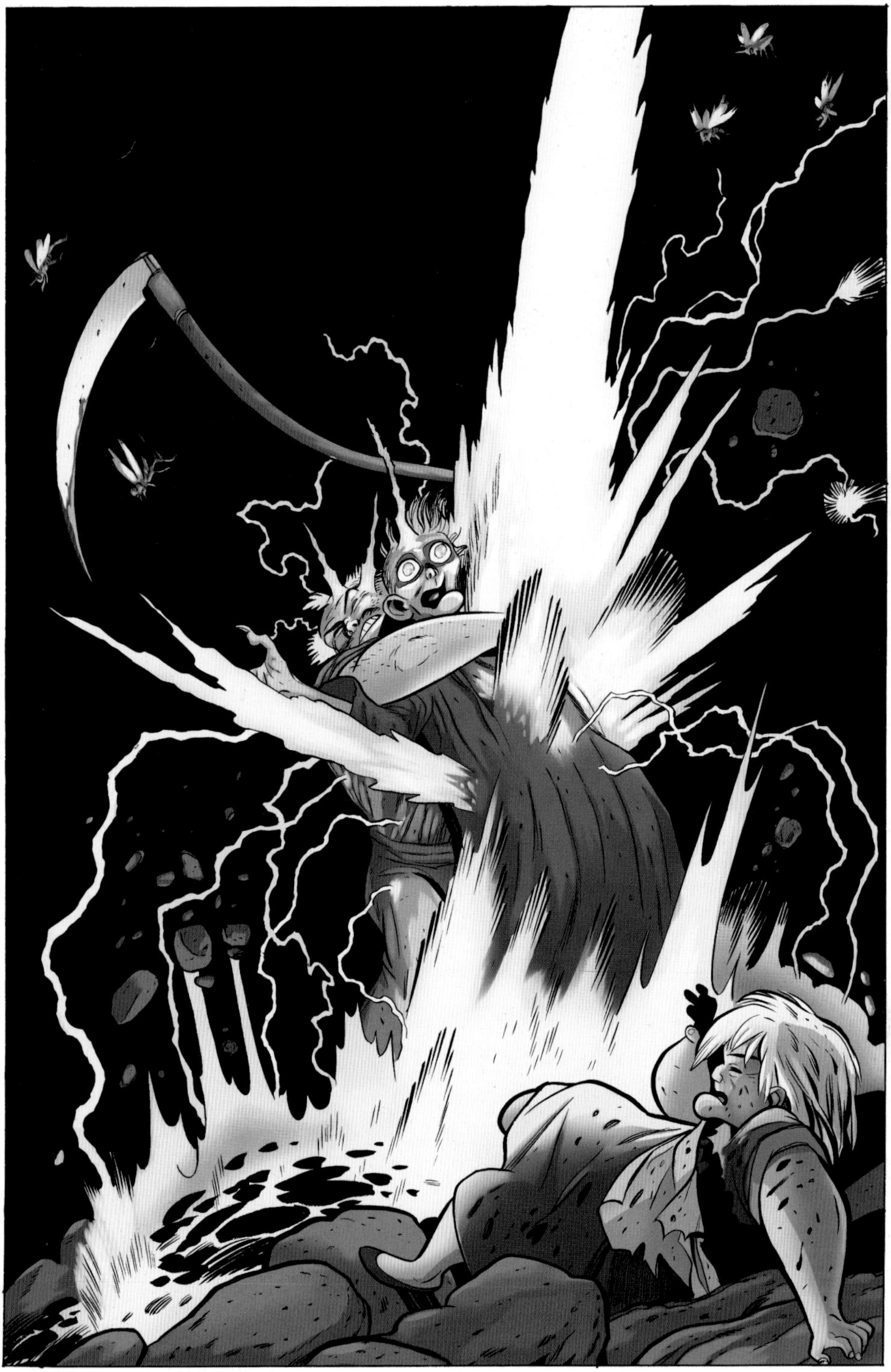

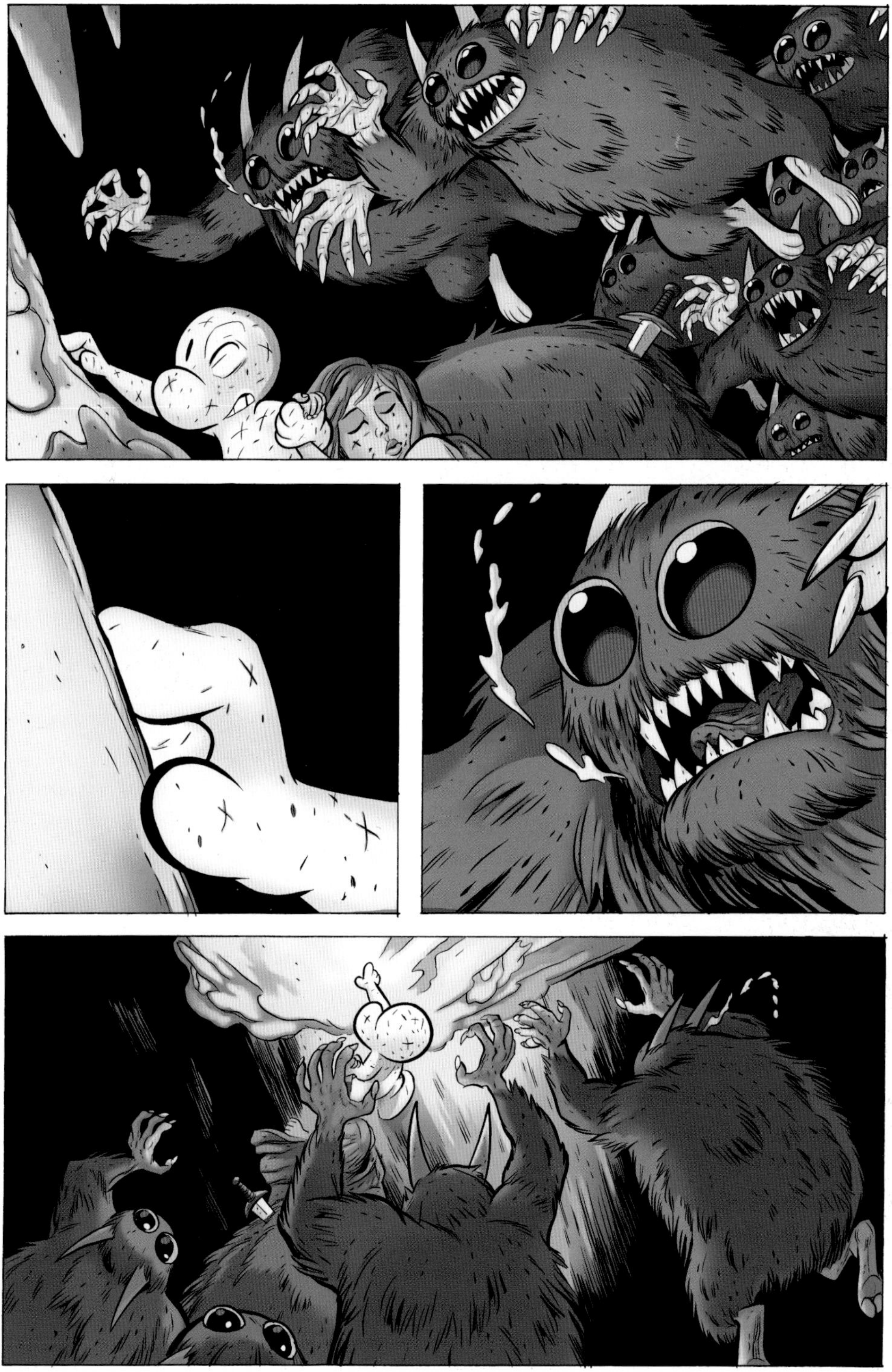

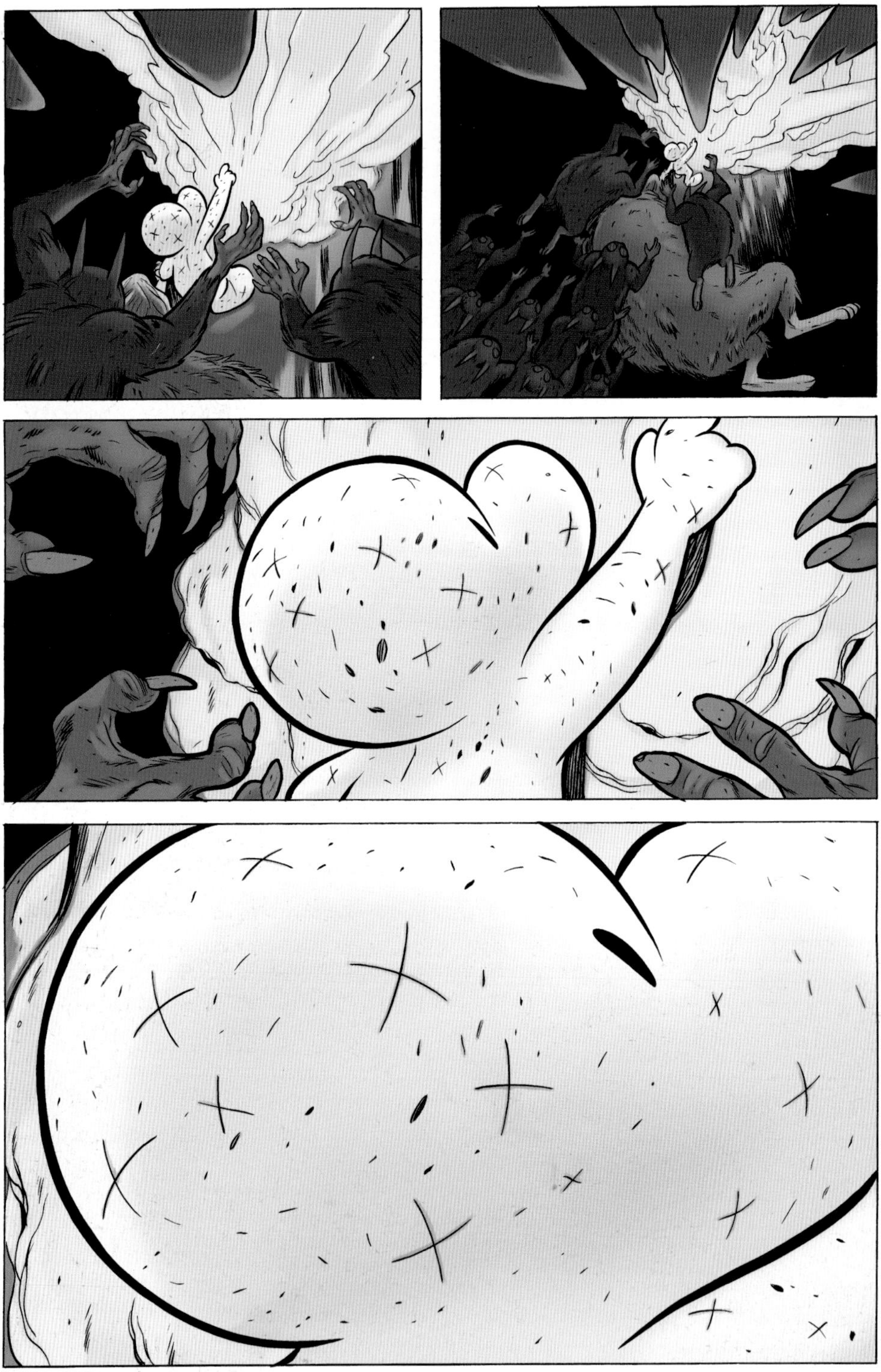

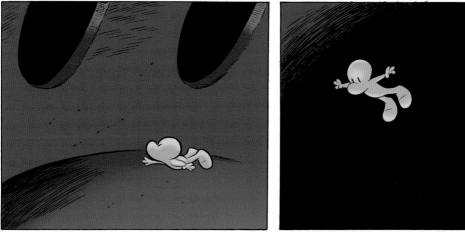

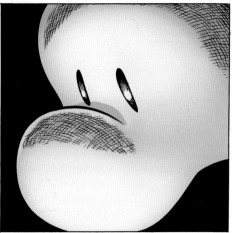

HELLO.

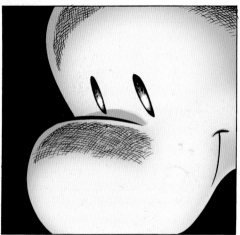

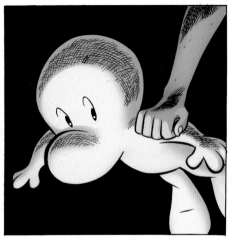

CHAMBER OF HORNS

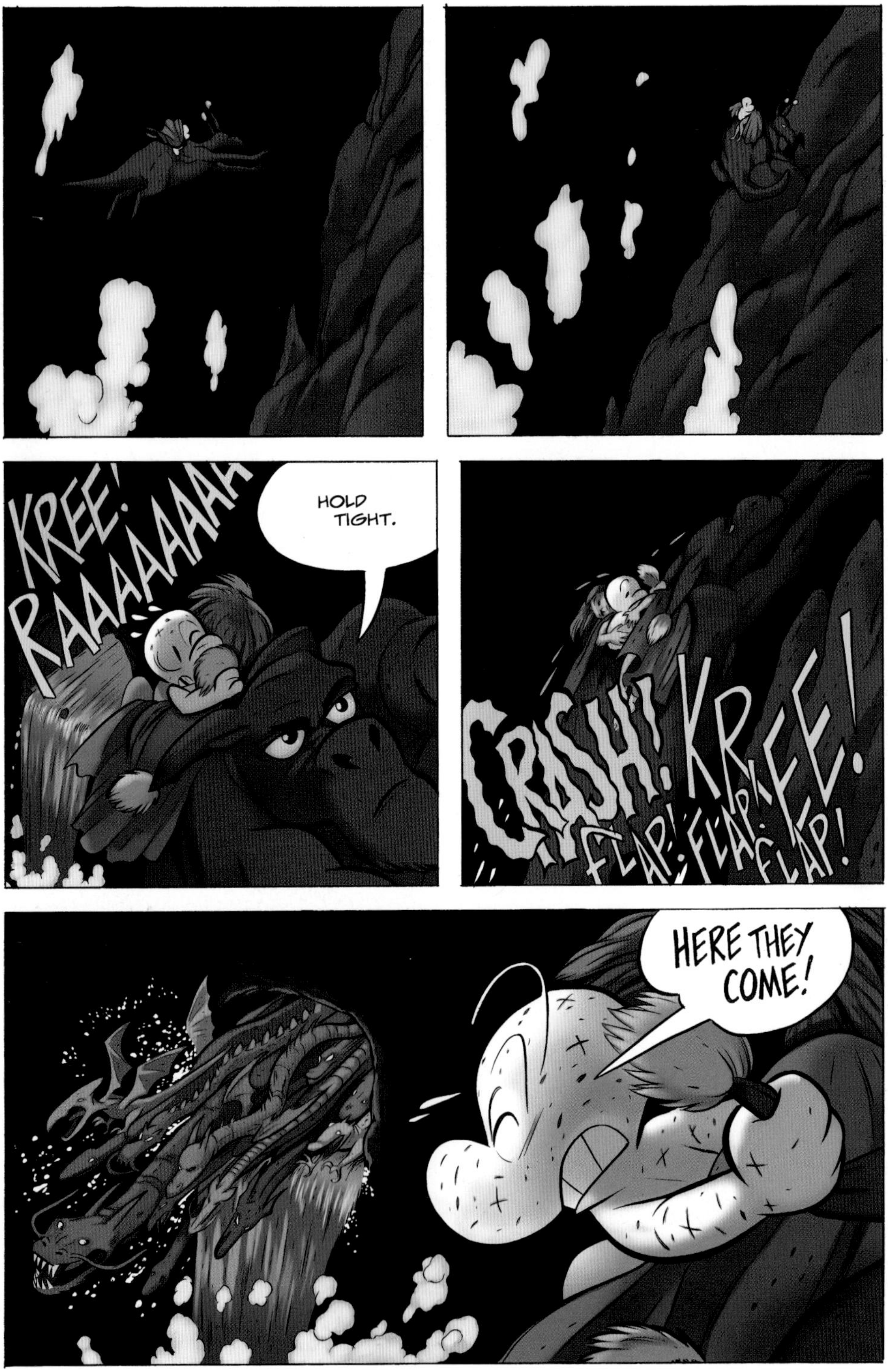
KREE! RAAAAAAAH
HOLD TIGHT.
CRASH! KR-EE!
FLAP! FLAP! FLAP!
HERE THEY COME!

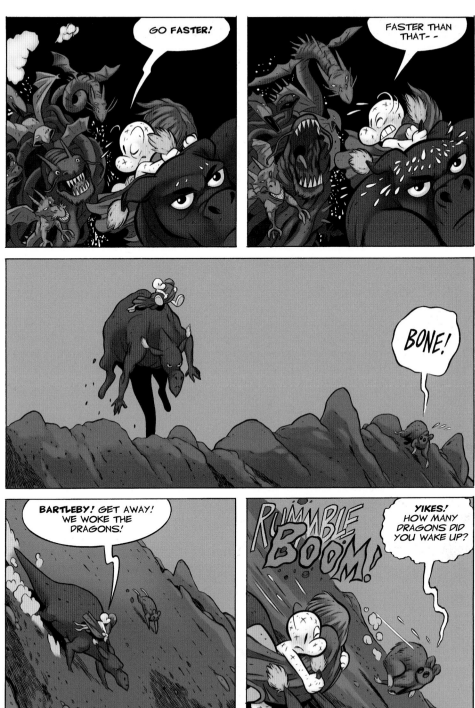

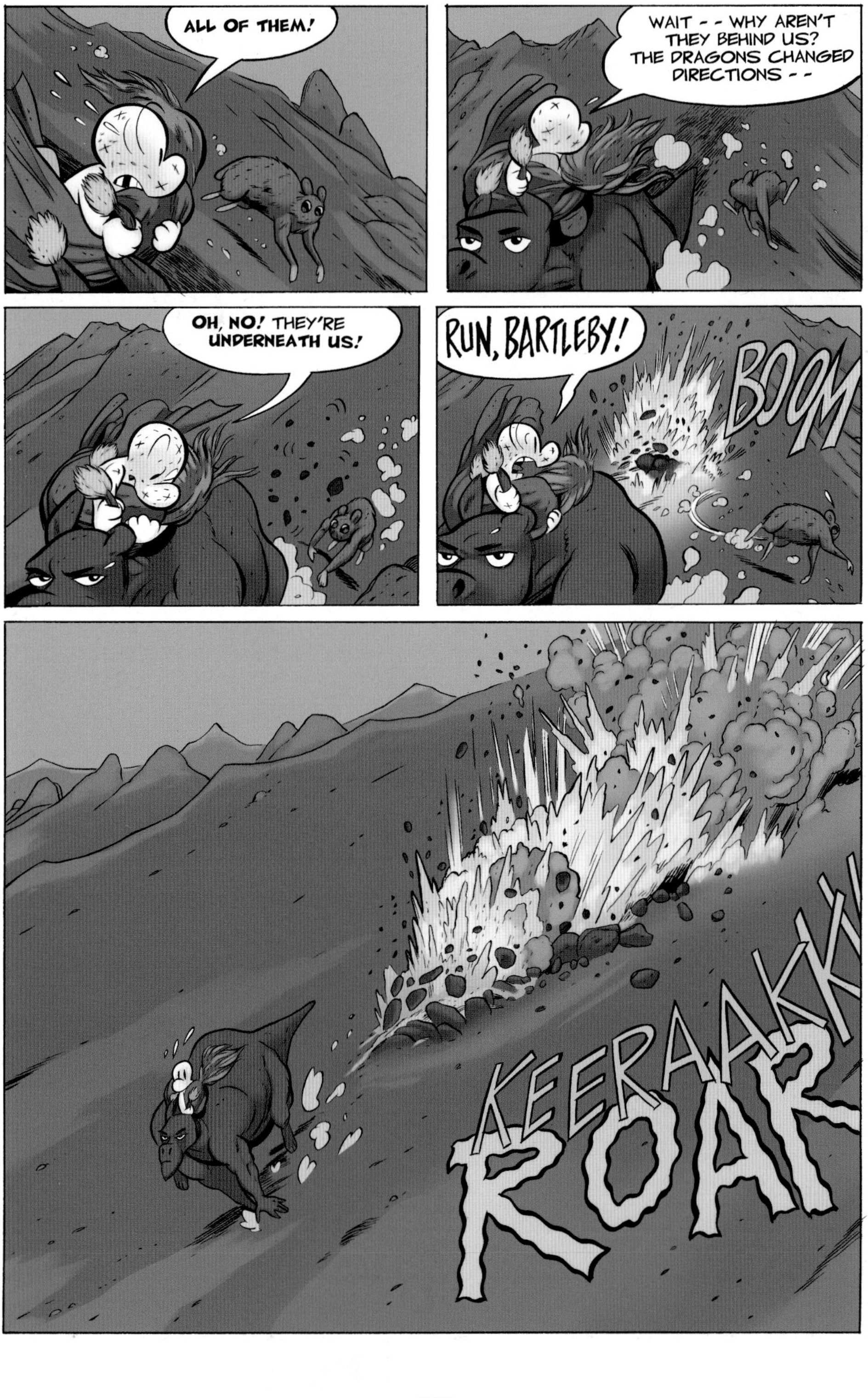
ALL OF THEM!
WAIT - - WHY AREN'T THEY BEHIND US? THE DRAGONS CHANGED DIRECTIONS - -
OH, NO! THEY'RE UNDERNEATH US!
RUN, BARTLEBY!
BOOM
KEERAAKK
ROAR

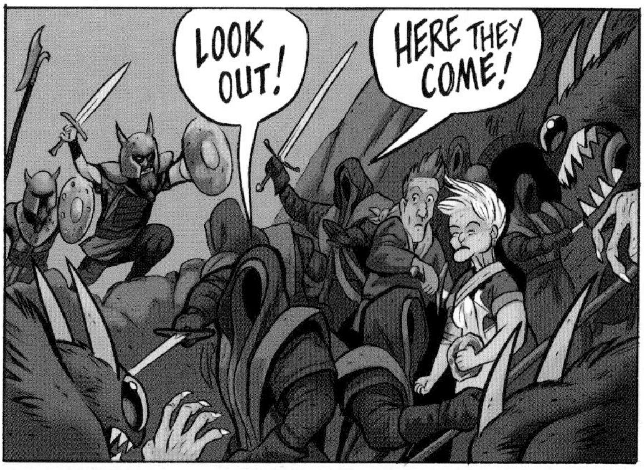
LOOK OUT!
HERE THEY COME!

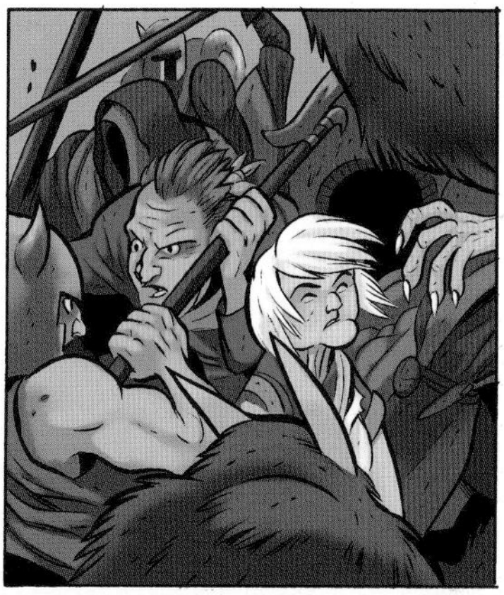

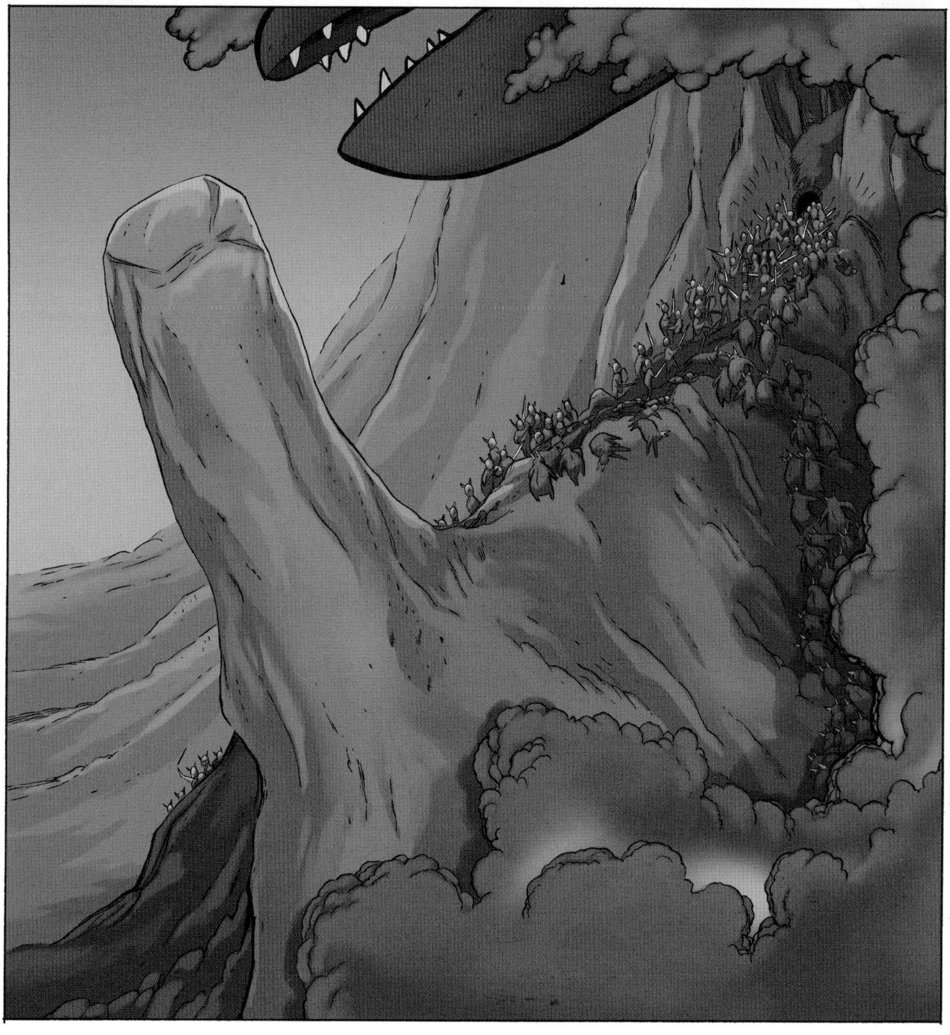

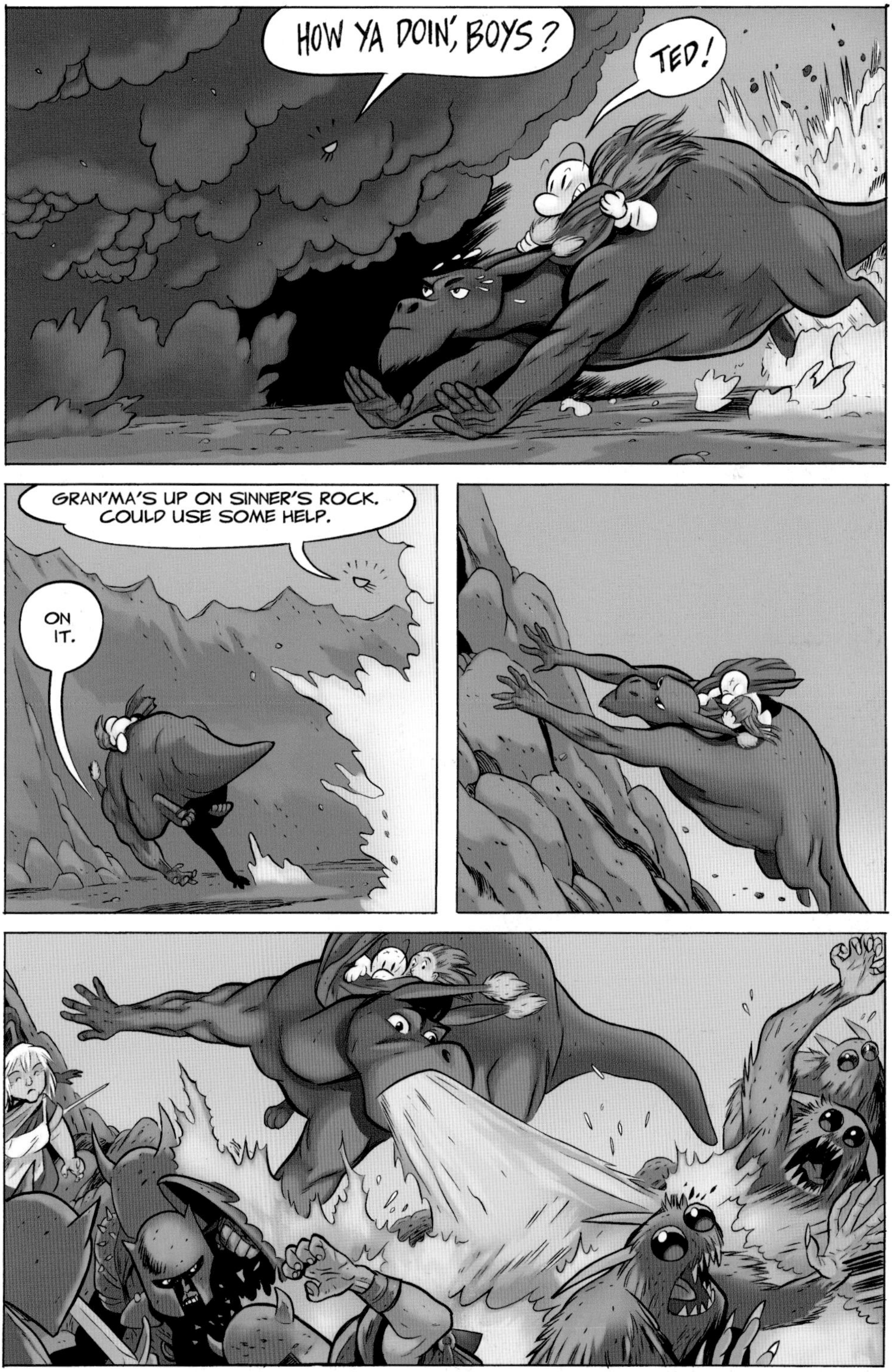
HOW YA DOIN', BOYS?
TED!
GRAN'MA'S UP ON SINNER'S ROCK. COULD USE SOME HELP.
ON IT.

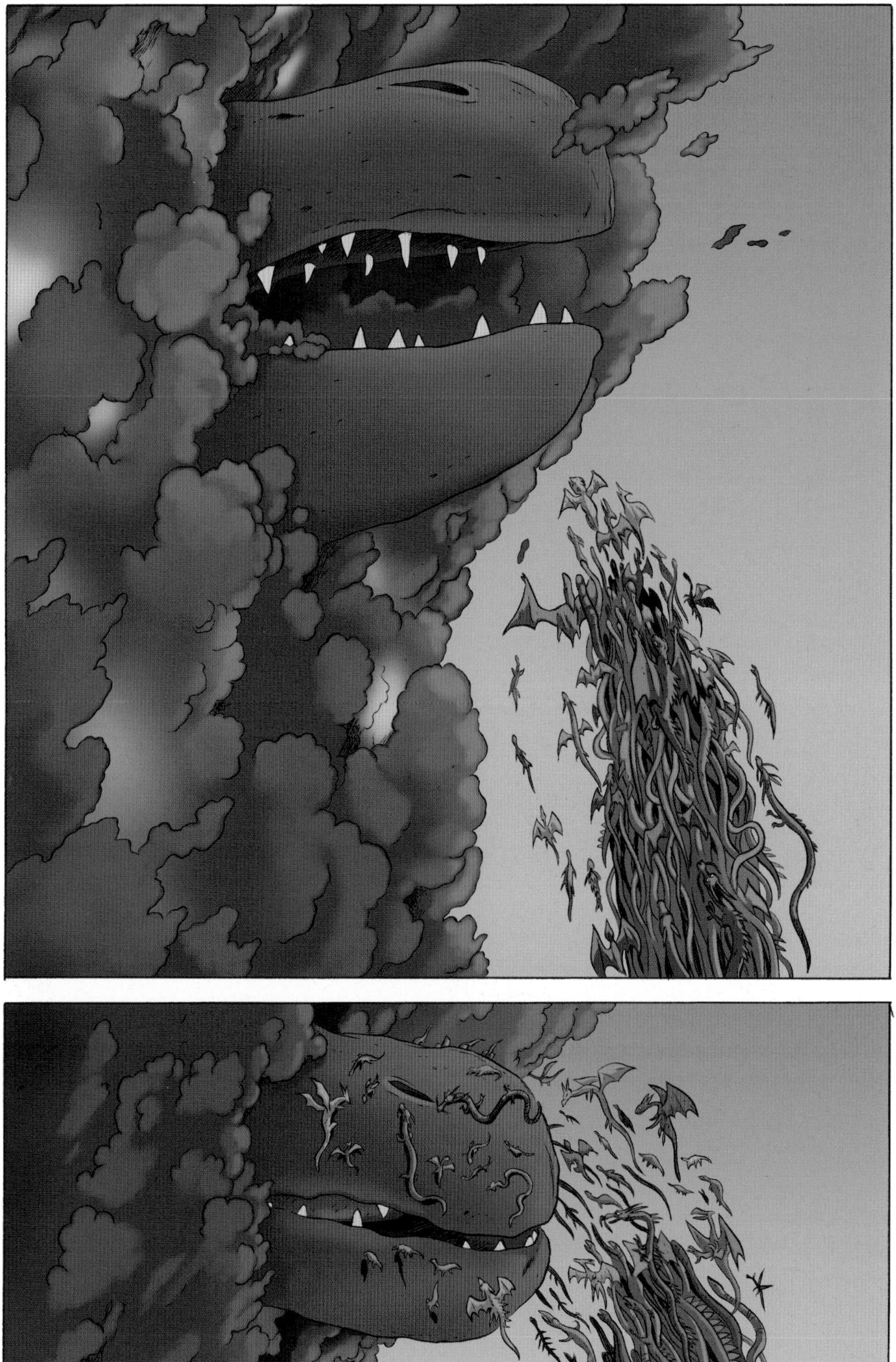

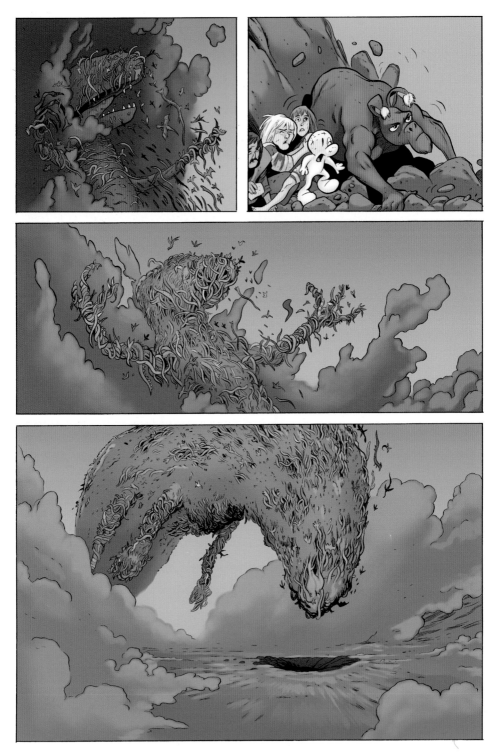

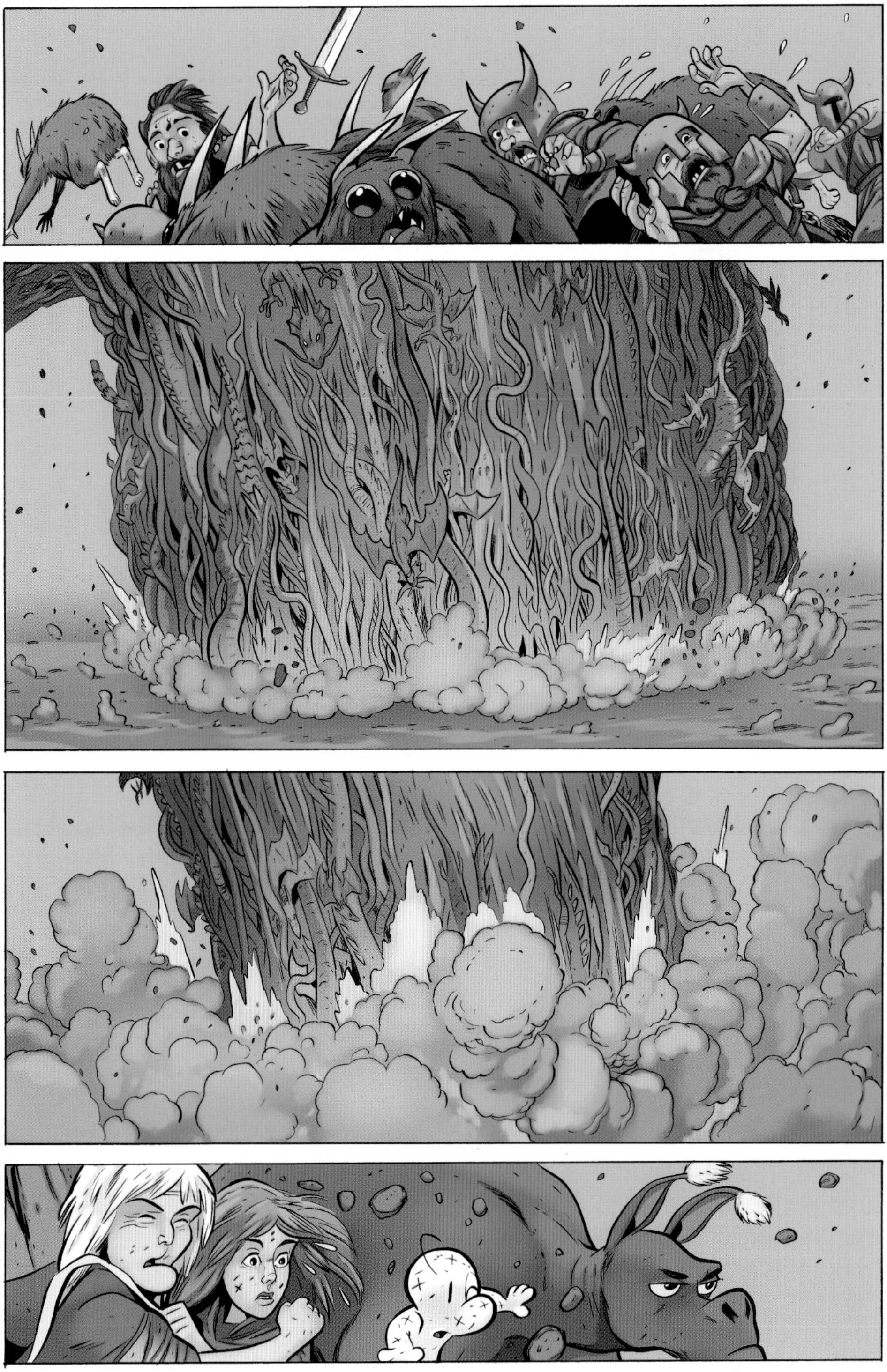

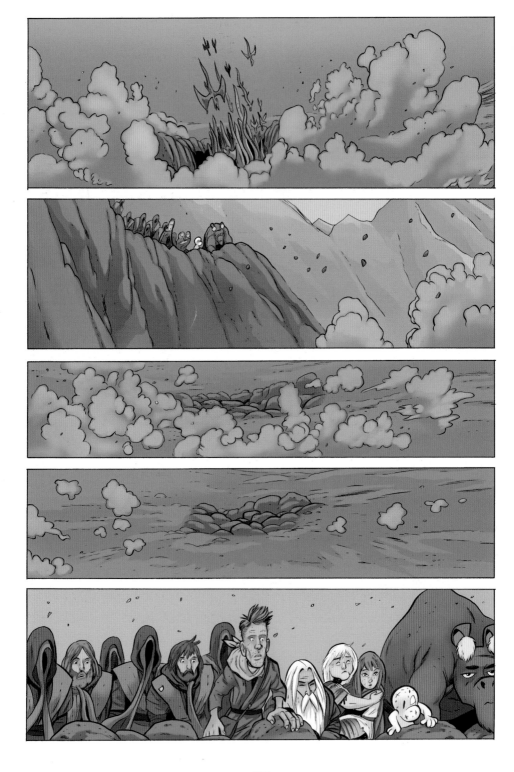

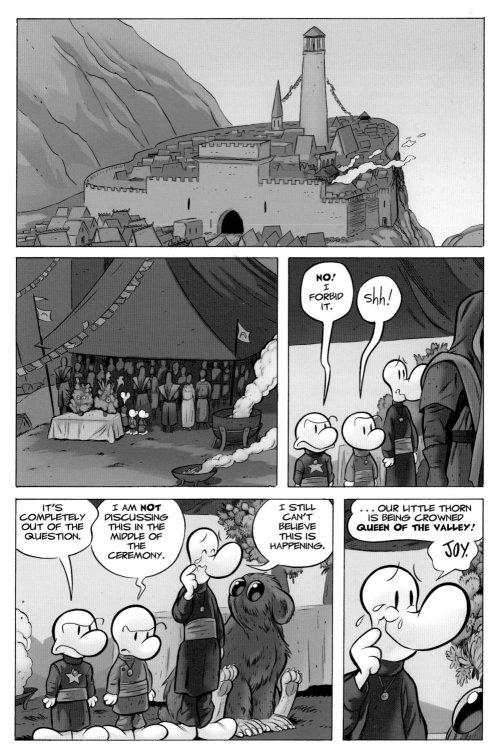

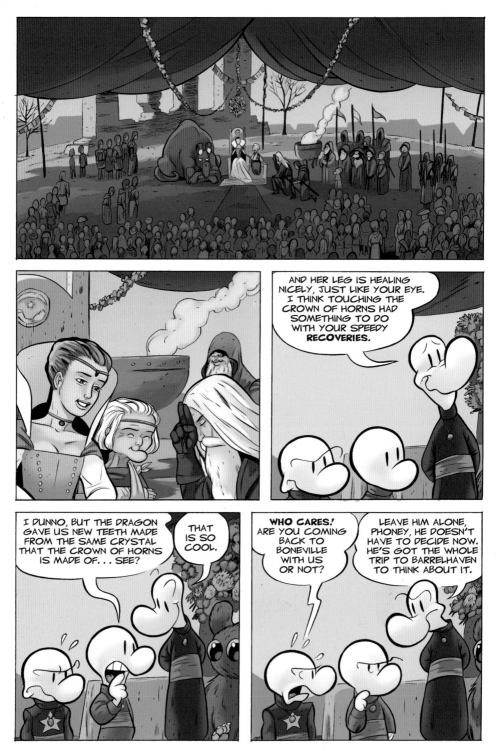

AND HER LEG IS HEALING NICELY, JUST LIKE YOUR EYE. I THINK TOUCHING THE CROWN OF HORNS HAD SOMETHING TO DO WITH YOUR SPEEDY **RECOVERIES.**

I DUNNO, BUT THE DRAGON GAVE US NEW TEETH MADE FROM THE SAME CRYSTAL THAT THE CROWN OF HORNS IS MADE OF... SEE?

THAT IS SO COOL.

WHO CARES! ARE YOU COMING BACK TO BONEVILLE WITH US OR NOT?

LEAVE HIM ALONE, PHONEY, HE DOESN'T HAVE TO DECIDE NOW. HE'S GOT THE WHOLE TRIP TO BARRELHAVEN TO THINK ABOUT IT.

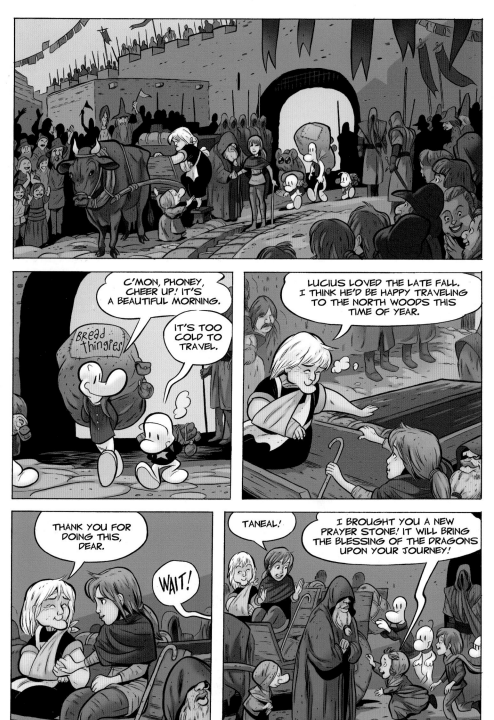

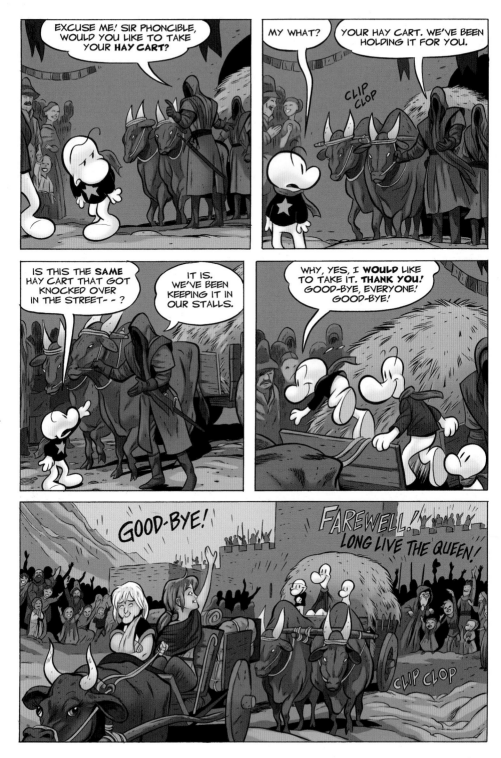

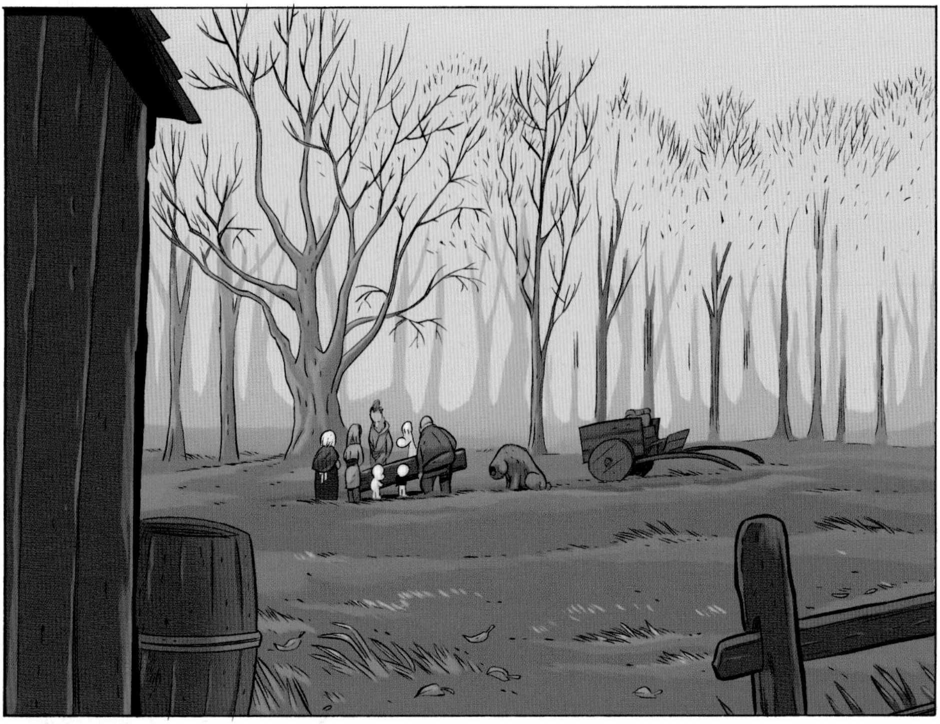

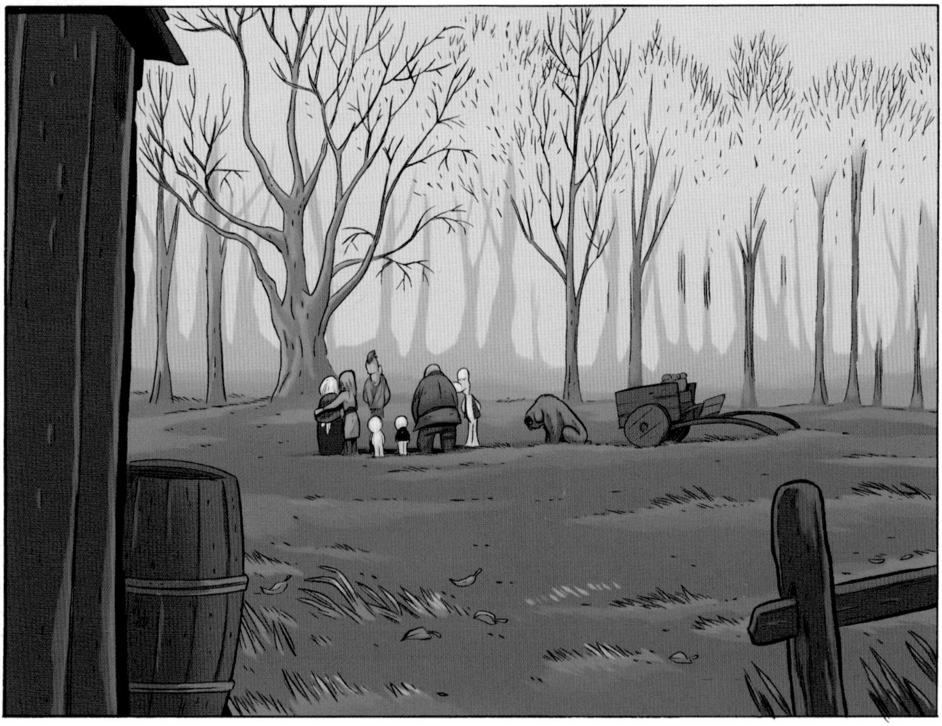

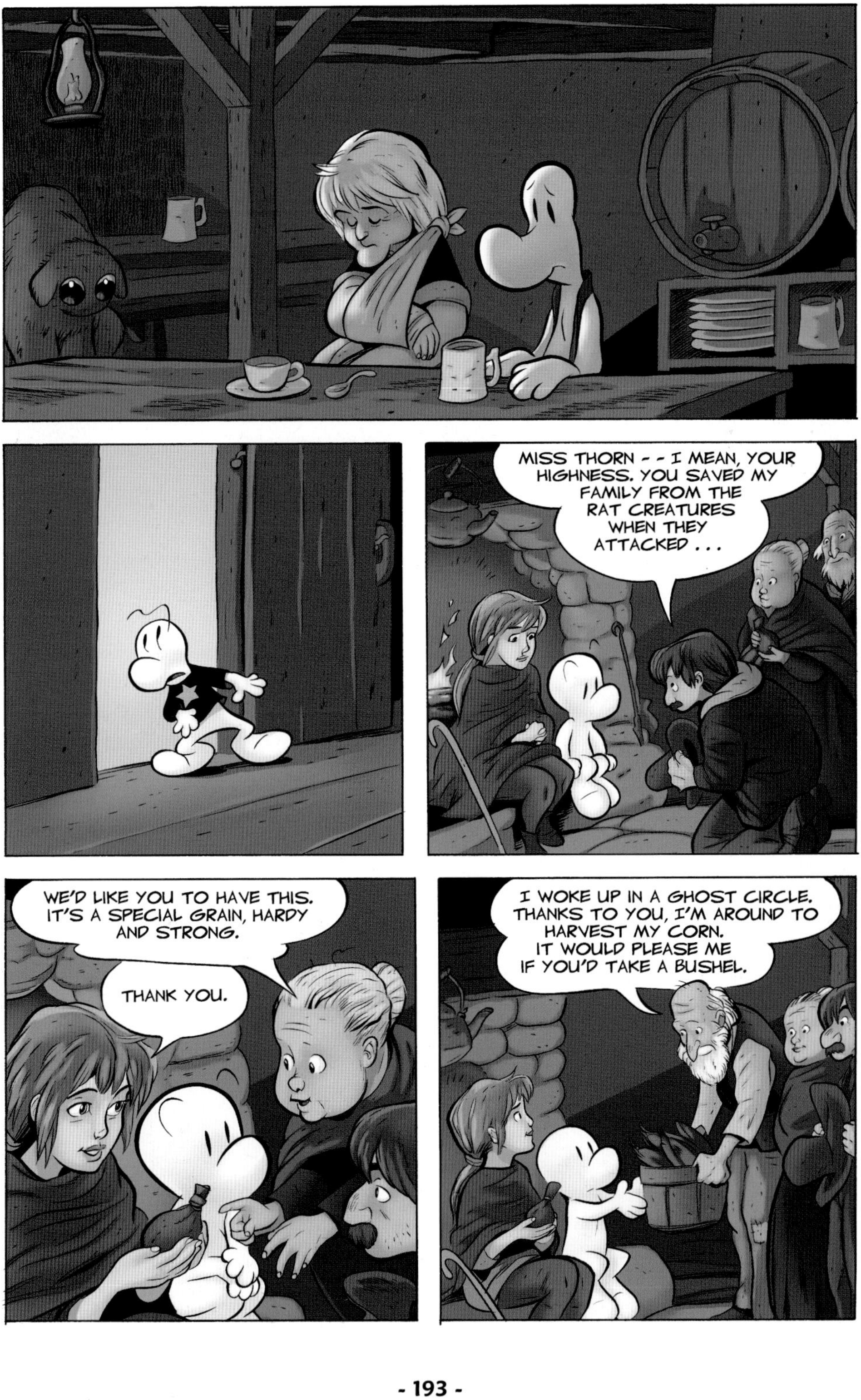
MISS THORN - - I MEAN, YOUR HIGHNESS. YOU SAVED MY FAMILY FROM THE RAT CREATURES WHEN THEY ATTACKED . . .
WE'D LIKE YOU TO HAVE THIS. IT'S A SPECIAL GRAIN, HARDY AND STRONG.
THANK YOU.
I WOKE UP IN A GHOST CIRCLE. THANKS TO YOU, I'M AROUND TO HARVEST MY CORN. IT WOULD PLEASE ME IF YOU'D TAKE A BUSHEL.

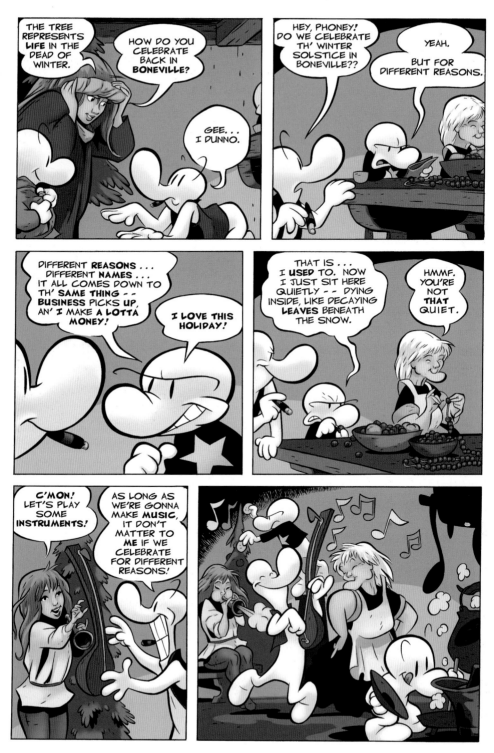

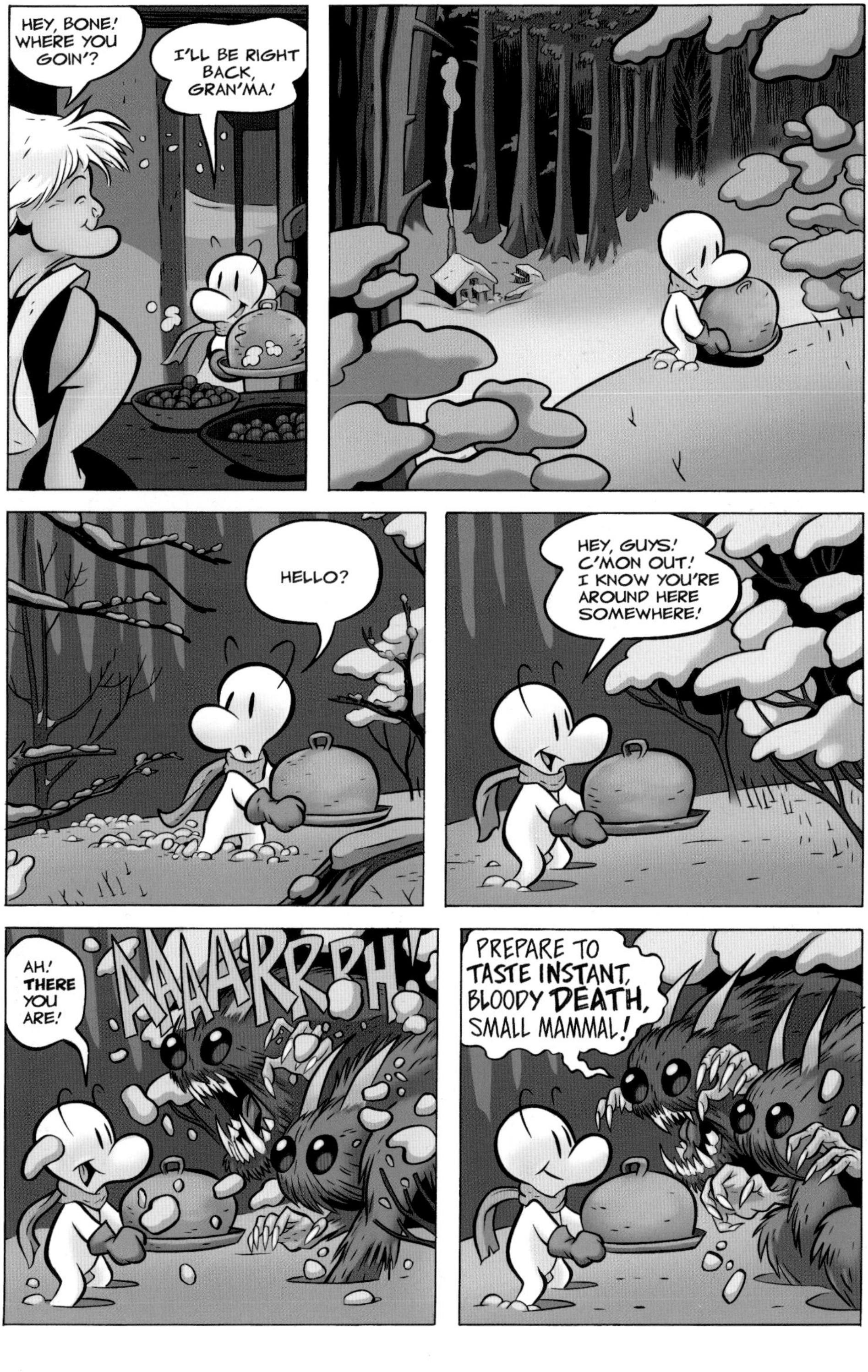
HEY, BONE! WHERE YOU GOIN'?
I'LL BE RIGHT BACK, GRAN'MA!
HELLO?
HEY, GUYS! C'MON OUT! I KNOW YOU'RE AROUND HERE SOMEWHERE!
AH! THERE YOU ARE!
AAAARRRGH!
PREPARE TO TASTE INSTANT, BLOODY DEATH, SMALL MAMMAL!

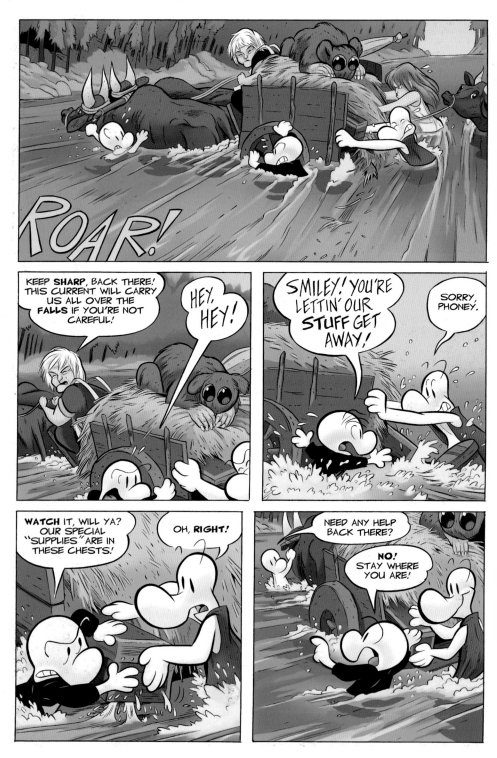

RIVER CROSSING

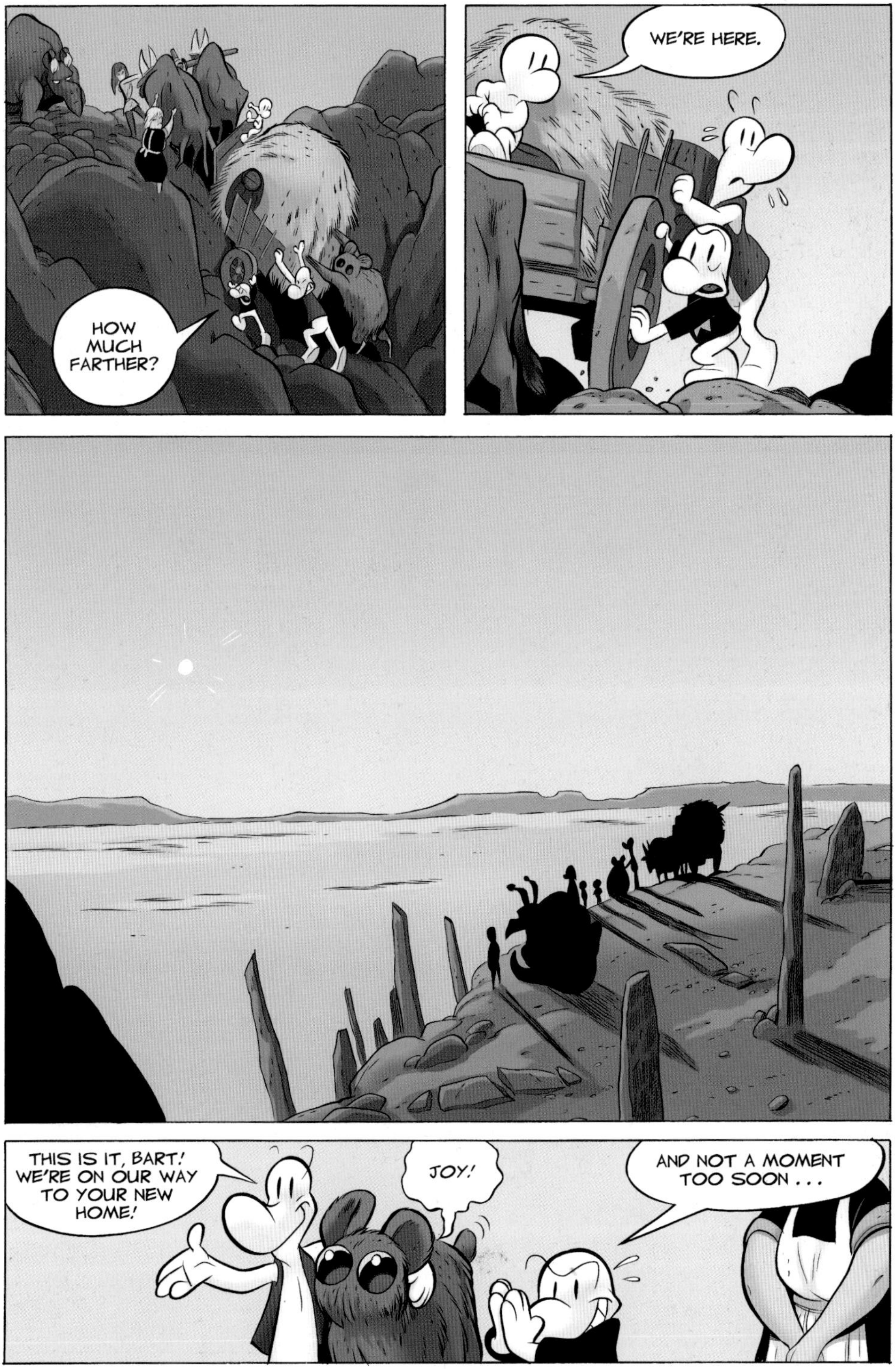
HOW MUCH FARTHER?
WE'RE HERE.
THIS IS IT, BART! WE'RE ON OUR WAY TO YOUR NEW HOME!
JOY!
AND NOT A MOMENT TOO SOON . . .

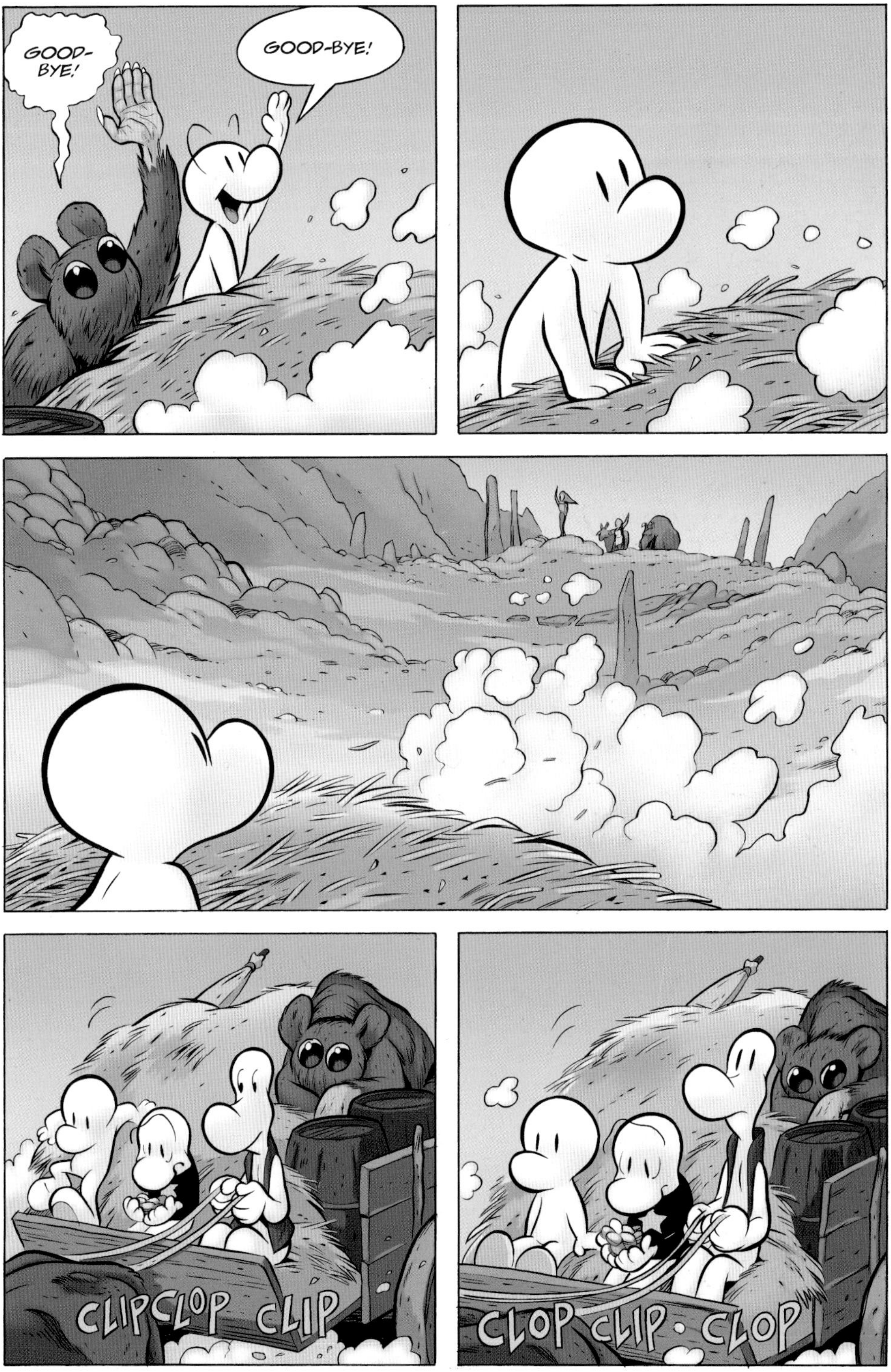
GOOD-BYE!
GOOD-BYE!
CLIPCLOP CLIP
CLOP CLIP CLOP

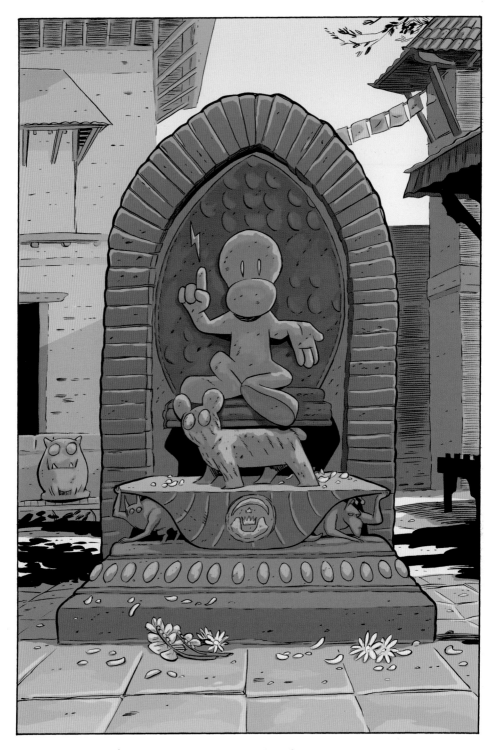

TANEAL'S SCULPTURE, QUEEN'S SQUARE, ATHEIA

About JEFF SMITH

JEFF SMITH was born and raised in the American Midwest and learned about cartooning from comic strips, comic books, and watching animated shorts on TV. After four years of drawing comic strips for The Ohio State University's student newspaper and co-founding Character Builders animation studio in 1986, Smith launched the comic book *BONE* in 1991. Between *BONE* and other comics projects, Smith spends much of his time on the international guest circuit promoting comics and the art of graphic novels.

More about *BONE*

An instant classic when it first appeared in the U.S. as an underground comic book in 1991, *BONE* has since garnered 38 international awards and sold millions of copies in 15 languages. Now, Scholastic's GRAPHIX imprint is publishing full-color graphic novel editions of the nine-book *BONE* series.

Look for the exciting prequel to the amazing *BONE* series, *ROSE*, written by Jeff Smith and illustrated by award-winning artist Charles Vess.

OTHER GRAPHIC NOVELS FROM SCHOLASTIC

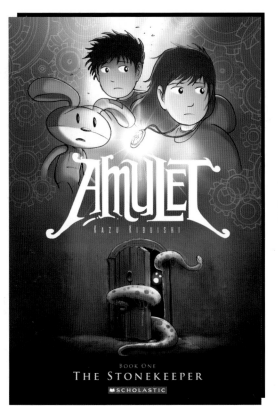

There's something strange behind the basement door. . . .

AMULET BOOK 1 - THE STONEKEEPER
By Kazu Kibuishi

After a family tragedy, Emily, Navin, and their mother move to an ancestral home to start a new life. On the family's very first night in the mysterious house, Em and Navin's mom is kidnapped by a tentacled creature. Now it's up to Em and Navin to figure out how to save their mother's life!

OTHER GRAPHIC NOVELS FROM SCHOLASTIC

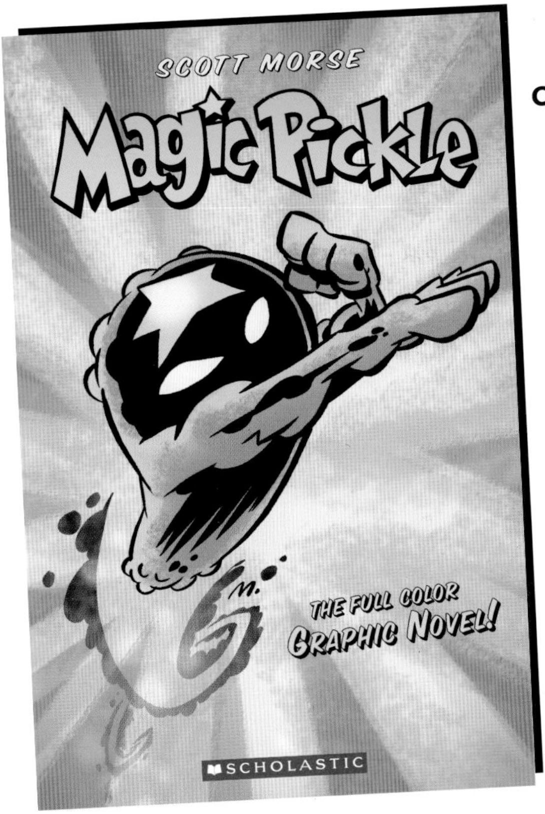
SCOTT MORSE
Magic Pickle
THE FULL COLOR GRAPHIC NOVEL!
SCHOLASTIC

One flying dill hero
TO THE RESCUE!

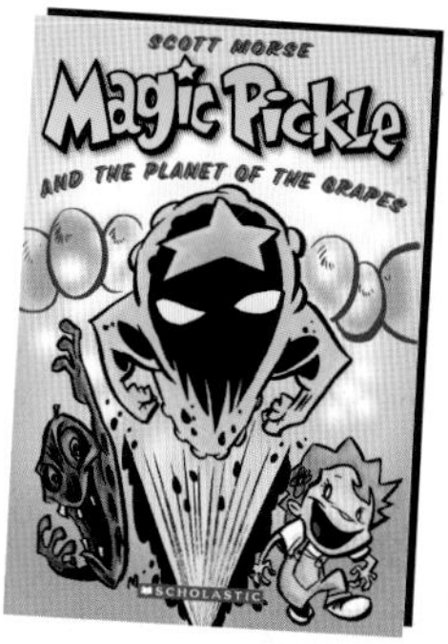
SCOTT MORSE
Magic Pickle
AND THE PLANET OF THE GRAPES
SCHOLASTIC

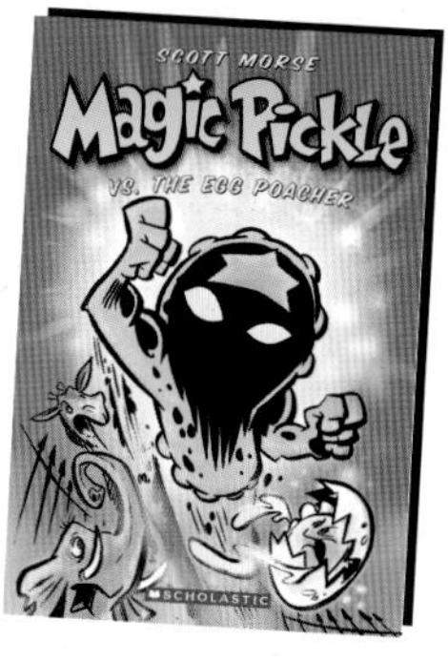
SCOTT MORSE
Magic Pickle
VS. THE EGG POACHER
SCHOLASTIC

MAGIC PICKLE
BY SCOTT MORSE

Meet the Magic Pickle, a flying kosher dill secret weapon created in a government lab under the floor of Jo Jo Wigman's bedroom. He's here to save the world from The Brotherhood of Evil Produce, who are threatening to take over the planet!

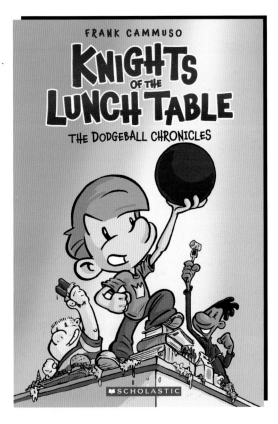

BEHOLD!
Artie King!
Ordinary hero!

KNIGHTS OF THE LUNCH TABLE
By Frank Cammuso

Artie King just wants to ease into life at Camelot Middle School. He's got new lunch buddies and a cool science teacher, but then there's the scary principal and Joe and the Horde, the brawny bullies who rule the school. The real trouble starts when Artie opens an old locker full of mysterious stuff, and Artie and his friends are challenged to a do-or-die dodgeball game. Losers get creamed!